I Love You When We're Together

Patsy Snowdale

Acknowledgements

I believe that everyone has a story to tell. Some are short, some are long, some are fact, some are fiction, some are pure and some are naughty. There were several things that inspired me to write this particular story. I had an obsession that could only be tamed temporarily by creating something of my own. I set out to accomplish a specific goal, but was unable to because the characters took on lives of their own and transported my story to unexpected places.

Everything starts with Elio and Oliver (and, by extension, AA), add a little Anastasia and Christian, and sprinkle some Doris and George on top. Voila! *I Love You When We're Together.*

It takes a village to accomplish anything and this book is no exception. I'd like to thank the people who read and offered suggestions for improvement prior to publishing: AC (the first ending made me sick), TRR (is that true?), CK (I learned a few tricks for my next girlfriend), KN (intellectual property!), HM (I've always wondered about that), GV (it made me cry!), and TP and LR who massaged the synopsis without ever reading the content (that takes talent).

Of course, none of this would be possible without the support of my family who let me spend hours at the keyboard without interruption and my husband who is always my most faithful champion.

Thanks to the talented Kristin A. Kahl for her cover art and bringing Catherine's journey to self-discovery to life in a creative and thoughtful way.

Finally, a special thanks to Barbara Mirell & Liberty Bell Publishers for putting the finishing touches on ILYWWT.

2005

It started with a donut. Or maybe a bagel that led to a donut. Once in a while, our office had breakfast gatherings. We were a small office, only fifteen employees. We were pretty close except for a few people. There was Victoria, who was a busybody. She was always stirring up stuff – creating additional work for people, starting, or, at least sharing rumors, things like that. Her cousin worked in another part of the organization so Victoria had a built-in friend in her cousin. I guess no one in our office tried to become really friendly with her because they didn't want to become a topic of conversation whether it be truth or fiction.

The other person I wasn't really close to was Paula. She started in our office while I was on maternity leave. My twins were born prematurely in 2002. Instead of the three months of maternity leave I planned to take, I was gone for six months. Logan and Bodie were in the NICU for two months. My husband, Drew, and I spent day after day in the hospital as the twins slowly grew strong enough to breathe on their own. Drew's paternity leave ran out before the boys left the hospital. I know he hated having to go to work and leaving me alone at the hospital. I spent all day with the boys when Drew returned to work. It was a difficult time for us. We had no time alone, no time to be "us." We were just the twins' parents for months. We spent our evenings taking turns sitting beside them in their incubators, until they were big enough to be held. I pumped breast milk for six weeks and we fed them with syringes, then tiny bottles, hoping that someday they could drink directly from my breasts.

We fell into a routine after the twins were released from the hospital. Because I had earned enough sick leave to stay home longer and the babies needed some extra care, I was their primary caregiver for several months. Each day, I would desperately attempt to get them to nap simultaneously so I could have a few brief moments to myself. Then I was faced with my biggest decision of the day – do I eat, shower or check email while they are sleeping?

Since I am an extrovert, being at home day after day caring for two little ones with mild health issues, I usually chose email to feel connected to friends. By the time Drew came home from work, the house was usually a mess, no dinner had been prepared and rarely did I complete a load of laundry. Even though our lives were crazy and hectic, we were pretty happy together, at least we were in my mind.

When I returned to work, Paula had already started her position as counsel to our Branch Chief and had formed her own routines. I usually welcomed new employees, showed them around the office complex, took them out for lunch and got to know them in an attempt to make them feel included. None of that happened with Paula. We were at an office breakfast eating bagels when she mentioned that she really prefers donuts, specifically toasted coconut donuts from Dunkin Donuts. I was surprised because she appeared to be athletic and very fit. Although I had reviewed her resume years before, I couldn't remember her exact age or much about her past experience. I know she had a military background, but I didn't recall if she came directly from the military to our office or if she had other jobs in between. I suppose none of that mattered at the time. I would learn everything there was to know soon enough.

A few days after the office breakfast, I was driving by a newly opened Dunkin Donuts on my way to work and decided to stop in to get a donut. As I maneuvered into the last open parking spot at 7 a.m., I remembered the conversation with Paula and decided to get one for her as well. I ordered my favorite, a Boston cream donut, a toasted coconut for her and two toffee nut lattes. I knew that Paula started her work day about a half-hour after my 7 a.m. start time. I wanted to hurry to the office since I was already late and leave it on her desk so it would be there when she arrived. Around 7:45 a.m., there was a knock on my office door. It was Paula. She figured the treat came from me and thanked me for it. She always dressed in nicely tailored pantsuits. Today's outfit was burgundy with a gray blouse beneath her jacket. She had a smile that suggested she knew something very secretive. It was oddly seductive and mischievous. I had noticed it before, but maybe not as obviously as I did that day. Her teeth were neither straight nor crooked, but they seemed to fit her face perfectly.

In late spring, Suzette, our human resources officer, emailed to tell me that Paula had been offered a position as an Administrative Law Judge in one of our field offices. It was a natural progression for a high-level attorney to take the ALJ test and be added to the national register of ALJs. She had been interviewed by a hiring committee and was rated as the best candidate. I knew that I would be responsible for hiring her replacement and planning a going-away party for her. She did not want a big party, just a luncheon with food brought in from the quaint Italian place across the street from the office. Our small group would eat in our conference room as we had many times before. I would acquire a government seal from our supply office, all the employees would sign it and it would be presented to her at her going away lunch. That was easy enough. I felt a little sad that I hadn't gotten to know her very well and she was leaving already.

Her last month in the office went by quickly. I created a job announcement to find her successor which was then advertised in all of the usual places, I formed an interview panel to meet the candidates and see who the most-qualified new-Paula would be. We made luncheons fun by playing guessing games or strategy games while we ate. They are supposed to be for team-building but end up being silly and creative ways to entertain ourselves. We also discussed two new television shows – Lost and The Office, which all of us watched and loved. As usual, the Italian restaurant did not disappoint. Paula ordered fettuccine alfredo with prosciutto, a specialty of Primi Pergola. Our less adventurous colleagues enjoyed spaghetti and meatballs, chicken parmigiana and lasagna. My best friend in the office, Bonnie, and I decided to split gnocchi with pesto and a small antipasto salad. On the rare occasions when we eat out, Bonnie always wants me to order food for both of us because she always likes my food better than her own. Rather than eating, Bonnie and I usually spent our lunch hours walking through a nearby park. We had started in our office two weeks apart twelve years earlier and had been best friends since then. Being the new women together created a very tight bond between us. We shared a very strong friendship, but it was almost exclusively at work. Unfortunately, she lived in Maryland and I lived in Virginia, almost an hour away from her. That made it difficult for us to spend time together outside of work. She had a husband and a son who was a bit older than my boys, so we didn't have a lot of overlap in activities. Bonnie was also very religious so she spent almost all of Sunday at her church. I am not religious, nor do I believe in God. Although we were opposites in many ways, we were remarkably well-matched in our friendship.

After the last of our meal was finished, and the seal and a small gift were given to Paula, we all returned to our offices to resume our work. A short time later, I heard a soft knock on my office door. "Come in please," I shouted. I was louder than I meant to be, but sometimes the air-conditioning in the office is very difficult to hear over. Paula walked in. Today's cream color pant suit was in startling contrast to her mostly dark hair. I noticed over the last year, there were more than a few strands of gray weaving their way into what had been thick black hair. Her hair cascaded to her shoulders in a flurry of unruly chaos that was unusual. She must be packing her office. I thought Chuck, our moving guy, would be helping her. "Is Chuck helping you?" I asked as she quietly closed my door.

"Yes, he took a cartful to the loading dock." Since she was transferring to a field office in our organization, the government was paying to move all of her office equipment to her new office in Pittsburgh. She had a week to pack up her house before she had to report to her new office. Paula's husband worked as a buyer for a big office supply company and could live anywhere since he spent three weeks each month traveling. His schedule made it easier for them both to move which allowed her to accept the new position that furthered her career goals.

"I want to thank you for all you have done to assist me with this move," Paula said to me. "Leaving our cozy little office and my life in Virginia will be a huge transition for me, but I am glad that I will still be part of the same organization. You helped make it a lot less tumultuous. I know I will always have great colleagues in Virginia. The luncheon today meant a lot to me...." Her voice trailed off and I wondered if she might cry. I stood up and walked around my desk, not sure what to do. She reached out to hug me goodbye. I embraced her. I never thought of smelling her hair before, but now it was next to my nose. I breathed in and could get a faint whiff of what? Fruit? No, it was a musky floral scent. Just as I was feeling that this hug was lasting a little too long and wondering whether it was enjoyable or uncomfortable, she slowly pulled away and smiled at me with her slightly crooked smile. I thought I saw something in her eyes that I just couldn't place. What was it? Longing? Desire? I was still trying to absorb what just happened, when she backed up to my office door, opened it and said, "Goodbye, Catherine."

Weeks went by and I wondered periodically about Paula. I decided to email her and see how she was settling in.

Hi Paula – or should I call you Judge now?
How are things in Pittsburgh? Do you like the new co-workers? Is

anyone taking care of your toasted coconut donut needs?

Catherine

I wondered if that sounded flirtatious? I didn't really mean it to be. It was nearly the only thing I knew about her. Except ... what happened during her going-away luncheon? She mentioned something about a trip she took with her husband to see Wimbledon. She plays tennis and her husband doesn't. He surprised her with a trip to Wimbledon for her birthday using his frequent flyer miles. I knew that she plays tennis, likes coconut donuts, and is obsessed with the television show, *Lost*, like I am.

Good afternoon, Catherine:
It is nice to hear from you. Pittsburgh is a great city. I'm discovering quirky restaurants, art galleries and many running trails along the rivers. Let's catch up soon. I'll call you next week.
~P

The following week, I was getting ready to go on a lunchtime walk with Bonnie when my phone rang. It was Paula on a break from court. The area of caselaw our office deals with is Mine Safety, so I suspected she was in court all day hearing about safety violations or accidents, usually resulting in injury or death. It must be draining. I am lucky that I am the administrator of the office, so I have only passing knowledge of the details of the cases. It is incumbent on me to ensure the office runs smoothly: people have computers, get paid, have professional development opportunities, benefits, stuff like that. I wasn't sure how long she could talk but I thought I'd better make myself available, so I quickly emailed Bonnie to tell her that I couldn't walk with her and I'd fill her in later.

Since our office was so small, we rarely called each other on the phone. We could walk to each other's offices or email each other. I think this was the first time I ever spoke to Paula on the phone. Just hearing her voice and not seeing her face was strange. I could imagine her face as she spoke the words. I focused on each word that I heard and the texture of her voice. She confided in me that her husband – Garrett was his name – had been gone all but three nights since they moved. She had been unpacking and arranging their house. She felt lonely. After about twenty minutes of conversation, she said "This might sound strange, but I really liked the way you felt when we hugged on my last day at headquarters." I had been thinking the same thing, but I would have never said it. Was this loneliness talking? Was she missing Garrett and transferring her need for him to me? I wasn't sure what to say. I didn't want to reject her, especially because I felt the same way, but how could I, in good conscience, encourage her? I was happily married – and she was too, wasn't she? My head spun with the suggestion of something illicit. I heard a loud ring. Paula said, "my mentor is calling, I have to go. Bye!" And she was gone.

I rushed down the hall passing filing cabinets and thriving spider plants to Bonnie's office, but I wasn't sure how much to share with her. Over the last twelve years, we told each other everything. I comforted her when her brother, Wayne, was killed by a drunk driver. I even went to court with her during the awful trial and sentencing of the alcoholic creep with the suspended license who hit Wayne while he was helping a stranger change a flat tire on a neighborhood street. I helped her find eldercare for her aging parents. And during that short time when she had an affair, I was her confidante. Actually, calling it an affair wasn't entirely accurate. Her husband, Javon, left her before she was pregnant with their son. While they were separated, Bonnie decided to attend different churches. She wanted to get away from the Baptist one she and Javon frequented. She tried services at a Methodist church, an Episcopalian church, Lutheran, and Presbyterian places of worship. One Sunday, she went to a Catholic mass and met Patrick, an Irish guy from New England. He was a recent transplant to the D.C. area. Bonnie was going through a dreadlock phase and Patrick was obsessed with her hair, her beautiful smile and her infectious laugh. He asked her out for coffee after communion hour. They went out and began a brief but crazy-passionate affair. It was the first white man she ever slept with and she couldn't get enough of him. She said he smelled different, his hair felt different, his lips were thinner and rougher than Javon's. She liked how his nose pushed into her cheek when they kissed. His hands were soft and she loved the paleness of his skin on her darker complexion. It was different and wild, and maybe it was too intense to last. She told me about the interesting and creative positions he liked to try, the places they made love: at Wolf Trap listening to a jazz band playing during a cool early summer night under an afghan his mother crocheted, on the balcony of his apartment in Cleveland Park, in restaurant restrooms. She was revitalized by the relationship. Wanted, needed, craved, loved. And she felt a passion that she had never known. But she knew it couldn't last and she was right about that. About nine months after she and Patrick started their fiery relationship, Javon returned home. Bonnie knew that the intensity with Patrick couldn't be maintained – it was all-encompassing and it had to end. I know that she still thinks of Patrick even now years later, but she belonged to Javon. She knew her life would always be with him. As quickly as Javon left her a year earlier, he returned like nothing had happened. They resumed their life and, a short time later, Bonnie was pregnant with Keith.

I decided to tell Bonnie that Paula called to tell me how things were going in Pittsburgh and nothing else. Besides what could I tell her? I really had nothing to say. Paula gave me an awkwardly long hug when she left and just referenced it in a phone call. It wasn't really creepy or suggestive. Was it? Those are two very different takes on the same event. Did it seem creepy? No, I don't think so. Except it was longer than a regular hug and I smelled her hair which was pretty delightful. I didn't think it was overtly suggestive at the time, but now several weeks later... what? I really just didn't know how to feel about any of it so it was better to say nothing.

I returned to my office. There was an email from her.

Catherine:
I hope I didn't freak you out. There's no one else buying me toasted coconut donuts. That honor belongs only to you.
~P

Wow. What am I supposed to think of that? The workday was over so I tried to push Paula out of my mind. I picked the boys up from preschool and drove home. They were at the charming age where one would try to annoy the other for no particular reason. Or maybe the reason was that they were three. Terrible threes or threenagers. They were loud and demanding. Logan put his fingers into Bodie's chubby cheeks and said "waff." Neither Drew nor I had any idea what that meant, but it made Bodie mad as hell. Bodie would try to bite Logan because he touched him and the argument would continue until I put them in time-out. We had a designated time-out chair in the corner of the dining room which was meant for one offender. Sometimes it was difficult to tell who the instigator was. I'm sure it happened frequently that the wrong little guy was in trouble. But the reality is putting one in the chair was bad for them both because each lost his partner-in-crime.

Because I had my monthly meeting scheduled with parents in the preschool co-op, Drew was bringing home some carry-out dinner. I usually cooked, but there wasn't going to be time tonight. He went to a Mexican place about a mile from our house and brought us cheese enchiladas – spicy for the adults and mild for the boys. We felt very lucky that the boys liked to eat many different types of food because we frequently had ethnic cuisine. That was one thing the Washington area is great for – the traffic is awful and the cost-of-living is outrageous, but we sure have a variety of food to try. I quickly ate my enchilada with rice and beans before an offensive smell reached my nose. Bodie had pooped in his underwear. Logan never had accidents since they were potty-trained, but Bodie was a different story. I scooped him up and took him to the bathroom, rinsed out his soiled underwear, cleaned off his bottom and put him in pajamas. I really didn't have time for that. I kissed both boys goodnight because they should be sleeping when I get home and rushed out the door for the meeting.

We were meeting in a late-night coffee shop because we weren't allowed access to the pre-school after hours. Everyone was already there when I arrived. I was hoping that I would have some alone time to think about Paula on the ride to the meeting, but since I was running late and realized that I forgot to put the rinsed underwear in the laundry basket, I couldn't think about what really needed to be sorted out. I was distracted during the meeting and then I was frustrated that I couldn't concentrate. I inadvertently volunteered to run the fall fun fair. Ugh! I really didn't want any additional responsibilities. I spent the ride home angry at myself for being so unfocused.

Another month went by before I heard from Paula again. She called late on a Friday afternoon. She had gotten out of court early. I had to leave work in a half-hour to get the boys from preschool. This was not a good time to call. But I had been thinking about her a lot over the past month and I knew I couldn't miss an opportunity to hear her voice – if only for a short time. I was surprised how much I looked forward to her call.

"Hey stranger," I tried to sound playful and not give away my growing infatuation.

"You may call me Judge Marlon," she answered.

"Ummm, ok." I didn't know what to make of that request.

"And from now on, you will respond with 'Yes, ma'am' or 'Yes, Judge.'"

Hesitatingly, I whispered "Yes, ma'am." Then I felt my heart race and a little tingle in my panties.

She said, "Catherine, I'm not sure you understand. When I told you to respond with 'Yes, ma'am,' I expect to hear you. Say it again now. This time so I can hear you clearly."

I wasn't sure where this was going, but secretly I liked it. And she knew it.

"Yes, ma'am," I said louder.

"Good girl."

I wanted to hear about her life, her caseload, her colleagues. There was a rumor that Judge Gelman was very unpleasant to work with and I was hoping she would share some stories about him. But it was obvious today would not be the day that we would engage in small talk.

"I want to play a game with you. If you don't like it, we can stop. I have been thinking about you a lot and I want to share more of myself with you. But it has to be just between us and it must be consensual. Are you willing to continue?"

Before thinking about it anymore, I answered, "Yes, Judge."

She went on, "From now on, you will not call or email me. I will initiate contact. Do you understand?"

"Yes, ma'am."

"Good girl, that is enough for today. I hope your panties are wet. Goodbye." She hung up. Nothing more.

Ugh! What am I doing? I suppose a little phone conversation with someone far away isn't the worst thing. Drew and I don't have a lot of time or energy for sex because the twins are so draining. I can see how this could actually improve our sex life. After ten minutes on the phone with Paula – er, Judge Marlon – I am feeling extremely horny. I wonder if I can maintain this feeling until the twins are in bed and take advantage of it with Drew. It sounds like a win-win to me.

It started with a donut, a long hug and then a phone call. I couldn't stop thinking about her. And yet, I knew almost nothing about her and I certainly knew nothing about being with a woman. Yet none of this seemed unnatural. Why did she pick me? Was it because I saw that something – a mischievous twinkle – in her eye? That look that said she knew something about me that I didn't even know yet. I felt a heady longing to hold her again.

But real life interfered. I was home, the boys were involved in a food fight and my desire was quickly leaving my body. Get these boys in bed, so we can make love, Drew. I thought it as loudly as I could. Each time the thought came, it was more intense. By 7:30 p.m., my brain was screaming "fuck me now and hard." Since I was rarely the aggressor in our sex life, I had to coyly express my interest as soon as we were alone.

"Honey, let's go to the bedroom."

"Do you want to watch some tv and eat ice cream in bed?" he asked.

"I had something else in mind...."

He joined me immediately. I didn't have to make that suggestion twice. I started to undress and he unhooked my bra and slipped his hands around my breasts gently squeezing my nipples. He pushed me onto the bed and pulled off my jeans. One deep kiss on my mouth and then he moved to my clit. He murmured a groan of approval when he saw how wet I was after easily slipping two fingers into my pussy. He masterfully moved his fingers in and out, once, twice and by the third time I had cum. My orgasm was intense and exhausting. While it seemed to have happened very quickly, the foreplay began hours before on the phone with my new favorite Judge. I tried to rally to please my sweet husband, but my mind was elsewhere. I went through the motions bringing him to orgasm while thinking of Paula saying "You will respond with 'Yes, ma'am'."

The remainder of the year was spent trying to find a few minutes to talk to Paula when she wasn't in training. I wanted to know more about her. I didn't know where she grew up or went to school. I didn't know if she had siblings or if her parents were alive. One day in the fall, I finally had a chance to ask her some of my questions about her background. What she told me filled me with sadness.

She told me that she was born in Vietnam in the late 60s. Her Vietnamese name was Lan, which meant orchid flower. She had an older brother and she was the beautiful flower, the precious baby of the family. Her family had a comfortable life until the war destroyed their quiet village. After the fall of Saigon, her family's lives were in danger. They were hidden in safe houses throughout the country for months until they could secure passage out of her homeland on a fishing boat. They left one night in October of 1978. She remembered some of the voyage. The sea was rough and the boat was not very sturdy. Many people were crammed inside with limited food and water, a few succumbed to disease. Her uncle washed overboard during a storm and, with no life vest, he disappeared quickly beneath the violent waves. Their rickety boat washed ashore in a remote area in Thailand which wasn't their intended destination. Armed men transferred them to a refugee camp. Several months later, they were resettled in the United States thanks to humanitarian efforts by the United Nations. Her family sought and gained legal status in the United States. She lived with her brother, parents and cousins in the Houston area. When she was seventeen years old, she became a citizen. Lan no longer existed – she converted to the American name, Paula. She shared all of her story matter-of-factly, as if it belonged to someone else. I had tears in my eyes hearing all that she and her family had endured.

Although her parents had limited English language proficiency and their ability to communicate in the U.S. was hampered, they had been well-educated in Vietnam and instilled in their children a drive to succeed academically. During high school, she played clarinet in the marching band and jazz band, but wasn't very athletic. During her senior year, she applied to several colleges and was admitted to three Ivy League schools on the East Coast. She chose Cornell University because they gave her an Army ROTC scholarship to ease the burden of the expense of college on her family. She earned her Bachelor's degree in Earth Science with a minor in Environmental Studies. She had a four-year commitment with the Army to fulfill after graduation. She went to the Officer's Basic Course in San Antonio, Texas, which allowed her to see her family regularly for nearly four months. After, she was stationed at Fort Wainwright in Fairbanks, Alaska. There she learned to ski, both downhill and cross-country, went snowshoeing, snowmobiling, spent time exploring the mountains, hiking and fishing. After her commitment to the military was finished, Paula went to Emory Law School in Georgia for her JD. That was where she met Garrett.

2006

It was an unusual start to the year. I arrived at 7:00 a.m. for work on my first day back after taking a few days off for Christmas and New Year's. A call came into the office a little after 8:00 a.m. indicating that there was an explosion at the Sago mine in West Virginia and several men were trapped. We had cited Sago several times in the past for having conditions that we call serious and substantial, meaning they could be unsafe for miners. Some of our safety experts and testers went to Upshur County where Sago is located. We were given periodic updates about the condition of the mine while the rest of the country watched rescue efforts on the news for two days until the fate of the miners was known. A crew finally reached the trapped miners and found twelve bodies and one man barely alive. It was a terrible tragedy that could have been avoided. Reports indicated that carbon monoxide poisoning was the cause of death. I suspected one of our judges in Pittsburgh would eventually be hearing the case against the mine owners for wrongful death and ignoring unsafe conditions for which they had been repeatedly cited.

I tried to remember the last time I talked to Paula. Oh yes, she called just before Christmas.

"Good afternoon, Catherine."

"Hello, Judge Marlon." Just saying the words put me under her spell again. I could feel the change in my breathing to deeper breaths trying to calm my racing heart.

"I've been thinking about you a lot. I love your smile and your perfect teeth. I would like to kiss your lips. Would you like that?"

"Yes, ma'am." I squirmed in my office chair, knowing that shortly I would again feel the tingle in my clit. Damn thing betrayed any type of indifference I could muster.

"You know what I would like to do before kissing you?" she asked.

"No ma'am, but I hope you will tell me."

"I would like to spank your ass."

I had to stifle a laugh. Why did I think that was funny? It sounded kind of hot.

"What do you think of that?"

"Ma'am, if you think I deserve to be spanked, you should spank me."

"Would you enjoy that?"

"My only goal is to make you happy, ma'am."

"Good girl. Are you wet now, Catherine?"

 "Yes, ma'am."

"I do not want you to go home and fuck your husband since I made you wet. Do you understand me?"

"Yes, ma'am."

"If you do, you will be punished. I will spank you and it won't be with my hand. Do you understand?"

"Yes, ma'am." Her voice sounded very stern – and very sexy.

"Ok, have a nice Christmas – and remember, no sex tonight."

"Thank you, Judge. I understand."

She hung up. I raced home, put on a video for the boys to watch and waited for Drew in a lacy soft pink teddy he had bought me for Valentine's Day years before the boys were born. I was sorry to not keep my promise to Paula, but I needed to have Drew's cock inside of me. He came home and entered our bedroom to take off his suit and change into sweatpants. I must have had a strange look on my face because he asked if I was sick. I was covered with our navy flannel sheets in bed on a Friday afternoon. I pulled the sheet off and exposed myself in lingerie.

"Hmmm, must have been an interesting day at the office." If he only knew.

"Honey, I've been thinking about you all day. How about a little "afternoon delight"? I sang the awful lyrics to the Starland Vocal Band's skeezy 70s hit.

Never one to reject his sexy wife in lingerie, Drew obliged. He quickly undressed, used the bathroom and joined me under the sheets. Our lovemaking was urgent, fast and thorough. We spent a few post-fuck moments cuddling tenderly before we had to make dinner for the boys.

I knew my transgression would not go unnoticed. In mid-January, she called me before her work day began.

"Good morning, Catherine."

"Good morning, Judge."

"Did you have a nice holiday?"

"Yes, ma'am. Did you?"

"Yes, I did. Thank you for asking. The last time we talked, I told you not to have sex with your husband that day. Did you obey me?"

Do I tell the truth and accept the consequences? Do I owe her the truth? Is the truth part of our game?

"No, ma'am. I did have sex with him that night." I decided to try honesty.

"Catherine, I appreciate that you told me the truth. But you know there are consequences for disobeying."

"Yes, ma'am. I'm sorry."

"You may respond 'Yes, ma'am. I am so sorry, ma'am.' Do you understand?"

"Yes, ma'am."

"Say it properly now!"

"Yes, ma'am. I am so sorry, ma'am."

"Good girl. Because I'm a fair judge, I think you should be involved in determining what your punishment should be. How do you think I should punish you?"

"Ma'am, I think you should spank me," I suggested.

"That sounds reasonable. How many times should I spank you, Catherine? What sounds fair to you for disobeying me?"

"Five times, ma'am?"

"Five?! You disobeyed a direct order. I made you horny and you fucked your husband to alleviate that desire. Do you think I make you horny so you can fuck him? I do not. I make you horny so you can think about me. Do you understand? I want you to have that bond with me."

"Ten spanks, ma'am?"

"That sounds fair. I think ten swats with a paddle ought to do. I think you need to understand there will be consequences for disobeying me. Maybe next time you will think twice before you disobey me."

"Yes, ma'am. I'm so sorry, ma'am. I will not disobey you again, ma'am."

"Good. I will trust you. Tonight, I want you to fuck your husband, but you do not get to have an orgasm. Only he does. Do you understand? That is your real punishment today."

"Yes, ma'am. Thank you for imposing a reasonable punishment." We both knew that she couldn't actually spank me since we lived hours apart. The idea of withholding my own pleasure to satisfy the judge's request was almost beyond erotic.

"Catherine, you are so hot. Thank you for being my submissive bitch."

This time I did not disappoint the judge. Drew and I ordered pizza to be delivered and played a game of memory with the boys before their bedtime. After cleaning the kitchen, putting a load of laundry in the washer, and paying some bills, I went to our bedroom. Drew was already in bed watching a murder mystery detective show on tv. I got into bed beside him. I waited to see if he wanted to fool around. After a long week at work, it was nice to unwind with a glass of wine and some sex on Friday night. It wasn't a regular tradition but it happened more often than not. He reached over to caress my cheek and pull me to his side of the bed. I rolled over willingly ready to engage in some foreplay. We kissed for a while and he reached between my legs, circling his thumb around my pulsing clit. I arched my back to force him to touch it and then realized that I wasn't allowed to cum. I pushed his hand away and mounted him. In this aggressive action of taking control, I ensured that he would orgasm first and forget about my needs. He knew that I was forgoing my own pleasure for his and entered me first gently and then with increasing force and passion. He finished within minutes. I was oddly quite satisfied mainly because I accomplished my mission of obeying the judge. It was amazing how not having an orgasm could be so stimulating.

Our office held biennial judges' conferences on even years. It gave them the opportunity to come together, share information on new areas of the law, hear from experts on mine safety, updates on Circuit Court decisions and other areas of interest. Because we hired three new judges last year, it would be the first time the new judges met all of the experienced judges since they are in three different cities. We currently have eight judges in headquarters, and five in both Denver and Pittsburgh. The conference is always held in Washington, D.C. Our training staff puts together the program, identifies speakers, develops the agenda, arranges the travel for the judges and all other minutiae to pull off this conference. I always attend the program, mostly to mingle with the judges and ensure things run smoothly. If the training staff needs additional help, I am there to provide support. This year's conference would be held in May. It would be the first time I had seen Paula since she left headquarters a year earlier. I was excited to spend time with her alone, but also very nervous.

Catherine:
I'm looking forward to traveling to D.C. for the conference. I think Garrett will be joining me because he has some clients to meet with in May. I hope to catch up with you soon.
Judge Marlon

Crap! She's bringing Garrett?! Why? I was not sure how to express my disappointment in this new information. I want to respond to her email without sharing my feelings. We both agreed that we need to be especially careful of emailing anything personal. With government computers, you never know who is reading.

Judge Marlon:
How wonderful that your husband can join you on the trip. I plan to be at the conference center for the entire week, maybe we can have lunch together one day?
Catherine

Rrrrrring. She's calling me.
"Good morning, Judge Marlon."
"Catherine, listen to me carefully. I will be arriving on Sunday night. Garrett will be coming on Tuesday. I expect you to come to my room on Monday morning before the conference starts. Call me from the hotel phone when you arrive at 7:00 a.m. Ask the operator for my room and I will tell you the room number. You should wear a dress with no panties. We will have two hours alone before the continental breakfast at 9:00 a.m."
"Yes, ma'am. Judge Marlon?"
I wasn't sure what to say except that I really enjoyed our conversations. I had never been unfaithful to my husband – this husband - and more importantly, I had never really been with a woman before. I had never really been attracted to a woman before. Well, there was one time that I found a friend of a friend really appealing. I met Hayley at a party my friend, Nicole, was hosting. It was one of those parties where a consultant comes with clothes. Only women are present and everyone tries on clothes and compliments each other. Then you can order whatever you like and it's delivered to your house a week later. Anyway, something about Hayley caught my eye. She was

beautiful in a non-traditional way. I think Drew would say that she's the type of woman that other women find attractive in a way that maybe men do not. She was wearing faded jeans that fit her perfectly, a button-down shirt, blazer and a striped scarf. She had bright blue eyes highlighted with just the perfect amount of eyeliner, mascara and very faint eyeshadow. She had short hair; sort of a pixie cut that Winona Ryder had in the 1990s that I generally wouldn't find attractive. But there was something about this woman. She exuded a quiet confidence that drew me in. Maybe it was her sexy boots? Anyway, I sat with her for a while and sipped wine. I asked how she knew Nicole, why we hadn't met at any of Nicole's other parties. I saw her only once or twice after that night. I was entranced with her, but from afar. I had no indication that she was interested in women, and I didn't think I was either – except there was something about her. Something I couldn't put my finger on.

"Catherine, don't be afraid. We will only do what you are comfortable doing. I promise. I'll see you on May 22nd at 7 a.m."

How could I simultaneously be excited for the 22nd and fearful? I was drawn to Paula in an erotic way that I couldn't describe. Maybe it was the way she took control of our relationship. She seemed to want me desperately which made me want her even more. I don't think I have ever felt so desired. One evening when Drew wasn't feeling well and went to bed early, I searched the Internet for some tips on being a lesbian. I know how crazy that sounds. I just didn't know what to expect. I have never been much of a porn-watcher so I didn't want to resort to viewing of lesbian sex. Several years ago, Drew and I went to see the Vagina Monologues in D.C. One speaker said that most women have not even looked at their own vaginas. She suggested that women get out a mirror and actually look at themselves. See where the labia are, how the entrance to the vagina is tucked neatly in between, locate the clitoris and the urethra opening. See what you really look like. How is it that our significant others know our bodies more than we do? I am certain Drew has seen my private parts thousands of times more than I have. Hell, my ob-gyn who only sees me annually sees me more than I do. After reading a couple of websites, I went to the bathroom. Drew was snoring so I knew I wouldn't be interrupted. I grabbed my mirror, the one that had both regular size reflection and ten times magnification on the other side. I sat on the cool tile of my bathroom floor and looked at myself. After re-discovering the intricacies of my own private parts, I realized that I really need to shave a bit.

The pubic hair around my pussy didn't make it look appetizing at all. I am surprised that Drew never mentioned it. He can't possibly think that looks sexy or even ok. I took his electric shaver and tried to remove a little hair. The vibrating of the shaver was sensual and making me horny. I wasn't sure how much more hair I could shave. I felt the strong urge to cum. I turned off the shaver and slid one finger inside of my dripping pussy. It felt great. It was warm and cozy inside, velvety even. I was dying to touch my clit, but decided instead to put another finger inside, then another. Three of my fingers moving in and out of my pussy. I was worried about the length of my nails and if they could possibly do damage to my vagina. I imagined scraping the inside walls and withdrew my fingers. I was desperate to have an orgasm and my throbbing clit could not be ignored. I looked at the mirror I had been using to view myself. The handle was round, thick, long and hard. I washed it and jammed it inside of me. I moved the handle of the mirror in and out, in and out. I squeezed my nipples with my left thumb and forefinger before reaching down between my legs and rubbing my clit. First, I did it very softly, then with increasing speed until it exploded with a fierce orgasm. As it turns out, I didn't need my husband – or a man – to have an amazing climax. That's not to say that I hadn't masturbated before. I usually just didn't care to. I didn't feel the need to have an orgasm any more frequently than I already did with Drew. I hated the idea of taking that intimacy away from him by doing it on my own. Sort of like how I disliked eating Indian food with Bonnie at lunch on a rainy day. I knew Drew and the boys loved that type of food and almost felt like I was cheating on them to eat it with someone else.

May 18, May 19, May 20, May 21. I couldn't decide what to wear to the conference. I knew that I had to wear a dress. I wondered how I would bring my panties with me – in my briefcase? That seemed bizarre. I carefully shaved my pussy the day before the conference, being careful to use a razor rather than the electric shaver. I couldn't risk having a repeat of the other night. I also shaved my legs and armpits using the same razor. Do women usually use the same razor for all three? It didn't matter. My shower time was limited. I had to accomplish a lot in a few short minutes. When I felt appropriately hairless, I left the shower and contemplated what to wear the following day. It's important to select something that is comfortable, flattering, not transparent as to not expose my panty-less condition. It is also late May in D.C. which means it could be 80+ degrees. I quickly check the forecast for Monday. Weather.com indicates that it will be unseasonably cool with a high of 70 degrees. I chose a short-sleeve violet dress with a matching sweater. Sometimes hotels are cool inside. Having a sweater will prepare me for whatever temperature I'm faced with. I have sexy pumps that complement the color of the dress. I can't remember the rule on wearing pearls in daytime? Is that ok or not? I picked some champagne-colored freshwater pearls because I have corresponding dangling earrings and a bracelet. I wondered if that is too matchy-matchy. Bonnie recently told me that wearing jewelry sets is not in fashion now. But I don't care too much about what is popular. I want to look comfortable, confident and maybe even alluring.

I am torn about possibly taking my relationship with Paula to another level. I feel as though I can justify it. Our minds are funny that way. Allowing us to make decisions not based in fact or logic, but using some primal part of our brains that work using emotion or fleeting visions, maybe even dreams. I have an example of this from my past life. In college, I was dating a guy who became my first husband, Thomas. We were together since October of sophomore year. We did almost everything together, had some of the same classes, ate our meals together, and worked together in the mall after classes. After I graduated, I worked a few jobs while waiting for him to graduate a semester later. I met a guy in one of my other jobs, working in a stained-glass lamp store. I had heard the guy's name, Mikey, from other employees who worked in both the store and the factory. One time he came to the store to drop off some lamps from the factory where he worked and we were introduced. I thought nothing of him. Really nothing. A few nights later, I had a vivid dream about a guy who swept me off my feet, who I had an intense connection with that was stronger than anything I had ever felt. My dream was eerie and powerful and yet calming in a way that demonstrated I had found my true soulmate. I woke up feeling unsettled but eventually forgot about it - until a week later when Mikey made another delivery of some new lamps to the store. Mikey was the guy in my dream. I fought the feeling that he was meant to be mine, but honestly not very fervently. He stayed around the store until closing time and walked me to my car. I asked him to sit inside the car with me. I debated whether to share the story with him and eventually decided to tell him about my dream and how it haunted me. I hadn't noticed how truly gorgeous he was until that moment. He had dirty blonde hair – not my typical type. He was a skier and he drove a red Subaru wagon – a weird car for a young guy, but it held all of his skiing equipment and it was rugged in the winter. His green eyes were warm and welcoming and I felt like the night wouldn't end until I kissed him. But I was committed to Thomas. Well as committed as two college kids could be. I thought I would marry him and be with him forever. Maybe the introduction of Mikey into my dreams should have foretold the trouble in my future with relationships and fidelity, but I was young and there was much left to learn about myself.

This was the first time I really struggled with making a decision like this. Could I in good conscience kiss Mikey, knowing that Thomas was waiting at our off-campus apartment for me? There were no cell phones then, so I couldn't call or text to tell him that I would be late. Even if I could, there would be no reasonable excuse I could make for staying out late with another guy. I didn't notify Thomas of my tardiness. I talked with Mikey for two hours and wondered if I could let him leave without kissing him. I didn't think I could let the moment pass without seeing how his lips felt on mine. Eventually, I quit fighting my desire and I kissed Mikey. It was amazing. I told Thomas when I returned home that I kissed someone else, that I enjoyed it and I wanted to do it again. For some reason, he wasn't completely angry with me. My relationship with Mikey lasted a few months. I wouldn't allow myself to have sex with him, believing that would really cross the line to become inappropriate, but he did teach me the art of dry-humping. And, for a time, that was good enough. I don't recall how our relationship fizzled out, but it did. It was intoxicating, but not really sexually rewarding since I didn't allow myself to be naked with him. I knew I couldn't trust myself with him if nudity was part of the equation.

I realized some of my reasons to be with Paula were not authentic, but instead ways to rationalize doing whatever I want to do. I felt like the last several years, I haven't been able to do things for me. I understand being a mother requires me to forfeit some of my personal identity and instead be just "mom." Occasionally I long for the opportunity to be "Catherine." Those chances are few and far between. Of course, my bigger concern is the idea that I could hurt Drew. I never want to do that. He is a good man. He is a good dad, a good provider, funny, handsome, smart, and a true partner to me. I would never leave him for someone else. I would never love anyone else. But what's the harm in fucking someone else? And do two women "fuck"? I'm not sure what the terminology is for that. Or is it the intimacy with someone else that is the problem? I have always been intrigued with what I believe was the premise of the movie Eyes Wide Shut. In the movie, the characters played by real-life couple at the time Tom Cruise and Nicole Kidman, are each confronted with temptations. She has an emotional affair with a man she doesn't know, while he actually has sex with strangers. So, which is worse? I have always thought that sex is a physical act – which can be complicated by emotions. Having an emotional attachment to someone outside the marriage is much worse. Is having sex with someone else a breach of our marital contract? Did I promise to forsake all others? Does that mean forsaking emotional relationships too? The point is I didn't take the situation of possibly being intimate with Paula lightly. I obsessed over it for hours and days, weeks and months, maybe even a year since we began our sexy phone conversations. I never knew what would happen.

BLEAT! BLEAT! BLEAT!

My annoying alarm was going off. It was 5:30 a.m. on Monday, May 22nd, the day the conference begins. The day I'm expected to show up at the JW Marriott on E Street, a few short blocks from the White House, wearing no panties to see a woman I haven't seen in a year who could change my life. I wasn't ready. At all.

I showered quickly, butterflies performing a wild Capoeira in my stomach. I attempted to style my hair, but gave up on it instead opting for a sleek ponytail. I put on my dress, jewelry, sexy shoes and carefully placed my panties in a Ziplock bag in the bottom of my purse. It seemed like a better solution than putting them in my briefcase. My nerves made my driving more erratic than usual. I half wished I would crash the car on the way to the city so I wouldn't have to realize my destiny. At the same time, my clit was starting to throb and I hoped that I wouldn't have a wet spot on the back of my dress. Why didn't I wear panties until I got to the hotel and then stop in the lobby bathroom to remove them? Rookie mistake, no doubt.

I forgot to check ahead of time to see if there were other cheaper parking lots nearby. I guess the government would cover the cost anyway. I pulled into the valet parking area of the hotel, left my keys with the uniformed man there and entered the hotel. I found the lobby phone; it was 6:50 a.m. I wondered if she would be displeased with me if I called earlier than she told me. I waited five minutes, popped an Altoid into my mouth to hide the flavor of the coffee that I gulped down before leaving home. I wished now that I ate a muffin or a scone. This could be an exhausting morning and maybe I needed nourishment for endurance. I called the young woman at reception across the lobby from where I was standing and asked for the room of Paula

Marlon. She connected me. Paula answered the phone on the second ring and told me that she was in room 735.

"Take the elevator to the right of the reception desk to the 6th floor. Get off there, walk down the hallway to the left and take the stairs to the 7th floor. Judge Kowalski is on my floor between the elevator and my room and I don't want you to be seen. My room is across the hall from the stairs. Do not knock. The door will be open, just walk in."

As I followed her directions, I remembered a conversation that we had about four months ago. She said that she couldn't wait to see me and she had specific plans for our time together. She wanted to assert her dominance over me and show me who the boss was. She would greet me at her door, kiss me once or twice to demonstrate how grateful she was that I came to her room. Then she would assume her role as dominatrix and I would be her submissive. She didn't want to start immediately on a basis of rewards and punishments, but only after appreciating me as I entered her room. I really had no understanding of how any of this would play out, but it felt enticing in a naughty way. I was equally reticent and anxious. A wicked smile crossed my face.

This was on my mind as I walked past the reception desk, took the elevator to the 6th floor, went left, found the emergency stairwell and walked up one flight. My toes were pinching in my pumps, but they would be off soon enough. I think my shoes really completed the outfit so I could endure the pain for a few more minutes. I opened the stairwell door and peeked into the hallway. No one was there. I stealthily crossed the hall and pushed open the door to 735. It was 7:00 a.m.

I entered her room, closed the door behind me and locked it. I turned around and Paula was standing there in a white hotel robe. She appeared to be freshly showered with no make-up and her damp hair falling below her shoulders. It had grown since I saw her. There were some new layers that framed her face in a really enticing way. She smiled warmly.

I put my purse and briefcase on the desk. The room was rather large. The bathroom and closet were immediately on the right. The closet door was open and I could see all of the suits Paula brought with her. I recognized two of them. There was a bed after the door to the bathroom, the desk and desk chair on the left, then a closed armoire which probably held the tv, another chair beyond that and a couch and coffee table near the window. The whole room was decorated with different shades of cream, gold and brown. It wasn't exactly my style, but it had the appearance of opulence. The Marriott does not disappoint.

"Catherine, it's good to see you." I nodded, not sure how to respond.

"Remember, I don't want to ever hurt you. If you are ever uncomfortable, we stop. Before we do anything, let's identify a safe word. You say the word if you want me to stop. How about 'Phoenix'? Yes, that will be it. Catherine, say 'Phoenix.'"

"Phoenix."

"Good girl. Now I hope I don't hear you say that again."

With that, she took a step closer to me. With my pumps on and her barefoot, we were the same height. She touched my face, put her nose next to mine, then tilted her head slightly and kissed me with her lips closed. I felt the strangest and deepest desire that I had ever felt. I wanted more. Her lips were soft and I could smell cinnamon coming from her mouth. Did she use cinnamon toothpaste? Suddenly, even toothpaste seemed sexy. She kissed me again with her lips parted, her tongue gently pushed its way into my mouth. Definitely cinnamon. We kissed for a few more minutes and then she pulled away. I wanted more. I wasn't done kissing her.

"I am pleased that you are here. Now we will play my game."

She walked to the couch that was across the room, past the king-size bed and near the window with the gold drapes closed. I imagined there was a view of Freedom Plaza with granite fountains and cars and buses driving by and people rushing to work. She sat there and asked me to follow her.

I approached the couch planning to sit next to her.

"No, Catherine. You will not sit. Stand in front of me and remove your dress."

Ummm. Ok. I knew I would feel exposed, more than just physically naked. Almost emotionally stripped. Maybe that was the point.

Even though the twins were born nearly four years earlier, I hadn't lost all of the baby weight I gained. I had about three pounds to go. Surprisingly, my little wobbly bits, as Bridget Jones called them, didn't dissuade me from removing my dress as instructed.

I lifted my dress over my head and placed it on a chair to the left of the couch. I stood in front of her in my bra, pumps and assorted matching jewelry. I realized how silly I felt that I had put so much time into choosing jewelry for this occasion.

"Turn around so I can see all of you. I have waited so long for this. I want to take it all in."

I obeyed her order and turned around. I felt the familiar twinge in my clit. Amazing how she could do that to me with just a few words.

"Take off your bra."

Again, I did as she commanded. I reached behind my back and using a finger-snap method unhooked my bra with one quick flick of my thumb and middle finger. I removed it and added it to the growing pile of my clothes on the chair.

"Ma'am, may I remove my jewelry?" I asked.

"Take off your bracelet, you won't be needing that. I'm glad to see that you didn't wear any rings. Let me look at your hands."

I took a step closer to her and put my hands out for her inspection. It seemed like an odd request, but it was her game.

"Catherine, I'm disappointed that you did not think to cut your nails before coming here. Go to my bathroom and get my nail clippers out of my green make-up bag."

I went from feeling horny to humiliated with one sentence. Was she going to make me cut my nails? They had been rather long since I quit biting them in third grade. Except for the year that I tried learning violin. That was 5th grade. My violin teacher did not approve of my nails either. He cut them in lessons one day. I was embarrassed. Somehow, my nails made it through the remainder of the school year but I quit playing violin after that. My nails were more important to me than becoming a violin virtuoso. Or was it virtuosa?

I found her make-up bag and the clippers were nestled in the corner inside. I returned to the couch with them.

"Give me the clippers."

I handed them to her.

"Now, let me see your hands again."

I put my hands out so she could reach them. She took her clippers and trimmed the nails on both index and middle fingers. She expertly used the clippers to ensure that no rough edges were left on my nails. While she was cutting my nails, I noticed her nicely manicured – and very short – nails. It looked like she put a lot of effort into having perfectly maintained hands, which embarrassed me even more. I had monthly pedicures to keep my toes looking attractive, but I never had my fingernails done. Maybe it was the trauma of having my violin teacher publicly cut my nails that I never overcame. She seemed pleased with her work.

"Put the clippers away now."

I quickly took them back to the bathroom, my toes aching in my pumps. I realized that they were a bad wardrobe choice as well.

"Catherine, in the future, ensure your nails are trimmed very short, particularly your index and middle fingers. I do not want to see any white parts extending beyond your fingers. Do you understand?"

"Yes. I'm sorry." She realized that I didn't answer her correctly before I did.

"'Yes, I'm sorry.' Is that how you are supposed to answer me?"

"Uh, no. I'm so sorry, ma'am." But the damage was done. I had earned my first infraction.

"I must punish you for breaking a rule. Do two spankings sound fair?"

This was really going to happen. "Yes, ma'am," I croaked.

"You don't sound convinced. Are two spankings a fair number for breaking the rule or would you prefer three?"

"Two, ma'am. I would prefer two. Thank you for including me in determining my punishment."

"Catherine, you understand that I make all final decisions, right? I am the boss and you are my submissive little bitch."

"Yes, ma'am. I understand completely."

"Good girl. Now bend over the chair."

I walked over to the chair and bent over. She smacked my ass. It wasn't very hard, but it definitely stung.

"Ouch!" The word escaped my lips. It was unintentional and I wasn't sure if it would be met with delight or anger.

"Did that hurt you?"

"Yes, ma'am."

"Good. Maybe now you will be more careful not to disobey me." A second, harder slap fell on my ass. I flinched.

The slight sting on my butt cheek was soon forgotten as she slid one perfectly manicured finger in my moist pussy. She fingered me from behind for a minute. Her finger filled a void that I didn't know I had. She then abruptly stopped. I wanted more. Even her brief connection with my pussy left me on the edge of orgasm. Her departure from my pussy hurt way more than any spanking could.

"Lie on your back on the bed," she commanded.

"Ma'am, may I remove my shoes?"

"No, you may not, but thank you for asking."

I stood up, walked four steps to the bed. The bedspread was neatly in place, remade after her night spent there. For an instant, I thought of Drew. The first thing he always did in any hotel room was remove the bedspread because he thinks it is dirty. While the maids change the sheets between guests, the bedspreads are rarely changed. My sweet husband attempted to keep germs away from us. My new lover apparently had no concerns about germs. I felt a pang of guilt, but the thought quickly left my mind as I did as I was told.

I climbed on to the bed and lay on my back. I was glad to be off of my feet, even though my shoes were still on.

"Spread your legs so I can look at you."

I spread my legs. Paula still wore the bathrobe while I wore nothing. I guess this is part of the dom-sub game. I am exposed, she is not. I still hadn't seen her naked body. I assumed I would in due time. There was no rush. Or maybe there was. We had to be at breakfast at 9 a.m. and I wasn't sure how much time had elapsed since I arrived. I was afraid to turn my head to look for the clock. I closed my eyes to avoid the scrutiny of her gaze. I wonder if I shaved enough or if pubic hair bothered her.

"Catherine, open your eyes. I want you to see me inspecting you."

I felt vulnerable which was understandable. I was lying naked having my most private parts analyzed. She touched my labia and smiled the sexy mischievous smile like she just discovered something no one had seen. I could tell that I was about to drip some pussy juice, I was so turned on.

"Now that I have met your beautiful cunt, I am going to name it. What do you think of 'Pam'?"

"Yes, ma'am. Pam sounds like a perfect name for my pussy. Does yours have a name as well?"

"Yes, you may call mine 'Sawyer'." She chose names from our favorite television shows – The Office and Lost. The connection was clever, the good girl of one show and the bad boy of another.

Prior to this relationship – if you can call it that – with Paula, I had never thought too much about women's bodies. There is a saying that women look at women more than men look at women. But when we do, we are sort of evaluating their shape, their clothes, their hair, and their jewelry, anything we could potentially covet. Sometimes we judge each other on those things, but mostly I think it's to envy other women. What does she have that I don't have? There will always be someone thinner, prettier, richer, smarter, whatever-er, so why beat ourselves up over those things we can't control? I have stopped being envious of other women after reading an article in a women's magazine. It said that it wasn't healthy to pick the best thing about a slew of different people and be envious of each. For example, Bob's car is better, Sally's house looks like a model home, Sandy's husband makes more money, Frank's kids went to Ivy League colleges. Basically, there isn't a single person who has everything. I thought of one neighbor, Jasmine, who seemed like she had a pretty perfect life: her husband is a partner in a law firm, she doesn't have to work, they have a beautiful house in the nicest part of our neighborhood and another one at the beach, her kids were athletic, attractive and smart, they took annual trips to Europe and the Caribbean. Seemed pretty perfect. But I took time to look beneath the surface and discovered that she was a recovering cocaine addict, her unattractive husband was a serial philanderer and her daughter was kicked off the high school lacrosse team for underage drinking during the homecoming football game last fall. If Jasmine was the best option of whom I could be jealous, I could do without it. I can't say that it's easy to not be envious of anyone, but I challenge myself to not use my energy for that.

One time I was looking for a suitcase under my parents' bed and I found a box of magazines. I'm guessing that it belonged to my father and my mother didn't know how to get rid of it after he died when I was thirteen. These magazines had glossy pictures of naked women inside. When I knew my mother would be at work, I looked at them. The women had glamorous names like "Misty" or "Trinity" or "Amber," names that seemed too sexy for regular people. Next to their photos, their measurements were listed and there was a place for them to fill in blanks in their own handwriting about activities they enjoy. Favorite hobbies? Roller skating, hiking, eating sushi, walking on the beach. They even had intriguing past times. No one said watching tv or hanging out with their little sister. Anyway, I was entranced by the beauty of their curvy bodies. Not an ounce of fat or a wayward dimple on their thighs. My teenage self hoped that wasn't how real women looked because I would never live up to that. I would be lucky if I had an interesting activity that I enjoyed when I became an adult. I realized that I really hadn't seen very many naked women in person. I didn't play sports in high school so there were no locker room opportunities and, when I had friends sleep over, everyone modestly changed in the bathroom. I had seen my mother, my aunts and my grandmother. While I love them dearly, they didn't really have sexy bodies that would inspire me to seek out more naked women. I thought back to those women in the magazines as I was anticipating Paula removing her robe and sharing her nakedness with me. Clearly, she was older than the women in the magazine, which reminded me that I forgot to check her personnel records for her birthdate. I guessed she was in her late 30s, maybe about five years older than me. But I really had no idea. Asian women can hide their age better than white women whose frown lines near their nose, mouth and between their eyebrows often betray their age before gray hairs supplant the natural color.

When Paula seemed sufficiently satisfied that my pussy had all of the usual parts and I was barely able to contain my heavy breathing, she offered me an option.

"Catherine, do you want to cum now or should I remove my robe first?"

I wasn't sure if this was a trick. Was she really allowing me to express my opinion or was it another opportunity for me to be punished?

"Ma'am, I am not comfortable making an important decision like that." I thought that was a safe answer.

"I didn't ask what we were going to do, I asked what you preferred. Make no mistake that I will be making the final decision. What is your preference?"

"I would prefer if you undressed, Judge."

She smiled.

"You may undress me, Catherine. Untie the belt to my robe and take it off me."

I quickly sat up, trying to be delicate yet accomplish my new task. I reached over to her robe and untied the belt. I reached inside the collar and touched her shoulders, gently pushing the soft material off of her. The robe fell from her arms and off her back onto the floor. I wasn't sure how much I should look at her. I wanted to take in every inch of her skin, see every freckle, touch every joint, fondle each muscle.

"Paula?"

"Catherine, please get on your elbows and knees with your ass in the air. If you feel the need to call me something other than 'Judge' or 'ma'am', you may call me 'Mistress'. 'Paula' is not an option."

As soon as I managed to get in the position she demanded, a felt a swift smack on my ass.

That stung, yet it was really sexy.

"Thank you, ma'am, for correcting me. I am so sorry for disobeying, Mistress. I request permission to look at your naked body."

From the position I was in on my elbows and knees, I could see the clock. It was 8:20 a.m. There wasn't a lot of time left to further explore her body.

"Catherine, in spite of your tendency to disobey me, I find you very attractive. I know you are inexperienced with women. Listen carefully and I will teach you how to make me cum."

She lay on the bed next to me and allowed me lay next to her. She kissed me forcefully.

"I want you to look at Sawyer."

I positioned myself between her spread legs. I wanted to touch her but I was afraid I would be clumsy. She had no pubic hair at all. Everything looked smooth and was glistening with her juices.

"Please, Mistress, tell me how I can please you."

"Put your right index finger inside of Sawyer. Do it very gently so you can see how it feels." I slipped my finger inside of her. It felt like mine except she squeezed her muscles and tensed around my finger. That was incredibly sensual. I wonder how to do that. She was so wet.

"Now put your right thumb on my clit and push up and in."

I did it.

"Again!" she urged.

I did it again and again. After about thirty seconds, her body shuddered. My hand was dripping wet. She squirted as she orgasmed. I made her orgasm! I felt proud of myself. She must have been very turned on by our game because that didn't take any time at all.

She groaned in approval and said, "You are a very good girl, Catherine. We must both get dressed now for the conference. I will give you a key to my room. You will return here at lunch time and I will return the favor. No panties for the entire morning. I want you to get wetter and wetter as you think about me this morning."

Holy shit, she was so hot. What an amazing morning. I'm learning to be submissive and it's inconceivably sexy. I wasn't sure if I could wait until lunch time to be with her again.

I put my dress on and left her room, using the stairs to go to the 6th floor and take the elevator from there. There could be no reason for anyone to think that she and I were anything other than acquaintances. Except, we sort of were just acquaintances. I didn't really know much about her except she was the hottest woman – ok, the only woman – I've ever known.

I went to the second floor where the conference center was. The hospitality staff was setting up a continental breakfast for our group. I didn't realize how starving I was. I needed food. I forgot Victoria was assisting the conference planner today. I will sit in some of the sessions to hear what the judges are learning about. Then I can simultaneously avoid Victoria and share what Paula is experiencing. I grab a croissant and some strawberry jam. I put my plate on one of the high-top tables in the corner and go in search of a drink. Coffee, tea, water and an assortment of juices are displayed across the room near the entrance to the conference room. I really needed water to hydrate, but I'd like some coffee too. As I'm adding creamer to my coffee, a group of judges enters the hallway. I see Paula with Judge Gelman and Judge Suitor. She is wearing a teal suit with a white ruffled blouse. I undress her with my eyes. I can't wait until her teal suit is draped over the chair in her room and she is in my arms again. But first, three long hours of the conference.

After I eat my breakfast and mingle with the visiting judges, I enter the conference room and sit in a chair in the back. All of the judges are seated at tables with their binders full of materials. The conference coordinator introduces the guest speaker and the attendees politely applaud. The speaker is talking about the increasing trend of fatal mine accidents and my mind starts to wander.

I think about giving Paula her first orgasm, how easy it was. I was afraid to lick Sawyer because I really had no idea how to do it so I was really glad that the first time was a simple digital manipulation. Damn it. I got wetter and wetter as I thought about it. And she squirted! I'm pretty sure that I don't squirt. One time, Thomas told me about an old girlfriend of his who squirted when she came. What was her name? She was a heavy girl who dated him before we met. Lisa? Liza? Lisette. That's it – Lisette. The first time she did it, he thought she peed on him. He was thinking "What the hell was that?" Then he discovered that she came almost like he did – lots of cum squirted out of somewhere – her clit? I haven't heard about women who squirt like that, but again, my research in this area is sorely lacking. Maybe I'm the odd one and everyone else does it that way? It would be pretty crappy for me to find that out at this point in my life.

Maybe I can read about that and how to tongue a clit or suck a pussy to increase satisfaction of my partner? Or maybe it would just come naturally? Do men have some kind of guide? It can't be intuitive, can it? Maybe I can assume that my Mistress will teach me, just like she did earlier today. I would think it would be difficult to belt out instructions when trying to focus on having an orgasm. I'm going to stop worrying. I'm certain she will tell me what pleases her. I think that is the point of the game, to maximize her satisfaction. She must be very in tune to her own needs and confident of her desires to ensure she gets what she wants in each scenario. And I am happy to play along.

Finally, it was noon and I took the elevator to the 6th floor, walked up the flight of stairs and used my key to enter her room. She was not there yet. I was unsure what to do. Should I undress and wait for her? That might be presumptuous. I wish she had given me instructions.

Click!

The door swung open and Paula walked in, locking the door behind her.

"How is my precious little sub?" was how she greeted me.

Tingle between my legs was my involuntary response.

"I'm happy to be back here with you, ma'am. Did you enjoy the morning session?"

"Not really, I kept thinking about getting back here with you. I am surprised you are not naked waiting on my bed."

I made the wrong choice. Was this a punishable offense or not?

I quickly removed my dress and bra. I kept my shoes on.

"Catherine, you were fairly obedient this morning, so you may remove your shoes now. Better yet, I will do it for you while you put your own two fingers into Pam. Lie down on the bed."

I did as I was told. I started to reach my hands towards my wet pussy when Paula screeched, "I did not tell you to put your fingers inside yet. I said *while* I take off your shoes! I have not even touched your feet yet."

I waited for my next direction. She started at my knee and licked the length of my shin until she got to my ankle. Then she put her fingers into my shoe under the arch. Who knew my shin could feel erotic? Everything with this woman was so sensual.

"Catherine, now put your two fingers on your right hand inside and I will remove your right shoe."

My two fingers easily glided inside my super-wet pussy. I moved them gently in and out as she slowly took off my shoe.

She noticed the movement of my hand. In. Out. In. Out. That was the final straw. She overlooked my earlier miscues, but not this one.

"I did not tell you to masturbate. I said put your fingers inside. Catherine, I am sorry but I can't overlook your disobedience. Please get on your elbows and knees with your ass in the air. This will be known as position number one. If I tell you to assume position number one, this is what I expect you to do. Do you understand?"

"Yes, mistress." I could barely say the words. Her words were taunting me.

"I am not trying to hurt you. I just want you to understand who is the boss, who dominates you. That is me. Please repeat after me 'I understand that you dominate me.'"

"I understand that you dominate me."

"I will not make any decisions or act without your permission."

I repeated her statement. "I will not make any decisions or act without your permission."

"Good girl. How many times did you move your fingers in and out of Pam just now when I only asked you to put your fingers inside?"

"Three or four, ma'am."

"Was it three or was it four? Those are two different numbers!"

"I believe it was four, ma'am."

"Ok, then. I will spank you four times." She reached into her briefcase and pulled out a spiral notebook.

"How do you think these metal spirals will feel on your bare ass, Catherine?"

"I think it will hurt, Mistress."

"Can you handle the pain?"

"Yes, ma'am." I gritted my teeth and waited to feel the sting of a new weapon.

Whap! Whap! Two very fast swats hit my ass. I kept my ass in place to not reveal the depth of the pain.

"How did that feel? Did you learn from your mistake or should I give you the remaining two?"

"I'm very sorry, ma'am. I will listen very closely to your demands. Please accept my apology." I sounded more desperate than I meant to. Even though my ass hurt, my pussy was still aching for attention.

"Roll onto your back. Let's see if I can remove the other shoe without any more problems."

I rolled over.

"Put your two fingers from your left hand in your pussy as I remove your left shoe. Ready?"

"Yes, ma'am." I positioned my hand near my hole waiting for her to make the next move.

She caressed my calf with her hand, tickled my ankle with her tongue, and then flipped my shoe off before my fingers entered Pam. Shit!

"You are not very good at this. Maybe I can help?"

She reached up to my hole and put her thumb inside. The fingers on her other hand circled my right nipple and she pinched it really hard.

"Uhhh!"

"Did I hurt you?"

"No, ma'am. You just surprised me."

"I want you to pinch your own nipples while I make you cum. Squeeze them now!"

I did as I was told. She slid her thumb in and out of my pussy and rolled her index and middle fingers over my clit in a titillating manner. It felt amazing and confusing. I wasn't sure what she was doing.

My fingers loosened their grip on my nipples which she noticed immediately.

"Harder!" I pinched and as I did, my clit exploded in orgasm. I felt a giant pulse as it felt like I fell off a cliff. How did she know how to make me cum like that? I needed to catch my breath, enjoy the moment. I felt like I needed a shower to clean myself off.

She laughed at her ability to make me cum so easily. She was so beautiful and that tauntingly sexy smile seriously made me swoon.

"Beautiful Catherine, you were a very good girl today. You may kiss me now."

I kissed her hungrily. I was grateful that she allowed me to cum. I felt that I should thank her to prove my gratitude, but I didn't want this moment to end. After several minutes, she pulled away.

"Thank you, Mistress, for allowing me to have such an amazing orgasm. I feel unworthy of your attention. May I make you cum again?"

"You are right that you are not worthy, but I expect that you will prove that you deserve my attention. You may not make me cum again today. But I expect to see you here at 7:00 tomorrow morning with no panties on. Now get cleaned up and get back to the conference."

I cleaned myself with a washcloth in her bathroom, got dressed and left. Back to the stairwell to the 6th floor.

When the conference ended that day, I used the restroom in the lobby to ensure I looked presentable before going home. I asked Drew to pick up the boys from preschool because I knew I wouldn't get out of the city in time to get them. When I finally got home ninety minutes later, Drew had carryout dinner on the table, the boys were bathed and in their pajamas. What a great husband I had. After a life-altering experience, I was back home with my family trying to forget the deeds of my day. It was surprisingly easy. There was much to do at home: the boys' laundry required folding, the bathroom needed cleaning, the dishwasher had to be emptied and refilled. By the time I was done with my household chores, I was ready for bed. Drew knew that driving in D.C. area traffic was stressful for me and assumed that spending hours in it today wore me out. He didn't complain when I went to bed early.

I had a restful night of sleep and woke up with lots of energy. However, I forgot to choose something to wear before going to bed, so that would waste time this morning before leaving. Ugh! After showering, doing my hair and minimal make-up, I rummaged through my closet to find an appropriate outfit. Let's see, what says "I'm trying to look sexy for my hot Dominatrix, but look business-like for my colleagues?" I chose a short navy skirt with a flowered low-cut blouse and a sweater that I could button at the top to hide my cleavage. I put on a push-up bra that would make my breasts look perky, round and full. I put a thong in my purse and found some very sensible open-toed sandals to complete my outfit. I skipped coffee, just grabbed a water bottle and left.

Traffic was worse this morning and I was terrified that I would be late. I was not looking forward to the consequences of tardiness, although it's possible Pam disagreed. I practically threw my keys at the valet and raced to the elevator. I was so glad to have comfy shoes on! The elevator opened quickly and I made a split-second decision to go directly to the 7th floor. Breaking a rule. Disobeying. I felt guilty about my choice but I was trying to be on time. I reached her door at 7:02 a.m. I put my key in and pushed the door, but the security latch was engaged. I knocked gently. Maybe she forgot to unlock it after waking up? She approached the door and saw me through the small opening.

"Yes?"

"Good morning, Judge. Can you please open the door for me?"

"Catherine, what time did I tell you to arrive?"

"7:00 a.m., ma'am."

"And what time is it?"

"7:02 a.m., ma'am." I felt ashamed and a little naughty having to whisper these responses from the hallway.

"Do you know what I do to nasty little subs who disobey me?"

"I'm so sorry, ma'am. I will accept whatever punishment you deem necessary." I knew it didn't matter if I was stuck in traffic or overslept. There was no good excuse. I didn't follow directions. I should have left earlier. I could have woken up earlier. Now I have started our day off in a bad place.

She unlocked the door and allowed me to enter.

"Before we start, safe word check."

"Phoenix," I replied.

"Good. Take off your clothes and sandals. Leave your bra on. Assume position one."

I fumbled removing everything as quickly as possible. I got onto the bed on my elbows and knees with my ass high in the air.

She sat on the chair across from me silently. "You made me wait for two minutes. Now you can wait for two minutes until I decide how I am going to punish you. You can think about what you've done and how we can rectify the violation of my timeliness request."

She came behind me and snapped my bra twice really hard. She unhooked my bra and re-fastened it on the tightest hooks. It was uncomfortable, the underwire was gripping under my breasts, pushing the cups in and forcing my boobs to appear even more voluptuous.

"Roll over so I can admire your beautiful tits."

I turned to my back. She was reached inside my bra cup to free my right breast and pinched my nipple. She produced a clothes pin from her nightstand and put it on my right nipple.

"Ow!" I softly howled.

"Catherine, you must learn to enjoy the pain I'm inflicting on you. You understand that pain and pleasure operate together. We cannot experience one without the other. I am not trying to hurt you, only control you and make you truly mine."

"Yes, ma'am. I understand completely."

"Good girl. You are starting to redeem yourself for your bad behavior earlier. Let me taste your wet pussy."

I opened my legs and she climbed between them, removing her bathrobe as she did.

"Mistress, may I have a clothespin on my left nipple, too?" I thought this request would please her because she would believe that I am embracing the discomfort.

"How badly do you want the clothes pin?"

"Very badly," I lied, but she didn't have to know.

"I will give it to you in two minutes. You must wait, like you made me wait."

"Yes, ma'am. I understand completely."

She flicked her tongue around my crotch, sucking on my thighs and biting my lips. She pulled on my pubic hair with her teeth. She did not, however, touch my clit or enter my pussy. I was writhing in anticipation. She stopped after two minutes and put the other clothespin on my left nipple. Damn, that hurt. But it was somewhat pleasurable, not just painful. I thought about channeling the pain into another dimension, perhaps bliss. Maybe I could learn to love this feeling?

"Catherine, I want you to make me cum now. Get up. I will tell you what I want."

She took my place on her bed and I stood at the end of the bed. She opened her legs and then scooted to the edge of the bed so her legs were dangling off the side. Sawyer was on display for me. So clean and perfect with no hair anywhere. I had to figure out how to shave all of my pubic hair without arousing suspicion. That really looked sexy.

"Get on your knees on the floor between my legs," she directed me.

I did. My face was right at pussy-level. I was a little scared of what would happen next. The clothes pins were pinching my nipples in a way that was becoming erotic and my pussy was dripping.

"I want you to put one finger inside of me and fuck me with it."

Done. That was easy.

"Now add another finger."

My two fingers with the nails she trimmed were inside of her. I slowly moved them in and out of slippery Sawyer. I remembered to cut all of the rest of my nails before leaving home this morning in case having short nails was a necessity today.

She was breathing harder and thrusting her hips in rhythm with my fingers. "Catherine, fuck me with three fingers."

My third finger went inside of her. It was getting tight. The movement created friction and the moisture created an arousing slurping noise. I wondered if I could fit another finger inside.

She was moaning in passion and could barely say, "one more finger. Now."

I added my final finger, pushing it in gently at first and then with more force. I was afraid it might hurt her but she was giving me no indication that I should stop.

"Thumb my clit. I'm ready to...aaahhhhh!"

Oh my god. She came the second my thumb grazed her clit. Her body shuddered and then went limp.

"You are getting very good at this. I want you to take your index finger and wipe my pussy juice behind your ears. For the rest of the day, you can smell me there like perfume. My juice is your perfume."

My Dominatrix Judge is so freaking hot. I can't wait for her to make me cum. My clit is throbbing and my pussy – her Pam – is aching to be filled with her fingers. I am so anxious to see what she has planned next.

"Come lie next to me, Catherine."

Without hesitation, I nearly leap to her side. We are both naked except I'm still wearing my push-up bra and her clothes pins are still on my nipples. She removes the clothes pins and massages my sore nipples, then places my breasts back inside the cups of my too-tight bra.

She reaches between my legs to feel my hot pussy and it doesn't disappoint her. Her index finger circles around my hole once, twice, then she plunges it in deeply and I catch my breath. She withdraws her finger, wipes it all over her lips like she is glossing them, then kisses me. I taste myself on her lips. So. Fucking. Hot.

"We are finished for today, my sweet Sub. Get dressed. You may wear your panties today and you will keep your bra how it is now, on the tightest hook. Every time you feel it around your ribs, your beautiful tits and on your back, you can think of me."

I was surprised that she wasn't going to finish me off. I wanted to beg her to let me cum, but I was afraid to invoke her wrath. Very sheepishly, I complied.

"Yes, ma'am. Thank you for letting me give you an orgasm."

"You are welcome. You must learn to control your urges better. I am withholding your orgasm to teach you control. That is your lesson for today. I do not want you to fuck your husband tonight. No more sex today."

I dressed myself, feeling empowered that I gave my Mistress pleasure and I was strong enough to abstain myself.

"Catherine, in no time, you will become my perfect Sub. Thank you for being such a willing participant and enthusiastic learner. My husband is arriving later today, so I think our games are over for this week. I can talk to you during the remainder of the conference, but I will be doing so with extreme indifference. Do not take it personally. We absolutely cannot spark any suspicion. We don't need to give Victoria anything to speculate about."

"Yes, Judge." What could I say but to agree with her?

She opened the door. I gathered my belongings and left. I went to the stairwell across the hall, walked down to the 6th floor and then used to elevator to go to the conference.

I ate a quick breakfast and asked the conference coordinators if they needed any help. I thought I should probably keep myself busy to keep my mind off of Paula. But I was drawn to her and I found myself in a session where she was listening to updates from the 9th Circuit Court. She knew I was in the back of the room. She made notes on a yellow legal pad and then she played with her pen. First, she rubbed one finger along it, then two, then three. She was trying to excite me, knowing that I would see her. And it worked. I watched her finger her pen and caress it. My breathing grew heavier. I felt like I would explode. She found the simplest ways to be totally sexy and used the most mundane objects to entice me. I found her irresistible and outrageous. I walked out of the conference room to get some air and some water. I could barely breathe and my mouth was drier than a desert.

At the next break, she approached me and asked if I was okay. She smiled her sexy mischievous smile and I melted. A man hurried toward us pulling a suitcase.

"Catherine, meet my husband." Garrett had arrived.

The next morning, I woke up on time, but realized that I really couldn't go back to the conference. I couldn't bear to see her with him. I told Drew that I was having cramps and I would probably sleep for a while and go to work late. He dressed and fed the boys and took them to pre-school. I was happy to have time alone to sort through everything that happened the last two days.

I stayed in bed until 11:00 a.m., thinking, analyzing and rethinking. While I felt a strong attraction to Paula, I didn't think I could continue our short affair. I'm not sure calling it 'an affair' was even accurate. It was a two-day fling. Or year-long foreplay leading to a two-day fling. However I characterized it, it still added up to being wrong. I was determined to go to the conference tomorrow to let Paula know that I couldn't be with her any more. Once I made the decision, I immediately felt a sense of relief. I jumped out of bed, showered, went grocery shopping and decided to make Drew's favorite dinner – shrimp scampi. A huge weight had been lifted and I felt free. I even bought myself a bouquet of flowers celebrating my good sense to not be involved in this marriage-crippling liaison.

I picked the boys up early from preschool. They had school in the morning, then lunch, nap time and recess. I felt a renewed connection to my family since my attention was no longer diverted. I didn't realize how much energy I had put into Paula – even though our phone conversations occurred irregularly and I had only spent parts of two days with her in person. I took the boys to their favorite park and we ran around enjoying the warmth of the spring day. Then we went on a secret mission for a little pre-dinner treat – ice cream. I swore them to secrecy because Drew didn't like them spoiling their appetites. I figured they would still be hungry even after ice cream at 4:00 p.m. since they burned so much energy at the park.

Dinner was delicious. The boys were well-behaved. It was a splendidly perfect family evening. I told Drew that I think my earlier cramps were likely a result of something I ate at the conference center the day before. But since I felt fine now, I wasn't really worried about it. One last lie before I'm out of this situation.

On Thursday morning, I didn't rush to the hotel. I had no reason to be there at 7:00 a.m. I told Drew to go to work early and I would take Logan and Bodie to preschool. I arrived at the hotel around 8:40 a.m., ate some of the continental breakfast that the hotel provided for our group and checked in with Duncan, the conference coordinator. He said that everything went well on Wednesday and asked if I was feeling better. He said a few judges asked where I was. I wanted to know which ones, but I was afraid to ask. Duncan ran off to ask the hotel assistant to alter the temperature in the conference room.

I was standing in the corner sipping my coffee when Paula emerged from the elevator. She looked strikingly gorgeous, the type of beautiful that people on the street would stop and watch her walk by. I had never felt she was that pretty before. It was as if she had something pulling me to her. It was an undeniable attraction. In a few short steps, she was next to me. I could smell her cinnamon toothpaste and perfume that I didn't recognize. In hushed tones she asked why I didn't come to the conference yesterday. I lied when I told her that I didn't feel well. This lie was getting a lot of use this week.

"I was worried that I left a mark on your beautiful ass and your husband saw it," she admitted.

"That is not something you have to worry about. He rarely sees me naked. I wake up before he does and I usually change clothes in the bathroom. When we have sex, it's in the dark."

"While I am happy to hear that your husband doesn't suspect anything, I am not ready to hear the specifics of your sex life with him. It makes me a little jealous knowing that he can fuck you anytime he wants while I cannot. Garrett has gone to Annapolis for the day, so I want you in my hotel room at lunch time. Do you still have my key?"

"Yes, ma'am. I will be there." I felt a little sad knowing that would be the last time I'd answer her with my submissive response.

The morning crawled by. I was both saddened and relieved to be ending this situation.

At the appointed hour, I took my last trip to the 6th floor to the stairwell leading to the 7th floor and paused at her door across the hall. I carefully removed the door key from the outside pocket of my purse and pushed it into the slot, turning the door handle as I did. Imagine my surprise to see her standing there naked when I opened the door. Holy shit, she was perfect in every way, even her slightly crooked yet alluringly mischievous smile. There went my break-up plan just like that. Her tits were round with perfectly quarter-sized areolas surrounding sweet pointy nipples. I couldn't wait to lick them and tease them with my teeth. Shit! Shit!! I stood there paralyzed by my change of heart, although I wasn't sure I was thinking with my heart. I felt the increasingly familiar pulse that would turn into a throb in my deceitful clit.

"Catherine, since you were my perfect Sub this week, I want to reward you with some passionate lovemaking. No games today. You may call me Paula."

"Yes, ma... Paula. That sounds wonderful." I was putty in her hands.

She approached me and kissed me; her tongue explored my mouth. She tasted of the cinnamon that I smelled earlier. Was it just a few hours ago that I thought I would be ending this crazy relationship? Now I couldn't wait to experience a different side of this complex woman. She lifted my shirt over my head with urgency as I fumbled with the button and zipper on my pants. Within seconds I joined her in nakedness. We stood by the door kissing and fondling each other, moving slowly in an awkward dance toward the bed.

I pulled the bedspread off, feeling a slight twinge of guilt. Life is short, enjoy the moment. It's all physical, not emotional. Go with the flow. I didn't need to convince myself. She climbed into the bed and beckoned me to join her. I kissed her toes, sucking each one individually. She closed her eyes and licked her lips indicating her enjoyment. From there, my tongue traced the arch of her foot and circled her ankle. I massaged her calf. Her skin was soft, yet I could feel hard muscles beneath. I inched my way up to her thigh, pausing to suck on her kneecap producing a small hickey. The anticipation of reaching Sawyer was almost too much for us both. I skipped over her entire pelvic area. I guess I could also play a little game of delayed gratification. I fingered, then licked her belly button. How could a navel be so flawless? I wished I could jump inside and swim around in her navel. I stifled a laugh when I thought of a leaked conversation between Prince Charles and his then-mistress Camilla Parker Bowles during which he wished he could be her tampon. I think navel swimming was a lot more provocative than being a tampon. But maybe Prince Charles was going for risqué or dramatic and not sensual like I was?

I went on to massage her flat stomach, drawing invisible circles with the pads of my fingers. She reached under my chin and pulled me close for another kiss. I felt like I knew her so completely when we kissed, like I knew all of her secrets and nothing would come between us. As we kissed, she reached between my legs. I reciprocated. She pushed her fingers inside of me and I mimicked her movements. She flicked my clit with her thumb and I did the same to her. We kissed hungrily and rocked our hips in unison and in tempo with each other's fingers. My clit was pounding and I could barely focus on continuing to finger Sawyer. But I wanted so much to continue to gratify Paula like she was doing to me. And like a hackneyed cliché, we reached orgasm simultaneously. My fingers felt her vagina clench as she came. We both trembled, then giggled. I removed my fingers from Sawyer and licked each one, savoring her taste. I wanted to remember this moment forever. We stayed in each other's arms kissing. I cupped her breast and felt the smooth skin leading up to her areola.

"If you continue to do that, we'll never get back to the conference."

She was right. The lunch hour flew by, filled with passion and tender love-making. I liked seeing this side of Paula, but I sort of missed the Judge. We got out of bed and used the soft hotel washcloths to wash each other's pussies. I used warm water and soap and slowly moved her lips from side to side cleaning every nook possible. She asked me to sit on the vanity and spread my legs resting my foot on the tank of the toilet for easier access. I felt her fingers through the washcloth and was tempted to have one more orgasm. She heard my breaths get deeper and chastised me, "No, no, no. We can't do that again." With that, my cleansing was over. We dressed and returned to the conference. We were both flushed and hungry. I retrieved two smashed granola bars from my purse, handed her one, and whispered, "I will get us some food while you go into the next session."

I walked around the hotel until I found a small café near the lobby. I purchased a couple of to-go sandwiches. They didn't look very appetizing but were certainly better than starving. As I returned to the second floor, I realized that we didn't even say goodbye in a meaningful way and it's likely that we wouldn't be alone again. Crap. Maybe that was better? Long, drawn out goodbyes are never a good thing.

When I rounded the corner, I saw Edwin, our Branch Chief, looking flustered. "Catherine! Can you help me? I just got a call from our Public Affairs staff. Some big-wig at the Department wants to visit our office tomorrow. The PA folks are going to be here at the conference doing the discussion on congressional inquiries, legislative updates and stakeholder outreach programs. There aren't many people I trust enough to handle this visit. Will you meet with them? I have all of the materials that they are interested in. I will email them to you. The timing of this visit is awful, but I just can't leave the Judges' conference."

"Of course, I can meet with them. Who is coming? Cal Johnson?"

"Yes, Cal and Samantha Snyder – do you know her?"

"I've heard her name, but never met her. It's not a problem. I'm glad to help out."

Except it sort of was a big problem. Being at the office meant I wasn't going to be at the conference. And not being at the conference meant I wasn't going to see Paula again. I assumed Garrett would be back so we wouldn't have alone time, but at least I could see her if I were at the conference.

I ate my sandwich outside the conference room where the continental breakfast had been served much earlier and waited for the break between speakers. Finally, Paula emerged from room. She looked at my face and said, "Who died?"

"Ahhh, if only it was that simple," I responded. "Edwin asked me to meet some of Department leadership tomorrow. They are coming to the office for a meeting and almost everyone will be here at the hotel."

"Well, aren't you important?" she asked jokingly.

"I guess so. I'm really disappointed that I won't be able to see you tomorrow." Tears started to fill my eyes. I didn't want her to see me upset.

"Hey, it's ok. I'm not going anywhere. We will talk on the phone next week. I have many more surprises for you! I can't wait to share new games."

"That sounds great. I can't wait to learn new games, ma'am," I winked at her.

Leaving her wasn't as difficult as I thought it would be since there were promises of more adventures.

Back to my normal life, where I get to be wife, mom, daughter, sister, friend, colleague and not anyone's Sub. The next week at work, Bonnie and I took our regular lunchtime walks. It was a beautiful time to be in the park. Since the spring came later than usual, the azaleas were blooming in late May. I loved the smell and sights of spring time, especially in Washington. The cherry blossoms around the Tidal Basin in April are magnificent. The throngs of tourists also come, which is one of the many downsides of living near the nation's capital.

As we entered the southeast end of the park, I finally told Bonnie about my experience with Paula. Bonnie and I were friends during my separation with Thomas and the steamy romance with Antonio that ended my first marriage. She had seen that not-so-flattering side of me. She reminded me that the stakes were higher now. I had a family.

"Thanks, Dr. Ruth. I don't need a therapist and please don't try to be my conscience. I just want you to be my supportive friend."

"Cath, I know how you get. You have an obsessive streak. Don't get in too far that you can't get out."

"I have a plan for that. I'm not going to fall in love with her. That was the problem with Antonio. I didn't leave it at just sex. Emotions were involved. I won't let that happen again."

"Many people can't separate sex and love. They become intertwined. How can you share that intimacy without feeling something?"

"I think I'm better at compartmentalizing now. I will not let anything jeopardize my family. I love Drew and our life together. I have no idea how this thing with Paula will go anyway. She lives in freakin' Pittsburgh! It's not like she's here and I'm seeing her every day."

I thought about that for a few minutes. Imagine if this relationship had started while she was here. That would have changed everything. I'm not sure I could have worked with her every day, seen her every day. That would have been like having a Viagra erection 24/7. I'm also not sure I'm good enough to have a poker face day in and day out. Maybe we would have gotten busted. At work. There isn't much worse than that. Everything happens for a reason and Paula happened just how she was supposed to – with her in Pittsburgh and me still in Virginia.

The few days I spent getting to know Paula during the conference were not enough for me. And our infrequent phone calls were not enough either. I was happy, when three or four days at a time, I would forget about her. Life was so easy then. Go to work, go home, take care of the family. Occasionally have a date night with Drew. I attempted to think about her when we talked and forget about her when we didn't. Sometimes that worked. I told her once that I would not fall in love with her – and I meant it. Our relationship would work better if there was no real emotion involved. I had made that mistake once before.

I remembered how innocently things had started with Antonio. When Thomas and I were married for three years, after we had dated for three years in college, we went to a party that one of his co-workers was hosting. Out of the twenty-five people there, I knew one person besides Thomas. I poured myself a dark beer and looked around for someone to talk to. A group formed in the kitchen and I joined them. They were mostly young guys talking about their research jobs, which I knew little about. One guy in particular seemed friendly, yet vulnerable and maybe broken somehow. He introduced himself as Antonio. We chatted for at least an hour. He was open about his life, including that he suffered from depression, his love for his family's summer house in Vermont and his cat. He was separated from a woman he met in a bar and married on a whim. She had been in the Navy but was now a stripper in a local club. None of what he said made any sense to me; it was so foreign from my own life. But I was intrigued so I listened. When the evening was over, I realized that I wanted to listen to him some more. I gave him my work phone number. I'm certain now that perhaps that wasn't the best idea I had ever had. But maybe it was the beer that shared my number and not me. He called me the next day and we talked some more. He told me about how he had two middle names, one that he saw in a dream and had his name legally changed to reflect the addition. He spoke about competing in a bodybuilding competition and modeling. He liked spelunking and rock climbing. He told me about his sports car, his sick grandfather, divorced parents and desire for a tattoo. Well, that was one thing we had in common – I wanted to get a tattoo, as well. We made an impromptu plan to get tattoos the next day after work. I met him at a tattoo shop in Arlington. It was near his sick grandfather's house. Antonio and his brother, Giorgio, took turns staying with their grandfather and ensuring all of his needs were met. They really thought he wouldn't live much longer. Antonio knew that he wanted a yin-yang tattoo to symbolize his quest for balance. Meanwhile I was obsessed with peace signs. I waited until I was in my mid-20s to get my first tattoo because I wanted to be sure that whatever I selected would not be a frivolous design. There was nothing trivial about peace. An hour after we arrived, we were both sporting our first tattoos. My purple peace sign was on my shoulder blade. His yin-yang was on his bicep. I went home to show Thomas, so very excited that I finally did it. I promised to talk to Antonio the next day. Thomas was shocked to see my peace sign. At first, he thought it was a stick-on tattoo. I had to convince him it was real. Eventually, he liked it a lot.

The next day, Antonio asked if I wanted to meet his grandfather. I agreed to stop at his grandfather's house on my way home. My visit was brief as it appeared that Grandpa Luca was, indeed, very ill. Even though I had worked with the elderly while I was in college, I felt out of place there. A week later, Antonio was back at Luca's house and asked me to come over. I picked up a six pack of Antonio's favorite beer and parked on the narrow street in north Arlington. He was waiting for me at the door. His grandfather was sleeping and he didn't want me to ring the doorbell and disturb him. He gave me a tour of the old bungalow. Antonio seemed pretty fragile; the truth of Luca's deteriorating health was taking its toll on him. I could tell how close he was to his grandfather. Giorgio stopped by to bring some food their mother had made. Even though their mother was a nurse, she would not spend time with her dying father because she refused to see him like that. I didn't understand why she wouldn't visit him, but it was not for me to judge. Giorgio, Antonio and I ate quietly in the small dining room and consumed the beer I brought. Giorgio was not as intense and brooding as Antonio was and I enjoyed his company a lot. When the meal was finished, Giorgio cleaned up the dishes and left. It was Antonio's night to spend with Luca. I called Thomas to tell him that I was seeing Luca and I'd be home later. It would have been more truthful to say that I was seeing Antonio. And that I wouldn't be home. That night was the first time we kissed. It was passionate and desirous. I didn't want to leave him. But my husband was home. So, at 6:00 a.m., I drove home.

Unlike the time I kissed Mikey years before, this time I did not admit my transgression to Thomas. I wanted to keep it to myself a while longer. A few days later, Antonio and I had sex for the first time. It was raw and wild. He said he liked rough sex. I didn't really know what that meant, having only been with my gentle Thomas for the last three years. Antonio was younger than me, very athletic, very inventive. He wanted to do it standing up, on countertops and tables. He sometimes wanted it fast and hard in his car. Occasionally the Italian lover in him would want to just fuck slowly for hours, never reaching orgasm. Just enjoying each other's bodies. I snuck to Luca's house as much as I could to be with Antonio. After four months of meeting secretly, Luca died. Antonio, Giorgio and their mother were all with him. Luca's house would be empty until it sold – and they were in no hurry to sell it. Our trysts became more frequent. And in my inexperience with being unfaithful, I made a critical error: I fell in love. My lovemaking with Antonio became more intense and sex with Thomas became non-existent. I actually felt like I was cheating on Antonio when I was with Thomas. What had I done to my life? Thomas was my dream man and I was throwing it all away to be with my hot Italian lover. I felt like a piece of shit. And I was certain that Thomas had no idea. It was easy to go to the gym after work for a half hour, then spend an hour with Antonio before going home. I was hot and sweaty either way. After nine months of deceit, I couldn't stand it anymore and I came clean with Thomas. We were on vacation when it happened. We woke up one morning in our hotel room and I was missing Antonio desperately. I started crying. Thomas said, "What's wrong?"

"I don't know how to describe it," I admitted. The thing was I had said it in my head so many times. I'm in love with someone else, but I don't want to leave you. I want you both. But those are not words anyone can say aloud. They don't work aloud. They barely worked in my head.

I cried some more and finally spoke. I knew I wouldn't be free unless I spoke the truth. "I'm seeing someone else."

He was genuinely shocked. He wanted to know who, why, where? I didn't want to tell him all of my secrets.

He said he was leaving. He packed his suitcase and went to the airport. He left me there. My flight was two days from then. I walked around the city alone, went to restaurants and shops and cried. Mostly I cried. I was heartbroken for what a mess I had made of my life – and our life together. Two days later, I took a taxi to the airport and flew home. When I got to our house, he wasn't there. He had left a message on the answering machine.

"Catherine, don't leave. I want to talk. I want to fix it. Stay there please." I could hear the desperation in his voice. I unpacked and waited. He came home a few hours later and we cried together. We decided to go to marriage counseling. We each had our own therapists and we went to a third one together. The one we saw together said I had to quit seeing Antonio. I tried. I didn't see him for a week. Then I saw him but didn't touch him. I couldn't stand it. I refused to let him go. As a result, marriage counseling didn't go well. Three months of trying to stay together until we gave up. We made a decision to separate the following month – conscious uncoupling before it became a thing. I didn't know that he had already met with a divorce attorney and emptied out half of everything from our bank accounts.

I told Antonio that I was leaving Thomas. I was going to get my own place so I could be with him whenever I wanted. He pleaded with me to only leave Thomas for myself, not for him. He didn't want to be responsible for the dissolution of my marriage. If I hadn't met him, I would have continued to be happy with Thomas. I wouldn't have known what I was missing in my life. Antonio could touch my hand and my panties would turn into a mushy mess. All of my senses were heightened with the promise of erotic ecstasy. Even remembering now, the nights we spent together more than a decade ago, leave me craving that intense passion. For six months after my separation, we continued our affair with candlelit dinners and adventures to abandoned barns that made him so horny. It was surprising how many empty buildings could be easily entered and fucked in. We spent weekends exploring rural areas and each other. Until one day, he decided he wanted to move to Vermont. Without me. I was devastated. Empty.

I heard the lyrics to the Cranberries' song, appropriately titled *Empty*:

> *Something has left my life*
> *And I don't know where it went to*
> *Somebody caused me strife*
> *And it's not what I was seeking.*
> *Didn't you see me? Didn't you hear me?*
> *Didn't you see me standing there?*
> *Why did you turn out the lights?*
> *Did you know that I was sleeping?*
> *Say a prayer for me*
> *Help me to feel the strength I did*
> *My identity has it been taken*
> *Is my heart breaking on me?*
> *All my plans fell through my hands*
> *They fell through my hands on me*
> *All my dreams, it suddenly seems*
> *Empty*

It was as if Dolores O'Riordan was singing the lyrics to my life. That song perfectly described how I felt. Completely empty. Because my relationship with Antonio was still secret, in spite of my being separated. I had to grieve quietly for the loss of the most intense relationship I ever had. It was the worst feeling ever.

I met Drew two months later.

2007

This was the year that the Department of Labor finally caught up with the rest of the government workforce and allowed select individuals to sign up for alternate work schedules if their positions permitted it. I was first in line to ask Edwin if I could do it. I figured it would be good for work-life balance. Having one day off every other week and working 9-hour days for the remaining days would be great. I could make doctors' appointments, go grocery shopping, do laundry and all kinds of things on my day off. It would make my weekends free for more family activities and decrease the stress in my life. Logan and Bodie had started playing soccer the previous fall. Weekly games and practices ate into time for errands and household chores. But Drew and I loved seeing them run around in their little blue soccer jerseys – it was so adorable. Edwin approved my request to change my schedule. Starting February 1st, I would have every other Friday off. I was more excited about that than I should have been.

On a Wednesday afternoon in mid-February, Paula called. I hadn't talked to her in a couple of weeks because she had to go to the Denver court to fill in for Judge Hernandez who was on maternity leave. I was happy to hear her voice.

"Catherine? Remind me never to go to Denver in January without my skis! What was I thinking? There are ski resorts everywhere. Have I told you that I love skiing almost as much as playing tennis?"

I wasn't sure which Paula I was talking to, so I decided to err on the safe side "no, ma'am. I didn't know that you loved skiing." I smiled at myself for allowing her to be dominant.

"Do you know how hot you are when you are acting like my perfect little submissive?"

"Yes, Judge. I think I do. Because I know how hot you are when you demonstrate who's the boss."

"Did you hear that Edwin is not letting the judges do the alternate work schedule?" she asked.

I had heard because I was administering the program. "The program is a pilot program anyway. He may change who is eligible after we see how office coverage is. Each branch chief is deciding how to run the program. He is allowing me to do it. I started last week and have every other Friday off."

"You are very fortunate. Don't you forget that." I had a feeling she was talking about something entirely different.

"Excuse me, Catherine?" Edwin walked in to my office.

"Judge Marlon, Edwin is here to see me. May I return the call?"

"No, I will call you in a few weeks." Paula hung up.

Dammit! I have to remember to close my door when she calls so we can have privacy to talk dirty and to decrease the chances of interruptions. I'm so disappointed that our call ended so abruptly.

After Edwin asked about who was covering Judge Hernandez's docket in March, he returned to his office. I emailed Paula immediately.

Judge Marlon:
I'm so sorry that we were interrupted, ma'am. I would really like to continue our conversation. Are you available?"
Catherine

That sounded tame enough.
The response came swiftly and succinctly.

Catherine,
I think you understand that I am very busy and my time is valuable. I do not have any more time for you today. Your opportunity to talk to me has passed.
Judge Marlon

Ouch. That stung as much as a slap on my ass. I know that is what she intended.

The days and weeks passed as I waited to hear from her again. Periodically, I forgot about her and occasionally I longed for her. Early on a Thursday morning in March, she called.

"Good morning, Catherine."

"Good morning, Judge." I tried not to sound excited to talk to her.

"Catherine, is tomorrow your Friday off?"

"Yes, ma'am."

"Great. The case that I had a hearing scheduled for tomorrow has settled, so I don't have to go to court. I have the whole day available."

I wasn't exactly sure where she was going with this since she is in Pittsburgh and I am in Virginia.

"I guess you will have time to catch up on decision-writing then, right Judge?"

"Yes, I will. But I will also have time for a new game. I want you to call me in my office from your bedroom at 10:00 sharp tomorrow morning. Do you understand?"

"Yes, ma'am."

Click. She hung up on me! I wonder what the new game is? What can she possibly think of doing from Pennsylvania? I couldn't wait to find out.

At the appointed time, I called her office. It was sprinkling lightly and I could hear the ping-ping-pings on my bedroom window. I glanced outside and saw the mailman crossing the street to my house wearing his rain gear.

She answered immediately, "Judge Marlon."

"Judge, it's Catherine. I am in my bedroom."

"Good girl. And you called on time. I can't tell you how important timeliness is to me. You have pleased me this morning. What are you wearing?"

"I have on sweatpants and a t-shirt."

"Tell me everything. Are you wearing socks? Panties? A bra?"

"Uh, yes," I reply.

"Uh, yes? Is that how you answer me?!"

"I'm so sorry, ma'am. I meant, 'yes, ma'am, I am wearing all three of those things.'"

"Catherine, I want you to remove your clothes. All of them. Tell me as you take each piece off."

It was hard to hold the cordless phone and report the removal of each item. But I told her as she requested.

"Tell me about your bra. What color is it? Is it underwire? Is it padded? Is it lacy? Sheer?"

"Ma'am, it is nude colored, it has a little padding and a little lace on the cups. Oh yeah and yes, it has underwire. I don't think I own any bras without underwire anymore."

"I want you to put your bra back on and put it on the tightest hooks like we did in my hotel room. Do you remember me doing that to you in my hotel room?"

I remembered. It was uncomfortable yet totally sexy.

I did as she told me. "I am finished, ma'am."

"Good girl. I want to invent a bra that has nipple clamps inside it. Would you like that?"

"Yes, Mistress, I would." Honestly, I wasn't sure I would, but it sounded like the best answer for the new game.

"Now that you are wearing a tight bra, you may not touch your tits or your nipples. They are off limits. Your bra is providing a barrier that you must not penetrate. Tell me that you understand that you may not touch any area covered by that tight bra."

"I understand." I swallowed hard. Even the way she repeated 'tight bra' was making me crazy.

"Catherine, please go to the bathroom and get your hairbrush and get one of your husband's shoes. Let me know when you have them."

I hurried to the bathroom, my breath getting deeper as I wondered what was in store for me. Then I looked around for a shoe. What was this scavenger hunt about? "I have them."

"Catherine, I want to tell you what position number two is. Go to the corner of your bed and lie on your stomach with your legs off the edge. Then spread your legs so they straddle the corner of the bed. Do you understand what I mean?"

"Yes, ma'am. I am doing it."

"Very good. You displeased me last month when we were interrupted on the phone. What do you think I should do about that?"

"I am so sorry, ma'am. I will keep my office door closed while we are on the phone in the future. I realized it was a mistake to not close it when you called."

"I don't need to hear excuses. What should I do?"

"Punish me, Mistress?" I offered.

"Yes, good idea. What type of punishment should I impose today? You may offer suggestions, although I will make my own decision."

"I could spank myself, ma'am."

"Oh, you are very naughty. Do you think I would trust you to punish yourself like that?"

"I could put clothespins on my nipples." Another possibility.

"Catherine, I am not sure that would be a punishment. You would enjoy that because I have taught you that pain can be pleasurable. Isn't that right?"

"Yes, ma'am. I am so sorry that wasn't a very good suggestion."

"Catherine, I want you to smack yourself on the ass three times and I want to hear it over the phone. You may choose the flat part opposite the bristles of your brush or your husband's shoe. Which do you prefer?"

"Ma'am, with all due respect. I want you to choose,"

"You will use your husband's shoe. You hold the heel and swat yourself using the bottom of the shoe near the toe. Do you understand?"

"Yes, ma'am. I understand completely."

"Begin when I say 'go' and remember that I want to hear it. That is how I will know if you are serious about inflicting your own punishment. If you do a good job, I may reward you. GO!"

I gripped the shoe with my right hand. This was the most erotic yet humiliating thing I have ever done. I was glad that she was on the phone and not here in person. I'm not sure I could do it in person, but then I guess I wouldn't have to because she would be glad to do it herself. I took the phone and held it close to my ass to amplify the sound.

Whap! Whap! WHAP! I pounded my own ass with Drew's shoe. The position was awkward. The pain was intense. But I did it. I followed my Mistress's order. I quickly put the phone up to my ear.

"Catherine, how did that feel?"

"It hurt."

"Good. Now every time you see your husband wear that shoe, you will know that I made you beat yourself with it. I am your boss. And you are my little submissive bitch. Say it."

"You are my boss and I am your little submissive bitch."

"That is right. Are you wet now, submissive bitch?"

"Yes, ma'am. I am."

"Do you think you earned the privilege of having an orgasm today?"

I really hoped so because I couldn't deal with being forced to deny this urge today.

"Yes, Mistress," I said sheepishly.

"I do too," she said.

I did something right! I wanted to cum more than I would admit. She has a way of making me so horny. I guess the new game is humiliation and reward. I could probably live with that.

"Are you still in position two?"

"Yes, ma'am."

"Roll on to your back and put your head on a pillow. Are your nails trimmed?"

"Yes, ma'am." I wasn't going to make that mistake again.

"Good. I want you to masturbate until you cum. I will tell you how to begin and then you narrate everything you do. How is that?"

"That sounds magnanimous of you, Judge."

"I want you to position two fingers at the opening of Pam. When I tell you to begin, I want you to forcefully jam your fingers inside. Not gently. Once they are inside, do not finger fuck yourself. I want you to feel the inside of your pussy and tell me what it feels like."

"Yes, ma'am."

"Ok, begin."

My pussy was so wet that my fingers slid in easily even though I was trying to ram them in.

"My fingers are inside. It is warm and tight. It feels like soft, wet sand."

"Squeeze your vaginal muscles like you are stopping your pee. Can you feel that on your fingers?"

I tried, oooh. That's how she did it. What a cool feeling that is. I felt a strangely sensitive area in there. Is that my G-spot?

"Yes, it feels amazing both on my fingers and Pam. You teach me the best things."

"You can thank me for that when you see me next. Now make yourself cum and tell me what you are doing."

I started stroking myself, I moved my fingers in and out of my pussy slowly at first and then faster. I realized that I forgot to tell her what was happening, although she probably sensed something with my audible panting.

"I'm fucking myself with my fingers, in and out, in and out faster and faster. Now I'm reaching for my clit with my index finger. Oooooh. Oh my God. Oh, that feels so good. I'm caressing it in a circle. Oooh. I'm going to cum. I'm about to. Mistress, may I cum now?"

I wasn't sure I could wait for an answer.

"Yes, Catherine, yes, cum now!"

I felt like I was falling off the familiar cliff. Falling, falling. My body involuntarily quaked in response to the explosive release. My God I felt dizzy and satisfied and wet and thirsty. Really thirsty.

"Judge, thank you so much for allowing me to have an amazing orgasm. Thank you for directing me how to masturbate. Thank you for teaching me your games and making me your submissive little bitch." I was feeling ridiculously thankful for our time together today.

"Catherine, you are amazing. You make me so wet because you are so hot. You are my perfect little sub. I hope I have time to think of you later and masturbate. That would be a wonderful gift."

"Ma'am, I hope you think of me later while you cum. I want that for you. I am feeling guilty that I had an orgasm without you today."

"Well our phone sex would improve if I also had a day off. I'll see what I can do about that. Now when you hang up, call another phone number so my number is not the last one on your phone. Every time we talk, you must call someone else afterward. Do you understand me?"

"Yes, ma'am. Of course, we must be careful."

"I'm risking a lot to be with you so don't make any stupid mistakes."

"I understand completely. Thank you again for the fun morning."

"You are welcome, beautiful Catherine. Enjoy the rest of your day."

I wished that my every other Friday off had a similar pattern but it didn't. Our phone sex dates were few and far between, but I enjoyed them immensely. Who knew phone sex could be so fun? May came and went with no conference since we were in an "odd year." I hated the idea that I would have to wait another year to actually be with Paula.

But June brought better news. One afternoon, Paula called.

"You know I love your perfect smile so much because my teeth are so problematic. We didn't have fluoride in Vietnam when I was growing up. My teeth have been plagued with problems my whole life."

"I think you have a sexy and mischievous smile. It was the first thing I noticed about you. It looks like you are up to something. Maybe you are!"

"That is nice of you to say. But my teeth are nothing but trouble. Because of my dental issues, I have to come to see my specialty dentist in Virginia. I have a new regular dentist in Pittsburgh but I have not found one that specializes in the types of problems I have and I really like my dentist in Alexandria. So, I am making an appointment to see her."

"You are? When?" I could barely contain my excitement.

"Either late June or early July. Will you be around?"

"Yes, but my sons are graduating from preschool at the end of the month. I hope you will have the flexibility with appointment scheduling to work around that."

"When do they graduate? I think Dr. Clayton will be able to fit me in because she knows I'm traveling from out of state to see her. I think she's flattered that I still want to use her, but the truth is, I really need her and I don't want to go through getting a new dentist updated on my dental history. It's too much. I call it catastrophic dentistry."

"They finish on June 28th. The school puts on a ceremony and they will earn certificates of completion of pre-school. It involves a significant amount of pageantry, but it should be fun. Then the school is closed the day after, Friday the 29th, and all of the following week to clean in preparation for their summer camps. Drew and I are taking turns being home with them that week. Then they will go to the pre-school's summer camp for the summer."

"Ok, so either before the 27th or after the week of July 4th? I will see what I can do and get back to you. Keep smiling, sexy!"

That may have been the most normal conversation I have ever had with my favorite judge. A few days later, she emailed.

Catherine:
I'm all set with my dental appointments. I will arrive on Tuesday, July 10 after dinner. I'm flying into National Airport. My first appointment is at 8:00 a.m. on July 11th and I have another at 10:00 a.m. on the 12th. Then I fly home at 2:00 p.m. that day. I'll call you to discuss specifics in a few days.
Judge Marlon

Good afternoon, Judge Marlon:
I'm sorry it has taken me so long to write back. Thank you for notifying me of your trip details. I hope we can get together for lunch or something while you are here.
Catherine

A minute later my phone rang. I jumped. It was her.
"Hello?"
"Catherine, why did it take you so long to respond to my email? Do you think I want to wait four hours for a response from you?"
Pulse....

"I'm so sorry, Judge. I don't have an excuse."

She cut me off "Of course, you don't have an excuse. There is no excuse. This will result in punishment."

Throb....

I swear every time she said the word 'punishment', Pam responded quickly. My breathing deepened.

"Yes, ma'am. I understand completely."

"Catherine, you will call in sick on July 11th and pick me up from the dentist's office wearing no panties. I will send you the address later. Be there at 9:30 a.m. and do not be late. I don't know how long the appointment will last, but you will wait in the parking lot for me until I get there. Then we will go to my hotel room and we'll negotiate how to deal with your delay in responding to my email."

"That sounds fair, Mistress" I whispered.

"I don't care whether it sounds fair or not. I am not in the business of being fair. Do you understand me, Catherine? I am in the business of dominating you. That is all." Click.

Note to self: respond to emails quickly. And do not mention being fair. Check. Geez, I feel pretty aroused. This could be another night of having Drew take care of my needs.

The boys finished pre-school on June 28th as planned. They were so stinking cute. They had little knit vests – navy for Logan and brown for Bodie - that it was way too warm for, button down shirts, clip-on neckties and new khakis. We took lots of photos with their teachers and other classmates. Only two of the kids would be going to kindergarten with them. Another one – Kayla – was on their soccer team. I promised to arrange some playdates with the other kids so they could keep a wide circle of friends. After the program, parents were invited to join the kids for lunch and recess on the playground. We pushed them on swings, helped them on the monkey bars and organized games of duck-duck-goose and steal the bacon. It was a fun afternoon that we capped off by indulging in ice cream. Next stop for these guys was kindergarten. It just seemed like yesterday that they were born and now they are five already. Wow. People always say how kids grow so quickly, it's true, they sure do!

After a week with no childcare, the twins started summer camp on July 9th at their old preschool. Most of their classmates were still there, although a few had stay-at-home moms so those kids stayed at home during the summer.

On July 10th, I had a pedicure on my lunch hour and asked the woman at the salon to also trim my fingernails really short. She offered to give me a manicure too, but I declined. I think I should go for the clean and plain look. That night I shaved my legs and armpits. I had trimmed most of Pam a few weeks before when our neighborhood pool opened. Bathing suit season seemed like a good reason to get cleaned up down there. And, best of all, it wasn't suspicious.

The next morning, I got up as usual, showered and got dressed for work. Because it was summer, I didn't dry my hair. My long curls could not be tamed in July and August, so I didn't even try. I wore a short white dress, beige bra, open-toed wedge sandals to show off my pedicure, and no panties. I took the boys to summer camp and signed them in. Before leaving the parking lot, I called my office to tell Edwin that I wasn't feeling well and wouldn't be at the office today. I drove to Old Town Alexandria and found street parking, which was pretty challenging on a weekday morning. I went to a small coffee shop on King Street and ordered a latte and a scone. I sat at a small table near a window and read the Washington Post. It was 8:30 a.m.

At 9:15 a.m., I walked to my car and drove three blocks to the dentist office. The parking lot was mostly empty, so it was easy to park. I arrived early and took out the newspaper to finish reading an article on immigration. I checked my watch at 9:45 a.m. and there was no sign of Paula. I had her cell phone number but vowed never to use it unless there was an emergency. At 10:00 a.m., still no Paula. I was still busy with the paper, but I wondered if I was at the right place. If I wasn't, I knew there would be hell to pay. I checked the address I wrote down and the dentist's name. I was in the right place. By 10:30 a.m., I was wondering if I should go into the dentist's office to see if she was there. But I knew that wasn't what she wanted, so I continued to wait. I worried about what was happening inside. Maybe her mouth would hurt too much when she was done? That would be terrible. I tried to wait patiently but I was anxious for many reasons.

At 11:00 a.m., she finally emerged. She found me in the car waiting. She climbed inside and without saying a word, spread my thighs apart and put her fingers inside of me.

"You are so wet. Good girl. My hotel is about a mile away. I'm going to play with Pam while you drive."

I pulled out of the parking lot and went north on Route 1. It was very difficult to concentrate on driving. She instructed me to make a few turns and thankfully we arrived at her hotel minutes later.

We entered the hotel using her key card through a side door so we didn't have to pass through the lobby. No evidence we were there together. Smart move.

She was on the ground floor four rooms from the door we entered. She unlocked the door and we went in. This place wasn't as nice as the Marriott from last summer, but it had all of the essential pieces of furniture – bed, sofa, chair, table.

She pulled me near her, kissed me passionately and whispered, "safe word?"

"Phoenix."

"I want to show you some new things today. It is important that you remember the safe word, but only use it if it's necessary."

I nodded. We kissed for a few more minutes. Then she said, "let's begin."

She walked across the room and sat on the sofa. I didn't move, I murmured "yes, ma'am."

"Remove all of your clothes and assume position number two."

I did as I was told, straddling the edge of the corner of the bed face down. She stood behind me and rubbed my ass and the back of my thighs. I anticipated a slap but it didn't happen. I think it was a test to see if I remembered her positions. She told me to sit and watch her undress. She was wearing capri pants and a cami with a sleeveless sweater over it. She looked like someone who would summer in the Hamptons or at least the type of person I thought would summer in the Hamptons. She removed everything, even her flowered thong. I thought for a minute about asking where she found that since all of mine were solid colors. She upped the thong game with that cute number. She neatly folded her clothes and put them by her suitcase on the luggage rack. At that time, I noticed a clarinet case on the table. Did she still play? Why would she bring a clarinet on this trip? My face betrayed my confusion.

"Do you want to know why my clarinet case is here? I brought it for you. Bring it to me."

She sat on the sofa and I carried the case over to her and placed it on the coffee table.

"Kneel beside the table and open the case."

I kneeled and opened the case. There was no clarinet inside. It was filled with vibrators and other sex toys! Wow! This was going to be an unforgettable day. I had limited experience with vibrators. The brother of my best friend in high school bought me one as a gag gift because I was so uptight. It stayed in the box for years. I tried it once with no batteries. It felt ok, not great. I always thought I'd get one someday but it just hadn't happened. My sex life with Thomas had been great, then Antonio was life-changing and Drew was pretty fabulous. I never had felt like I had to supplement intercourse with anything. Oh – maybe this was because there wasn't a dick between us. I hadn't felt like I was missing it with Paula, but maybe this would make things even better. Was that possible? I wasn't sure how to react. I waited for Paula to speak.

"Catherine, I have brought some toys for you. That white one shaped like a cock is a regular multi-speed vibrator. The purple one is a vibrating butt plug. It is the small one for training. As your asshole is stretched out or if you want to experience more pain or pleasure, there are larger sizes. You see the nipple clamps? They have a screw that can increase the tension level – and the pain. The chain that connects them can also be used to intensify the pleasure. There are orange plastic ben-wa balls – those are for beginners. There's a blindfold, pretty standard. I have wrist and ankle restraints. My favorite toy though is the pink one in the middle. You'll notice is has three distinct parts. The short prong in the front stimulates your clit. The longer one in the middle dives deep into your pussy and the shorter curved part is for your beautiful ass. I am ready for some new games. How about you?"

"Mistress, I have almost no experience with sex toys. I would appreciate your tutelage."

"Oh, my naïve little sub. I will be instructing every step of the way. You don't have to think about a thing. Stand in front of me and present your tits to me by holding them out on display."

I stood up, placed me hands under my tits and showed them to her.

"Very nice. Sometimes I will spank you on body parts other than your ass, like your thighs or your tits." She swatted my right tit, then my left tit as she said it. It stung slightly. I continued holding them out for her to enjoy.

"I am going to put the nipple clamps on you now. I will not tighten the screw. I want to inflict a slight pain at this point, just to dominate you."

"Yes, ma'am. I can handle it."

She took the nipple clamps out of the clarinet case and put them on my nipples. It hurt intensely for about five seconds and then subsided. That wasn't bad at all. The chain that connected them dangled between my breasts. She tugged on the chain and it pulled on my nipples. It seemed there was a direct correlation between my nipples and my clit because the latter was throbbing in anticipation because of the clamps.

"Catherine, you are pleasing me. So, I want to please you. Assume position one."

I climbed on the bed on my elbows and knees. I needed to keep my breasts off the bed because I assumed that any pressure on my nipples would really hurt.

"Have you ever had anal sex, Catherine?"

"One time on our honeymoon in Barcelona. Drew and I had too much red wine at dinner and went back to our hotel feeling very drunk and ready to experiment. He wanted to fuck my ass and I let him. It hurt a lot, so I never let him do it again."

WHAP! WHAP! Two swift slaps landed on my ass.

"I asked you a yes or no question! Do you think I want to hear a story about you fucking your husband?"

"I'm so sorry, Mistress."

"I am going to put some lubricant on this butt plug and jam it into your ass. And you are going to like it, do you understand me?"

"Yes, ma'am." She sounds so authoritarian and it really turned me on. I was a little afraid of the pain though. She removed the butt plug from the case, opened a small tube of lube and spread it all over the plug.

She raised my hips higher in the air and said "relax your asshole. If you fight against it, it will hurt more."

I wasn't sure how to relax it, but I guess I won't tense it – that should help. I took a deep breath and she pushed it in. Owww, ok it wasn't bad once it was inside. Then she turned on the vibrating mechanism. Holy shit. That felt amazing. I felt like I could cum between the nipple clamps and my vibrating asshole.

"How do you like that?"

"It feels reallllly good, ma'am."

"Ok, roll over gently. We don't want to disturb any of the toys."

I did as I was told. If I rocked my hips slightly, I could make the butt plug move just a little bit, almost like I was butt-fucking myself.

"Oooh, my little bitch, you like the butt plug so much, you are trying to fuck yourself with it? You are very naughty!"

I was busted. I should have known I wouldn't get away with that. She pulled on the chain between the nipple clamps. It pinched. Punishment. Pain and Pleasure. I could barely handle the erotic dichotomy of the feelings.

I felt like I would explode if she got anywhere near my clit.

"For that little indiscretion, I think your punishment will be to wait a little longer on your orgasm and make me cum first. I really wanted you to experience the pink passion before me, but I can't wait. Get off the bed, make sure you clench your asshole so that plug does not come out. Walk over to the clarinet case and get the pink vibrator. We are going to call it pink passion."

Walking with a butt plug in my ass was challenging. The natural instinct is to push it out like a shit, so I had to really focus to hold it in. And feeling the vibration was tantalizing. Where did that word come from? I don't think I have ever thought anything was tantalizing, but there really wasn't another word that came to mind. It really was an incredible feeling. I grabbed the pink vibrator with 3 parts that sort of resembled a saguaro cactus and carried it back to the bed. Paula was lying diagonally across the bed.

"Kiss me passionately," she said.

I put pink passion on the pillow and carefully climbed next to her, being careful not to get my nipples too close to anything. I licked her lips playfully and forced my tongue into her mouth. For a minute, I felt like I was dominant. I kissed her hungrily, getting wetter down below.

"May I kiss your perky tits?"

"Yes, Catherine, kiss them and bite them gently, pulling on my nipples."

I loved her breasts. They were perfect, soft and round slightly paler than the rest of her skin, little pink nipples sitting atop quarter-sized areolas. I wished mine were as lovely as hers, but I guess months of breastfeeding take their toll. Her tan line told me that she wore bikinis in the summer. I imagined her in a cute bikini at the pool or hot tub or beach. I longed for a tropical vacation with her. With or without the bikini.

I kissed all around the mounds and sucked gently on her nipples, tugging each one with my teeth. Her breathing came faster indicating that she was really turned on. I loved foreplay with her but I also really wanted to see what pink passion could do. I reached for the vibrator.

"Catherine, put all three parts of pink passion in your mouth, one at a time, making each section very wet. Your saliva will be the lubricant."

I licked the small part meant for her clit, then put the big part into my mouth. I sucked it like it was a cock, in and out, making it very wet. She groaned while watching. I felt a little self-conscious sucking on a fake dick knowing that our relationship was not based on penises at all, but she enjoyed seeing it anyway. Then I moved to the curved part meant for her ass. I wanted to ensure it was well-lubed for her. I wanted her to have only pleasure and no pain. I am certain that is what a good sub would do. I wanted to be the perfect sub for her so she would never want anyone else.

"Mistress, may I fuck you with pink passion now? I really want you to have a satisfying orgasm."

"Hahaha! Satisfying? I'm going to have an explosive orgasm – and you, my perfect little Catherine-sub, will give it to me. Yes, you may fuck me with pink passion now."

In my excitement to try out the new toy, I realized that I had no idea how to get all of these parts in the right spot at the right time. This could be embarrassing. Time to improvise. I grasped the base and put the big part into Sawyer after slightly fingering her first. It slipped in easily. Then I slowly maneuvered the curved part toward her asshole. I hadn't been close to her asshole before, but there it was – a tiny sunshine between her luscious cheeks. Man, she had a beautiful ass. I should take the time to admire it more. I forced it into her ass inch by inch. And her ass ate it up like it fit in there perfectly. She squirmed a little enjoying the pain-pleasure combination. Next, I twisted the base to start the vibration. I thought I should do that before touching her clit – and I wanted to fuck her with pink passion before allowing her to cum. I was momentarily in the driver's seat and it felt good. She was moaning and thrusting her hips to the rhythm of my hand on the vibrator. In and out, back and forth.

"Oh my God, Catherine, this feels soooo gooooood."

"Do you want to cum now, ma'am?"

"Yes! Make me cum!"

I put the small part on her clit. As I did, I shifted my weight so I was sitting fully on the butt plug vibrating in my ass. Holy crap, that was so amazing. I felt like we were sharing the pleasure. I moved pink passion forward a little so the clit stimulator was all over her clit and a few seconds later, she squirted, screamed and shuddered. Wow – that was explosive.

I removed pink passion from her private parts and set it carefully on the carpet near the bed.

Paula lay there recovering from the intensity of her orgasm. I felt proud that I did that. I made her cum so hard, it was super-sexy and made me hornier if it was possible. I really wanted to cum too, but I knew I shouldn't ask just yet. I moved beside her and held her while she came down from the high. I still had the nipple clamps on and the butt plug deep inside me and my clit was throbbing from the excitement of her orgasm and the anticipation of my own.

After what seemed like entirely too long, my sexy Mistress rallied and reached between my legs.

"Dang, Catherine, I've never seen you so wet."

"Ma'am, that was the most intense orgasm I have ever experienced and it wasn't even my own! You make me so horny."

"Well, let me see if I can fix that."

She put one finger inside of me, then another. Slowly moving them in and out.

"How many fingers do you think fit in here?"

"I don't know. That feels really good and I'm very wet."

"I'm going to put a third one in. How does that feel?"

Mmmmmm.

"Oh, you like that? I'm going to put a fourth one inside."

She added another finger inside of me. It didn't hurt, it felt pretty good.

"Catherine, you are so hot. I want to fist you. Can I put my whole fist inside Pam?"

"I don't know. I've never done that before. I ..."

"I'm putting my thumb in now and I'm going to try to spread my fingers, just to widen your hole a little. I won't make a fist."

All five of her fingers were inside me. Instead of moving them in and out, she was spreading her fingers stretching my hole. It was a different type of pleasure that I had never felt before. Then she moved them in and out and turned them around. She removed her thumb and it pressed on the butt plug. My God – so many feelings at once. It was hard to concentrate. She removed her fingers from Pam and just put pressure on the butt plug, then bzzzzzz, she turned it up! I didn't realize there were multiple speeds on it. I could barely focus on anything. My asshole was the pleasure center of my whole being. I was trying to cope with the intensity of the feelings when she put her mouth over my clit and circled it with her tongue. She flicked her tongue up, then down, then UUUUUHHHHHHHH. My whole body shook with orgasm.

I felt like I was cumming and cumming and cumming. It wasn't ending. I was falling off a cliff and rolling in the sea overtaken by the strong waves, pushing me down deeper and deeper until I could finally catch a breath of air. I collapsed on the sand gasping for breath, exhausted.

Before I could get myself together or process what just happened, she reached up and removed the clamps from my nipples and massaged each one tenderly. I didn't realize how much they pinched until they were off. The whole episode was an intense mélange of pleasure and pain, more pleasure and pain and the most complete and profound orgasm I had ever experienced.

She carefully pulled the butt plug out of my asshole and turned it off. I would be tempted to have another orgasm if that stayed in there any longer. It was definitely the catalyst of something great.

We turned on the bed so our heads were on the pillows and we cuddled lovingly. Then I woke up in a panic. We had fallen asleep. What time is it? Only 2:00 p.m. – whew! I was starving and thirsty and still exhausted. I nudged my sleeping beauty to awaken her. She woke with a start like I did seconds before. How is it possible that she could be even more beautiful when just waking up? I kissed her mouth, her nose and her eyes.

"My, my, are you ready for some more games, amor?"

"Actually, I am really hungry. Can we get some lunch and then play some more?"

"That sounds good. Let's get cleaned up and get dressed. I know a little Mexican place we can walk to – does that sound good?"

"Perfect, ma'am," I winked at her.

Her crooked sexy smile let me know she appreciated my response.

"Before we leave, I want you to try something. Please get the orange Ben-wa balls out of the clarinet case. I'm going to gently push them inside of Pam. When you walk, they will jingle inside of you. It's an amazing sensation. It will drive you crazy and make you very ready for our afternoon."

I wasn't sure I needed help getting ready for the afternoon, but I was willing to try new things and I was especially willing to please my Mistress.

"Lie on the bed and pull your knees toward your chest with your legs spread apart."

As I pulled my knees in, she popped the balls in her mouth one at a time for lubrication, then pushed them inside my vagina. There was a point that it was obvious they were inside, almost like a "pop." The string hung outside my body.

"I don't feel anything."

She giggled "oh you will. Get up, put on your shoes and we'll walk to the restaurant."

I walked across the room to get my shoes and I immediately knew what she meant. There must be some kind of shifting weight inside the balls that moves when I walk. Wow. It was subtle yet intense. How can that be? I'm not sure I could walk all the way to the restaurant like this.

We walked to the Mexican place. The orange balls rattled silently inside of me. The sensation was distracting. It was making me wetter and wetter. I need to focus on something else. For a moment, I imagined what people must think about us. I'm sure we appeared to be two friends having a late lunch. I guess that wasn't too far from the truth, but at the same time, it couldn't be farther from reality.

I was glad to be seated at the restaurant and not moving at all. Only then the balls wouldn't jingle and tingle. I looked over the menu briefly and asked her to choose. I think she liked having that additional bit of control. At that point, I honestly didn't care what I ate. I just wanted food and water and to get back to the hotel and remove these damn balls. We shared the chicken and steak fajitas. I was so famished that I couldn't resist putting all of the toppings – peppers and onions, cheese, sour cream, salsa, even guacamole - all over the meat on the tortillas. I really wanted a frozen margarita but it's not a great idea for me to drink at lunch time, so I passed on that. I made a mental note to go back some time for dinner to try one. I realized over lunch that we never discussed her dental appointment.

"Paula, what happened at the dentist? What took so long?"

"Dr. Clayton had an emergency. A mother came in with a young child with tooth pain. I knew you were waiting for me but there was no way I could share that information. I had to let the other patient go first. After she handled the emergency, I went back to the exam room and she took new x-rays, took a mold of my teeth and did a thorough exam. I have to return in the morning to discuss additional treatment options."

"You didn't seem to be suffering from any pain."

"No, not today. Actually, I don't think she blocked enough time tomorrow so I think it will be more of a consult to determine next steps. The treatment for my catastrophic dental problems is commencing. It's going to be a long haul."

Although I didn't want to see her in any pain, the idea that she might have to return to Virginia for additional appointments was appealing to me.

After we gorged on fajitas and chips, queso, and salsa, Paula paid the bill. I offered to pay, but she rejected my offer. I didn't really want to feel like a kept woman or like I was taking advantage of her. She insisted, so I dropped the topic. We walked back to the hotel. Jingle, jingle, jingle.

While I was looking forward to some more play time, I had something I needed to ask Paula. I don't know why the topic never came up before, but it seemed to me that she was more experienced than I was when it came to being with another woman. Her tongue so deftly pushed me to orgasm in a matter of seconds and I didn't think it was by chance. When we entered the hotel room, I said, "Can we talk for a minute before our afternoon session?"

"Session? That sounds very formal. I like to think of our games as scenarios that I dream up and hope someday to carry out. You know I spend a lot of time thinking of you and ways we can enjoy each other's company?"

"That makes me happy. I think of you, too. I'm not as creative as you, however, so I could never come up with the ideas you do."

"I will teach you, Catherine. You will have many amazing ideas and I'll show you how to communicate them to me – both over the phone and in person."

"Paula, this is awkward, but I feel like I need to ask you something. Today was the first time you performed cunnilingus on me. It was overwhelmingly amazing. Like you really knew what you were doing. I think I told you that I had never been with a woman before. But you didn't tell me about your experience with women. What's the deal?"

She looked a little surprised but realized that it was time to have a talk with me.

"Catherine, remember I told you that I was in the Army between college and law school?"

"Yes."

"I was stationed in Alaska. While I was there, I met a woman named Joan. She was also an Army officer. Although I dated men at Cornell, something about Joan felt familiar. We spent time together enjoying the rugged terrain of Mount McKinley, white-water rafting, developing a love of tennis, and engaging in other outdoor pursuits. We started as friends, but Joan pursued me until I surrendered."

I was listening intently. One minute I was enjoying her story, then I became jealous of Joan and their relationship – young and unencumbered. Two things I would never have with her. But I suppose all of our experiences brought us to where we were today. I started telling myself that now.

"I learned how to love women from my relationship with Joan. She was more experienced than I was and we tried everything. I really thought I might never go back to men after being with her. Everything seemed so instinctual and natural. I felt like she was the person I was meant to be with. She promised to be faithful to me and love me exclusively. And I felt deeply loved like never before. But it turned out that she was lying to me the whole time we were together. You see, Joan had a fiancé in North Carolina. She married him after finishing her tour of duty and leaving Alaska. I was crushed, devastated and afraid to trust people in intimate relationships."

"Wow. That's terrible. I'm so sorry." I guess I'll stop being jealous of Joan now. What a mean bitch.

"I left Alaska shortly after Joan did and moved to Georgia to go to Emory. It was good that I could focus exclusively on law school while nursing my bruised ego. I didn't have time for dating and I couldn't envision putting myself in a situation that could result in my being hurt so thoroughly again. All of my effort went into schoolwork – until I met Garrett in my third year."

Ok, so the story was coming together now. I wasn't sure how to feel. I was hurting for her, but jealous of the amazing love she thought she had. I wonder if Garrett is just a rebound, someone safe for her to be with so she isn't alone? That's a long-lasting rebound, so maybe it's true love? She settled for safe love with bland Garrett – and now she had me on the side for some real fun. I can't judge her as I am in a similar situation. Although I'd never say I settled for Drew. He is great in every way – almost.

"I don't know what to say. I'm glad I know about Joan but it sounds like she hurt you so much."

"She did, but it is in the past. Is there anything else you want to know? I want you to feel comfortable asking me anything."

"No, ma'am. That's enough reality for one day. What scenario do you have planned for the rest of the afternoon?"

"Let's see – how do you feel about being tied up and blindfolded?"

"Whatever you desire, Mistress."

"Undress first. Then open the clarinet case, get the red satin blindfold and matching wrist and ankle restraints and bring them to me. Assume position number two."

Like a good little sub, I did as I was told collecting the requested items and handing them to Paula, then lying on my stomach on the corner of the bed.

"I'm sorry to do this, but I'm feeling such a strong urge." She spanked me three times. Then she blindfolded me and ordered me to put my head on the pillow near the headboard.

She took each wrist, wrapped the restraint around it. There was a loop that my hand went inside and it was velcroed tightly around my wrist. She pulled it taut and fastened the other end to something. I couldn't see what it was but I'm guessing the legs of the bed frame. She tightened the strap so that I couldn't move my outstretched arms any closer to my body. She did the same thing with my ankles, leaving me vulnerable in a spread-eagle position. Even though I was immobile and exposed, I felt fairly safe with her.

I heard a strange noise. It seemed my sense of hearing was heightened because of my inability to see. I couldn't figure out what it was – maybe a snapping sound or some kind of unfastening. A zipper? More Velcro? She was trying to keep it quiet to not arouse suspicion but I was on to her. I knew something was going to happen but had no idea what.

I felt something soft on my nipple. It tickled me. A feather! She was teasing me with a feather. It was an unusual sensation. I was afraid I might giggle and perhaps that wouldn't be appropriate. The smirk that came across my lips was short-lived. Whap! She whipped my breasts with something. Ouch. Tickle, whip, tickle, whip! What the hell? It was a whirlwind of pleasure followed by a sharp burst of discomfort. I hesitated to call it pain, it was an erotic sort of pain. The tickle-whip cycle moved from my breasts to my stomach, then my pubic mound, then my thighs. Each location presented a new feeling of painsure. I created a portmanteau to describe the combination of the words of pleasure and pain into one word that defines them together. As this series of repetitive sensations decreased in tempo, I smelled something sweet like honeysuckle. Was it herbal tea? How could I suddenly be smelling tea? My mind was trying to make sense of something that was nearly incomprehensible. That's when I felt something new. Hot wax. Paula poured hot wax from a honeysuckle candle on my left breast. It burned slightly. She rubbed it into my skin. Then she repeated the offense on my right breast. Burn and rub.

"Do you like it, Catherine?"

"Yes, ma'am. So many competing sensations. It's almost

overwhelming."

"It's amazing what you can enjoy, particularly when one of your senses is absent. You know I could do anything to you when you are defenseless and naked – both physically and psychologically. I could have someone else in the room with us and you wouldn't know it. I could have a male prostitute fuck you and you would think it was a dildo."

The silence hung like a heavy overcoat in the room. I felt betrayed and sick. She wouldn't do that, would she? Had I trusted her too much?

She continued, "of course, I would never do that because I want you all to myself. You won't be with anyone else, will you?"

"No, ma'am. I only want to be with you." I almost cried. I could feel the moistness in my pussy dry up as I felt deceived and threatened.

She immediately sensed my aloofness. She had to win me back – quickly. I was so close to saying "Phoenix" and getting the hell out of there. But we had such an amazing morning, I had to think this through. Maybe I was feeling paranoid because of the sensory deprivation. It started out thrilling but then turned dirty. Maybe I wasn't cut out for this type of adventure?

I heard the hum of a vibrator. That got my attention quickly. I thought of pink passion and how quickly she came after seconds in contact with it. The sound wasn't getting closer to me. I heard her groan. She was using it on herself and making me listen to her masturbating. That was really hot. I wanted to see her do it but I couldn't see a thing.

"Ooooh, Catherine. This vibrator is filling me up. Would you like me to use it on you instead?"

"Yes! Please!"

"Yes, please *what*?"

"Ma'am! Mistress! Judge! Please. Is it pink passion? I would love to try pink passion."

"No, Catherine. I have something better for you. But first I am going to remove the balls from Pam."

I had almost forgotten about them. I wasn't moving at all since I was tied down so they stopped jiggling long ago. But I was still wet down there so they slid out pretty easily.

"Open your mouth."

She put one of the balls in my mouth and one in hers. I tasted my juices. It wasn't bad, although I'm certain Paula enjoyed the taste more than I did.

She removed the balls from her mouth and mine and kissed me deeply, her tongue reaching for my tonsils. We were both now drooling the pleasantly pungent fluid. I made a mental note to get some mints before going home. There is no chance I could go home tasting like that.

She moved away from me and I heard the soft hum of the toy again. She came closer and touched the tip of my clit with it. I was glad to be so open to her now. She had full access to all of my fun parts and I was dying to have a full-blown orgasm.

"Catherine, meet Super-Blue."

Super-Blue? I didn't see anything that was blue in the clarinet case? But suddenly I was feeling Super-Blue. It went deep inside of my pussy. It seemed like it was touching my cervix – it went in that far. It hit the wall, the end of Pam. I didn't know there was an end, but Super-Blue found it. She fucked me with it for a few minutes. I felt like I was being stretched in ways I didn't know were possible. It touched everything with a mild vibration. I almost felt like I could orgasm without clitoral stimulation, but I was pretty sure that was impossible. I never had before.

"Relax your asshole."

I took a deep breath and she forced the rigid protruding part of Super-Blue into my ass. It felt bigger than pink passion looked or the butt plug she used on me earlier. My asshole strained against the intrusion. Relax! I shouted it in my head. Enjoy every feeling.

"You are such a willing little temptress, always wanting to please your Mistress, Catherine. I can't tell you how much that pleases me. I think I will let you have another amazing orgasm."

She increased the intensity of the vibration of Super-Blue and moved it in and out of both my pussy and my asshole simultaneously. I felt powerful painsure. When I felt like I couldn't bear the anticipation of my impending orgasm, she turned Super-Blue off. Screech! What the…?

"Catherine, you are about to experience maybe the best climax of your life. But you need to request my permission before you cum. Do you understand me?"

"Yes, ma'am." I could barely whisper the words. I was so close and she stopped. I was teetering on the edge of the cliff. A gentle breeze would push me off, tumbling to the sea below. But I was just pulled off the edge in an aggressive way. I longed to get back where I was seconds ago.

She turned it back on, she thrusted it in and out and she changed the angle ever so slightly so the stubby tip grazed my clit. Holy shit! I was back on the edge; I was about to tumble –

"Mistress, may I please, PLEASE cum now?"

"My, my Catherine. You sound very bold and anxious." And she turned it off again.

"You must learn to control yourself a little better. I will allow you to cum when I am ready. Do you understand that? If you are going to be disrespectful to me, I may withhold your orgasm. You wouldn't like that, would you?"

"No, ma'am. I'm so sorry, ma'am. You make me so horny and it's hard to wait."

"Patience is a virtue you need to learn."

She walked away. I heard the bathroom door close. The toilet flushed, the water turned on and off. She returned to me and wiped her cold, wet hands from my belly button to my breasts drying her hands on my skin. The cool water made my nipples harder than they were before. I was thinking of begging her to let me cum. I wasn't sure if that would make her feel more domineering or if it would make her want to teach me patience and restraint. WWPW? I played the "What Would Paula Want?" game. While I tossed the ideas around in my head trying to make the right decision, the vibrator turned on again. I tried to slow the climb to the edge of the cliff. Maintain control. If I wanted to achieve my goal, I had to play by her rules. I asked for permission earlier than necessary.

"Mistress, may I have an orgasm?"

"Catherine, you sound greedy. I'm assuming that is not your intention."

She was taunting me. I was racing to the edge with the threat of withholding. Panic was about to consume me. I had to stop before I went over. I had to win this game, but she was pushing all the right buttons and I couldn't wait.

"Please, Mistress, I am begging you." I felt like I was selling my soul to the devil. I was about to make other concessions, make deals that I might not be able to keep. All for the promise of an orgasm or the permission to have an orgasm.

"Yes, Catherine, you may have an orgasm after you say 'my Mistress controls me in every way.'"

"My Mistress controls me in every waaaayy."

If I were an action film, this would be when some big, fiery explosion occurred that blew people off their feet and back fifty yards into some empty barrels or something. With a cloud of flames and smoke billowing through the night sky. The survivors would look dazed as if a catastrophic event occurred. That was my orgasm.

She removed the blindfold and I squinted at the afternoon sun peeking through the hotel curtains. This woman. This woman makes me insane. I feel a crazy surge of a panoply of emotions. Too many to count, too conflicting to comprehend. She loosened the bands on my arms and legs so I could free myself. I wanted to curl up in a ball just to have my muscles in a different position. But first I knew I needed to thank her. The game wasn't over yet.

"Thank you for allowing me to have the most intense orgasms of my life, ma'am. You are teaching me so much about myself. I can never repay you."

"Catherine, all I want is for you to remember that I am the best lover you have ever had. We are perfectly naughty counterparts to each other. There is no one else like us. There are so many more things I want to show you. Be patient, beautiful."

I knew my time was up for today. I had to get home to my family. As I put my clothes back on, I noticed a secret compartment in the clarinet case.

"You are very sneaky," I said gesturing toward the case.

"I can't give up all of my secrets at once, remember patience – and a little surprise occasionally."

I had to admit that I liked her surprises, but I wasn't that good at patience. Of course, having an amazing lover once a year certainly does test one's patience. Maybe I was better at it than I thought?

"I'm really sorry that I have to leave you. I had an unbelievable day. When can I see you tomorrow?"

"We can't arouse suspicion if we want to maintain this relationship. I know you have to go. Drive carefully, be on time. Can you pick me up around noon from here and take me to the airport? Use your lunch hour. You must go to work tomorrow. Edwin will be suspicious if you miss two days of work."

"Yes, ma'am," I kidded her. I reached for her face bringing her close to me for one final kiss goodbye. I breathed in her scent, trying to remember everything about it. I ran my fingers through her thick hair, feeling each strand memorizing the texture of it. I hated goodbyes – even if it was just for a day. I hugged her too close and for too long and then I walked back out the side door of the hotel to my car.

The drive home took a little longer than I expected. I wasn't used to that route and there was more traffic. I listened to the radio trying to clear my head. I had an 80s station on. After a bunch of commercials, the Divinyls came on singing about Pleasure and Pain. Really? Was the radio narrating my life now?

It's a fine line between pleasure and pain
You've done it once you can do it again
Whatever you done don't try to explain
It's a fine, fine line between pleasure and pain
It's all the same
It's all the same
It's all the same

I listen to the lyrics, I'm pretty sure it's about domestic abuse. But I just spent the day experiencing the highs and lows of pleasure and pain. Painsure. My erotic painsure.

Next up – Def Leppard's Love Bites.

I don't wanna touch you too much baby
'Cos making love to you might drive me crazy
I know you think that love is the way you make it
So I don't wanna be there when you decide to break it
No!

Love bites, love bleeds
It's bringin' me to my knees
Love lives, love dies
It's no surprise
Love begs, love pleads
It's what I need

I turn the radio off. I need to be in family mode, not Paula mode. Goodbye, 80s songs.

I feel like it's been weeks since I've been home. Did I have a plan for dinner? Maybe I took some meat out of the freezer to thaw for tonight? I've got to focus on my real life, not my annual fantasy world. I was so distracted trying to remember my dinner menu that I missed my exit off the highway. Get it together, girl. In spite of my roundabout route, I managed to get home fifteen minutes before Drew arrived with the twins. For an instant, I felt guilty. Then I pushed all thoughts and memories of Paula aside and became immersed in the flurry of activity that comes with two active boys. Logan and Bodie went on a field trip to a local water park and had wet swimsuits and towels in their backpacks. Each one was trying to out-yell the other to tell me about the adventures of their day.

"Slow down, guys! I want to hear from each of you. Pick a number between one and ten." I held two fingers behind my back.

"Seven" shouted Logan.

Ever the analyst, Bodie knew his chances "six," he said.

I showed them my two fingers. "Bodie talks first."

As I listened to each of them, Drew went upstairs to change his clothes and check his email. I asked the boys to pause for a second so I could order Chinese delivery. I don't have the energy to make dinner.

Dinner was delivered and eaten. After the boys bathed to remove all chlorine from their little bodies, I read them each two bedtime stories. They had their own rooms, but usually slept together in the same room. Old habits, I guess. I kissed them goodnight and pulled the door almost closed.

Drew and I collapsed in bed.

"Some days these guys wear me out. I think it's supposed to get easier, right?"

"Yes, I think it'll get easier. The good thing about us is we seem to complement each other, like when you are tired or fed up with them, I am usually in a better place. And when I've had enough, you have the energy to take over," I said. I always have felt like Drew and I made a great parenting team. It's not to say we are perfect, but we work very well together. It is rare that we both have off-days at the same time. I can't think of a time when it's happened.

The next day, I woke up as usual, took the boys to summer camp as usual and went to work as usual. At 11:30 a.m., I drove to the hotel north of Old Town Alexandria. I realized on the way there that I didn't have a plan to contact Paula when I got there. Should I go in through the lobby and go to her room? I can't go in through the side door without a key. And I can't call her. Geez. Poor planning. I pulled up to the parking lot and she was waiting outside holding her purse, rolling suitcase and clarinet case! Oooh, the clarinet case. Who knew a "clarinet" could be so fun? I parked and helped her put her stuff in the trunk.

"Hello, beautiful, right on time!"

I think we both remembered what happened the time I was late. Sadly, there was no time for punishments today, although the reminder of it was starting the little pulse in my panties. Paula looked fabulous. I was always envious of women who looked put together on planes. I felt like I was always walking around with vomit or breast milk or something staining my shirt. I preferred yoga pants or leggings and shoes that slip on easily and are comfortable, like sneakers without shoelaces. I'm clearly going for comfort over fashion. And although I'm covetous of these fashionable women, I do think that I will be more agile in the case of a water landing than someone in 4.75-inch Louboutins. But that's just me. Paula was wearing more sensible shoes than something Sarah Jessica Parker would wear while walking down the streets of Manhattan in Sex and the City. Otherwise, I'm pretty sure our relationship wouldn't work.

"How was the dentist today?" I asked feeling like an old married couple.

"It was about what I expected. I definitely have to undergo more significant procedures. Dr. Clayton thinks it'll probably make sense for me to have a specialist in Pittsburgh. She is going to ask around for recommendations."

My heart sank – no more dental excuses for trips to D.C. She saw the look on my face.

"Don't worry – next year is a conference year. We will still talk on the phone. I even have more phone sex scenarios for us!"

I know what she was saying made sense. It was exhilarating to be with her. But my family came first.

"Ok, I really enjoy our time together and I wish it could be more frequent. I often wonder what would have happened if we got together when you still worked in Virginia. I have stupid fantasies about sitting under your desk in your office, fingering you while you attempt to work. Seeing if you could carry on a conversation if Victoria or Edwin walked in."

"Haha, I see I'm rubbing off on you. You know we could never have been together while I was still at headquarters. I like your fantasy though. You will have to share more of them when we talk on the phone. I want you to talk dirty to me and not just listen. That will be the next goal we work on."

"Yes, ma'am. I will try."

"Good girl."

And with that comment, we arrived at the departures section of

Terminal B at National Airport. It's funny how I don't get stuck at red lights when I'm not in a hurry to get somewhere, but when I am in a hurry, I hit them all.

"I'd like to try to get my clarinet case back inside my suitcase. I'm going to check them in because I don't want to go through security with the contents of the clarinet case."

"I can help. I'm a really organized packer."

We opened up her suitcase, shifted some items around. I told her to put on her heavier sweater rather than packing it since the planes are sometimes cool. That freed up a lot of space. Voila! Her clarinet case full of fun toys now had room inside the rolling bag.

I hadn't thought to ask before, but now I was curious. "Do you use those toys with Garrett?"

"Not usually. He travels a lot. I have to keep myself entertained."

She was so hot. I imagined her using some of the things she brought. Honestly, it was a little sad that she was alone so much, but how liberating to be able to take care of your own needs so easily with the twist of a base? She was so free to explore her own sexuality and make no excuses about it. I wish I could be more like her.

I lifted her suitcase out of the trunk and placed it by her feet. How do we say goodbye in a public place? I look at her, my blue eyes lost in her endless brown eyes. Sometimes I feel like I can see through her eyes into her brain, her heart, see into everything she is. And other times, she is but a beautiful stranger. Yet a beautiful stranger who touches parts of me so deeply that it is likely they'll never be touched that way again. I reach out to hold her in one last long embrace. The type that two years ago seemed a little comforting but mostly awkward. I want to touch her everywhere. I want to kiss her passionately. I want to know her carnally again immediately. But I know this isn't the time and it isn't the place. And, if anyone were watching, it would be good for us to appear to be old friends saying goodbye.

"You feel so good and so right to me."

"Catherine, my baby. Please don't make this any harder than it has to be."

Why does it feel like something changed in our relationship over the last twenty-four hours? Did we share more of ourselves with each other than before? Is each dalliance intensifying our relationship? Bonnie's words fill my head "Don't get obsessed. More is at stake."

Time to separate. Channel your indifference, sister. I tell that to myself over and over. The last thing I want to do is cry.

All right then. One last hug. For real.

"Goodbye, Paula. Have a safe flight. Let's talk soon." I tried not to sound desperate.

"Bye, Catherine. There's no one like us."

The last comment was meant to tether me to her for eternity. Is that a mind game? Does she believe that? Am I a stand-in for G.I. Joan? Myriad thoughts filled my head as I drove back to the office. I'm glad that I can close my door when I return and spend the afternoon unpacking the events of the last day. After an hour of self-reflection, I determine the best approach, of course, is to put it all away. I'm locking the door on Paula until next time. She's gone back to Pittsburgh. My life and my family are here in Virginia. She can't control me from there – until we talk again, but who knows when that will be?

2008

My conversations with Paula were irregular. She was busy in court and had a new law clerk that helped her draft decisions and do legal research making her less available. I started volunteering at the boys' school on my day off after they started kindergarten. Occasionally the timing would work so that we could talk. Sometimes when we talked, we did not have phone sex. We talked about our lives, our office, politics, music, films and books. I liked getting to know her more. She didn't have any close friends in Pittsburgh, but she played in a tennis league or two. She went to the gym every day after work and usually picked up dinner on the way home. She hated to cook and since Garrett traveled so much, she didn't bother learning to cook for herself. She usually read after dinner. She went through a book or two each week. I wish I had that kind of time to read. I struggle to get through a magazine a month. Maybe I'll make a very late New Year's resolution to read more this year? I was a little envious of her life without kids, although I would never want to get rid of mine. They are my life. I delight in every silly thing they do. I love seeing the world through their innocent eyes.

After years of going to friends' clothing, kitchen items, make-up, and jewelry parties and occasionally hosting my own, I was invited to a sex-toy party! My friend, Nicole, who hosts all kinds of parties sent the evite that she was having one in March. I was a little apprehensive about going, but also very interested. Many of my neighborhood friends were invited and some already responded affirmatively to the invitation.

"Drew? Guess what? Nicole is hosting a sex toy party and she invited me!"

"What? There are parties for everything nowadays. Are you going to go?"

"I'd like to. Do you mind?" I asked.

"No, it sounds fun. You should go."

"I think I told you about Tyleah-Shay and her collection of vibrators, right?"

Tyleah-Shay was my college roommate. She is the only person I knew who brought vibrators to college. Her high school boyfriend went to college several states away and she was a horny co-ed. She was desperate to stay faithful but needed to take care of her needs personally. Our whole floor had small white boards on our dorm room doors – mostly so friends could leave us notes if they stopped by. There were no cell phones then or texting to stay in communication non-stop. She had a little spot on the top left corner of the white board where she would draw a blue circle if she needed alone time. That way I wouldn't interrupt her. We knew each other's schedules so she could definitely have the room to herself when I was in class and she wasn't. But the blue dot was added security that she wouldn't be disturbed.

Tyleah-Shay and I saw each other once in a while after graduating. After a few glasses of wine, the topic of our sex lives would inevitably come up. She always told me about new things she was trying – positions, places, toys, and other accoutrements. She didn't marry the high school sweetheart. In fact, I found out after graduating that most of the time the blue dot was on the whiteboard, she was fucking one of her economics professors. Who says economics isn't fun?

Before she married Rook, she told me about the men she met on business trips, personal travel, the gym, clubs, anywhere she went. She had a varied and interesting sex life. I never really had anything interesting to share when Tyleah-Shay and I talked about sex. I didn't tell her about Antonio because she knew Thomas from college. I didn't want to admit that I cheated on him and that caused the end of my first marriage. I would never tell her about Paula. While she was very inventive in her sex life, it was always heterosexual sex. I'm not sure I would ever discuss this relationship with anyone. I only told Bonnie very vague stories, nothing too racy. No dom-sub, no vibrators, no bondage.

"Oh yeah. I wonder how Rook handles all of her imaginative ideas."

"What is that supposed to mean? Isn't variety the spice of life? If you don't want me to go to the party, I don't have to."

"No, please go."

"Is there anything in particular you want me to purchase or avoid? I understand orders are made privately. There's a website we could look at beforehand."

"Let's look at the website before the party," Drew said.

The night before the party, after the twins were in bed, Drew grabbed his laptop and jumped in bed. I sat beside him with pillows propped behind me. He opened the website of the party consultant. I can't believe that someone has a job of selling sex toys. Of course, people have all kinds of jobs, but I never thought about that being someone's job. Imagine having to demonstrate different vibrators to a group of women – or men – on a daily basis. I think I'd be aroused all of the time. Lucky husband of the sex toy consultant.

Although I was still fairly naïve about these things, the website seemed very thorough. There was a section for women, a section for men, a section for couples. There were games, oils, sex toys, bondage items. There were handcuffs, whips, spreader bars and swings. Who knew there were all of these items? They could all be ordered online also – no need to attend a party. I sort of assumed that people wanting to purchase sex toys would have to go to some dirty part of town, where there were warehouses, alleys and doorways covered in beads, maybe you could buy pot pipes and incense there too. But this is clean and easy.

I saw nipple clamps and butt plugs. There were even vibrating nipple clamps and fur-lined handcuffs. All of these things reminded me of Paula and I started getting very wet. Drew noticed the change in my breathing.

"This is making you horny!"

I giggled. "I had no idea there were websites like this – don't you find it erotic too?"

"Sort of, but I mostly like how it's affecting you. What things interest you?" He reached between my legs and felt my wetness.

"Well, that does. But stop for a minute so we can select a few things."

"A few? Aren't you adventurous?"

"Why not? It can't hurt. If we don't want to use them, we won't. But we'll have them available in case we do."

We clicked through several parts of the website.

"I definitely want to get a regular vibrator. Maybe one of those things for the butt?"

"Whose butt – yours or mine?" Drew asked.

"I meant mine, but we can get one for yours if you like."

"No thanks. My college girlfriend put her finger in my butt once when she was sucking my dick and I couldn't concentrate at all. It was distracting and unpleasant."

"Thanks for the story, hon. Tyleah-Shay said that it increases the intensity of her orgasms like ten-fold. I can't imagine having a ten times better orgasm, but it would be fun to try. Do you mind if I get something like that? I'm guessing you're not a fan of butt-holes based on your inability to change a poopy diaper without gagging."

"I can manage it, I think. I'm all about giving you pleasure." He reached inside my panties.

"What do you think about these other things? What's a ball gag? There's a section called role playing. Cock rings! Masturbation sleeves – I don't think you need that."

"Why don't you keep it simple? Get a vibrator – maybe a multi-speed one. And try one of the butt beads or plugs. I bet another of your friends will host a party after this one, so you can order more stuff from the next one after you try the ones you buy from the first."

"That sounds like a plan." I kissed my husband as he put the laptop on his bedside table.

"It seems you've been a little naughty, m'lady. Lusting over items online when I have all that you need." He pulled a bandana from his drawer and covered my eyes. Who needs a blindfold?

I drew in a deep breath and he bit my nipple through my night gown. He kissed me and slid down my body, pausing to bite my nipple again and to push my nightgown up to my neck exposing my breasts and stomach. He fumbled with my panties, pulling them off with more force than he meant to.

"Sorry, are you ok?" he mumbled.

"Yes, fine. Don't stop."

He gently pushed his finger inside of me, groaning as he enjoyed my soaking wetness.

"Wow – who knew sex toys would make you so ready?"

He removed his finger and put his thumb inside. The difference in the girth of the two digits was obvious. He thumbed me in and out. And with the dexterity of a pro, removed his thumb from my pussy and slipped it into my asshole. No warning. He put two fingers into my pussy and in unison fucked both of my holes simultaneously. I was riding this erotic wave as he put his lips on my clit. It was throbbing. I didn't need much contact to peak. His tongue flicked my clit and I exploded. My body quaked uncontrollably. I felt like I was sinking into my bed never to be seen again. My mind went blank and my body was numb, coming down from the orgasmic high. I felt my clit pulse again as the blood left it. I removed the bandana from my eyes.

Drew jumped up and ran to the bathroom to wash his hand, mostly his thumb. I have to give him credit for trying something new, something he probably wasn't terribly fond of. He returned saying, "My turn!" He jumped on the bed in a supine position. I knew what that meant. Even though every ounce of energy had left my body thanks to that soul-draining climax, he wanted me on top.

"Drew? Please."

"My thumb is going to smell like shit for a week. Catherine, please."

"Ok, you win." I climbed on top of him positioning my knees by his hips and glided my still-wet hole onto his rock-hard cock. I thrusted my hips from side to side like I was riding a wild bronco. I knew he liked that better than going straight up and down. It felt better to me too because his penis would stroke other parts deep inside of me. Drew had a beautiful cock. That isn't something I'd say ordinarily. In general, I think penises are rather unattractive, the ugly step-sister of genitalia. But his was perfect, a creamy color, no big veins, it was straight. I'd seen some that were curved, almost bent. Drew's was not like that. Also, it was fairly large. I don't think size matters, per se. Don't "they" say it's how you use it that counts? Anyway, his was clean, always smelled nice and fresh, just a gorgeous specimen. The one time it wasn't so perfect is when I had to suck it. Its size made it difficult for me to enjoy the art of fellatio.

I remember long ago in college, there was a Greek guy I dated for about a month. His name was Gus. I didn't have sex with him, but I did give him a blow job once. He had a tiny penis, about the size of my pinkie finger. I could put the whole thing in my mouth, so that his pubic hair was tickling my nostrils. And he had a lot of unkempt thick Greek pubic hair. His tiny dick was lost in my mouth. I had to curl my tongue around it just to feel anything. I'm sure the experience was as unpleasant for him as it was for me. I'm not sure I saw him again after the blow-job night. I told Tyleah-Shay about that night and she still harasses me about him.

It isn't as if my experience with penises is extensive, but I do feel confident that my husband's is one of the best. I rode the bronco with a fervor that I didn't know I had. Drew's panting became extreme. I knew he was about to cum and I almost laughed. I imagined for a minute that panting was an Olympic sport. Right now, Drew was in the lead in the extreme panting competition. But look out! The Russians have Oleg Debrov about to overtake him. And Austria's Franz Heinsmith, who medaled in the last Olympics, is also a contender!

I had never heard a noise like the one that escaped my husband's mouth when he came. It was like a wild hippo giving birth or an elephant grieving over a lost member of the herd. I was afraid it would wake the boys.

"Good grief, are you ok?"

He struggled to catch his breath. "That. Amazing."

"I guess it was if you can't even use verbs in a sentence to describe it."

I cuddled up next to him and reached for a glass of water. I took a quick sip and handed it to him. If just talking about sex toys results in such great sex, imagine what will happen after we actually own some.

The following night, I went to Nicole's party. I told her that I would come early to help her with arranging food and drinks. I mostly wanted to be there first so I wouldn't awkwardly walk into a room full of people ogling sex toys. I had no idea if they would be displayed or if demonstrations would be offered. The consultant, Trudie, was already there when I arrived. I greeted her nervously.

"Catherine, you seem nervous. Don't be. Most people haven't been to a party like this before. They are just coming to the D.C. area after our company had great success with markets in New York and San Francisco. We will do a game or two as an icebreaker and the ladies will drink some wine so everyone loosens up a bit."

"Ok, sounds good."

In the next half hour, about twenty women arrived. I knew about fifteen of them because they were neighbors or parents of kids from school. A couple were Nicole's work friends. I wondered if Hayley would come. Not that I needed to see her. She was nice to look at and talk to, but I must put that idea out of my mind. I already have enough confusion in my life.

Trudie welcomed the group.

"Ladies, grab a glass of wine or beer. Take a big gulp and set it aside. We're going to play a game and you can't use your hands. Everyone, stand in a circle."

We drank, set our glasses down and moved to form a circle in the middle of Nicole's family room. She handed Nicole a large grapefruit. "Hold this between your neck and chin and pass it to the person on your left. Then you do the same." She was pointing at Lorrie.

I was between Devorah and a woman I didn't know. I was introduced, but couldn't remember her name. Ugh. Shahi? Salahi? I guess it didn't matter. This game was harder than it looked. We watched as the grapefruit was passed from person to person. There was a lot of laughter and a little swearing. Devorah collected it from Sharon very easily and tried to transfer it to me. My neck was short. Yikes. I tried to grab it but it was difficult. Finally, success! I turned to my left to give it to Shahi-Salahi. She had long dark hair that was partially pinned up and smelled of sandalwood, one of my least favorite smells. I didn't notice it until I got this close to her. The smell made me feel a little sick. I had to do it quickly to get away from the smell. My head hit her jaw. Ooops. How could I be so bad at this game?! We eventually made the connection and the grapefruit was no longer my problem.

Trudie began to speak again, "That game took longer than I expected. You all were very determined to finish. Good job. Everyone, eat and drink for about ten more minutes and then I'll demonstrate some of our products."

I made a beeline to the table of food. I didn't have dinner before the party and I was famished. I snacked a little as I was putting the food out, but I realized that the wine was going to my head and I needed to counter it with some sustenance. I grabbed some hummus and veggies, some cheese and crackers and a few meatballs. Then I refilled my wine glass and sat in a safe corner. I heard some nervous conversations, each woman curious about what was under the cloth covering the table across the room. Sharon sat next to me.

"Have you been to a party like this before?" she asked.

"No. What about you?"

"No. My husband said he'd like me to host one. He thinks he will get to see what everyone orders. Sorry – that sounds creepier than it is. You know Ivan – he isn't creepy!"

"Haha. No worries. I'm sure all of the husbands would love to know what happens at these parties!"

Just then Trudie approached the mysterious covered table and removed the cloth. "Good evening, ladies. I hope everyone had a chance to enjoy some of Nicole's delicious spread and drink some adult bevvies. Now, what you've all been waiting for! I kept these items covered because I wanted to ensure I show you each featured item and, more importantly, demonstrate how to use them to maximize your pleasure."

She continued, "If anyone has any questions, please feel free to ask. There are no stupid questions. I'm sure everyone has different levels of experience with sex toys or pleasure enhancers as we in the business like to call them. And all of our company's consultants like to employ the Vegas Rule: what happens at the party stays at the party. Capisce?"

We nodded in agreement. I hadn't heard anyone say capisce in years. Must be that I don't hang out with many Italians any more.

"First, maybe we should start with terminology. All vibrators are dildoes but not all dildoes are vibrators, got it? Some people do not like the intensity of vibrators, it's too much for them. We offer dildoes that are just penis-substitutes essentially. They do not use batteries or move at all unless operated manually."

She went on to discuss the different types of toys for anal stimulation and recommended that everyone try it at least once because of the perceived increase in intensity of climax. I could attest to that, but I won't. There were vibrators with separate controls that one's partner could turn on remotely. Everything could be used alone or with a partner. There were contraptions for holding legs in the air or apart, bands that bind wrists to ankles. She talked about items for role-playing like whips and blindfolds, but cautioned everyone that the products they sell are for consensual usage only. She strongly recommended using their lubrication products – some were flavored or spicy to create additional warmth – and their cleansing products. She said regular soap and water should never be used on the silicone the toys are made of because it degrades the material quickly. I think Paula cleaned all of her toys with hot soapy water. I wonder if she knows about that? I will have to tell her during our next conversation. Even though I know I'll probably never get to use my toys with her, I can't help imagining what she would want me to purchase. And what she would do to me with them.

After Trudie finished talking, she passed around the toys and other products for us to touch. All of the vibrators had batteries so we could turn them on and feel the difference amongst the different levels of vibration. Some pulsed, some twisted, some had ridges while others were smooth. Some were water-proof and some were glow-in-the dark. So many choices!

Each person took turns going into Nicole's dining room to place her order. I brought a catalogue with me when it was my turn.

"There are so many options. It's hard to decide," I admitted.

"That is why so many women decide to host their own parties. You get a 20% discount when you host and free items based on how much money in sales your party generates. You also get additional bonuses if anyone books a party from your party. Are you interested in hosting a party?" she asked.

"Not right now, but thanks for letting me know about the opportunity. I'd like to get a multi-speed vibrator and some type of thing for my butt," I said embarrassed.

"I'm happy to make recommendations for you. Why not try this pink pulsating vibrator? It has a massager for clitoral stimulation and it's slightly curved to hit your G-spot, too. It has ten speeds for mild to massive intensity. It takes two AAA batteries. We don't provide those."

I thought of pink passion. I could have my own pink vibrator! "Yes, that looks good. I'll order that one. What do you recommend for my ummm...?"

"Your anal enjoyment? Don't be afraid to ask for what you want. Your partner can't read your mind. You know men aren't afraid to ask for what they want – that is why they get raises at work more than women do. Empower yourself, lady."

I felt admonished by the sex toy consultant. That is just great. I know she is right. That will be my second very late New Year's resolution: Ask for what I want.

"Yes, I'd like something to increase my anal pleasure," there, I said it.

"Good girl," she said gratified with her lesson.

Whoa – that one term put me back in my lover's arms. My clit pulsed in a Pavlovian response. Down, girl. Finish the transaction, go home, fuck Drew. Repeat.

"I don't know what your experience is with anal play and you don't need to tell me, but there are a variety of shapes and sizes. There are beads, plugs and anal vibrators, too. I'd recommend something with a base for easy removal. You don't want anything getting stuck in there."

"That sounds like good advice. How about the blue one?" I pointed to one with pleasure beads on it.

"Good choice. I strongly advise getting some lube and cleanser to keep your toys performing at the optimal level and to protect yourself from injury."

Injury? I never thought I could be injured by a sex toy. "Yes, can I get a cinnamon flavored lube and the medium-size cleanser?" I am obsessed with cinnamon since I first smelled Paula's toothpaste.

"Yes, I'll add that to your order. Remember you can contact me any time to order more lube or cleanser or additional toys. Your total is $120 and your order will be shipped directly to your house in about a week. It will come in a plain brown box with no return address. If your mailman is nosy like mine, he won't know a thing!"

I gave her my credit card to complete the order and left the dining room, allowing the next person to place her order. I picked up a few dirty plates left around the family room, thanked Nicole for the fun evening and went home. Drew was waiting up for me. He wanted to hear everything. I just didn't have the energy. Too much wine, too many decisions, being reprimanded for not advocating for myself, thinking of Paula and her toys, I was drained.

"Can we talk about it tomorrow? I really just want to sleep."

"Are you ok? Wasn't the party fun?"

"Yes, it was fun. I think I drank too much. I'm really tired. I'll give you the full report tomorrow. Love you."

"Love you, too, hon."

As expected, my package came a week later. I was anxious to try everything. So was Drew. Unfortunately, there was a late PTA meeting and no time afterward. The next night we discovered that we had no batteries in the house. Who doesn't have extra batteries lying around? Apparently, us. The next day I made a point to go to the drug store on my way home from work. I know poor Drew has been walking around with a three-day old erection waiting to test my loot. The twins were in rare form. They were arguing, having food fights at dinner, splashing water everywhere at bath time. It was challenging to transition from the chaos that enveloped our evening to having romantic time. When I finished the bedtime stories and went into our bedroom, I noticed an odd flicker. Drew had lit some candles and put on soft music. Way to get me in the mood.

"Come here, you little vixen." He could be so romantic. Dang, I love this guy!

I took off my clothes and climbed next to him on our queen size bed.

"Mama!!!" Crap! Bodie was calling me.

Drew still had his pj bottoms on, so he went to see what the screaming was about. He comforted our little monster and returned to our room.

"Where were we?" he nuzzled my neck where I'm ticklish.

"I think you wanted to see what new fun I can inject into our boring sex life."

He tickled me under my arms and down my sides to my hips, I laughed out loud at my joke and his attempts to tickle me.

"You think our sex life is boring, huh?" he grinned. He was very sexy and the soft light of the candles made him even more appealing if that was possible.

I had the new toys already out of the boxes, filled with batteries and washed with cleanser prior to their maiden usage. The lube was handy nearby if necessary. I remembered that another item Trudie was selling was an anal numbing gel. I didn't order any. I hope it isn't necessary. The beaded wand wasn't that big and I thought I could probably handle it. And even if it hurt a bit, a little painsure never killed anyone.

"Tell me what you want to do with your new toys."

"I'd like to think they are *our* new toys," I corrected him.

"I'm pretty sure you are going to get a lot more enjoyment out of them than I will."

"Ok, fair enough." I handed him the pink vibrator. He turned it on.

"Whoa! That's powerful." I wonder if it'll be too much. I would guess that I could be overstimulated to the point of losing the ability to orgasm. That would suck.

Even though we didn't engage in much foreplay just talking about and handling the vibrators was exciting. I decided to save the wand for another day.

"Drew, please see if I am wet enough to insert the vibrator."

He obliged by feeling between my legs. "Yeah, you are very moist, my love."

"Ok, good. That feels good. Can you rub the tip of the vibrator around my hole, but don't turn it on yet and don't put it in?"

"Ok. I just realized that this vibrator is going to stretch you out so I don't get to feel that with my dick. You know the feeling I get when you are so tight and I'm pushing myself in there?"

"Don't be dramatic, I think it'll still be fine for you. The vibrator is smaller than you are!"

"We shall see. What's next?"

"Put the big part inside of me and go in and out a few times, then turn it on low and do it some more. Don't let the small part touch my clit yet please."

"Yes, ma'am." Drew sounded like me talking to Paula. I don't want that thought in my head now. Focus on Drew. Focus on the new pink vibrator.

This vibrator felt so good. I really wanted to cum. He tilted the vibrator so the small part was near my clit. But it wasn't on it. Or it wasn't on the right part. It felt good but it was a little frustrating because it wasn't where I needed it to be. I adjusted my hips to force the small thing on to the sensitive area of my clit, but it wasn't working. In order to complete the task, I knew I needed to take over. I grabbed the vibrator and shoved Drew's hand away. I pushed it in and out of my hole a little more aggressively, turned up the vibration a notch and forced the small nub onto my lonely clit. OooOoooh. That felt so good. One little tilt of my hips to grind the vibrator into my clit and that was it. Boom! It was swift but intense. The pink vibrator made quick work out of satisfying my needs. Once again, I'm satiated and must tend to Drew. He mounts me, driving his cock in and out repeatedly. I try to match his rhythm but I can't keep up with the urgency. The headboard knocks against the wall. I'm glad we no longer live in a townhouse where the neighbors could potentially hear the collateral noise that comes with the activity of sex. He collapses in a heap on top of me. Finished. His body moist with sweat.

"What happened to using the blue thing?"

"I thought we'd save it for another day."

"Yay! We get to do this again." Sure, sweet, Drew, we'll do it again.

The office's annual conference was not held in the spring time this year. We had to wait until the fall because of the lack of funding. The government's fiscal year starts in October, so the conference was scheduled for then when we would have additional money to pay for it. Because of budget constraints, we shortened it to three days rather than a business week. That allowed the participants to travel on Monday and Friday and the conference itself would run Tuesday, Wednesday and Thursday.

I thought I would die waiting to see Paula again. We had a few hot phone sex sessions after I bought the new vibrators. Although, initially she was not pleased that I had my own and used them with Drew. When I first told her, she punished me by not calling for two months. I knew that was part of her game, so I was willing to accept the punishment. Then I promised not to use them with Drew until she gave me permission. I kept my promise. It wasn't that hard. Although I had amazing orgasms with the toys, Drew wouldn't initiate using a vibrator unless I asked for it. All I had to do was not ask for it. He didn't know the difference. I was abstaining from using them for her. It made me even more horny to know that I was sacrificing my pleasure to please her – even from afar. What a good sub I was. This was the first time I recognized her jealousy. We both knew that we were married to other people and our relationship was mostly getting together on an annual basis. Phone calls were an added bonus, but did not occur regularly.

The week before the conference, the office was busy firming up all of the details: ensuring speakers knew where and when they were speaking, making binders, reserving hotel rooms for attendees. This year we centralized applying for Continuing Legal Education credits for attending certain conference sessions. We had to identify the requirements for each state that the judges and law clerks were members of the Bar in and complete individualized paperwork for each attendee using each state's forms. It was a headache administratively, but it would be very beneficial for our attorneys, judges included. Also, allowing them to use the conference to obtain these credits would mean they would not have to take time off from work to attend other training sessions offered elsewhere to earn their CLEs. I volunteered to handle the CLE program for this year's conference. It would guarantee my attendance.

Paula called on Thursday afternoon, minutes before quitting time.

"Catherine, are you off tomorrow?" No greeting.

"Yes, ma'am."

"Call me at 11:30 a.m. from your house. Can you do that?"

"Yes, ma'am."

I called at 11:28 a.m. the following day.

"Good morning, Judge Marlon's office," she answered.

"Judge? It's Catherine."

"You're early, that's a nice change. I'll award some good girl points for that."

Yay, good girl points! I hope they add up to something!

"I'm surprised you are off right before the conference."

"We have Monday to prepare as well. It's your travel day, but I'll be in the office. Are you coming alone?"

"Yes, Garrett is in Las Vegas for the week for a trade show. We don't have to worry about him. Listen. I have decided to institute a theme for us for next week."

"Okay."

"Okay?!"

"I mean, that sounds like a great idea, ma'am. What is the theme?"

"Since the length of time that the conference is this year is smaller and the amount of time we'll have together is smaller, the theme will be 'too small'."

"What does that mean for me, Judge?"

"Excellent question, Catherine. Do you own any pantsuits?"

"Yes, ma'am."

"On the first day of the conference – Tuesday – I'd like you to wear a pantsuit – one that is a little smaller than your size. I'd like it to be a little tight around your waist. You may wear a thong with it but I want a visible camel toe. Are you able to accomplish that?"

I caught my breath to slow my racing heart. She is really inventive.

"Yes, ma'am. I will do as you wish."

"Very good girl. I also want you to bring your two new toys. I cannot bring my clarinet case. It's way too risky, so you must bring your toys to me. My flight lands at 2:00 p.m. on Monday. Call the hotel before leaving work that day to get more instructions. Are you wet now, Catherine?"

"Yes, Mistress." I could call her my favorite name from my house. I couldn't try that from the office – just in case anyone was within earshot.

"Good. You may not fuck your husband this weekend. I want you fresh and tight for me on Tuesday. Do you understand?"

"I understand completely, ma'am."

"And you will obey me, right? No masturbating either! Nothing. You must save yourself for me."

"I will obey you." I am not sure I ever said those words before. My stupid clit was throbbing. All of the different ideas that this could play out were running through my mind. I could obey her. I could disobey and use my vibrator, tell her and accept my punishment. I could disobey and use my vibrator and not tell her. I could disobey, use Drew, tell her and accept the punishment or I could disobey, use Drew, and not tell her. As strange as it sounds, I felt the need to be honest with her. So not telling her my misdeeds was not an option. Maybe I enjoyed her punishments more than I cared to admit.

"Catherine, I will find out if you disobey. You know that, right? You aren't very good at being untruthful to me." She was reading my mind.

"Yes, ma'am," I responded.

"Ok, I will talk to you when I am at the hotel on Monday."

"Thank you, Judge, have a safe flight."

It didn't take long for me to decide that I had to disobey her. I need to cum right away. She made me so horny. I got out the pink vibrator and slammed it into Pam before I changed my mind. Ahhhh. That felt so good. I tipped it forward, rubbed it against my clit and the deed was done. It took less than a minute. I felt such relief. But I was such a failure at keeping my word. And I knew there would be a punishment. Thinking of that made me want to cum again. Tuesday couldn't come soon enough.

On late Monday afternoon, I called the Omni Shoreham at Woodley Park where the conference was being held and asked for Paula Marlon's room. "Just a moment."

"Hello?"

"Good afternoon, Judge. How was your flight?"

"It was very nice. Thank you for asking. I am in room 513 on the west side. I hope you will join me at 7:00 a.m. tomorrow morning for some pre-conference fun."

"Yes, ma'am. I will be there."

"Very good. Don't forget to bring the items we discussed. See you then." She was gone.

I really needed to tell her that I had to manage the CLE table at lunch time so I couldn't be with her then. I'm sure that will make her angry. I guess I'll share the bad news in the morning.

I had to get up earlier than usual because getting to Woodley Park wasn't easy. The Rock Creek Parkway only operated in one direction during the rush hours. In the morning, that was toward downtown. I needed to go away from downtown, which meant I had to be off the parkway by 6:45 a.m. I needed to leave home by 6:00 a.m. to accomplish that.

I woke up at 5:00 a.m. to shower, trim my nails, and get dressed in a tight suit. I chose the navy one the night before. I had two suits – one navy and one brown – that were too small. The navy one was slightly more fitting for this occasion. I wore a nude cotton thong, navy lacy bra, opaque yellow blouse with small navy flowers on it and my suit. I chose low navy pumps, elegant but a little sexy. I put the two vibrators in my briefcase the night before.

I checked the mirror before leaving to ensure my required camel toe was visible. It was. I felt excited already just following her directions. My pants pinched at my waist so I decided to skip breakfast to limit my discomfort.

I drove quickly to the hotel, parked in the garage and took the elevator to the lobby. I had only been in this hotel once years before when the parents of a friend stayed there. I forgot how opulent it was. I felt wealthy and important just walking through the lobby. I glanced around trying to find the west wing without appearing lost. I noticed a small sign pointing to the west wing elevators. I pressed the "up" button and waited for my elevator to arrive. It opened immediately. I entered and selected "5." She didn't tell me to go to a different floor first so it must be safe. The hotel was huge and we had fewer than twenty judges and maybe another twenty law clerks staying there. It seemed unlikely I'd see anyone I knew, particularly at that hour. That reminded me to glance at my watch to see what time it was. I know I parked around 6:40 a.m. It was 6:50 a.m. Even though I was very anxious, I wasted five minutes ambling down the hallway to her room. I wasn't sure if being too early would have the same result as being late.

I approached the door with the gold placard indicating 513 and knocked gently. She opened the door, wearing only a bathrobe. This reminded me of our first time together. The sight of her took my breath away. She wasn't perfect, but she was perfect for me.

"Good morning, Mistress." My clit tingled in anticipation and I felt it rub against my tight pants. Smart move, camel toe.

"Good morning, Catherine. Please come in." She locked the door behind me. I entered and placed my purse and briefcase on the chair tucked into the desk.

"I want to kiss you before we start, ok?"

"Yes, ma'am." I fell into her arms and we kissed for several minutes.

"I don't think we'll need your safe word this morning, but please tell me it."

"Phoenix, ma'am."

"Good girl." I was glad to hear her say that because I was certain I would be displeasing her soon enough. I need to build up my – what did she call them? – 'good girl points' whenever I could.

"Please remove everything from the waist up and keep everything on from the waist down."

I took off my suit coat, blouse and bra and made a pile of my discarded clothes on her desk. She sat on the love seat across the room and watched.

"Come over to me so I can inspect you," she commanded.

I walked over feeling like a petulant child and stood in front of her. Her face was close to my crotch level.

She reached out and touched me, pushing my pants around my labia even more than they already were. Then she tried to put her fingers inside my pants around the waist. She couldn't.

"Are your pants uncomfortable?"

"Yes, ma'am. A little bit."

"Good. Catherine, tell me, did you fuck your husband last Friday?"

"No, Mistress." I dodged a bullet.

"Did you masturbate after we talked?"

Gulp. Not so fast. "Yes, ma'am. I am so sorry. You really turned me on. And..."

"Catherine, you know I don't want to hear any excuses. I appreciate your honesty, but there will be consequences for disobeying. Do you understand?"

"Yes, Mistress. I understand completely and I'm willing to accept the punishment."

"Present your tits to me."

I cradled my breasts with my hands and held them out for her to see.

"From now on, when I tell you to present your tits, I want you to push them up from underneath with the backs of your hands, you may not fondle them with the palms of your hands."

I quickly inverted my hands to do as I was told. Whap! Whap! She slapped each one. They stung briefly.

"Today your punishment will be more psychological than physical, Catherine. Can you handle that?"

"Yes, ma'am. I am prepared."

She removed her robe and climbed on the bed. "Go get your toys."

I fumbled through my briefcase. I had placed them inside an old make-up bag to protect them and keep them away from my notebook.

"Today you will make me cum using your mouth and your toys. I know you have never sucked on Sawyer before, but I am confident that you will enjoy it and do a good job. You want to please your Mistress, right little sub?"

"Yes, ma'am. I will do whatever you ask."

"Good girl. I want to suck on your titties first. Bring them to me."

I got onto the bed next to her and brought my breasts to her mouth. She sucked then bit each one. She clenched her teeth harder than she had in the past. It was truly painful. I knew this was part of my punishment so I didn't moan to indicate distress or pleasure. I attempted to act indifferent.

"Let me see your toys."

I opened the bag and pulled out the pink vibrator. She touched it, turned it on, turned it up higher, then turned it off and put it on the bed. I handed her the blue beaded butt wand. It was firm yet flexible. Drew and I had only used it once and I had a memorably fulfilling climax. I would not be sharing that information with Paula now. She tried to bend it to test its malleability.

"I'd like to think that you made these good choices based on your experience with me last summer?"

"Yes, ma'am. Do you approve of my purchase?"

"I will let you know after they have been indoctrinated by me."

"Mistress, may I completely undress now?"

"No, you will keep your pants on today. You may remove your shoes after I spank you. Assume position one."

I got onto my knees and elbows on the bed, my waistband digging into my stomach even more in this position. She went to the bathroom and emerged with her hairbrush. "How many swats does my disobedient little bitch deserve?"

I wasn't sure if that was a rhetorical question or if she was waiting for an answer. I decided to hesitate momentarily before responding.

"Well, I guess I'll add one to whatever suggestion you give since you didn't answer me promptly."

"Four?"

"Is that a question? Do you want four spankings? If you do, then say it."

"Yes, ma'am. I would like four spankings for disobeying."

"Ok, four plus one for not answering."

She used her brush and spanked me five times. It didn't sting as much through my pants but I could still feel it. I could also sense the increasing wetness soak through my thong. She was making me crazy and she knew it.

"Time to eat. Get up."

I leaned back on my knees and she got onto the bed again. She lay spread-eagle before me. I looked at her naked body in front of me. Unlike men's bodies, women's bodies were an intricate work of art and hers was no exception. I looked at all of the soft parts and curves, muscles and angles. I saw the perky mounds of her breasts with the pink nipples perfectly perched on top and, closer to me, the little fluff of newly-grown dark pubic hair serving as the gateway to her wet pussy. I was anxious to please her, but still a little terrified of failing.

"Catherine, look at Sawyer. See all of the parts. You have already touched everything. Now you can taste everything. Put your nose in my pubic hair and smell it. When you do that, your mouth will be next to my clit. Don't touch it yet though. I want you to take your time. Savor each moment."

I felt powerful being able to give her an orgasm in the most intimate way possible. I was confident I could do it. I knew what I enjoyed; it must be similar for her. I circled her wet hole with my forefinger. Going closer and closer to entering, teasing her just a bit. For this one minute, I wanted a little control. I reached her right nipple with my left hand, fondled it and then gently squeezed. Paula moaned. The transition of power occurred. I pushed my finger inside of her, then added another. I fingered her slowly, then withdrew my fingers and licked them, sucking the juice off each one. She tasted good. I grabbed the pink vibrator and poised it at the opening of her pussy. I let the tip enter her, then I turned it on. I increased the intensity as I pushed it in deeper and deeper filling her. Her breath was coming faster and her hips were swaying with acquiescence. I turned the vibrator so the clit stimulator was not near her clit but the vibrator was inside of her as far as possible. I was ready to bring her to climax. I put my nose near her pubic hair and put my lips on her clit, using the fingers on my free hand to expose it by moving the hood. There it was. Sweet little pink bulge. I licked it slowly, trying to feel every part of it, imagining I was trying to free a pimento from a green olive with my tongue. Simultaneously sliding my pink vibrator in and out of Sawyer. She started saying my name "Catherine, Catherine." It never sounded better coming from anyone else's mouth. Then she erupted, her hot lava spewing everywhere. I tried to capture it in my mouth but there was too much. It was almost the taste of sweet sweat, honey sweat. Sticky, warm and complete. I made my Mistress come in my mouth. There was no better feeling.

I removed the vibrator and found myself in her arms. I kissed her sharing the sweet taste that came from her. She was still panting heavily. I was looking for some positive feedback, but she didn't say anything. A tear rolled down her face into her hair.

"That was beyond amazing. You were incredible. You knew just what to do. Perfect Catherine."

We kissed and held each other for several minutes. She was naked and I still had my damn tight pants on. I wished I could remove them, but I knew better than to ask again. Even after I gave her what she wanted.

"You poor girl. You still have your pants on. I'll tell you what. I like to think I am a fair person, so I'll make a deal with you. I really hate to withhold an orgasm from you when you have just done such a stellar job licking my clit. So, I will let you cum. But there will be strict conditions. First, I will not touch you. Second, you will not have direct contact with yourself either. But you may use the pink vibrator on the outside of your tight pants. I will watch you. We'll see how creative you are now."

This will be an interesting challenge. I don't think I have ever cum without contact. But I was certainly horny enough to try. Paula moved off the bed to the love seat across the room. I positioned myself so she could see me. I took the pink vibrator that I brought with me and just fucked her with and turned it on almost as high as it went. I bent my legs and spread them apart and touched my clit through my pants with the vibrator. I could feel the movement. I wasn't sure my tight pants were helping. They almost provided an additional barrier because I couldn't move the fabric around to help me. It felt good but I wasn't sure if it was good enough to climax. As my right hand forced the vibrator closer and closer to my clit, I reached with my left hand to squeeze my nipple. I thought that might help drive me up the cliff.

"No touching skin, naughty girl!"

Scolded again. I wondered if she'd slap me. I think she knew this lack of contact was punishment enough. She was cruel but in a super-sexy way. She also knew that a smack on any part of my body would arouse me more than deter me. Maybe I should continue to disobey until she had to take more drastic measures?

I continued rubbing the vibrator on my pants-covered clit, almost feverishly with intent. I felt close, then the urge went away. I felt desperate to cum, having her watch me as I tried to orgasm was both humiliating and erotic.

"You have one minute to cum or I'm taking the vibrator away."

Oh, this was horrible. I needed to cum. My clit was throbbing. Please, please, please cum. I begged my clit to let this indirect contact be enough to satisfy me.

"Thirty seconds." She was taunting me. I tried to focus. Please, stupid clit, do your job. I was so wet that my thong was stuck to both my pussy and my pants.

"Time's up. Turn it off. Now!"

I turned it off.

I was hoping this failed experiment would result in some pity for me. And the orgasm I needed.

"Catherine, I'm so disappointed in you. You can't even masturbate. What a failure."

Believe me, she didn't need to say it. Her words stung.

"Come here."

I got off the bed and walked to the love seat. "Kneel in front of me with your hands clasped behind you."

I did what she asked. I looked at my pants.

"Look at me."

I was afraid of her gaze. I was so horny that I couldn't sit still. I wanted to rip my stupid pants off and do whatever it takes to cum. Oooh. I now see the lesson. That is exactly what I did last week when she told me not to. Punishment or was it revenge for disobedience?

"Catherine, you were naughty last week when you disobeyed me. Now you are suffering the consequences. You must sit in your wet pants at least until lunch time. I want to see the wetness on your camel toe and know that I made you that wet and only I will decide whether or not you will cum at lunch time. Do you understand why you should obey me?"

"Yes, ma'am. I will not disobey you again. It is too painful."

She smiled. She knew how desperate I was for a release of this tension and she didn't care. She owned me and my sopping camel toe.

"You meet me here at lunch time and if you are a very good girl all morning, maybe your afternoon will be more pleasant."

"Judge, I am so sorry, but I have to be at the CLE table all during the lunch hour so people can collect their forms. I told Edwin that I would stay at the table for the entire hour and a half."

"Catherine, you naughty little sub. I will think of an appropriate punishment for not telling me this earlier."

I was pretty sure that stewing in my own juices with an engorged clit was punishment enough. But maybe she would come up with another plan.

"I can stay late after the conference if you like."

"Yes, that might work. I'll let you know during the afternoon break. Put the rest of your clothes back on."

I got up to find my bra and blouse. I also wanted to wash off the vibrator and put it back in the make-up bag. I found it folded into the bedspread and walked to the bathroom to wash it. I didn't bring my cleanser, opting for the warm soapy water that seemed to be Paula's preference. After washing and drying it, I put it back inside the make-up bag and put the make-up bag back into my briefcase.

"Not so fast there. I am keeping your toys for the week. Leave them on the table."

I didn't love that idea but I wasn't sure I could protest either. "Mistress, why do you want to keep my toys?"

"Does it matter why? Maybe I'll use them. Maybe it's to keep you from using them while I am in the same city as you. This week they are mine. End of discussion."

I felt oddly violated. I really didn't want her to use them without me. It didn't seem worth an argument though. She wins. She's the boss.

I put on my bra, blouse and jacket. Then I slipped on my shoes. She disappeared into the bathroom while I fixed my hair and checked my make-up. I was sitting on the bed when she returned. She was wearing a pant suit very similar to my own, except hers fit her properly. She looked stunning, a little blush on her cheeks that made her appear youthful and exuberant.

"Catherine, before you leave, I'd like to inspect your camel toe one more time."

She sat on the bed and I stood before her. She looked at my crotch, nearly burning a hole in it with her eyes. She flicked Pam's lips with her fingers. They didn't move.

"Do you approve, Mistress?"

"Very much, two good girl points for those plump lips."

Gosh, I hope no one else noticed them. Maybe I'll stay seated all day?

"Time to go downstairs to the conference center. We need to leave here separately. Take a key card so you can return when I tell you to. No more kisses for you now. I want you to think about me, crave me and remember how naughty we are together. There's no one else like us, Catherine. Be a good little sub and rub your dripping pussy lips together with every step you take. That is how wet I make you and you accept it."

"Yes, ma'am." I barely caught my breath. She was so demanding and intense. I liked being with her a lot. There was no one like her.

I left her room and walked to the elevator. I remembered the words in a book that the boys have – squelch-squerch. It's supposed to be the sound of someone walking through mud. I think it is now the sound of my labia rubbing against my pants and the ridiculous wetness that is enveloping everything down there. Squelch-Squerch. Gross. Erotic. Squelch-Squerch.

When I arrived outside at the conference center, the continental breakfast was already available. I was starving, but my tight pants reminded me that I couldn't eat very much and have any level of comfort. Maybe I could unbutton my pants and have my blouse cover it up? Was that against the rules? I guess that it was and nibbled on fruit. I was afraid that drinking coffee or even water would bloat me to the point that the button on my pants would pop off. I sipped a little water. The too small theme might have been the best idea Judge Marlon dreamed up in terms of creating discomfort and making me think about her incessantly. If that was her intended goal, I think she achieved it remarkably.

I greeted all of the attendees and told them to visit my CLE table at lunch time to complete their forms. I hadn't met any of the new law clerks in the field offices before so I spent a little time trying to put names with faces and create connections with my colleagues. Little did I know that Paula was watching from her table. I saw her out of the corner of my eye talking with some other judges. I, of course, did not approach them because it was important for us to maintain our distance in public. We did not want anyone thinking we were anything but co-workers. I knew she was great at showing a face of indifference. I suppose she did it every day on the bench. But I wasn't as good at that. I tried to busy myself with the young law clerks and find topics of conversation to keep us talking.

Duncan walked around the breakfast spread with a triangle, dinging it to notify people that the opening remarks would begin in five minutes. People started filtering into the meeting room. I wasn't sure how much I would listen to today. I loved sitting in the back of the room, hearing what everyone else was hearing, but also watching Paula from behind. I liked seeing the shape of her head, her hair as it swung when she moved, hearing her laughter when something amused her, watching her mannerisms as she tapped her pen or asked a thoughtful question asking for clarification on some obscure point of law. I didn't have time to stare at her when we are alone, which really sounds ironic.

Before she entered the conference room, Paula passed by me and said, "What was that about?"

"What?"

"Did you have to talk with the young handsome law clerk for so long?"

"Who? Colby?"

"Yes!" she almost yelled.

"I was asking how he liked his court. Are you... jealous?"

"Why would I be jealous? Because he's young, attractive, and a guy?"

"Please, Judge, I am not interested in anyone but you," I whispered.

"You better not be. Camel toe check."

I stepped away from the table to expose my tight pants to her.

"Good girl." She walked away and entered the conference room.

I decided to stay out of the room for a while. Was she really jealous? Did she think I had time or energy for *another* affair? I could barely handle her. I walked around the hotel for a while thinking.

When I returned to the area where people congregate during breaks, Duncan said, "Someone from the hotel just told me that Drew has been trying to reach you."

"What?"

"He called the hotel to try to find you because you weren't answering your phone."

"Oh, ok. I had it turned off. I'll call him. Thank you."

I found my phone in the bottom of my purse and saw there were four missed calls from Drew. I hope the boys are ok. Pangs of panic and fear subsided when Drew told me that he had to go to work early the next morning, so he needed me to take the boys to school. I can manage that. I'll get to the conference late though. Which means Paula will be unhappy. No morning play time. I have to find someone to man the CLE table for me during Wednesday's lunch. I have to see if Bonnie can come to the conference to cover for me if Duncan doesn't have anyone available.

During the lunch time break, I stayed at the table and talked to about half of the attendees. They were happy that we were managing their training requirements. It was better for everyone. My thong had dried a bit so I wasn't terribly uncomfortable due to wetness, only tightness. I guess that was a step in the right direction.

As the afternoon session was about to begin, Paula came to the table. She was a member of the Georgia bar. I found her forms, showed her what needed to be completed and told her that I could collect them when she was finished.

"Thank you for your assistance," she said distantly. "I forgot that I made plans to have dinner with some of the other judges at one of the restaurants in the plaza down the hill from the hotel. Consequently, I can't see you this afternoon."

My cheeks flushed with confusion. Is this a valid excuse or a punishment? I never can tell. I had to dish it back to her all the same.

"That's too bad because I can't come early tomorrow morning. My husband has to go to work early so I have to take the boys to school."

"Isn't there anyone else to do that for you?"

"Not since my in-laws retired and moved to Arizona. There is no one else. But I will get someone to cover my duties at this table tomorrow at lunch if you want to see me then."

"If I want to? Of course, I do! You know I think about you all the time, even when we are not together. I spend hours creating new scenarios. I will see you tomorrow at lunch. For tomorrow's way to incorporate the theme, I'd like you to wear a tight bra. It needs to be tight around the band and on the tightest hooks, not tight on the cups. I do not want your tits popping out the top so that the young attorneys drool over you. Those tits are mine and only mine. Do you understand?"

"Yes, Judge. I understand completely." My damn clit pulsed as I said it.

"I think I mentioned before, but I'm glad to remind you – absolutely no sex with your husband this week. And I'll babysit your toys to ensure you don't use them either."

"Yes, ma'am."

Duncan appeared with the triangle – ding-ding – indicating it was time to go back to work. I had some filing and organizing to do, but then I would go into the break-out session that Paula was in and watch her for a while silently in the back.

My night didn't go as planned because my period started. I had cramps and blood everywhere. I took a shower after putting the boys to bed to clean myself up. Usually my periods were heaviest in the middle of the week, but this seemed like a lot of blood. I secretly wondered if my tight pants stressed my body into an early period with heavier flow. I tried to laugh at the absurdity of it, but I really felt awful. After showering, I took some Advil and went to bed.

I slept in the next morning because I didn't have to rush to get to the hotel early. I was going to have to find a different route because I couldn't use the Rock Creek Parkway at the hour I'd be traveling in that direction. It would probably take me twice or three times as long to get that far up Connecticut Avenue. I wasn't going to be able to be with Paula anyway since I now had my period. It was so inconvenient, but I was lucky this hasn't happened before – with either of us.

After I got the boys up, dressed and fed, we left for school. Even though I knew my day with Paula wasn't going to be as she planned, I decided to wear the tight bra that she demanded. It was hot pink and it used to fit me well, but it shrunk in the dryer. I never dried my intimate apparel but once or twice when Drew did the laundry, he forgot to hang things to airdry. This bra was a victim of one of those times. It was cute and a little sexy but definitely not comfortable. I had matching panties which had no use for my day today, but again I wore them anyway. My dress was attractive enough but nothing to get excited about. In fact, I looked pretty bland and it mirrored exactly how I felt.

I arrived at the hotel around 9:20 a.m. and everyone was already in the conference. I set everything on my CLE table, grabbed a coffee as the hotel staff was removing the leftover continental breakfast items and looked around for Duncan. He was always handling some emergency. I walked down the hall and decided to use the bathroom to change tampons. Then I went toward the lobby. I could sit there all day and watch people go by. I was surprised at the number of people with kids there. It was mid-week in October. Didn't they go to school? Who are the people who can afford to stay at the Omni with their kids? When Drew and I traveled, we often stayed at Homewood Suites or Embassy Suites – something with a good breakfast and a pool. We clearly were not Omni people. These Omni moms were probably the same ones that looked good on airplanes. They wore suits without wrinkles or sundresses with perfect tans. Their nails were done and their hair was newly-coiffed. "Excuse me, Mrs. Rothschild, the valet brought your Rolls Royce around." Sometimes I entertained myself with stories about the lobby people.

"What are you smirking about, Catherine?" It was Duncan.

"Hey, I was looking for you, but I ended up doing some people-watching instead. I made a plan to eat with some of the judges today, can one of your folks watch my CLE table then? There are only a couple of people who I haven't talked to yet, so it shouldn't be very busy. I can also make an announcement during the next break to remind everyone to do their paperwork."

"No problem. Glad to help. A couple of my people took too long of a lunch hour yesterday so I'd love to have an excuse to keep them near me today. This is perfect."

"Thank you so much. I owe you one!" I headed back down the hall to the conference center.

I would have skipped down the hall if it wouldn't have been out of place, I felt so creative in my lying skills. But then I remembered that maybe I wouldn't need that lunch time anyway. I hated to tell Paula about my period. Bloody hell. What a waste the rest of this week would be.

At 10:30 a.m., everyone emptied out into the break area to stretch their legs, get a snack and mingle. I talked to a few judges who hadn't done their forms yet. Then I saw her. She made my heart skip a beat. I thought of those movies when the leading man sees the object of his affection who is running in slow motion toward him. That is what I saw. She was approaching me at half speed. I could see her sexy crooked smile, her hair dark flowing around her shoulders, the confidence in her step, the tailored fit of her peach pantsuit. I looked at my dress and immediately felt frumpy. Why did I pick this dress? It was like I forgot to care what I looked like. Hopefully she'll forgive me – or maybe she will approve that I was trying to not bring attention to myself? The truth is I could never guess what she was thinking or how she would react.

"Catherine, can I ask you something?" she put her hand on my back, directly on my bra band and gently led me to the corner as if her conversation would need to be private. She was assessing whether or not I obeyed – in public. She was really gutsy.

"Yes, Judge?"

"I can tell that you did not disobey. What color is your tight bra? I want to have something to think about for the next two hours until we are alone."

"Ma'am it's hot pink, but... I'm not sure how to tell you this. I have my period."

"And?" she questioned.

"I didn't think we would be able to ... do anything."

"I'm not afraid of a little blood, are you? You still have my room key, right? I will see you there at 12:15."

"Yes, ma'am."

"Good girl," she whispered as she walked away.

I'm surprised to see that the throbbing down below isn't impacted by its neighbor, the tampon. I wonder what she will do with me while I'm bleeding. It didn't sound that sexy to me, but I guess she now has two hours to dream up a new plan.

At 12:15, I went to her room and used my key card to open the door. She was already there. She met me at the door and locked it behind me. She pulled me into her arms and rubbed my back, mostly to feel my tight bra. I think it excited her as much as it did me.

We kissed with urgency. Our time was limited to a lunch hour and a half.

"Do you feel ok? Do you have any cramping or discomfort?"

"I'm fine today. I had some pain last night when it started."

"Excellent. I'm guessing that you did not have an orgasm last night even though you were super-horny all day?"

"That's right ma'am. I obeyed – for a change." I winked at her, hoping the playful Paula would be present for a few more minutes.

"I'm impressed. I think we should celebrate your good behavior with an orgasm. What do you say?"

"I'm intrigued. I don't usually have sex when I have my period."

"There's a first time for everything. Please remove your dress. I want to look at your bra and panties."

"Yes, Mistress."

I took off my dress. I felt a little bloated and not very sexy.

"Turn around so I can look at you."

I let her look at me from the front and behind. She snapped my bra band.

"How does it feel knowing that you wore a tight bra for me?"

"It feels like I am obeying your orders in secret, which makes me feel special and sexy."

"You know why? Because you are special and sexy. We do things that only we know about and feel erotic even when we aren't together. Isn't that great? It's only for us. Please take off your bra and panties now."

"Yes, ma'am. I'd be glad to."

As I removed the remainder of my clothes, she also rid herself of her clothes.

"How long ago did you change your tampon?"

"About a half an hour."

"Are you bleeding heavily?"

"Moderately, I'd say."

"Ok, then let's keep it in there for now. Please assume position number two."

I lay down on the edge of the bed on my stomach with my legs spread.

She massaged my ass for a few minutes and teased me with a gentle scratch of her very short nails.

"I'm going to insert the blue beaded wand into your asshole. I want you to suck it first to lubricate it. Get it nice and wet." She handed me the wand.

I licked it over and over ensuring it would be wet enough to glide into my asshole without pain. It was ironic that my ability to lubricate it would influence how much I'd feel. Just the thought of it entering my ass made my clit begin its dance: first a tingle, then a gentle pulse, followed by the full throb. When I was certain it was wet enough, I handed it back to her.

"Relax." I barely felt the first bead enter. Each subsequent bead was a little larger. No discomfort at all. I could get used to this. She was gentler than usual as the wand entered and nearly exited several times. Just months ago, I could not have imagined enjoying being fucked in the ass. My, how things have changed.

"Roll over carefully," Paula directed. I needed to ensure I wouldn't impale myself with the wand. She massaged around Pam and tugged on the tampon string but didn't remove it. The immobile wand was vibrating inside of me.

"Do you feel good?" she asked.

"Yes, really good."

"I want to make you cum now. Do you prefer the pink vibrator or should I eat you?"

"Surprise me."

She put her lips near my clit and moved her pointy tongue up one side and down the other. Then she flattened her tongue and did it again. I felt so many different sensations, each one equally stimulating. She grabbed the wand and started fucking me with it again while licking up one side and down the other around my clit as if she were trying to catch a drip of ice cream. I worried for a minute about my period and the tampon. I felt very wet in that area and I hoped I wouldn't bleed through. My distraction momentarily threw off my progress. I reminded myself to focus. I thought of her talking dirty to me on the phone, telling me how hot I was, how there was no one like us in our shared naughtiness, when she spanked me or inspected my camel toe in public. My hips reached up to grind her lips into my crotch as I put my hand on her head and pressed down. I needed to finish. It felt so good. I felt my back arch in anticipation and finally I let two days of build-up escape me. The denial of yesterday's orgasm coupled with the excitement of having her eat me while I was bleeding created the apex of my sexual experiences with Paula. The wand was the cherry on top. I totally believe Tyleah-Shay's theory that orgasms are exponentially better with some anal stimulation. I felt like a wet noodle, devoid of bones or muscles after that.

Paula carefully removed the wand and put it aside. She crawled next to me and kissed my mouth. I could taste the warm sweetness from my own orgasm. She licked the taste off my lips.

"You didn't remove my tampon, did you?" I was worried I could be bleeding all over the bed.

"No, I didn't. You know that bleeding usually stops when you are aroused, right? Your body knows to lubricate your vagina for sex and pauses menstruation."

"Really? I had no idea."

"That has been my experience."

"Oh, with G.I. Joan?"

"Yes. I'm sorry, I didn't mean to talk about her."

"I usually avoid sex when I'm having my period. But I'm glad it didn't bother you. That was fantastic."

"At your service, today only!"

"You know just the right time to be dominant or be passionate and loving."

"Don't get mushy on me, Catherine. That wasn't our arrangement."

"I know. But I've been re-thinking that. I know I told you that I wouldn't fall in love with you because I wouldn't ruin my family for you. I will never give them up. They are too important to me."

"Yes, that's right. This relationship isn't real anyway. It's for fun. We meet once a year for a day or two and play out our fantasies. It couldn't be maintained in a daily situation. It wouldn't be like this. There would be laundry to do and trash to take to the curb, grocery shopping and cooking – and you know I don't cook."

"Haha. Well, I was going to say that when we are together, I feel like I love you."

"So do I."

"My thought is that I can say 'I love you when we're together.' That's it. I'm not going to love you when you return to Pittsburgh or even when we're having phone sex. But when I'm alone with you, then I do."

"I'm ok with that. I love you when we're together, too."

"Do you want to cum before we have to return to the conference? We have about fifteen minutes."

"No, today was about you. I wanted you to feel good. I think I accomplished that goal."

"Did you ever! That may have been the most erotic orgasm I've ever had.

I feel like I say that a lot with you, but there was something different about today. It seems like we ascended to a different stage in our non-relationship. Having you near Pam when I am having my period is a game-changer for me. It reflects a rare level of intimacy. Something I've never experienced. You find new ways to surprise me every time we're together. You are the most amazing lover and beautiful woman and there's no one else like us."

"There is no one like us. I want you to remember that I'm the best lover you ever had."

"You are. Thank you for being mine today, Mistress."

"You are welcome, my hot little sub. Let's get ready to go back downstairs."

I knew this meant putting my tight bra back on along with the unflattering dress and changing my soaking tampon.

I spent the afternoon hungry, feeling post-orgasm drained of energy, yet mildly turned on because of this stupid bra and obeying the good judge. After the afternoon break, Paula dropped off an Omni gift bag containing my well-hidden make-up bag and the two vibrators and said that she felt it was too risky to get together tomorrow. I nearly cried but tried to hold it together. What was that about? My admission of having emotions? This rollercoaster ride with her is too much. I'm diverting energy from my family for these irregular flings. Why? Do I need the excitement of our relationship for my self-worth? Do I try to reason with her or let it go? I know she's right in terms of the riskiness, but we have limited time together and I like to use it to the best of our ability. I decide to let it go, sleep on it and see what happens tomorrow. If I didn't have to manage the CLE table, I would probably call in sick and avoid the whole situation. But maybe she would change her mind? Maybe she wouldn't be able to be so close to me and not be with me? I'm not sure if her actions would lead me to believe that or if it was wishful thinking. I tried to look on the bright side – at least I wouldn't have to wear shoes that were too small or some other painful feat tomorrow! That is a small victory. It almost made me laugh except I really felt hurt.

I gathered all of my files and papers and told Duncan I was leaving for the day. He would store them for tomorrow in one of the locked offices that we used during the conference. I grabbed the Omni bag and put it in my briefcase. I went through the lobby watching the people who were in D.C. on business or vacation, trying to imagine their stories. Is anyone there having an affair, having an illicit rendezvous? Probably.

I called Drew on the way out and said that I could likely get the boys on my way home since I was leaving a little early. Traffic was just starting to pick up. I managed to get on the Rock Creek Parkway before it turned to one way in the other direction. The ride home was easier than I expected and I made it in time to get the boys from school. I asked them what they wanted me to pick up for dinner since I couldn't devote any thought to preparing food.

"Pupusas!" yelled Bodie.

"Burritos!" suggested Logan simultaneously.

"Ok, guys. Do you want to compromise or pick a number one through ten?"

"Mama, we learned rock-paper-scissors-shoot today. We can do that three times and see who wins."

"That's a great idea, buddy," I said to Bodie. I let them decide in the back of the car as I rounded the corner away from the school.

Bodie won this time, so we headed toward the Salvadoran place to order pupusas. The restaurant had chalk the boys could draw with on the sidewalk while we waited for the food to be prepared. That gave them some entertainment while I turned inward once again to analyze what happened today. All of the thinking and not coming to any other outcomes was tiring. I can't read her mind. I really have to quit thinking about Paula and be in the moment with the boys.

"How about a game of tic-tac-toe?" I suggest.

"Yes! Yes!"

I played with each one separately. Occasionally one would make a mistake allowing me to win. I don't feel great beating a young child, but I also don't want to purposely lose. I want to give them the tools to strategize how to win. After about twenty minutes, our food was ready. We paid Yelka, our favorite server, and took our pupusas and fried plantains home.

Drew was happy to have pupusas – it was one of the meals we all really enjoyed and I always ordered extras so we could have them for leftovers another night. After dinner, Drew cleaned up and put away the leftovers. I thought it would be nice to get outside and clear my head. I suggested to the boys to get their scooters and I would walk around the block with them. They always got ahead of me, but I shouted for them to stop and wait. Sometimes I ran a little to keep up. But I wasn't in a running mood with my period. I really wanted to stay a bit behind them and enjoy the fall evening. The leaves were changing colors a little earlier this year but they were nowhere near peak colors. In the D.C. area, thousands of people head to the Shenandoah Mountains each fall to see the autumn colors. Skyline Drive, that winds through the mountains, is packed with cars on several weekends in October and November. Some people park and hike on trails or to waterfalls while enjoying the leaf-peeping. It is truly a majestic sight. One time in the summer, we took the boys tubing down the Shenandoah River. It was fun, refreshing and a little dangerous because there were very small rapids. They loved it so much that we might make it an annual tradition. We really enjoy making small traditions for the boys to have fun memories of growing up. One of our favorites is the annual "ice cream for breakfast day." It falls on the first Saturday in February. We get a huge bowl and fill it with two half-gallons of ice cream and add a bunch of topping – sliced bananas, strawberries, caramel, hot fudge and, of course, homemade whipped cream. I think they would like to do it every month, but once a year is the tradition.

We ran into a neighbor, Tessa Powell, with kids a bit older than our boys. She was clearing some weeds from her yard.

"Hi Tessa! How does your daughter like high school?" I hadn't seen her in the month since school started.

"She loves it. She joined the football cheerleading squad. She's making new friends which is great." I knew her daughter went to private Catholic school through 8th grade so the move to the neighborhood public high school was a huge transition for her.

"I'm so happy for her. That's wonderful. We want to bring the boys to a football game sometime. Are they still going on?"

"Yes, games go through the beginning of November. The freshman team plays on Thursday nights at 5:30 p.m. She is a cheerleader for that team, although sometimes she is asked to join the junior varsity cheerleaders. Both JV and varsity play on Friday nights. The JV team plays at 5:00 p.m. and varsity at 7:00 p.m."

"I didn't realize they had three different teams. I guess I don't know much about high school sports since we are far from that age." The boys turned the corner and were circling in a cul-de-sac while I talked. Sometimes I was amazed at how they entertained themselves without my intervention.

"That reminds me, we have some old books that we'd like to give you for the twins if you want them. We've been cleaning out some of Emmy's old toys and books to donate."

"We'd love them. That is very generous of you. Is Emmy babysitting yet?

We'd love to have her help us out sometime if she's interested."

"Yes, in fact, I was just going to mention that. She did some sitting over the summer. As soon as football season is over, she'll have more time. Please let us know if you ever want her to watch the boys while you and Drew go out. We're right down the street if she runs into any problems."

"That sounds great. We will be in touch. Have a nice night and please tell Brooks 'hello'."

"Will do. He's inside repairing a broken light fixture in our spare bathroom. There's always something that needs to be done with these old houses," Tessa shared.

"No kidding! It's exhausting. You are lucky that Brooks is so handy. Drew is pretty good at fixing things too, but sometimes we have to call a plumber or electrician. I'd better catch up with the boys and get home before dark. See you later!"

"Bye."

I reached the corner and shouted for the boys to join me. They caught up in a flash. Earlier in the year, I bought an adult-sized scooter and used it for a few weeks. The boys thought it was hysterical. It did make going down the block quicker but it was more tiring than I recalled. I used it occasionally since then but I preferred walking. The boys were also learning to ride bikes without training wheels, but that was Drew's area to instruct. Before the boys were born, Drew and I took a few very long bike trips. One was forty miles toward West Virginia. Another time, on one of the many local trails, I lost my balance, fell off and broke my wrist. After that, I have limited my time on my bike. I think it's great exercise, but I don't feel as steady on it as I used to. Whoever coined the phrase about riding a bike being something people don't forget how to do was wrong. Unless I'm some kind of anomaly. And, in spite of some of my emerging fetishes, I still feel like a pretty average person.

The twins don't bathe every night, but after their scooter trip around the neighborhood, it seemed like a good night to get cleaned up.

"Mama, can I take a shower tonight like you and Daddy do instead of a bath?" Bodie asked as I was running the water in the tub.

"Sure, I guess so. Let Logan take a bath first, then you can take a shower. Ok?"

"Yippee!! I'm going to be a grown up! I'm going to take a shower!" Bodie exclaimed with excitement.

The things these guys get excited about is really entertaining sometimes.

If small things make them happy, I'm fine with that. Logan wasn't bothered that his brother wanted to shower either. That was another bonus. No competition. No arguments. What a great night.

Of course, Bodie's shower wasn't without a little drama. Keeping water inside the shower curtain is not an easy feat for a little person. He didn't want any help, so I let him do it independently. He smelled delicious when he got out. I'm not sure if it is the Dove soap we use or the baby shampoo, but I could smell the post-bathing boys every day and never get tired of it. I helped each of them brush their wet hair and reminded myself that it was probably time for haircuts – maybe we could fit that in this weekend. They put on clean pajamas and Drew got bedtime book duty.

I wanted a glass of wine, but I was a little dehydrated from the walk so I thought water would be a better choice. I didn't want to go to the conference tomorrow with a headache. I needed to be as fresh and alert as possible for whatever was coming my way.

I fell asleep in my sweatpants while Drew was reading to the boys. I woke up at midnight in my dark room. Drew was snoring next to me. I heard the rhythm of his breath with each exhale. I hadn't set my alarm since I missed my usual night time routine. I'm so glad I woke then or I would have overslept in the morning. I went to the bathroom to pee, change my tampon and put on my nightgown. I filled a glass with water and drank the whole thing before returning to bed. I felt very tired, but my mind started to think about the coming day. I felt a bit of dread. I hadn't let my mind go to the inevitable very bad place. What happens if Paula doesn't want to see me ever again? What happens if our relationship is really over? I tried to remember exactly what she said when she handed me the Omni bag. Oh crap! The Omni bag was still in my briefcase! I forgot to take it out because I stopped to get pupusas and then I carried the food inside and left my briefcase in the car. Should I go get it now? Would I be able to do it in the morning before leaving? Shit! Shit! Shit! I have to go to the car and get it now. I quietly left my room, tiptoed down the hall, unlocked the front door and raced to the driveway. I found my briefcase on the floor of the backseat where I left it. I brought it inside, set it on the chair by the door and carefully took the Omni bag out. We kept the vibrators on the top shelf of the linen closet. It wasn't an ideal place, but we didn't put much thought into it. It needed to be someplace the boys would never look and they couldn't reach the top shelf at this point. I took the make-up bag out of the Omni bag and put it back in the closet. Done.

Now what was I going to do with the Omni bag? It's funny that I am not that worried being deceitful about Paula, but I'm not sure how to handle the complicit Omni bag. I am going to put some sneakers inside it and put it near the closet. That way it might appear that I had extra shoes with me at the conference. I'm not sure Drew would notice it anyway, but it's better to have a plan and not be caught off guard. Whew. Back to bed I go worrying about my future – mostly with Paula. What was the look in her eye when she gave me the bag? One that indicated she was saying goodbye forever? Or she really believed that it was too risky to spend another day in her bed? She had often told me that she loved her job so much and it was the best job she ever had. She would never risk it. I personally think my family is more important than her job, but I didn't think it was taking a risk. The two things – my relationship with her and my marriage – were completely separate. As long as emotions didn't seep into my relationship, everything was good. I think the ability for me to compartmentalize my feelings, and love her only when I was with her, was a perfect solution. I think our affair can be maintained as long as no one finds out. I drift back to sleep feeling that I have the future resolved.

But when I woke up, the calmness of my sleep was gone. I rushed to shower, dress and eat. I wanted to look attractive but not provocative. I wanted Paula to see what she was missing if she decided to go through with her idea that we weren't going to be together today or in the future. And since I really didn't know her intention, I was preparing my mind and, honestly, my heart for whatever eventuality I might encounter that day. I felt jittery on the drive to the hotel, almost like I was driving to my own execution. I remember feeling a similar nervousness on the first day I was going to be with her. Yet this is entirely different. The other time it was butterflies of excitement. This was moths of dread. Or maybe even bats – they were bigger, more erratic, crashing into my stomach lining with a ferocity I've never known. I wish I never agreed to be responsible for the CLE table. Then I could have called in sick, stayed under the covers of my warm bed and watched game shows or talk shows all day while avoiding the real world. My fantasy about television-viewing collided with reality as I passed the turn for the hotel. That was not a good error to make. I would have to travel several blocks before I could turn around. What was I thinking? I was two blocks from the hotel when I saw her. Paula was out jogging. She was with other people. Is this the Administrative Law Judge jogging team? I noticed one law clerk that

I had talked to the day before. I couldn't tell who everyone was since it was not totally light out yet. One person had a hood over his or her head. There were six or so people. Fortunately, they didn't notice me and I moved ahead when the traffic light changed. I felt sick again, almost betrayed. Is that what she does when I'm not around? Jogging with others isn't the worst thing one could do, but I feel replaced somehow. Am I being a baby? She's *running* for Christ's sake, not fucking them. Or maybe she is doing both – running with them and fucking them?! Wow – I'm going to make myself crazy. I must stop this line of thinking immediately. When I see her, I'll ask what she did this morning without me and I'll see what she says. If she tells the truth, then clearly, she has nothing to hide. If she lies, then maybe I have something to worry about. I want to turn left onto Garfield Street but there is no traffic light there. I wait for oncoming traffic and almost hit a driver who didn't put his headlights on. There are a few pedestrians trying to cross the street as well. I finally make my turn, drive a little while. My plan is to make two more rights and end up back on Connecticut Ave near the zoo.

I remember when we had the boys' birthday party at the zoo the previous year. We had a choice of three different areas – the otters, the bears or the rainforest. One kid wanted the rainforest and the other wanted the bears. Wouldn't it be great if they agreed on something? Fortunately, the zoo made the decision for us. The rainforest only accommodated sixteen party-goers and we had eighteen. We had to go to the bear habitat. I was glad we reserved the bear party because it included the pandas. The pandas in the National Zoo are on loan from China. When they reproduce, the cubs must return to China when they are old enough to leave their mothers. I have always enjoyed panda-viewing so I was particularly happy to have a private tour of their den. The boys each got a bear plush animal for having their party at the zoo and all of their guests were given explorer hats that were very cute. I don't know why we don't go to the zoo more often. It's not hard to get to and it's free to enter, although the treats and gift shop are not cheap and it's hard to escape the zoo without visiting a snack bar or gift shop. I'm going to suggest to Drew that we plan a zoo trip soon.

The next thing I knew I was pulling into the long driveway of the hotel, leaving my car in the garage and heading to the best lobby for people-viewing in the D.C. area. I just made that part up, but I wonder if there is a better place? Since I am early, I will get a coffee in Morsel's, the lobby café, and watch the guests for a while. I brought my newspaper with me just in case there is time to read. I settled into a subtle paisley-print wingback chair with my latte and the paper, half reading and half looking around taking in the surroundings. This was my last day at the conference and maybe my last day at the Omni since Duncan usually finds new places to have the conference at each year we hold one. It gives the judges and their families new areas to explore. The location of the Omni is good for judges with kids to visit the zoo, a few blocks away that is pretty easy for walking in spite of the hills. Of course, the timing this year wasn't good since the conference was held in October. Often the judges came a few days earlier or stayed a few days later so they could enjoy the city with their families. The hotels we use extend the government rate for lodging for additional days to accommodate their travel plans. We don't pay for their additional days, of course, but they have a cheaper rate if they want to stay.

My latte is delicious and I contemplate getting another when I see Paula standing in front of me.

"May I join you?" she asked.

My face flushed and I said, "of course, Judge."

"You're up and dressed early. The conference doesn't start for another half hour."

"I went for a run this morning with some of the others. The city is nice before it gets crowded with the hustle and bustle of the business day." I was glad to hear her tell me the truth.

"I agree. Although I do like when I have to come downtown for meetings. It makes me feel grown up in a way that I don't really feel working in a safe office park in Virginia."

She smiled warmly, her crooked gorgeous smile.

"Did you have a nice evening last night?" she inquired.

"Not really, I spent too much time worrying about you. Then I woke up in the middle of the night and realized I left the vibrators in my briefcase in the car. I retrieved them and hid them very quietly."

"Why were you worrying about me? Because I said we shouldn't be together today?"

"Yes, of course. I thought maybe you were dumping me after I told you how I felt."

"Oh no, Catherine. I'm sorry. If we ever split up, I will be clear about it. I have no intention of letting you go. I enjoy our time together way too much."

"Then why...?"

"Sometimes I just worry. I can't risk my job. If it seems like we might appear to be more than colleagues, I have to back off a little, but it's not from you or us. It's just to maintain appropriate space in public. I just felt like I needed to have a little space. I know when I'm back in Pittsburgh, I'll miss you like crazy. I don't want to ever hurt you."

"I'm happy to hear you say that. You know I volunteered to do the CLE table so I'd be here with you all week. Last night I wished I could call in sick to avoid coming today. I couldn't stand to see you if I couldn't be with you. I understand what you are saying about being careful. I am taking risks for you too; I just don't think we will get caught. I'm very careful."

"I'm glad you are very careful. How's Aunt Flo?"

I hadn't heard my period referred to like that since high school. "Still flowing."

"Maybe we can get together for a little while at lunch or on a break. Just to spend a few minutes alone – nothing too intricate."

"Yes, ma'am. I'd enjoy that a lot. I will make myself available whenever you want."

"Good girl, Catherine. You mean so much to me. I love being naughty with you."

"So do I. Last night when I thought you broke up with me, I worried that I might never be spanked again. Or punished. Or have to assume any positions. I thought of everything we do and how much I'd miss it." I wanted to say that I hope we stay together forever, but I knew it would sound needy. I didn't want to do that. I think she needs me as much as I need her. But tipping my hand might make her withdraw.

"We have plenty of years of fun left. I have scenarios planned for a dozen more conferences."

"A dozen? Wow. You have a lot of time on your hands."

"You know I go to the gym every day after work. I run on the treadmill and think of you and the great things we can do together. I tell you some of them on the phone and we try a few ideas when possible. But we have only scratched the surface of the things I want to do. That reminds me, when I return to Pittsburgh and we have phone sex, I want you to be more vocal. You can make suggestions to me. Say things like 'I really don't want that big vibrator in my ass' or 'you can blindfold me if you want to'. You can do it in a way to suggest what you want. But you know I will always make the decisions."

"Judge, you know I'm not as good as you are at being dirty on the phone. I will try though – anything to make you happy."

"The better you do, the more good girl points you will earn. When you earn enough, you will be able to have a voice in our games. Ok?"

"Yes, ma'am. I will do my best to talk dirty to you."

"All right. I need to get some coffee and head over to the conference. I'll stop by the CLE table during the break."

"See you then."

Even these brief conversations make me aroused. She really is the most erotic person I have ever met. We would never have been able to maintain a relationship if this started when she was here. I would break my own rule of never getting emotionally involved with anyone other than Drew. She is hard not to love. But I can keep her and Drew separate in my mind and in my heart. That is the only way this works.

Maybe I'll make a scenario for her when we talk. One in which she's on the bench in her robe and I'm hiding beneath it playing with Sawyer. Maybe she's actually hearing a case and I'm making her wetter and wetter, almost to the point of cumming. And she has to act like she is just working like usual and keep her impartial judge face, no sexy mischievous smile that would give me away. I think she would like this scenario. I have to remember it, tell her and earn good girl points. Whatever they are. I guess they are another fictional way to control me and I'm ok with that. It's all part of our sexy game.

I fold up my newspaper and go to my table outside the conference room. I want to organize all of the forms to ensure everyone has already completed them. Then I really won't have any work to do and I can be available if Paula wants to see me in her room. It took me half an hour to alphabetize the forms, check to ensure each set was complete and cross off the names on my master list of attendees. One person took the forms and didn't return them to me. It was Colby, the young cute attorney that Paula accused me of flirting with. I wish she knew that I don't need any other distractions. And, frankly, I don't have time or energy for other distractions. Also, I have Drew if I need a man. He takes care of my needs quite well. And Paula helps with my other intermittent needs that, until recently, I didn't know I had. She is enough for me. I'm going to have to ask Colby on the break if his forms are done and risk her jealousy or wrath. Lucky me.

I packed almost everything up. All of my boxes will be brought back by our office courier at the end of the conference, so I don't have to carry anything. I went into the ethics session to listen while waiting for the break. While the Ethics Officer was sharing important and required information, it isn't the most interesting topic except when they are providing examples. She finished and everyone left the room looking for coffee to make it through the rest of the morning. Paula was no exception.

"Did you hear any of that? It's the same boring information year after year. I wish they'd figure out a more interesting way to present the topic."

"Yes, it's rough. I'm sorry you have to get trained on that annually. Do you like the computer-based training better on the years we don't have conferences?"

"Not really. Ethics is a dry subject. There isn't really a way to inject much excitement into it. Listen, I'm sorry but I can't see you at lunch time. The judges want to have lunch together to discuss an important topic. I'll tell you the results on the afternoon break or at the end of the day if you can stay late. In the meantime, will you please see if you can find us a place to eat at the hotel that is somewhat private?"

"Sure, I'll be glad to. I can't stay late though because I didn't make arrangements for anyone to pick up my kids so I have to. But I'm curious about your topic so I hope we can talk during the afternoon break. Table for eighteen?"

"Yes, that sounds good. Thank you so much."

"You are welcome, Judge." I winked at her. I don't want her to forget who her best girl is. I spent the rest of the break at Robert's, the restaurant in the hotel. I was trying to secure a somewhat private area for the judges. It sounded like they wanted to speak with some level of confidentiality. The maître d' suggested they could move some decorative screens to provide additional seclusion. I think that will be perfect. I hope this earns the elusive "good girl points," the fictional reason for me to do anything nice and potentially influence the direction of a future scenario.

I wrote a quick note on a sheet of paper and handed it to Paula as the last session for the morning was starting. "Robert's Restaurant, table for eighteen reserved, somewhat private location, in your name at 12:30 p.m."

She mouthed "thank you" as I left her the paper. Sadly, I had no plan for lunch. Maybe I could eat with the law clerks. I wasn't sure if they had been to Lebanese Taverna yet. It was just across the street from the Omni and one of my favorite places. I hadn't been able to eat there this whole week because I was busy on my lunch hours. Now it seemed that I had some free time – if I could get Colby's paperwork. I was on a mission to get him to complete the forms and maybe have lunch with me, too.

The judges left the conference room with great speed and went down the hall toward Robert's. I was very curious about the topic of their discussions. I temporarily forgot about it when I saw Colby. I grabbed him on his way out of the conference room. I guess I didn't pay that close attention to how cute he really is. He was tall with very dark hair. I couldn't guess his ethnicity.

"Colby, you didn't turn in your CLE forms. Did you do them?"

"Oh, sorry, Catherine, I haven't heard if I passed the Bar yet." His green eyes flashed when he spoke.

Oh! Of course, he was a first-year law clerk. He shouldn't have been on my list.

"I'm sorry. You were on my list and you shouldn't have been. My fault. Hey, do you have lunch plans? I wanted to go to Lebanese Taverna across the street. Have you been?"

"I haven't been but I heard it's great. I'd love to join you. I think I missed the others so I'm not sure where they are. Let me use the restroom and I'll be ready in five minutes."

"Perfect." I crossed off Colby's name, packed up the remainder of my files, and was ready when he returned.

"Can we walk there?"

"Yes, it's just down the hill and across Connecticut Ave. For a change, I have comfy shoes on, so I'm all set."

We walked out of the hotel, down the long driveway and crossed Connecticut Avenue. The restaurant wasn't very busy at lunch time. We occupied a table for two near the window, ideal for people watching. I ordered the fatteh bel bathenjan, a delicious eggplant, yogurt and pita dish with pomegranate seeds in season! There is a Lebanese Taverna in Virginia near us, but we haven't been in ages. The twins love hummus so they would undoubtedly enjoy the place as well. I made a mental note to go there again soon.

Colby and I spent the hour talking about his family, his move to Denver, how he likes Colorado in general, people in the office, topics at the conference, etc. It was a very tame conversation until he said, "Do you know Judge Marlon well?"

"Why do you ask? She used to work at headquarters before she became a judge and moved to Pittsburgh." I hoped I didn't give anything away. I was going for a neutral response.

"I get the feeling that she doesn't like me. Maybe I'm reading too much into it. She seemed a little short with me when I was asking about some case law during the session that she presented."

"I'm sure she was just tense because she had to prepare for the presentation. She understands the law very well. It doesn't really sound like her to be brash." I didn't want to make excuses for her.

"Mmmmm. This food is delicious. I've had Mediterranean before, but not Lebanese specifically." I guess we were done with the Paula-talk.

"It is one of my favorites. There are so many great ethnic places here. What is the food scene like in Denver?"

"I've only been there for two months. I think the culinary options are emerging. I did try Ethiopian and Thai food. Those restaurants were good. There are also quite a few brewpubs around Denver and the suburbs. The brewpubs used to just focus on beer, but now they are making better food to go along with it."

"I guess I should add Denver to places I'd like to visit. I've been to Colorado, but not Denver. When my kids are older, I'd like to take them skiing out west."

"I snowboard and I can't wait for winter. I want to go to Vail and Aspen, Beaver Creek, Breckinridge and Telluride. So many places, so little time!"

"Yeah, you don't earn a lot of annual leave when you first start with the government. You have to use your leave wisely. Take days off in conjunction with holidays to maximize your travel time. Are you able to do an alternate work schedule yet?"

"Not yet, but I like the idea of using my leave when we have holidays. That's a smart move. Thanks for the advice."

"No problem. If you ever need any guidance, please let me know. I'm happy to help." With that, our waiter dropped off our check and I decided to pay for both of us. After all, he's just out of law school, not making very much money and probably has a lot of student loan debt to pay. Of course, he is on per diem and I'm not. But that's ok. It'll be my treat today.

"You don't have to do that, Catherine."

"It's ok. I want to."

"That's very kind of you. Thank you so much."

"You're welcome." We walked back to the hotel and who did we run into as soon as we entered the lobby? Paula. This might not go well.

She was waiting in the foyer for Judge Kowalski who was outside smoking. I knew Paula hated smoking, so that must be why she wasn't with him.

"Well, well, it looks like you two had a nice lunch."

"We did, Judge Marlon. Catherine recommended Lebanese Taverna. It was fabulous. Have you been there?" Colby tried being extra nice to her.

"No, I haven't." She was purposely abrupt with him – and I think it was because of me.

"You should try it sometime. Thanks again, Catherine. See you later." Colby walked away.

"You seem very comfortable with the young law clerk, missy."

"Seriously? Please don't act jealous even if you are joking," I whispered. I wasn't about to apologize for something that didn't happen.

"I thought I was pretty clear that I don't trust you with him."

"Trust me? Please! I don't have time for anyone but you." I hated to act disgusted with her because I knew she could probably walk away from "us" easier than I could. But I wasn't going to let her accuse me of things that were blatantly false.

"Ok, ok, let's not escalate this. We'll discuss it later."

"Fine. What was your lunch meeting about?"

"Just a minute." She walked outside, said something to Kowalski, and returned to me.

"Let's walk. I don't want anyone to hear."

"Is it that secretive?"

"Some of the Administrative Law Judges want to unionize to have more power to make some demands as a group. We want alternate work schedules one or two law clerks per judge, more time to draft decisions. Our case completion goals are on a tight deadline that sacrifices due process. We want more judicial independence and potentially more pay. We are forming a committee to research the possibilities. We have unanimous support among us. Please do not discuss this with anyone, particularly not Edwin."

"Wow! I'm sort of surprised no one formed a union before now. Do you know if other federal ALJs have unions? Is there a precedent for this?"

"We aren't sure. That is why some judges are going to look into all of the regulations and the Administrative Procedures Act. Sworn to secrecy, got it?"

"I won't tell a soul," I promised.

"Good girl. Do we have time to run to my room and make out?"

"Nope! Back to the conference. Last chance will be on the 2:30 p.m. afternoon break."

"I can't wait for 2:30!"

"Me either," I confessed. I guess we made up just like that.

Surprisingly the next two hours of the conference flew by. I went up to Paula's room just prior to the end of the session before break and was waiting when she entered. I wanted to do something crazy like stand there naked before her, but because of our limited time and my lingering period, it didn't feel right.

"Hey there," she said when she entered.

"Good afternoon, Judge." I wanted to portray the obedient sub one last time. Do I wait until she beckons me or run into her arms? Time is running out.

"Come here, sexy Catherine."

It was remarkable how quickly I could be someplace I wanted to be. She held me and kissed me, first very gently and then with increasing passion. I took off her jacket and fumbled to reach beneath her blouse to feel her nipple. I wanted more time with her. I want to be inside of her and feel her inside of me. I need to taste all of her and hear her breath quicken as her back arches and she squirts into my mouth. I want to love her while we are together one last time for the year.

"Where are you?" she noticed my far-off stare.

"I don't want you to leave." My lip trembled and I felt that awful lump in my throat. My eyes filled with tears. I insistently begged my tears: please do not trickle down my face, smearing mascara, making my cheeks blotchy. I didn't mind showing her my emotions, but was afraid that my face would not recover quickly enough for my return to the conference. Why was I worried about my appearance when my heart was aching in anticipation of her departure? I was experiencing the adult version of separation anxiety. Certainly, I can let her go when she's gone. Out of sight, out of mind. This transition time when she's all mine, but leaving shortly is what kills me. I can barely enjoy being with her because I'm obsessed with her leaving and the months or years until I see her again.

"Don't worry, my love. We will talk on the phone. You know how much fun we have on the phone. This isn't goodbye. It'll never be goodbye. There's no one like us. We have a bond that can't be broken by space or time."

This comforted me more than it should have. I know she's right. I know when I leave this room, all of the complexities of my real life will return and she will be back in her little compartment of my brain – and my heart – until I see her again. The phone conversations are just to keep the spark alive.

"Ok. I miss you sometimes. I wish we could talk more." I don't want to give away the depth of my neediness. I know that, in reality, it is only transition time neediness. I have to enjoy the moment and let the transition of her being in my life to being hours away come and go. This is easier said than done.

"Don't be sad, baby. Kiss me."

Kissing makes things better. There's no doubt about that. I worried that our alone time was up and I spent it all being a moody mess. But I won't have regrets. It's important that she understands my feelings. Then she will leave and my feelings will disappear into the dark nothingness inside of me.

We kiss deeply. I want to feel every crevice of her teeth, every ripple inside her cheeks, have her tongue dance with mine in a tango of passion. I run my fingers through her thick hair pushing her head closer to mine taking control of our proximity. My shift of power does not go unnoticed. Paula grabs my hair and pulls my head away from hers. Pull me close, push me away.

"Who is in control here?"

"You are, ma'am," I whisper.

"I'm glad you remember that."

She is so hot and forceful in the sexiest way. God, I'm going to miss her. *But we have the phone.*

We spent twenty minutes in her room. The break is officially fifteen minutes long. Time is up. We both know it. We kiss. We hug. We gaze lovingly in each other's eyes like a pathetic Hallmark movie. We hold onto one another as if it's the last time we'll be together although we both know it's not.

"What has changed? Why is this so hard?" I said the words aloud but was hoping to just ponder them.

"Our connection is deeper. Our relationship has morphed into something slightly different than we anticipated. It's ok. Go along for the ride. I love you when we're together."

She said my thoughts.

"I love you, too."

For months afterward, I thought about our last moments together. I didn't dwell on them. I have too many things to manage – busy twins, a fulfilling marriage, a house, a demanding career – but those words, my words, coming from her mouth kept ringing in my ears.

I love you when we're together.

2009

Drew and I were busy preparing for our first spring break trip with the twins. His parents invited us to their house in Arizona and offered to pay for our plane tickets. That offer was hard to pass up. The boys had never been on a plane before and they were so excited. I wrote a million checklists – activities for the plane, decisions about whether to bring car seats or rent them when we get our rental van, bathing suits for all of us since the country club my in-laws belonged to had golf, tennis and a pool. There was so much to do and we were leaving in less than a week.

I fell into bed exhausted. Drew was trying to help, but, honestly, he wasn't great at the minutiae of preparing for anything. He often found other priorities like cleaning out the garage when I was packing suitcases or re-arranging the container cupboard when we were having friends over for dinner. I really needed him to focus on trip preparation. I knew logically that if we forgot anything, it could be purchased in Arizona. Certainly, there were Walmarts or Targets there. It was also possible to just do without. I discovered that on one trip to the Caribbean prior to having kids when I forgot to pack panties. We spent most of our days on the beach so I wasn't missing them. At night, I wore sundresses for dinner. It was actually quite freeing to do without panties. I'm not recommending that my sons go without underwear of course. But it is possible to go without essentials for short periods of time.

"Cath, I'd like to talk about something."

"Hmmmm," was all I could muster.

"Let's have another baby. Let's make the daughter you always wanted. We don't have a lot of time left. I'd like to do it before we don't have energy to run around with her."

"What?" This conversation woke me up.

"I've been thinking about it for a while."

"You have?"

"Yes, the boys are getting big. I miss having a little one. The boys could help us. They'd be such good big brothers."

I agree that they'd be great influences on a younger person. They often demonstrate empathy beyond their young ages and are compassionate, as well. Once they found a baby robin that had fallen out of her nest near our driveway. She was clinging to life. There was no mother around. They carefully scooped her up, brought her inside and made a nest, lining an old shoebox with cotton. They went outside digging for worms and somehow convinced me to use my kitchen hand mixer to grind them up to try to feed the bird using an ear dropper. She chirped weakly in the warmth of our house for two days, but then died. The boys were crushed. I was proud of them for trying to help her survive. I'm not equating a baby human to a baby bird, but I think they have a proven ability to see beyond themselves and try to make the world better.

"Let me think about it when I'm not exhausted."

That night I had the eeriest dream. I dreamed that my dead father was trying to teach my sons how to fish. He seemed so real. We were camping in the mountains by a fast-flowing stream. I could smell hot dogs being cooked by the campfire. I felt the coolness of the country air and saw the stars sparkling at night. My dad asked what he had missed since he left. It didn't seem that he meant since he died, but like he just went on a trip. He definitely knew my boys in the dream and they knew him. We had a nice time together. It was comforting to be with him. I woke before finishing the dream and realized that Drew wasn't in it. He was always a little mournful that he hadn't met my dad. I tell him stories of the things I remember about him. I really have to concentrate to remember anything – his voice, his cologne, his gait, the repetitive jokes he'd make. Sometimes I wonder if they are actual memories or games my mind plays to fill in the gaps in my memory. Having dreams about my dad always make me feel calm, like he's guiding me. I appreciate the visits he makes to me in my dreams even though they are few and far between. So, what did it mean that he visited on this night when Drew talked about having another baby? I wished I had the answer to that.

The days leading to the trip passed quickly. In fact, the trip passed quickly, too. The boys were great on the plane. They were worse on the car ride to Dulles Airport than they were on the entire flight. I think they were very excited to fly and couldn't keep from being obnoxious, loud and belligerent toward each other on the way to the airport. The hour wait to board the plane allowed the boys to run around a bit and get some their energy out. The airline representative announced via the loudspeaker the pre-boarding would begin for people with small children for our flight to Phoenix. Phoenix. Our safe word. I hadn't thought about it for almost six months. We didn't discuss our safe word during phone sex anymore. It was easy enough to avoid something dangerous, shocking, or painful on the phone. But hearing someone else say *our word* was strangely intrusive. I realized that Drew and I always said we were going to Arizona without mentioning the city. Phoenix. Phoenix transported me back to sensual days in hotel rooms with my lover. It was funny to call her that even in my head, but that is the truth. She's my lover, my dom, my judge, my Paula. My panties grew damp with each time the word "Phoenix" was mentioned. I have my own Pavlovian responses to so many things because of that woman. I guess it's "response," not "responses." The response is always wet panties. The stimulus is many different things.

Once we got on the plane, the pilot let the twins look into the cockpit and they were fascinated. They enjoyed the honey-roasted peanuts the flight attendant gave them and, because they were so polite in thanking her, she snuck them some Häagen-Dazs ice cream from first class. What a treat that was. Then they read their books, colored some pictures and were a joy to be with. I imagined what life with three kids would look like. What's the saying? You go from man-to-man defense to zone defense? I have heard that it's easier going from two to three than it is going from zero to one. And we went from zero to two! We must be some kind of superheroes already. Did we need to add to our superhero family? What happens if baby number three was another boy? I mean of course we would love him, but another son isn't our goal, right? And somewhere in the back of my head and in the deepest catacombs of my heart, I wondered how this would impact my relationship with Paula.

Two weeks after I returned from Arizona, Paula called to tell me that her life was about to get more complicated. Funny how I jump to conclusions. Did Garrett find out about us? I'm not sure how that would happen, but I suppose it's possible. We don't leave any kind of trail when we talk. We only see each other once a year. Maybe she yelled out my name during an orgasm? I doubt it. It was humorous to envision, however. Could she be pregnant? Moving? Retiring? She isn't old enough. What is the big change or complication?

"Why?" I asked.

"Ken is moving in."

"Ken?"

"Kenickie, my brother."

"Wait. What? Your brother's name is Kenickie??" I tried to contain my laughter.

"I've never told you his name? You know, I told you that we arrived in the U.S. in the late 70s? When we picked our American names, my brother was obsessed with the movie, Grease. He didn't want to be Danny though, he wanted to be Kenickie. We didn't realize it wasn't a common American name until years later. We just call him Ken now."

"Oh my God, that is hysterical. Why did you pick Paula?"

"I loved the Beatles, especially Paul McCartney. I wanted to be as close to him as possible, so I chose Paula. I know that is not as intriguing as Kenickie, but that is what happened. I guess I could have chosen something more exotic like Eleanor, Lucy, Rita. Martha, Michelle or Sadie from one of the Beatles' songs, but I liked the sound of Paula. It's so weird that we haven't talked about that. Did you know I love the Beatles?"

"I remember you humming a Beatles song once, maybe when we were having Mexican food. Maybe it was Lovely Rita to your margarita? Haha."

"We didn't drink at lunch that day, but maybe I hummed it thinking about having a margarita."

"What's going on with your brother?"

"He worked for Lehman Brothers as a financial analyst. He was always so good with numbers. He went to MIT to study statistics and moved up the corporate ladder very quickly. He had a beautiful house, expensive cars, exotic vacations, but he worked a lot so I didn't see him very much. After the financial crisis last year when Lehman Brothers closed, he lost most of his savings because they were tied to stock in the company. His wife went into a deep depression and killed herself. He has been trying to pull himself together, but his house was just foreclosed on. So he's moving in with Garrett and me."

"Holy crap! That's terrible. I had no idea. How is he doing?"

"Not well at all. He is really broken. I have never seen him this way. He spent years building up his reputation, his earnings, his wealth and it was all gone in the blink of an eye. He can't find another job since the markets haven't rebounded and not many in the financial field want to be associated with former Lehman Brothers employees."

"Wow. How will this impact your life?"

"Our house is too big for the two of us, so it won't matter in that regard. Garrett is traveling a lot so it will be nice to have company. I don't think that Ken is good at many household chores though because he had a maid, a chef, and a gardener. I also don't think he will contribute much financially because he is unable to. But it's important for me to help my family. We stick together. We have been through so much together and try to land on our feet, so it's my turn to support him."

"You are so wonderful to help him."

"If you only knew all of the times he helped me, you would see why I wouldn't hesitate."

"Will he get a job or will you be supporting him?"

"I don't know the answer to either of your questions. I have to emotionally support him now."

"Please let me know if I can do anything to help you from here."

"I will. Catherine, thank you for listening."

"You're welcome, Judge."

Drew and I continued our conversations about having another child. I recalled someone telling me about a way to nearly ensure the gender of a baby. Who was it? I wracked my brain to remember. I thought of my work colleagues, neighbors and friends. Who would I have had such a conversation with? It had to be someone with whom I shared some level of intimacy to have such a conversation. It took me several days to remember that it was Tyleah-Shay! I emailed her right away asking her for the details. She wrote back days later saying that we should get together in New York City this summer to have some girl time and reminding me about the Shettles method that her cousin used to conceive a daughter after three sons. This theory supposes that sperm carrying the Y (male) chromosome "swim" faster than the sperm carrying the X (female) chromosome. So, if intercourse were to occur during ovulation, say day 14 of the woman's menstrual cycle, it would produce a male baby because the faster swimming Y sperm would reach the ready ovum and fertilize it. However, Shettles postulates that the X-carrying sperm are heartier and live longer. While the Y-sperm rush up to fertilize the egg, if the egg isn't there, they die. The idea is to have sex on the tenth day of the regular menstrual cycle and hope that the faster Y-sperm wither away, while the strong X-sperm lie in wait for the innocuous ovum to saunter through the fallopian tube and meet up, thus, creating a zygote. Couples should try intercourse on the tenth day of the month for several cycles and, if it doesn't work, move to the 11th day of the month and so on. I wondered if there were any statistics on how often this works. It sounds like it makes sense, but what is the data that backs up the hypothesis. I'll plan to do some additional research on this when I have time. I almost laugh at the idea of having extra time to do that. I still haven't agreed to the idea of having another baby, but if there were a pretty good chance we could choose the gender, I'd be more willing to try.

Each year, Tyleah-Shay and I promised we would get together. We picked different cities and said we'd meet there. The truth is we had only seen each other about 6 times since college graduation. Her wedding, my wedding, a quick getaway to Boston that Drew and I took years before we had the boys, another wedding of a mutual friend, her visit to D.C. for a training class and an actual girls' trip to Cape Cod. I'm disappointed that we don't make more time for each other. Life gets in the way. Even though we don't see each other, we email and talk occasionally so we are still involved in each other's lives. But there is a chasm in our closeness due to the distance. I have shared so much of my life with her, but I would definitely hold back information about Paula. She would probably see through me like I was hiding something from her. It's funny how girlfriends know the truth whether you say it or not. I wrote her back saying that we should try to meet in the fall. I really would like to spend time together, especially if I am going to have another baby. I need to see her this year because I won't be able to abandon Drew with three kids until the new baby-to-be is potty trained at least.

As spring stretched into summer, the days dragged on like walking through quicksand. I'm not sure what I was waiting for, but it seemed like something was about to happen. The boys finished first grade and were going to summer camp at the local YMCA. They had a variety of different activities – adventure week, outdoor fun week, movie week, sports week, writing week, etc. In July, Drew and I decided to try for another baby. I explained the Shettles method and we agreed to try it. This meant having contraception-free sex for the first ten days of the month and then using condoms or abstaining for the remainder of the month. I wasn't sure he would go for either of those options, but those were my conditions. Because of the timing of our decision, we couldn't try until the beginning of August.

I decided not to tell Paula about this. Since this was not a conference year, I wouldn't see her until the following year. We didn't know our conference budget yet so there was no telling if it would be a spring, summer or fall conference. And maybe I wouldn't get pregnant at all? I didn't want her to get upset if there was no reason to. I once heard someone say there are crimes of omission and crimes of commission. I was going for the crime of omission. That seemed safer in this circumstance.

On the tenth day of my cycle in August, Drew and I had sex. It wasn't sexy sex. It was sort of forced and mechanical. I didn't really enjoy it. We would have to wait another month to see if we were successful on our first try. We didn't have any trouble getting pregnant with the twins, so I wasn't expecting any difficulty this time either. Sometimes, I'm naively optimistic I admit.

In early September, my period came. No success on the first try. Neither of us were seriously disappointed. More time to try. I decided that this month I would fix a romantic dinner, have some candlelight and soft music on day ten. Maybe the mood was off last month? I can fix that.

On the third day of my cycle, my cell phone rang with a call from an unknown number. I frequently don't answer unknown numbers, but I felt compelled to.

"Cath?" the voice was crying. I didn't recognize it.

"It's Tyleah-Shay."

"Oh, hey. What's wrong?"

"Did you see the news about the fire in Pittsburgh?"

"No." My heart raced. What happened in Pittsburgh? She didn't know about Paula so I wasn't really sure why she is crying about it. What is her connection to Pittsburgh?

"My dad, sniffffff, that was my dad who was killed."

"What??? Aren't they in Minneapolis?"

"No, they retired last year and moved to Pittsburgh to be close to my Aunt Helen. <sniff> He was bored at home, so he joined the volunteer fire department."

I had a very vague memory of her telling me they were moving to Pittsburgh, but I guess I didn't realize that it already happened. Tyler Dean, Tyleah-Shay's dad, was a fireman in Minnesota. We used to worry about him when we were in college. He earned a variety of awards from the city of

Minneapolis – awards for valor, service, life-saving efforts. He was even honored with a key to the city for his achievements.

"What happened?"

"There was a house fire on the west side of the city. Dad was in the firehouse when the alarm went off, so he was on the first truck to leave. When they got to the house, it was fully engulfed in flames and neighbors were screaming that there were a mother and child inside. Dad had his gear on first and ran into the house. The others started dousing the flames. <sniff> The fire ignited the roof and the whole thing collapsed trapping Dad inside. They didn't find him for hours. He made it to the back of the house where the bedrooms were and was stuck under rubble and fallen debris."

"Oh my God, Tyleah-Shay. That is horrible. I'm so sorry. How is your mother?"

"The worst part is, the family wasn't even home. He knew the risks. He rushed in to save them, but no one was there." She was wailing. How awful. I wish I could comfort her.

"Oh crap. What can I do?"

"Please come to the funeral. I don't have the details yet. I just wanted you to know. My parents loved you so much. You were their favorite out of all of the friends I've ever had."

"They are my favorite, too." I visited them in Minneapolis over quite a few summer vacations while we were in college. They invited me to their lakefront cottage in the country. I loved watching fireflies, making s'mores, swimming, canoeing. I fell in love with the land of 10,000 lakes because of Tyler and Leah Dean. After my dad died, I never really felt connected to a group except when I was with them. They made me feel so welcome and like a part of the family. Every night after dinner at the cottage, we would play card games and drink wine. What wonderful memories I had of them and what a tragedy to lose Tyler that way.

"Of course, I'll be there. Let me know when it is. I can come earlier if you need me. Anything you need. I'm so sorry, Tyleah-Shay. Is Rook there with you?"

"Yes, he's here. I'm so glad you can come. I couldn't go through this without out you and Rook."

"I love you, Tyleah. Call me as soon as you know anything." I hung up, my heart aching for my dear old friend and her sweet mother.

She called two days later to tell me the funeral would be in four days,

Saturday, September 12ᵗʰ. The city wanted to honor him for his service, so they planned a special event with local firemen. They are adding his name to a tribute to Pennsylvania firefighters killed in the line of duty. I told Drew that I was going to Pittsburgh to the funeral. My plan was to fly there on Friday morning and return on Sunday night. I could rent a car and find a hotel for two nights.

Good morning, Judge.

I have news, sort of very bad and sort of very good. The father of my best friend from college was the volunteer firefighter who died in the house fire last week in Pittsburgh. I am coming for the funeral. I know you said that you would give me a tour if I were ever in Pittsburgh. Any chance you have some free time on Friday afternoon, Saturday morning or Sunday morning?

Catherine

My phone rang immediately.

"Hello?" I answered breathlessly.

"Catherine, I'm sorry for your loss. Were you close to him?"

"Yes, ma'am." My response told her that I was in the mood to be playful.

"Are you coming alone? Where are you staying?"

"Yes, I'm coming alone. I don't know where to stay. Can you recommend a place? The funeral home is on the east side of the city. Jones, I think it's called."

"All right. There's a Hampton Inn on the east side. I drive by it when I go to work. I'd like you to stay there. What time is your flight?"

"I arrive at 10:00 a.m. and will arrange for early check-in. I am renting a car."

"Excellent. When is the funeral?"

"It's Saturday in the early evening. I'll see my friend late on Friday night after she sees family coming into town and be with her on Saturday night as well. Is your husband traveling?"

"Yes, he's in Seattle this week, but Ken is around. I don't have to worry about him. He knows I play tennis frequently so I'll tell him that I'm out playing."

"I hate to be excited to see you when I'm coming to town for this terrible reason, but I can't wait."

"Call me at the office when you get into your hotel room and I'll be there as soon as I can."

"Sounds good. Any special requests?"

"One word – thongs! I want to spank your beautiful ass while you are soaking through a tiny thong."

"Yes, ma'am. Consider your request fulfilled."

"Catherine, it will be the first of many. Be a good girl."

"I intend to stock up on good girl points."

"I am happy to hear that. See you on Friday."

My heart skipped a beat or three. I am feeling a little guilty making this trip about fucking, but I don't have many chances to see Paula. I never thought I'd get to go to her town and now it's happening. I will give Tyleah-Shay all of the attention I can when I'm with her and, when I'm not, I will be perfecting my role as a submissive to my dominant judge.

I just realized that I would be flying on September 11th. Ugh. That diminishes my sexy feelings about this trip. What a tragic day to fly. I have to focus on the reward of my strength. Drew suggests I drive instead. It would save on airfare and car rental, but it'll also take at least four hours instead of one. I want to arrive as early as possible and still have stamina to fuck for most of the day.

My flight lands at 9:50 a.m., ten minutes early. Getting the rental car was surprisingly easy. I called Drew to let him know that I made it and I'd check in with him later. I needed to use my phone for driving directions, so I couldn't talk long. According to Mapquest, I have to get on Route 376 east and drive for about thirty miles. I estimate my check in time to be around 11:00 a.m. That should work perfectly.

The drive was easy enough. I have only visited Pittsburgh once before on my way to Chicago. It is a nice stopping point from D.C. to split up the drive. Drew and I visited the Warhol Museum and wandered around the city. I liked it more than I expected.

I checked in at the Hampton and went to my room on the 3rd floor. I called Paula to let her know the room number. She would be with me in about twenty minutes. I know I shouldn't have waited until the last minute, but I planned to use that time to cut my nails. I retrieved my toiletry bag from my suitcase. My clippers were missing! I looked through every pocket and pouch. Crap. I ran to the registration desk hoping to score some there and they were out. Double crap. They had plenty of toothbrushes and sewing kits. Not very helpful to me now. I don't have time to find a drug store, so I return to my room and attempt something I hadn't done since third grade. I bite my nails. Chomp on a corner, break off a piece and try to pull off the remainder. It was sort of gross and definitely not fun. I managed to remove several of them and the filed them to tame the jagged edges. Then I heard the knock at my door. I did the best I could in the time I had, but I was certain it wouldn't be good enough. Maybe she wouldn't notice?

I opened the door. She was wearing cropped pants and a shirt with a wildflower print on it. Her hair was swept to one side and hung almost to her breast. I smelled cinnamon before she entered. The door slammed. She was in my arms, kissing me. She looked great, smelled fantastic and felt better than she looked or smelled.

"Hi Catherine. Nice to see you."

It was then that I noticed her purse and her clarinet case.

"Good morning, ma'am."

She put her purse and the clarinet case on the desk near the phone.

"Let me kiss you some more before we start with today's scenario."

"Yes, please," was all I could muster.

She made me feel so wanted. I couldn't wait to be naked with her. We had all afternoon to spend together. I hoped to savor every minute and not rush it, but I was so anxious. My clit was alive with the excitement of being with her.

"Are you ready?" she asked.

"Yes, ma'am. I'm always ready for you." That was not a lie.

"I am going to sit on the chair over there. I'd like you to kneel in front of me and present me with your tits. You remember the proper way to do that, right?"

"Yes, ma'am." I remove my jeans, shirt, bra and start pulling down my thong when she stops me.

"Keep your thong on."

I kneel in front of her with the backs of my hands holding my tits up for inspection. Instead of looking at my tits though, she notices my nails.

"What is going on with your nails? Catherine, they look awful."

"I'm so sorry, ma'am. I lost my clippers and I tried to –"

She cut me off. "I know you aren't making excuses for the condition of your nails. That would demonstrate a lack of preparation. Open the clarinet case and get my clippers out. Also bring the ping pong paddle that is in there."

I open the case. It is filled with things I haven't seen before. The little compartment that usually contains extra reeds has clippers and a nail file. I grab the clippers and a ping pong paddle with a red rubber blade.

"What do you think I'm going to do with this ping pong paddle, Catherine?"

"I think you are going to use it to spank me."

"That is right. Kneel in front of me with the clippers and the paddle."

I do as I'm told. She takes the paddle and places it on the table. She takes the clippers and inspects my nails more closely. There are only two that look bad – the middle finger and ring finger on my left hand. She trims them both down to the quick, a little shorter than I would have liked.

"Assume position two."

I get up and lie on my stomach on the corner of the bed, my legs spread. "How many times should I spank you? You may make a suggestion, but I will make the final decision."

"Two, ma'am."

"Why two? Because you thought that you would leave two nails long? Do you realize it took me five minutes to trim them so they would be usable?"

"Five then?" I suggested.

She caressed my ass before swatting it with the paddle. Whap! Caress. WHAP! Caress. She stopped after two thankfully. The paddle hurt more than her hand did. It covered more surface area. The rubber covering also provided an additional sting factor. It wasn't an entirely painful hurt though – it was an erotic hurt. Painsure. I began to soak through my thong.

"Two for now. I want you to have strength for all that I have in store for you today and tomorrow." She smiled her mischievous smile. It was sexy and secretive. I can't wait to see what she has planned.

"Roll over and close your eyes," she instructed.

I hear her fumbling with items in the clarinet case.

"I have such a nice surprise for you."

I hear a faint vibration as she attaches a vibrating nipple clamp to each of my nipples. They were not the metal ones with the chain that she used before. They were softer - maybe plastic?

"Open your eyes."

I was right – they were pale green plastic vibrating nipple clamps. They felt great – just the right amount of tension pinching my erect nipples. The vibration was an amazing bonus. I wasn't sure whether to let her know how good they felt in case she was trying to cause more pain. I moaned softly. Let her figure out what that means. I feel like such an easy target, between the spanking and the nipple clamps I am ready to cum. I suspect that I should try to contain my enthusiasm since it might be a long time until it actually happens.

"Is your clit throbbing, little sub?"

"Yes, mistress." My deep breathing gives me away.

"It's not time for you to cum. In fact, I think you should make me cum first today. You can wait. Do you understand?"

"Yes, ma'am. I understand completely."

"Go to the clarinet case and get the clear glass dildo and put it in your freezer. Then bring the white vibrator to the bed." She removed her clothes while I did what she requested.

I have never seen a glass dildo before. It seemed delicate. It was transparent, but had pink ridges along the shaft, apparently for added sensation. The hotel freezer was tiny, but very cold and it fit in there perfectly.

I brought the white vibrator to the bed where my mistress was waiting for me without a shred of clothing on her athletic body. Seeing her nakedness took my breath away. She was the type of woman that other women couldn't take their eyes off. There was something about her that was seductive and open, confident and sexy. I suppose I was a bit biased and probably not thinking very clearly since my nipples were fluttering with painsure, Pam was hot and wet and I was dying to have an orgasm.

"Please make sure I am sufficiently lubricated, then gently insert the vibrator into my pussy and asshole. I want you to fuck me with it for a few minutes, then turn it on the lowest setting to just slightly vibrate."

"Yes, mistress." For a moment, I felt powerful. I had control over the vibrator and I could fuck her with it as slowly or quickly, gently or forcefully as I wanted. I know if I take advantage of the situation, there will be consequences that have the potential to be unpleasant. I watched the vibrator go inside and out disappearing from sight and re-emerging again and again. Paula can't keep her eyes open. Her mouth is agape, she's panting heavily. It is so erotic watching her hips keep pace with my thrusting. I reach my left hand up to squeeze her right nipple. She moans louder. I think she is nearing orgasm. I push the vibrator in as far as it will go and increase the vibration by twisting the base. My lips move toward her clit. I kiss it, then swirl my tongue around it in a counter-clockwise motion. My tongue is a hula hoop twisting around her clit. Just as I get into a rhythmic beat, her ass clenches and she grabs my head smashing it closer to her wetness. Her clit explodes into my mouth and she collapses limply onto the bed. I turn the vibrator off and slowly pull it out. I put it on the pillow as I move closer to her to cuddle and help her recover from the intensity of the orgasm. I kiss her gently and circle her areolas with my fingertips. Even though only one of us is post-orgasm, I use this opportunity to engage in some tender loving.

"Catherine, you are amazing. Thank you for making me feel so fulfilled."

"I learned from the best."

"Oh my God! You still have those nipple clamps on! How do they feel?"

"They are making me very horny – between them and Sawyer – whew! I'd really love to cum now. Will you allow me to, ma'am?"

"I am happy that you are asking for permission. You have been a very attentive submissive today and I want to reward you for that. If you could choose how to have an orgasm today, what would you choose?"

"I want my orgasm to be just like yours. I would like you to use the same vibrator and do the same thing I just did to you. I want to experience what you did."

"Ok. Please wash off the vibrator and bring it back to me."

"I don't want it washed. I want everything that is yours to be part of me." I hand her the vibrator.

"May I remove my thong?"

"Yes, and spread your legs."

I take my thong off, feeling the wetness wipe along my leg as I pull it off. Then I lie on the bed and open my legs as wide as possible. My nipples are continuing to tingle. Paula puts her finger inside of Pam withdrawing some of the juice and smearing it around my asshole sharing the natural lubricant that I created. She then pushes the vibrator inside of both my pussy and asshole simultaneously. It feels so good that I can concentrate on nothing else. She gently fucks me with the vibrator turned off, then turns it on the lowest speed and continues in and out.

"I love watching Pam swallow the vibrator. It is magical and erotic. I think about this when I am in court sometimes. It's so hot."

I am panting and dying to cum. But I'm afraid to ask for exactly what I want. I don't think it's appropriate in this scenario. I will be patient if it kills me. She increases the intensity of the vibration and fucks me harder with the vibrator. Between my ass being fucked, my pussy being fucked and my nipples being both squeezed and vibrating, I feel as though I might cum without her even touching my clit. I move my hips slightly to see if I can manage to rub my clit on the moving vibrator. She reads my movement and senses my urgency. She reacts swiftly tonguing my ripe clit. I feel myself approaching the edge of the cliff. One more flick of her tongue and I'm airborne, flying, falling, floating in the weightlessness of this inebriating climax. I am breathless, exhausted, thirsty and grateful.

"No one makes me feel this good. You are incredible."

She reaches up to remove the nipple clamps. "And you are naughty. You didn't ask permission to have an orgasm." She winked as she said it.

Her comment made my clit pulse. Instead of the blood flow leaving it as it usually does post-orgasm, it was re-filling the tiny appendage. Damn it. I want to cum again.

"I am so sorry, ma'am. May I try again? I promise I will ask for permission."

"Sexy, little Catherine. You want to cum again? You are a needy, naughty nympho."

"Yes, mistress. You made me this way."

"Ok, get the glass dildo from the freezer."

I jump out of bed with new-found energy and retrieve the curious item, handing it to her as I return. The coolness of it is enticing.

"No more butt fucking for you. Focus on the feeling." She slid the cold glass dildo inside of me. The cold sensation rubbing against not only the opening of my hole but the inside of my pussy was stimulating in a way I can't describe. I was surprised how titillating it was. I wanted to enjoy the feeling, but my desire to orgasm again was strong. I kept thinking how right she was that no one was as naughty as we were.

She rubbed her finger around my clit without touching it directly. I was about to climb out of my skin. Then she abruptly stopped.

"Catherine?"

"Yes, ma'am?"

"How do you feel?"

"I was feeling really fabulous until you stopped."

"I'm happy to hear that. Did you want to ask me anything?"

"Yes. Will you please continue?"

She slapped my nipple. "Not that."

"I'm so sorry, ma'am. May I have an orgasm?"

"Yes, you may. Thank you for asking permission."

She resumed fucking me with the cool – no longer cold – dildo and pushed in and out on my clit like she was calling an elevator. That was a different feeling, the pressure centered right on my clit. Within seconds, I was cumming again. The second one was more intense. I felt drained of every ounce of energy that I previously had. I curled up in the fetal position and let Paula spoon me from behind. I felt vulnerable and naked in the basest form. She held me as I cried. I couldn't really tell why I was so emotional except I felt like she had given me two of the most profound gifts – herself and the experience of what is possible. She made my body feel things that it never had before. I felt a depth of intimacy that I had never known because Paula intuitively knows how to maximize my pleasure in a way that I, myself, do not know. I wanted to lie in her arms, share the warmth of our bodies and never move again. She turned my head toward hers and licked the tears from my face. What's hers is mine and what's mine is hers.

Our tender moment was interrupted by a loud growl. I giggled. "Are you hungry?"

"Yes, I skipped breakfast. I'm starving."

"I brought you some cinnamon pop-tarts and peanut M&Ms."

"You remembered my favorite things? You are really thoughtful. I'd love to have a pop-tart even if it's cold."

I got out of bed, went to my carry-on bag and brought her the snacks.

"I just want to eat a little because I want to take you out for lunch at a cool local place. Let's get cleaned up and go."

Fifteen minutes later we were in my rental car driving to Pam's Diner. How coincidental that it had the same name that she had given to my pussy. She wanted to eat in Pam's Diner after having eaten Pam. It was only a mile away and it was nice enough to walk, but Paula had other plans.

"I want to go someplace after we eat so we need to have a car. I'll tell you about my plans over lunch."

She ordered banana chocolate chip pancakes for us. It was a specialty of the diner. She said that President Obama had eaten there while campaigning and really enjoyed it. If it's good enough for our president, it's good enough for me.

I realized how famished I was as well. I had eaten breakfast at home several hours ago and there were no snacks on the plane. I smelled bacon in the diner. Mmmm bacon.

"What's the plan for this afternoon?" I asked.

"After we eat, I am going to take you to a local Farmer's Market."

"Ok." That wasn't what I was expecting.

"We are going to look at some of the fresh vegetables they have."

I'm certain I had a very confused look on my face. I clearly wasn't connecting the dots to figure out what she was intimating.

"Should I tell you more now or do you want to be surprised?"

I really hate surprises and I was intrigued at how she was going to turn this into a fun activity, worthy of my limited time with her.

"Please tell me more. I'm curious."

"Catherine, I want you to select three zucchinis. One that will fit perfectly in your ass. One that will fit perfectly in Pam and one that is just a little too big for Pam."

I swallowed hard. This is a provocative new game. I'm not sure what I think of it. It sounds enticing and different. I can't say that I have ever thought about fucking vegetables before.

"You look frightened." She didn't exactly read my expression correctly.

The server appeared delivering our food. The pancakes looked great and the bacon was perfectly crispy. I wanted to douse my food in syrup and dig in, but we were in the middle of a conversation that needed to be finished.

"I'm not frightened, more like intrigued."

"That's not bad. One of the fun things about our relationship is being able to test boundaries of what is possible, do things that we can't do with anyone else."

I guess today is the day that I will be fucked by food. I almost laughed; she did correctly interpret the amusement in my new expression.

"You are willing to accept this challenge, aren't you, Catherine?"

"Yes, of course. Whatever you want, ma'am."

"You are such a good submissive. I'm awarding you several good girl points for that answer."

I felt a tingle in my clit. There were certain words she said that could really trigger me. Sub. Punish. Obey. Good Girl Points. Even though they were imaginary. Earning them made me horny. When she said my name, it sounded so sexy.

I wanted to rush through eating to go to the market and pick my fuck buddies for the day. The pancakes were delicious and the bacon hit the spot, but my mind was elsewhere. I offered to pay the bill, but she insisted that she cover it.

She directed me to the Farmer's Market. It was the nearest one open on a Friday. We found street parking and walked to the market. We looked at apples, peaches, and blueberries. There was corn on the cob. I was glad that wasn't the vegetable she was envisioning. We saw peppers, onions, and potatoes. There was a dairy with fresh milk and cheese. There was a butcher-type stand with sausages, steaks, and hamburgers made of things like bison and ostrich. Next, we saw a rainbow of fresh flowers, then a bakery with fresh scones, pastries, breads, cakes and pies. Dessert sounds good. But we were on a mission. The great zucchini mission. Success! The next table had yellow squash, eggplant and the elusive zucchini. I touched the form of the yellow squash; it was curved almost like a hook. A small end followed by a larger bulbous end. I passed by the eggplant. There were a variety of sizes of zucchinis. Baby ones not much bigger than my thumb. Also, there were ones the size and length of my calf. Who knew they could grow so big? She watched me inspect them. One thing she probably didn't know about me was how terribly bad I am at spatial relations. I am shocked when I see cars on display at the mall. I wouldn't have guessed that cars could fit inside the mall. I never can tell what size container to put leftovers in. How will I ever determine what would fit comfortably and not so comfortably inside my own vagina, much less my ass?

"Catherine, please choose carefully. If you select something that is obviously way too small, I may buy my own for you."

"What do you think of this one?" I held up one about seven inches long and not very wide in diameter. It seemed like it might be the size of the glass dildo. I held it in my hand and fondled it a little. I tried to remember what the size of any of the vibrators were. I can't figure out why this is so perplexing to me. Size matters when it comes to zucchini selection.

"You can choose. Just remember that you need to pick three of them."

I spent more time than I should have trying to decide. Each zucchini I touch makes me feel wetter between my legs. I put on a clean thong after our pre-lunch session and I can tell that it's soaked already. I am glad I packed a few extras.

I pick my three partners and allow Paula to inspect them to approve or disapprove. She tells me with her mischievous sexy smile that I was successful in my choices. I pay for the zucchinis and they are placed in a plastic bag. I want to skip out of the market and return to my hotel room, eager for the afternoon's scenario.

As I pull out of my parking spot, she tells me that we need to make another brief stop at the drugstore. There is one a few blocks away from the hotel. We stop at CVS.

"You need to buy lubricated condoms for your zucchinis. I will be in line behind you buying gum. I want to see you interact with the cashier. You and I both know that you are buying condoms so you can be fucked by vegetables."

Gulp. She is wickedly sexy and creative. I know this activity is designed to be a little humiliating and embarrassing and to allow her to control me in public. I am only slightly intimidated by it. I can do it and I know it will make us both feel like we are sharing a great secret that only we know about.

We enter the store separately. I look around for the condom aisle. I hope there is a condom aisle – I would hate to have to ask the pharmacist. But I would do it if I have to. People buy condoms all the time. I, of course, have never bought one in my life. But no one needs to know that. Nestled between feminine protection products and medicine for yeast and urinary tract infections are the condoms. I wonder if the product placement is purposeful to deter people from purchasing condoms? I had no idea there were so many choices. There were different colors, flavors, lubricated or not, ribbed. Wow. I choose Trojan brand because I have heard of it. Lubricated ten pack with ribs. Sounds like a good time. I walk slowly toward the cashier. Squelch Squerch goes the wetness in my thong. I'm getting crazy aroused buying condoms. This is a new low. I know it's so much more than just buying condoms. It is obeying my mistress. It's the humiliation of the purchase. It's her watching me interact with the cashier. It's the second step in the rest of the afternoon that will at some point include fucking a vegetable. I see her near the cash registers perusing some items, obviously waiting for my return. I pass her and she follows me to register two. I realized that I hadn't thought about what kind of cashier would be ideal for this transaction. I didn't really want to go to an older woman and probably not a teenager either. My cashier is a male college student, he had the appearance of a frat boy. I take a deep breath and act like this is a usual purchase. This box of condoms is really some Flintstone vitamins for the boys. Not a big deal at all.

"A ten pack, huh? Sounds like a fun weekend," Fratboy comments.

"Yes, I hope so."

"That's $16.95."

I hand him a twenty-dollar bill, wishing I could let him keep the change and get out of there.

He hands me my change, puts the box of condoms and the receipt in a small bag.

"Have an excellent weekend," he chortles.

I walk out of the store and look over my shoulder to see Paula watching. I think she was pleased.

"I love when you obey me so perfectly," she said as she got into the passenger seat of my rental Ford sedan.

"I hope that earned some Good Girl Points."

"No, that just means you won't be punished for disobeying."

I guess that is just as well. I return to the hotel parking lot, get my two bags of newly purchased items and walk to my room with Paula beside me.

Inside the room, I await instructions on how to deal with my zucchini-lovers.

"Are you wet, Catherine?"

"Yes, ma'am."

"Come here."

I walk over to her and she begins to undress me. She removes my shirt, unhooks my bra and fondles my breasts. Then she licks them and gently bites my nipples. I want to caress her head, feel her soft hair, but I stand at attention instead letting her have her way with me. She unbuttons my pants and slowly pushed them over my hips letting them fall to the floor. Then she kneels before me gripping my ass and circling my pubic mound with her nose. She licks my lips through my thong mingling her saliva with my juices. Then she stands up.

"Please undress me in an identical fashion."

I removed her shirt and bra, then fondled her breasts and bit her nipples. I took her pants off and kneeled in front of her. She grabbed my head and pushed it toward her crotch. I licked her lips hungrily, moving her panties aside. I slipped a finger inside her.

"Off, off, off!" She pulled her panties down and motioned that we move to the bed.

I pulled the bedspread off and we climbed between the sheets. In a rare moment of pre-sex closeness, we laid facing each other kissing. Our breasts touched and I pressed my stomach close to hers. I wrapped my leg around her hip pulling her even closer. I want to have unlimited access to her and touch her everywhere. I want to be inside of her. I imagined having a penis that I could enter her with, feeling the deepest part of her pussy and moving our hips together in synchronicity as I made love to her.

"I wish I could make love to you the way your husband does."

"My husband likes to do it on the floor so there's no bounciness like the bed provides. It's not that fun. It feels ok, but it's not romantic or even really love-making, it is more like having intercourse. It's not even fucking. It's neutral. You do not want to do that with me. What we do is much more special."

I'm sorry to hear that sex with Garrett is not satisfying to her. I have great sex with Drew, but I don't tell her that. I am pretty sure that would annoy her and I don't want to annoy her. I am thrilled that she enjoys what we do more than she enjoys sex with her husband, but that instantly makes me feel very sad for her and her crappy sex life.

"I meant that I want to be inside of you and feel you from the inside. I want to be closer than we are."

"There are a couple of ways to accomplish that. We can try one of them. Let's 69. While you are eating me, I will be eating you. We will experience the same thing simultaneously. It is very sensual and intimate."

I, of course, had done the same thing with Drew, but I didn't love it. Mainly because his cock was choking me and I couldn't focus on sucking on him while he was eating me. It took more mental energy than I could devote to it. Nevertheless, I am happy to try it with Paula. I know I won't be choking on a cock – that's a bonus.

"Yes, let's do it. I want to try anything to be closer to you."

I remove the blanket from us both. I don't want to suffocate underneath it. As I move closer to Sawyer, I wonder how the zucchini will play a role in this session. I will not ask. It is strange how comfortable I feel eating her after only doing it a few times. She's such a responsive lover that I am not intimidated that I can't satisfy her. That certainly boosts my confidence.

Our naked bodies face each other, stomach to breast, but my face is between her legs and her face is between mine. My top knee is bent allowing easier access. I push one finger, then another into her pussy. I am relieved my nails are short and don't hurt her. I finger her gently before licking her inner thighs. I want to prolong our foreplay allowing myself to enjoy the texture of her skin, her unique smell, the smooth muscular walls inside Sawyer. I want to focus on each feature individually and memorize it. I wish

I could close my eyes and create a clay mold of this beautiful woman from memory. I want to remember every bit of her, counting her freckles or very few gray hairs, the lines that form her smile, the distance from her belly button to the beginnings of her pubic hair. I realize that she is teasing my clit while I am dreaming of her body and my lackluster abilities as an artist. I need to focus on pleasing my mistress instead of creating a statue of her. I nose her clit and push my tongue inside her pussy. It tastes a little salty and very warm. I am French kissing Sawyer while Paula contracts her pussy in a kegel. It almost feels like her pussy is kissing me back. I make a mental note to remember to kegel in my spare time. She has amazing control of her pelvic floor muscles which I assume is more sensuous for both of us. I deep throat my thumb making it super-lubed and press it into her asshole. She relaxes and allows a very easy entry. I put my middle and ring finger inside of her pussy allowing my index finger to reach her clit. I once heard Drew refer to this as the bowling ball grip. I circle her clit with my finger while gently fucking her with my other 3 fingers. I move my index finger aside so I can lick her clit. As I move toward it, I feel her change her finger fucking to the bowling ball grip as well. I love feeling her thumb in my ass. I imagine the zucchini sliding in and out of my ass. I wonder what that will feel like. My clit is throbbing. I might cum before she touches my clit directly. Her breathing is getting heavier. I can't wait to have her cum in my mouth. I lick her clit up and down this time like I'm trying to turn on and off a switch with my tongue. It feels so easy to do. She starts licking my clit like a switch as well. I'm surprised at how she can mimic what I'm doing so quickly. I am laser-focused on making her cum while feeling my own ascent to orgasm-land. As if on cue, we both convulse in unison, twins in ecstasy. My own cliff-dive occurring as Paula explodes in my mouth. I lap up some of her cum and rub my face in her pussy. I want her to see that I will wear her cum like a badge of honor. I roll over to come face to face with her, collapsing in her arms.

"Lick my face now."

"Mmmmm. Is that me?"

"Yes, it is all over my face."

"You are so hot – and naughty."

I kissed her and whispered "I love you when we're together."

"I love you too, Catherine," she said.

What an idyllic afternoon we spent together. I glance at the clock. I need to meet with Tyleah-Shay at 8:00 p.m. It's nearly 6:30. I feel tired, sore and in love. What a combination.

"When do you have to leave?" She noticed me looking for the time.

"A little before 8:00."

"Tomorrow I will come by first thing in the morning for bright and early veggie sex. I want you to take the zucchinis and condoms out of the bags and leave them on the desk next to each other. You will do this so you can see them whenever you are in the room. If the maid comes, she will see them too. You may not touch them until I return. Do you understand?"

Tingle. Dammit. "Yes, ma'am. I understand completely. You want me to be crazy horny in anticipation of your return."

"I am glad that you are excited about trying my next scenario. I am certain it will be pleasurable for us both."

"I have an unusual request, if I may ask."

"Of course, Catherine. What is it?"

"Does your clarinet case full of tools of the trade contain a ball gag? I saw one in the catalog of the sex-toy party I went to and it looked kinkily appealing to me."

"I don't have one, but I know where I can get one. On my way home tonight, I will pick one up when I stop to buy dinner for Kenickie and myself."

"Have you ever used one? Do you think I would like it?"

"I haven't used one, but I'm sure you will like it. I'm also certain that if I ask you to use it, you won't want to disobey me. Thank you for taking the initiative to ask for something. That earns you some good girl points."

I kissed her again and pulled her closer. I can't believe how lucky I am to have this wonderful woman with me even if only once a year. We explore the limits of our sexuality in a safe and sensual environment. I can't wait until tomorrow morning, but I know that first I must comfort one of my oldest friends.

After saying goodbye to Paula, I shower and attempt to fix my hair and make-up and look presentable for the decidedly less-sexy part of the day. Except... I had been avoiding one thought. Yancy-Bo, Tyleah-Shay's brother.

On the drive to the Deans' house, I remember the summer that Yancy-Bo and I had sex. Between my junior and senior years of college, Thomas had to do some internships required for his major. They were all out of state. He insisted that we take a break that summer since we would be so far apart. I reluctantly agreed. I spent a month at the Deans' lake house. Tyleah-Shay and I were alone for most of the time, but occasionally her parents would spend a few days there. Tyler often had mid-week days off from the fire department, so they would just show up. It was a wonderful time spent with my second family. After two weeks, Yancy-Bo came. He was a couple years younger than Tyleah-Shay. I hadn't seen him for quite a while and he had changed a lot. He had been a zitty, gawky teenager when we met three years before. But the Yancy-Bo that arrived that summer was manly. He had just graduated from high school and played several sports. His previously-lanky physique changed. He had broad shoulders, six-pack abs with just a hint of light brown hair on his chest. His smile was magnetic and the intensity in his gaze was mature beyond his years. I tried to keep a friendly distance.

One day we went water skiing and Yancy-Bo was driving the boat. When my turn came, I wanted to try to slalom ski. I had been unsuccessful years before but I felt confident I could do it. Tyleah-Shay's job was to watch in case I fell. I loosened the wingnut that kept the ski heel in place and tried to slide it back. This was difficult because I had to bend down to reach the ski while ensuring my knees had the flexibility to absorb any waves and keep my balance. I managed to push the heel back and returned to a near-standing position. I shimmied my foot out of the ski and let it fall behind me. After balancing on my left foot for a few seconds, I moved my right foot into the back binding. I managed to do that without falling. My dominant right foot was able to steer the ski. I leaned back to enjoy the ride. We went half way around the lake when Yancy-Bo turned the boat to the left. I tried to stay inside the wake, but his turn was too sharp and I found myself riding the wake wave until I went over. I nearly lost my balance but recovered. The water outside the wake was calmer and easier to ski on. But I knew I couldn't stay there. I would have to go back into the boat's wake. I attempted it, but wiped out. It wasn't pretty. I couldn't get my left foot out of the ski, it twisted my foot around before releasing. Fortunately, I remembered to let go of the tow rope, so I wasn't being dragged behind the boat. That ended my skiing adventure for the day. I climbed back into the boat trying not to put weight on my foot. Later it was slightly bruised and swollen.

After dinner, Tyleah-Shay suggested a game of whist. Whist is a card game that Norwegian settlers brought to Minnesota and I had played it with the Dean family for years. It is typically played with four people, but we only had three players that night. She wanted to see if one of us could manage the fourth hand and our own. We tried, but strategically it didn't work. After a few beers, Tyleah-Shay went to bed. Yancy-Bo and I sat on the couch and I quizzed him about his plans for the fall. While we were talking, he reached over to grab my foot.

"Catherine, I am sorry about your foot. I feel like it's my fault since I was driving the boat."

"It's totally not your fault. I couldn't get back inside the wake. I'm so impressed with myself that I finally was able to slalom this year. I have never been that successful before – even though right now, it doesn't feel like I was that successful."

He laughed easily and his face lit up. I noticed dimples that I hadn't seen before. Maybe he spent too many years being an angsty teen and now this was the nearly-mature Yancy-Bo. He massaged my foot and ankle. In spite of the bruising, it felt really good. He tickled the arch under my foot, interlaced his fingers with my toes. It was the most sensual foot rub I ever experienced. I was starting to feel aroused. But – yikes! – it was Yancy-Bo, my friend's little brother. Although, he didn't seem so little or young anymore. Maybe it was the lack of inhibitions because of the beer we consumed or my loneliness being far from Thomas, or the maturity of the new Yancy-Bo, but when he massaged further up my leg from my ankle to my calf to my thigh, I didn't stop him. Before I had a chance to rationally think things through, we were kissing. He was confident and kissed me with urgency and abandon. I sat on his lap and felt his hard cock through my pajamas. I grinded my crotch against his, wanting him inside of me. He flipped me on my back on the couch and pulled off my pj bottoms. He reached beneath my t-shirt and fondled my breasts. Then he put his face between my legs and licked me everywhere. His finger deftly entered my hole and he tickled my g-spot. Holy shit. I don't think I ever felt that sensation before. How did young Yancy-Bo know about that? He continued to lick my clit. I felt close to cumming several times but it just didn't happen. I begged him to stop and put his cock inside of me. Eventually he obliged. He fucked me deeply and with youthful passion that was enticing. He asked me to look at him when he came. I opened my eyes and looked into his. He wanted me to see him climax, to enjoy every emotion that passed through his face. He was young. He was mature. He was agonizing. He was concentrating. He was pushing through an invisible challenge. He was free. He was smiling. He put all of his weight on me, wasted in his fatigue.

I held him, shocked at what transpired. I don't feel any regret, except that I'll have to tell Tyleah-Shay at some point. He lifts himself off of me, looking at me.

"Catherine, you are so amazing. I hope you aren't upset with me."

"No, I'm not. That was unexpected and incredible. Actually, I had been thinking about you for the last several days."

"You have? What do you think I've been thinking about for the last three years?"

"What? Me?" I blushed.

"Yes, I have been dreaming about the day that you would look at me as something other than Tyleah-Shay's little brother. There was always something in the way. Usually it was my awkward body and lack of confidence. I'm sorry I used your injured foot as a way to get closer to you."

I wasn't sure whether to be offended or flattered, but I prefer the nicer approach. "Yancy-Bo, you really surprised me. That was a lot of fun, but you know it can't happen again."

And that was my plan – until the next night. After dinner and cards, Tyleah-Shay went to bed to read and Yancy-Bo sat next to me on the couch. I couldn't resist being next to him and he knew it. My labia were swollen for several hours after sex the night before. I wasn't sure why – maybe because of all of the contact there or the lack of orgasm. They were sensitive and misshapen for a while, but back to normal and ready to experience the lust of the teenager nearby.

That night I had an orgasm on the couch and the same thing happened each night for the remainder of the week. Tyleah-Shay went to bed early. Yancy-Bo and I enjoyed each other's bodies. Sometimes on the couch or his bed, once in the yard on the side of the cottage away from the neighbor's place, once on the dock over the lake. He was very creative in trying different positions. I blamed it on his youthful imagination, believing everything was possible. I was surprised to see that more things were possible than I knew.

He left at the end of the week to attend a college orientation session in Minneapolis. He would try to return to the lake before I left. I tried to just enjoy his company while he was there and not have another thought about it. He hugged me goodbye and said it was fun seeing me again. Neither of us wanted to arouse any suspicion in Tyleah-Shay, but she was smarter than that.

After he left, she said, "I noticed Yancy-Bo seemed to take a liking to you."

"Yes, I guess he did. Was it that noticeable?"

"Not initially, but by the end of his stay he couldn't take his eyes off you.

What happened? And what about Thomas?"

"Thomas said we are on a break for the summer. Yancy-Bo massaged my foot after I fell while skiing and it went too far. I'm really sorry."

"You fucked my brother, Catherine?" I wasn't sure of her tone.

"Yeah, several times. It was actually really great. I hope you aren't mad at me."

She laughed. "Mad at you? Why would I be mad at you if you made my brother feel good? Don't we all need to feel that kind of connection once in a while?"

That response perfectly encapsulates everything Tyleah-Shay is to me. Understanding, forgiving, able to see the big picture and not get caught in unimportant details.

I haven't seen Yancy-Bo again since he drove away that day in his silver pick-up truck. The dry dust from the dirt road the cottage was on flew up behind his truck as he left. It was almost as if he disappeared from my life in a cloud of dirt.

After all this time, I will be seeing Yancy-Bo again. I have heard about him through the years when Tyleah-Shay provided nuggets of information about him: when he finished college, went to grad school, got his first job, changed careers, got engaged, broke it off, etc. I know a lot of guys I went to high school and college with have ended up being bald and overweight. It seems like the women have aged so much better than the men. I am curious to see if the years have been kind to Yancy-Bo.

I arrived at the Deans' house around 8:15 p.m. Tyleah-Shay was out the front door before I got out of the car. We hugged for a long time.

"How are you, friend?"

"It's been such a crazy week. I'm so glad you are here. Mom is inside. She is looking forward to seeing you."

We enter the house. Leah Dean is sitting at the island bar in the kitchen.

"I'm so sorry about Tyler. He was like a father to me." I hug her tightly.

Leah is more stoic than I expected. "Catherine, thank you for coming. Your presence here means a lot to our whole family."

I sat at the bar and a glass of red wine appeared in front of me. Rook, Tyleah-Shay's husband, and Leah's sister, Helen, were there as well. I had met Helen briefly at Tyleah-Shay and Rook's wedding a few years before. It seemed that the events of the week had taken their toll on everyone as they appeared worn out and weary.

I wanted to talk to everyone and get caught up on their lives, but it didn't seem to be the right place or time. Tyleah-Shay nudged me to follow her to the living room. I grabbed my wine and went.

She and I sat next to each other on the couch. She put her feet on the coffee table and turned toward me. She hadn't aged since college – same shape, same hair, she probably could wear the same clothes. She had no kids, so she had time to take care of herself. I guess I always felt a little out of her league, but I am sure she didn't see it that way.

"How are you, Catherine? How are Drew and the boys?"

"We are all fine. Same old, same old. What about you? This has been a terrible week for your family. What can I do to help?"

"I think everything is in order. Mom is a little frustrated that the city wants to honor dad because he is a fallen firefighter. She understands the sentiment and the importance of the city wanting to honor its public servants, but it's taking a deeply personal tragedy and turning it into a bit of a public spectacle."

"Is it too late to undo the service they want to have?"

"Oh yes. I tried to convince the mayor through a series of emails that my family didn't need this recognition, but his office insisted. They are going to have a brief service at the fallen firefighter memorial and eventually his name will be on a plaque there."

"That doesn't sound too bad. Your mom seems to be holding up ok."

"I think we both have cried all of our tears. We know tomorrow will be emotional, so I think we are trying to temper our emotions for the time being. It's exhausting crying all the time. I'm not sure if she will stay in Pittsburgh after this. Maybe she will move closer to me or Yancy-Bo?"

"Where is he now?"

"He lives in Nashville. Still not married. I think I told you about his broken engagement to Yuki. He was engaged another time too, but broke it off. He'll be here first thing in the morning."

"What time is the service tomorrow?" I asked.

"The calling hours are 2-4 p.m., then the firefighters service is at 5:00 p.m. Close friends and family will come back here at 6:30 p.m."

"Ok. Do you need help with flowers? Food? Transportation? Anything?"

"You know we'll probably need more ice. Can you bring some when you come back to the house after the service?"

"Of course. Ice is easy. You have my cell phone number if anything else comes up, but I will be with you all afternoon. Whatever you need, I'm here."

"Thank you again for leaving your family for the weekend to be with us."

I feel a little guilty because I wanted to see Paula too. I didn't come to Pittsburgh just for Tyleah-Shay.

"Your family is my family. I never felt close to anyone's family like yours. Your parents really made me feel welcome from the moment we met the first day at college. Remember your dad helped carry my boxes to our dorm room because my mom couldn't do it? He was always looking out for me and helping me, making me feel like part of the family."

"I forgot about that. Haha. He was very helpful, wasn't he?"

"Remember when I got my first job during college and I had a problem with my boss – what was her name? Alice Zee? Your dad gave me talking points to communicate with her so I could stay employed. My mom couldn't have done that. And your mom would always send my favorite cookies back with you after winter break so I'd have treats too. Your family is so generous and thoughtful. I wish I could have seen them more often. I don't think I've seen them since your wedding."

"Don't beat yourself up for that. You have a job, husband, two kids – you are super-busy. I bet you don't even have time to do things for yourself. When was the last time you took a "me day" and had a massage or a mani-pedi or went shopping for you? When did you stay in bed and read a book or take a bath and enjoy a glass of wine?"

"Um, almost never since the twins were born." Although I do have a fabulous relationship with a judge, who, by the way, is female. I guess I do take a little time for myself, but it's not in the way she would expect. And now is not the time or place to tell her. There may never be a time that this conversation would come up. I'm a pretty open person but I guess there are parts of me that need to be hidden away forever. There isn't much I don't tell Tyleah-Shay because I know she would support me and be my friend for the rest of our lives. She proved that when I told her that I slept with her brother years ago. Paula would flip out if she knew I told anyone about her – and I did already tell Bonnie. Paula has to remain my secret, maybe forever.

"Girl, you need to take care of yourself. You can't be a good mother or a good wife if you aren't taking care of you first. You will have nothing left to give."

Sometimes Tyleah-Shay said the most insightful and profound things. Sometimes she says things that I am thinking but can't really articulate. I know she's right, but I'm not sure I can afford to take much time for myself. When you're a parent, you give up a part of yourself. There's no doubt about it.

I yawn. It's been a long day. I got up early, flew to Pittsburgh, spent the day fucking and now I'm drained emotionally and physically from being with the Deans who just suffered a terrible loss. The wine isn't helping my alertness or ability to stay awake.

"I guess the wine is getting to me. It's been a long day."

"I guess you are no longer the party girl who would blast retro-80s music from our dorm room and wear crazy fedoras, inviting strangers in to dance with us and drink jungle juice?"

"Yeah, I'm pretty sure that girl is gone. Now I'm the girl who barely drinks and collapses in bed by 10:00 p.m. I own one floppy beach hat and haven't had grain alcohol since I was twenty-three. I've turned into a loser, haven't I?"

"I think you turned into a mom. That's all. It's not bad, just not the old Catherine."

That's the truth. I have my foot in two competing worlds – one that is the same old me and one that is totally someone else. I am not sure which face is presented to the outside world on most days. Maybe it doesn't matter.

I say my goodbyes, locate my purse and drive back the hotel. I realize that I forgot to call Drew. He's probably still up. I put on my pjs and dial the phone.

"Hi hon," I said.

"Hey Cath. How are you?"

"I'm drained. I napped for part of the afternoon. I just came back from seeing the Deans. They are holding up pretty well. How are the boys? I'm sorry I didn't get to say goodnight to them."

"They are fine. Bodie got in trouble at school for pushing that annoying kid, Nicholas. Nicholas was bullying Abby, the red-headed girl. He was calling her names. Bodie had enough of it so he pushed him. Of course, the teacher saw that and nothing else. He has to write an apology note to Nicholas and it will be forgotten. I didn't discipline him because I don't think what he did was wrong. We did talk about other ways to express himself though."

"Oh, poor little guy. I'm sorry I missed it. Are you ok?"

"Yeah, I'm thinking that was a parenting win for us. Our kid was demonstrating empathy and sticking up for the victim. I wonder if Nicholas's parents know how poorly he treats other kids?"

"Who knows? I met them once at a school event. We'll just keep an eye out and make sure this doesn't happen again. I can also mention it to Bodie's teacher so she can check on Nicholas's behavior. It's likely that she already knows that he's a bully. Teachers have an amazing grasp on what's going on."

"I guess you are right. Single parenting is tough work. I hope you are coming home soon."

"You know when I'm returning. I'm sorry your day was rough. I'll call you tomorrow at some point. Good night. Love you."

"Love you too. Bye."

I fall into bed exhausted. I spend a few minutes thinking about my day. Visions of Paula, nipple clamps, pancakes, Yancy-Bo, zucchinis, Leah's soft pink pashmina wrap, red wine, Nicholas the bully, my bruised foot, Yancy-Bo's orgasm face.

I sleep deeply and seemingly dreamlessly for nine glorious hours and awaken to hear my door opening. Paula entered using my extra key card. She carried two bags – one containing warm bagels, cream cheese and coffee. The other remains unopened. She's wearing a fashionable sweat suit. I realize that sounds like an oxymoron, but the woman can make anything look great. She served me breakfast in bed. I could get used to this. We kiss and eat bagels playfully smearing cream cheese on each other's lips and licking it off. After drinking the coffee, I excuse myself to use the bathroom and brush my teeth and hair. I bought some cinnamon toothpaste to try. I want to taste like her and share with her how she tastes to me. I leave my pajamas in the bathroom and emerge naked.

"I hope you don't mind, my sexy mistress, that I left my clothes in the bathroom. I thought I would save you the trouble of having to remove them."

"Very kind of you, Catherine. Are you clean down below?"

"Yes, ma'am. Would you like to inspect me?"

"In fact, I would. Come here. Lie on the bed."

I lie on the bed in a supine position with my legs spread wide open.

"Bend your knees and lift your hips please."

She pokes around my privates, sniffing and scrutinizing. Her touch is tantalizing. I feel very vulnerable and exposed. "Is everything ok down there?"

"Catherine, I take cleanliness very seriously. I would like you to be quiet.

I am going to thoroughly wash you."

I'm not sure where this comes from, but maybe it's part of today's game. She goes to the bathroom and returns with a soapy and very cold washcloth. She cleans from my pubic hair, around my clit, in and around my labia. She returns to the bathroom, rinses the soap off the washcloth and then wipes it off me. She returns to the bathroom, rinses the washcloth again, adds more soap and then returns to clean my asshole. She repeats the rinsing process. I am wet from the washing procedure and from her attention to my privates.

"Did you touch the zucchinis since last night?"

"No ma'am." I told the truth.

"Please wash them with warm water and then sit on the edge of the bed."

I took my three zucchinis and cleaned them in the bathroom. I then sat with them on the edge of the bed. Paula removed her sweatshirt. She had on an athletic shirt like she was going to the gym and a not-very supportive sports bra. I could see her nipples through her top. They were perfect cherries on top of a sundae. I wanted to eat them and rub my face in the melting ice cream of her creamy white breasts. I assumed this would not be a day where I would be doing much of what I wanted to do. It was a day to be dominated and make my mistress happy. After yesterday afternoon's lovemaking session, I am content pleasing her anyway possible.

"Catherine, I would like to see you suck each of your zucchinis like they are cocks. Start with the smallest one."

"Yes, ma'am."

The smallest one is the one I chose for my ass. It is not too much bigger than my thumb in diameter but the length of at least two thumbs. I put the end that was not attached to the vine in my mouth and suck it. I try to make it seem sexy but I feel kind of ridiculous. I hold the vine end with my fingertips and push it in and out. After a few minutes, she stops me.

"Good girl. Move on to the next one."

I take the one that is supposed to fit comfortably in my pussy. It is almost too big for my mouth. I'm going to be in trouble with the bigger one. I lick around the end and up the sides, then put half of it in my mouth. My mouth can't hold too much more. Paula grabs the vegetable and pushes it deeper in my mouth.

"Good God, Catherine, can't you suck more than that?"

I try my hardest but start to gag. Tears come to my eyes and my tongue starts pushing up and out.

"Relax your throat! Flatten your tongue."

I try what she says, but my stomach contracts and I'm afraid I might vomit. That would be very un-sexy. My throat closes up and I can barely breathe. I pull the zucchini out of my mouth.

"I am so sorry, ma'am. I would like to try again. Please."

"My poor useless sub. Have you never been taught the proper way to suck a dick? Lie down on the bed with your head off the side. This will open up your throat and create a straight passageway from your mouth to your esophagus."

I hang my head off the bed as she takes the medium sized zucchini from my hands. She stands in front of me with the zucchini in front of her crotch as if it is her large green penis. She pushes it into my mouth and it goes down my throat. I gag again.

"Relax your freakin' throat or I'm going to spank you."

Tears spring from my eyes again, but I am determined to do as she wishes. I try to take a deep breath and relax my throat, but my nose starts plugging up from being upside down. The blood is rushing to my head. Maybe I should give up on this attempt and request a spanking instead? My clit starts tingling at the thought of a spanking. I blink my eyes to keep the tears in and relax my throat. My tongue is flattened and the zucchini slides in, touching my uvula and tonsils. I concentrate on not gagging. My lips are getting dry. She fucks my mouth with her zucchini penis until she is satisfied that I have obeyed her and then she stops.

"You have redeemed yourself. Get the largest one."

I grab the large zucchini. I'm fairly certain now that this will not fit in my mouth.

"Catherine, do you think you can suck the large zucchini?"

"I am not sure, ma'am."

"For the remainder of this scenario, I expect you to call me 'Dominant Mistress,' do you understand?"

"Yes, mm – Dominant Mistress. I understand completely."

"I would like you to try to suck it."

I put the end of the zucchini in my mouth. It goes in about an inch. She sees my mouth stretched to the max.

"Do you think the zucchini is too big or your mouth is too small?"

"Maybe the zucchini is too big, Dominant Mistress."

"Do you think it will fit inside Pam?"

"Yes, Dominant Mistress."

"I bought you a little gift. Go to the bag near my purse and open your new ball gag."

I had forgotten mentioning that yesterday. I was excited to try it out. I opened the bag and removed a plastic-wrapped ball gag. It was a red silicone ball maybe an inch and a half in diameter with a black leather adjustable neck strap.

"I am going to fuck you with the zucchinis while you are gagged. We need to have a gesture instead of your safe word. Can you snap your finger?"

"Yes, Dominant Mistress." I demonstrate my ability to snap my fingers.

"You need to listen carefully to ensure you don't get hurt. Do you understand?"

"Yes, Dominant Mistress."

I handed her the ball gag.

"Do you have a ponytail holder?"

"Yes, Dominant Mistress."

"Please bring it to me."

I went to the bathroom into the outside pocket of my toiletry bag, retrieved an elastic hair tie and gave it to Paula.

She put my hair into a high ponytail using the holder and adjusted the length of the ball gag so it would fit snugly around my neck. "Do you want to say anything to me before I put this in your mouth? Once I do, it'll be there for a while unless you snap your fingers."

"No, Dominant Mistress. I am ready."

She put it in my mouth and fastened the buckle behind my neck. The ball went behind my teeth and limited my ability to move my tongue or speak. It seemed very naughty and erotic.

"Catherine. I want you to open the box of condoms, remove and open one condom and put it on the medium zucchini."

I nodded in understanding. Putting a condom on a zucchini is not as easy as it would seem. But I managed to do it. There was a little reservoir tip at the end for collecting semen. That wouldn't be necessary here. I felt proud of myself for being able to condomize the zucchini.

"Good little sub. Now I want you to masturbate with the zucchini. Put your knees up and have Pam face me. I am going to sit in the chair at the end of the bed and watch you fuck yourself."

I turned myself so she could get a clear view. I took the zucchini and positioned it at the opening of my hole. I hoped that my ability to select the right size was somewhat accurate. I rubbed the zucchini around my hole ensuring that I was wet even though I knew the condom was lubricated. Ready, set, go! I pushed it inside. It felt fleshy and quasi-penis-like. It was actually more penis-like than the vibrators we used. It felt pretty good. I masturbated with the zucchini, slightly moaning. It sounded more like a dying cow wailing but I think Paula could appreciate the pleasure I was giving myself. I was longing to touch my clit with my other hand, certain I could climax in a few moments. I wasn't sure that was her goal and I certainly couldn't ask her with the ball gag restricting my ability to speak.

"Catherine, you are enjoying that entirely too much. Please stop. Open another condom and put it on the large zucchini."

I hoped the condom would stretch far enough to cover the larger vegetable without breaking. I really hoped my pussy would open wide enough to allow it to enter. I broke the first condom I tried which resulted in a spanking. Whap. That felt so satisfying. My ass ached for another spanking. Paula really turned me into a perfect sub. I was craving ass-whippings because they made my clit throb like nothing else did. I thought about breaking another one on purpose, but I wasn't sure the punishment would be the same. I got the second condom on the large zucchini and waited for a minute for instructions.

"What are you waiting for? Fuck yourself with it!" she said in a condescending tone meant to humiliate me. It worked. Throb.

I was quite wet from the medium size zucchini followed by the spanking. If the big one didn't fit after that, it wasn't meant to go inside. Once again, I positioned the zucchini at the edge of my pussy and pushed gently. My hole opened up and swallowed the zucchini. The fit was tight. It was difficult to have the whole thing enter me. I had to have enough on the outside to maintain a firm grip on it. I am fairly certain nothing this large had ever been inside of me. It felt oddly satisfying and a little painful. A little squeak emerged from my gagged mouth which made Paula looked pleased with herself.

I squeezed my vaginal muscles to push it back out, but not all of the way. I firmly grabbed the end and fucked myself with it. In and out. In and out. The inside of me seemed more elastic and flexible to accommodate the zucchini but my hole seemed to experience the brunt of the displeasure. I continued masturbating until Paula told me to stop.

"I want you to use your vaginal muscles to hold that zucchini inside of you."

My muscles wanted to involuntarily push that sucker out. I used all of my energy to hold it in place. I could not think of anything else. But it was being expelled slowly. Maybe it was some kind of horizontal gravity? Before long, I felt it on the bed mostly outside of my body. I was embarrassed that I couldn't will my mind to make my muscles contract. Maybe the contraction that I thought would hold it in actually pushed it out. Either way, it appeared to be a willful act of disobedience.

Paula watched the whole thing occur. I waited for her reaction.

"Catherine, Catherine, Catherine..." she paused.

"First, I want you to remove the tiny part of the large zucchini that is still left inside of you. Then put the condom on the small zucchini."

She waited while I followed her orders.

"Go to the clarinet case and find the vibrator with the harness on it." I found it. What the...?

"That is a strap-on vibrator. You fasten it around my waist."

She stepped inside of it. It fit like panties but needed to be buckled in the back to fit her waist. Protruding out the front of her pleather panties was a latex penis, complete with veins, a realistic-looking head and balls. There was a knob on the waistband to make it vibrate. She put a blindfold over my eyes and instructed me to assume position number one, reminding me of our safe gesture. I climbed back on the bed on my knees and elbows. My mouth was gagged and my eyes covered. If I thought I felt vulnerable before, it was nothing compared to how I felt now. She pushed me forward gently until my head touched the headboard of the bed. There was nowhere to go. She caressed my ass and then spanked each cheek once with her bare hand resulting in a sexy little sting.

"That was for letting the zucchini come out of your pussy. Now relax your asshole."

Holy shit, she was going to fuck my ass with that giant strap-on. I took a deep breath and gripped the sheets on the bed preparing for the impending pain. My clit throbbed in anticipation and I felt new wetness form around Pam. I must remember to snap my fingers if it hurts too much. I have never used our safe word. Maybe today I'll have to use the safe gesture. I am angry at myself for suggesting the ball gag. What happens if Paula doesn't realize I snap my fingers and I can't get away since my head is against the headboard?

I feel anxious and scared. I really want to be the perfect sub for Paula, but I am afraid. Maybe my asshole will expand and accept the pseudo-penis. Focus, relax. Focus, relax. I keep telling myself. Suddenly I feel it poised to enter me. I take a very deep breath and relax. In it goes. It was the zucchini! Not the strap-on. It fits nicely. The lubrication of the condom squishes around inside of me. She fucks my ass with the zucchini. I welcome the feeling of the vegetable. She pushes it in deeper and mounts me from behind. She slips the strap-on cock into my dripping pussy and uses her pelvis to keep pressure on the zucchini ensuring it won't leave my ass. She tilts her hips back and forth in rhythm fucking me doggy-style with the vibrator. It feels so good that I can barely form coherent thoughts. Then she turns the vibrator on. I feel the buzzing deep inside of me. It is so erotic and sensual, especially since I am deprived of my sense of sight. My other senses are heightened. Being on my elbows allows me to reach up and squeeze my own nipple. Just a tinge of pain shoots up to my breast. I moan like an aching beast and within seconds shudder with an epileptic orgasm. My whole body shakes uncontrollably and I sink into the bed. Paula falls on top of me, both the vibrator and the zucchini fall out of me.

"Holy shit, Catherine. Are you ok?" She unhooks the ball gag as I push the blindfold off my eyes.

"Uh, yes." I try to catch my breath. Once again tears are forming in my eyes.

"That is the first time I have ever had an orgasm without direct clitoral stimulation. It was different and vivid." I wipe my eyes.

I don't know how else to describe it. Words are failing me. It was so intense. I assume this wasn't exactly the way Paula thought this scenario would play out. I have to get myself together to allow her to climax in a way that she would enjoy. I just want one more minute to come down from that amazing high. I feel the blood drain from my unused clit.

She looks pleased with herself.

"Dominant Mistress. I apologize for cumming so quickly. Please tell me how I can best serve your needs."

"Catherine, you are a beauty to behold, so perfect, pliable and submissive. Please unfasten the belt on this strap-on and help me out of it."

We throw the strap-on over to the chair. I am eager to please her and wait for some direction.

She lies on the bed and motions for me to join her. I climb into her arms.

"We are running out of time. I'd like to have lunch with you before you have to go to the funeral."

"We still have tomorrow morning before my flight," I reminded her.

"Oh – sorry. I forgot to tell you that Garrett is coming home tonight. I can't see you tomorrow."

I tried to hide my disappointment.

We kiss like we are discovering each other anew. I trace her facial features with my fingers, trying once again to memorize every contour, every pore, every smile line, every eyebrow hair. I want to burn every inch of her into my memory. I want her demands and her laughter in my ear. I want her fragrance in my nose. I want her cinnamon breath and her silky clit in my mouth. Everything about her seems so perfect when I know our minutes together are dwindling.

Paula didn't climax that day. We spent our last hour in bed touching each other, reminiscing about our two days together, and expressing our love for each other. Then we showered together for the first time. I watched the warm water fall onto her head like a summer storm and form little droplets that made their way to her stomach, the curves of her hips and finally dripping down her legs to her perfect little toes. I lapped up the waterfalls as they careened over her breasts like ski jumpers in the winter Olympics. I washed her hair, massaging her head like an expert hairdresser. I washed her labia, clit and asshole how I would wash my own, except with extra attention and care. Our chaste shower was as sensual as any lovemaking session I've ever experienced. I wished we had time for one more brief scenario before having to leave. In a rare moment of creativity, I actually thought of a possible scenario for sex play. I often thought of ways to improve her plans although I never told her. I didn't come up with my own ever. Actually, this plan for only a small part of a scenario, not an entire one. This is why I wasn't good at this game. The only part I thought of was Paula making me stand while I had an orgasm. I am not sure I could manage to be upright. I think I would fall over or not orgasm. I spent too much time envisioning this challenge and its probable unsatisfying outcome. I was prepared to forego lunch to spend more time in bed with her. Fortunately – or not – she had the sense to make me get dressed and join her for lunch. We walked a couple of blocks from the hotel and ate at a riverfront restaurant. I had forgotten that she eats out for almost every meal since she doesn't like to cook and Garrett is usually gone. I wondered what her poor brother did for food each night.

I ordered a steak salad with a gorgonzola dressing and crispy onions and a glass of red wine. She ordered a club sandwich with a soda. I usually do not drink at lunch time, but I figured that I might need to relax a little before the afternoon. She tried a sip of my wine and licked her lips hungrily. I imagined what a drunk night in bed with her would be like. Could we be any more uninhibited? I suppose I would be more willing to try things and not have the foresight to be afraid. However, I am not sure how we would ever manage to be drunk together.

"I have a little surprise for you," Paula said.

"You do? What is it?" I asked.

She handed me a tiny gift bag. What on earth could she have bought me? And how will I get this home unnoticed?

"When I was shopping last night, I came across a little tourist shop. I thought I'd like to get you something to remember your trip to Pittsburgh."

"How thoughtful." I opened the bag and removed tissue paper to see a small velvet pouch. Inside the pouch was a nail clipper keychain with PITTSBURGH written across it in black and gold.

"Do you like it?" she questioned me.

"I'm not sure whether to laugh or cry. It's a useful souvenir - sort of a perfect reminder of our weekend together. Thank you."

"It wasn't supposed to be a grand gesture or anything. But I thought it would be meaningful to you. You can take it with you everywhere and always think of me."

"I will keep it with me always. You are kind and controlling."

"Haha." I loved hearing her laugh. I put the velvet pouch in my purse.

After lunch, we walked back to her car. She had purchased a new Lexus sports car recently and was happily showing it off to me. I wondered why we didn't take her car the day before when we went to the farmer's market, but I think she was worried someone might recognize her car. We couldn't be too careful – even in a town where neither of us knew many people. We paused in a doorway of a closed business to kiss goodbye. We had never kissed in public before. It was exhilarating and bold. I felt oddly free.

"Sometimes I wish we could really be like this forever."

"Catherine, you know this isn't real life. This is our fantasy. If we were together, we wouldn't have the romance, the lust. We'd have to go grocery shopping, take out the trash, do laundry. It wouldn't be all fun and games."

"I think we could make it fun. I could make you breakfast and burn the eggs. You would spank me and then we'd fuck all day on the kitchen floor."

"Catherine, I'm not sure if you are a hopeless romantic, a perfect sub or just living in make-believe land."

"Maybe it's a combination of all of those things. I miss you when I'm away from you and I love you when we're together."

"I love you too. I hope you can enjoy some time with your friend today in spite of the occasion that brought you together. I read another article about her dad in the paper. That fire and his death were so tragic. I'm sorry for your loss as well. I don't want to make you late. Goodbye, my love."

"Not goodbye. Don't ever say goodbye. We are never really apart. You are always in my head."

"Ok. Talk to you soon."

"Yes, we'll have phone sex soon, ma'am."

She got into her sporty Lexus and drove away. I rushed back to the hotel room to make sure I looked presentable for the afternoon. The funeral home was just a couple of miles from the hotel. I easily found a parking space and wandered into the entrance. My mind was on Paula and her departure. I had to change my focus and get into the present. Upon entering, I ran right into Yancy-Bo. My focus changed promptly. If it was even possible, Yancy-Bo in his 30's looked even better than Yancy-Bo at eighteen.

"Hello, Catherine," he smiled warmly.

"Yancy-Bo, I am so sorry for your loss." I hugged him gently.

"It was your loss, too. You are like family to us."

"Your parents are – were – like parents to me, too. How are you holding up? You just came in today from Nashville?"

"I am doing ok. I didn't want Dad to volunteer with the fire department after retiring. I thought maybe he'd sit still, read a little, garden or something. Maybe I had a premonition or vision? I just didn't want him back in the business."

"He was still in great shape, Tyleah-Shay said. He was doing what he loved."

"Third best outcome," he said.

"What?"

"Living doing what you love is the best outcome. Living doing something you hate is next best. Then dying doing something you love and, last, dying doing something you hate. I'd say Dad's death was the third best outcome."

"I see your logic. Very clever. Where's your sister?" I wasn't sure where else to go with that conversation.

"She's in the visitation room with Mom. Come with me."

"Let me grab some tissues first." There were tissue boxes on every horizontal surface that I could see so finding some was not difficult. I followed Yancy-Bo into a room down the hallway. The funeral home had soothing sage walls with an occasional pop of floral wallpaper accents. It wasn't distracting nor was it particularly calming.

We entered through double oak doors on the left. There were rows of chairs and a center aisle. At the front of the room stood a closed metal casket with a photo of a smiling Tyler Dean beside it. After that was a huge photo display with photos from Tyler and Leah's wedding, Tyleah-Shay and Yancy-Bo's births, graduations, wedding, and myriad other occasions. In the corner was a photo of Tyleah-Shay, Yancy-Bo and me at the cottage on the day I fell water-skiing. Evidence of the time that things changed for a few days between Yancy-Bo and me.

I greeted Leah and Helen, her sister, then went to stand with Tyleah-Shay and Rook. Many other people were filtering in through the room, expressing condolences, telling stories about Tyler and moving on.

"How are you holding up?" I asked Tyleah-Shay.

"I've been better," she said.

"Your mom seems like she's handling this situation well."

"She's on a lot of drugs to hold herself together," was Tyleah-Shay's response.

"Oh no. I'm sorry. What can I do? I feel pretty useless."

"I'm just glad you are here. Rook isn't a fan of these events. He doesn't like making small talk with strangers. If you keep him busy, that would be great."

"I can do that. I'm happy to do whatever you want – really."

"There are so many local friends and neighbors that I don't know. Not many people made the trip from Minnesota and a lot of their hometown friends had already died or moved to Florida. My parents might be the only people in history who retired to Pittsburgh!"

"That's probably not true, but I guess it is unusual."

I greeted guests for a while. When Rook was tired of that, I went outside with him for a breath of fresh air.

"How's Tyleah-Shay really?" I asked.

"She's doing pretty well, better than I expected."

"How are things with you two?"

"Great. I never thought I'd meet anyone like her. I try to make her happy every day that we are together. I cherish every minute we are together. How about you and Drew?"

"We are fine. I haven't told anyone this, but we are trying to have another baby."

"Get out!"

"We are. He wants a daughter. I'd like one too. So, we are giving it a try."

"You know you don't get to pick the gender of your baby, right?"

"Well, there are some techniques that could work." I explained the Shettles Method and that we are attempting that, but it is not for the impatient.

After two hours, the visitation and service, complete with multiple eulogies, was over. A small group of us went to the fireman memorial for the program during which the city honored Tyler Dean for his sacrifice. It was very moving. Many firemen were present and several spoke sharing stories of Tyler.

When we left there, Yancy-Bo asked if he could ride back to his parents' house with me. He didn't get a rental car and was tired of riding with his mother who was not a good driver. Leah Dean drove with one foot on the gas and one on the brake and was constantly jerking along in a way that would make anyone succumb to motion sickness. I was happy for the company.

"What have you been up to lately?" I asked Yancy-Bo.

"I've changed careers a few times. Now I'm teaching at Vanderbilt part time."

"That sounds very prestigious. What's your area of expertise?"

"Foot massages," he joked.

"I hope you've mastered that. From what I recall, you get easily distracted and don't ever really finish foot massages."

"Touché, Catherine."

I was glad to see he still felt comfortable with me after all of these years. Although it would be too easy to stray off my path of pseudo-fidelity with him. He was a known quantity, not a stranger who trickily seduced me. Gosh, why was I even thinking this way? I am happily married and happily involved with my woman on the side. I definitely didn't need a guy on the side as well.

And maybe he wasn't really flirting with me anyway. I sure let my imagination run away with me. "Get it together, woman," I told myself.

We arrived at the Deans' house for the post-funeral gathering. I just realized that I forgot to get the ice. The only thing I was responsible for and I didn't get it.

"Tyleah-Shay, I forgot the ice. Your brother was distracting me! Should I go out to get some?"

"Yancy-Bo, please leave my friends alone! You are trouble, dude."

Did she say friends plural? Was I one of many friends that he slept with? Ick. I started to feel used and dirty. I had just been flattering myself with his attention. What was wrong with me?

"Catherine, why the look? You know you are the only one for me," he whispered so only I could hear.

"Yancy-Bo, I don't know what you are talking about. I'm happily married. Do we need ice or not?" I was starting to feel confused and really wanted a glass of wine. I couldn't decide if I wanted to go get ice to be out of this situation or if I should just sit and drink wine.

"Nah, we're fine without additional ice. I'll get you a glass of wine. Do you still prefer red?"

"Yes, red would be great." Did he remember that I liked red wine when I was 21? I'd really like to know why he broke off two engagements. I hope he wasn't harboring any feelings for me. That was a very pretentious thought. He brings me a stemless glass of Syrah I thank him and try to find Rook. He's safe for me to be with.

I didn't have to try hard to avoid Yancy-Bo for the rest of the evening. He was busy with family. I was very curious about him, but I had the moral strength not to ask. I could get all of the details that I want from Tyleah-Shay another time.

I excused myself around 11:00 p.m. and went back to my hotel tired from the excitement and sorrow of the day. My flight was at noon on Sunday. I suddenly felt quite anxious to be home. I knew I wouldn't see Paula again and I missed Drew and the boys. Maybe I would try to get an earlier flight and get home sooner to surprise them? Everything I came to do in Pittsburgh was finished. I wished I could close my eyes, tap my shoes together and be magically transported to my own bed. Sadly, nothing is ever that easy.

After returning home, the next several months were pretty similar. Each tenth day, Drew and I would try to make a baby. Each 28th day or so, my period would come. I talked to Paula as often as I could. Frequently we would have phone sex resulting in me having an orgasm. However, she could not since she was usually at work. I tried to talk dirty to her as she requested, but she never seemed satisfied with my attempts. I was actually very good at thinking dirty, but not verbalizing it. I often used thoughts or memories of her words to force an orgasm while I was making love with Drew. She told me that she thought about me every day and masturbated in the shower while thinking about me and inventing new scenarios. I was happy to be her muse.

2010

When the new year came, Drew and I decided to start having sex on day eleven to increase our chances of getting pregnant. Our love-making became boring and mechanical, something neither of us wanted. I still hadn't told Paula that I was trying to get pregnant. I didn't want to upset her. I was trying to have my cake and eat it, too. I'd tell her if I had to, but not until then. It was best to keep my home life and my life with her as separate as possible. It was the only way I could continue having this long-distance love affair and maintain my sanity.

In February, a big local news story became national news. There was a British man renting a large house in Montgomery County in Maryland just a dozen or so miles from me who was hosting BDSM parties. He charged people for entering and they could live out their fantasies in a variety of different ways. The neighbors discovered what was going on and tried to shut him down. The government got involved and said that he was breaking zoning ordinances for having a business in a residential area. There were ways around the law like making the gatherings part of a club that members paid dues for and could enter as they wish without money exchanging hands at the door. The whole story was fascinating and perverse in a way that demanded my attention.

During one conversation with Paula, I mentioned the party house. "Did you see about the BDSM house in Montgomery County?"

"Yes, I did. What do you know about it?" she asked pointedly.

"Just what I saw on the news. Can you believe places like that exist? I know I'm naïve but that sounds like an innocent way to get needs met: being with like-minded people."

"Catherine, if you ever went to a place like that, we'd be done. You know that, right?"

"How would I find out about a place like that? No one can go there anymore. It's not secret. Thanks for the threat though." I felt angry with her for saying that and didn't care if she knew it.

"I can only be with you if I am the only one. I can't risk you giving me a disease or talking about us with anyone."

"Are you kidding me? When do I have time to be with anyone else? How would I start a relationship like this with anyone else? I don't want anyone but you! Please don't think I am with anyone else. Your jealousy is irrational."

"Catherine, I won't tolerate your being irate with me. Please think about your tone before we talk again." Click. She hung up on me. That is infuriating! Who does she think she is? Sometimes this game goes too far. I brought up the topic of the BDSM house parties because I thought it was amusing and something we both could relate to, but I was clearly mistaken. I wanted to cry, but I was at work. I hate being emotional with her and have no outlet because there would appear to be no reason that I am upset. That has got to be one of the worst parts of being in an illicit relationship.

After that call, we didn't talk for a month. I missed hearing her voice, but I was hoping she would initiate contact. I waited and waited.

Hi Catherine:
How's the nightlife in MoCo? I am sorry I overreacted. Forgive me?

What do I make of that? She is trying to make a joke out of her irrational behavior. Sometimes I wonder if she needs me more than I need her. I like to think our relationship is symbiotic. We are each fulfilling the needs of the other. Although I didn't think I had these needs until I met her. But now I can't imagine life without my dominant mistress. She makes everything more exciting. She helped me understand my own body – its desires, abilities and limits. I know if we ever split up, while physical proximity would keep us separated, we would always be connected through our shared experience. We will always have memories of our times together, her imagined scenarios acted out, our passion together, and our collective naughtiness. There is no one else like us and we both know it. I will never have another lover like her. She made me say that to her once. I never realized how true the statement would be.

Judge Marlon:
There is nothing to forgive. Nightlife anywhere is not the same without you. Hoping we can catch up soon.

YLS,
Catherine

I hope that wasn't too forward of me. Seemed like it was innocuous enough.

No sooner do I hit send that my phone is ringing.

"Hello?" I see it is Paula's number.

"YLS?"

"Your little submissive," I answered.

"Ahh. You're so hot. I miss you."

"I miss you, too," I admit.

"Let's have phone sex soon. Is this Friday your day off?"

"Yes. Should I call you around 10:00 a.m.?"

"Perfect. Catherine?" She whispers my name.

"I really miss you. There is no one like you."

I feel the familiar tingle in my panties. I know she means it because it isn't easy for her to say.

"I feel the same. I'll call you on Friday."

"Say 'goodbye.'"

"I can't. You say it."

Silence. We listen to each other breathe.

"Are you still there?" I whisper.

"Yes." Her breath deepens.

"Let's hang up together on the count of three. No goodbyes."

"Ok."

"One, two, three."

Silence.

"Are you still there?" I ask.

"Yes. Please say 'goodbye' Catherine."

"I don't want to."

"Ok. I will talk to you on Friday." The line went dead.

On Friday at 10:00 a.m., I was alone in my house. I dialed her phone number. She answered on the second ring.

"Judge Marlon's office."

"Hi, it's me."

"Why don't you say 'Good morning, Dominant Mistress, it's your little submissive, Catherine'?" she whispered.

I swallowed hard. We're starting already with a tingle in my clit. I don't understand how one sentence from her can make me feel so horny. I took a deep breath and said what she suggested.

"Good morning, Dominant Mistress. It's your little submissive, Catherine."

"Very good. Catherine, I'm afraid that I won't be able to make you cum today. The maintenance guys are on our floor cleaning the inside of the windows of our building. So our time together will be brief."

"I'm so sorry to hear that, Dominant Mistress."

"You are so hot. You make me wet just hearing you say that. I want to reach my hand under my desk and rub my clit. But it's way too dangerous today. I can't even close my office door because the window cleaners will be here momentarily. I want to talk about last September for a minute. What was your favorite part of our weekend together?"

"Let me think a minute. Um, I enjoyed when we went to the farmer's market and I was touching all of the zucchinis trying to decide which to buy. You looked so strong and sexy then. We both knew why we were buying the zucchinis, so it was really erotic, but it was also a little embarrassing. So many different emotions. I didn't know your specific ideas about how they were going to be used so it added a little mystery to it as well. You really have the cleverest ideas. Each part of your ideas is woven into something bigger and better than I could ever imagine. I really appreciate your creativity and insight into making the best scenarios ever."

"Thank you. That is quite a compliment. You know I spend a lot of time thinking of ways I can dominate you and make it pleasurable for us both. My favorite part is something you might not even remember. When you were blindfolded with the ball gag in your mouth and I had the strap-on poised to fuck you from behind, I told you to put your head up against the headboard, remember?"

"Yes, I remember. I try to remember everything we do in great detail." My breathing slowed and my heart was racing with the memory.

"Just when I told you to relax before jamming the zucchini in your ass, you gripped the sheets in anticipation of the pain. Seeing you prepare for the inevitable was so hot. I wasn't expecting that. I think of your fingers gripping the sheets when I masturbate some mornings in the shower. That has been my favorite orgasm thought for the last six months."

"Wow. I didn't know I did that. I guess it was involuntarily. You know I thought you were going to fuck me in the ass with the strap-on. I was really afraid and I didn't want to disappoint you by using our safe word – uh gesture – to get you to stop."

"I am not sure if I would be disappointed. I want you to always feel safe. But sometimes I want to punish you and have you feel pain too."

My clit was in a full-on throb when she admitted how she enjoyed punishing me. Just hearing the word made Pam leak. I felt desperate to masturbate under her direction.

"Dominant Mistress, you are making me so horny. I need to cum. Will you please tell me how to accomplish that now?"

"Catherine, I really can't. The cleaners are two offices away. I'd hate to start and have to hang up. I don't want you to cum today. I want you to think about how horny you made me when you gripped the sheets. Today will be a day of withholding orgasm. You need to control your desire. Do not disobey me."

"Judge, please. I'm begging you."

"I appreciate your desperation, but the answer is no. Do not touch yourself. Do not cum today. Do not fuck your husband. Do you understand me?"

"Yes, ma'am. I understand completely."

"The cleaners are here. I have to go. Catherine, be a good girl."

"Yes, ma'am."

"Goodbye."

"Goodbye."

Shit. I was so horny, I thought I might explode. One minute with my vibrator and the deed would be done. I am resolved to obey her for the morning. Today was day eleven, so I will just maintain my wetness until bedtime and then have sex with Drew. It was going to be a long-ass day.

I spent the day doing errands and cleaning the house. I picked up Kentucky Fried Chicken for dinner, a rare fast food dinner. The boys wanted to have friends sleep over but I managed to convince them to wait for Saturday night. I couldn't imagine having a bunch of kids running around and not sleeping when Drew and I needed alone time. By the time it was bedtime, I had been ready to make love for over twelve hours. I put on a short nightgown rather than my usual pajama pants and t-shirt.

Drew looked at me and said, "oh no, is it day eleven?"

"Yes. Did you forget?"

"Yeah and I have a headache."

"I'm sorry. Take some Advil. I've been thinking about this all day."

"Catherine, do we have to? I am not sure I feel up to it."

"Yes, we have to. I'll do everything if you like. Just get in bed."

"Yes, ma'am," he said jokingly. But it sounded too much like my response to Paula and it instantly made me wet again.

He swallowed two Advil, took off his clothes and laid motionless on the bed. He wasn't going to make this easy for me. I climbed on top of him and kissed him. He grabbed my breasts through the top of my nighty and squeezed my nipples gently. I wanted to tell him to pinch them or bite them, but maybe today wasn't the day that I would be demanding. I reached behind me to stroke his cock. In spite of his indifference, he had an erection already. He groaned as I touched it. Sometimes his sex noises were really hot and sometimes they sounded like moans I envision a porn movie actor would make. I realized it's not good to laugh when I'm in bed with a man – even if it's my husband. I convince myself that his moans and groans are sexy and not vile. In spite of the day-long desire I have been saddled with, I think I really do have to forego my own pleasure in order to accomplish our mission. I hate giving up my orgasm, but I will be half faithful to the demands of Paula. No orgasm for me, but yes orgasm for Drew. That is what is necessary to make our baby – his orgasm, not mine.

I slide myself onto his cock and ride him with more energy that I have expended in a long time. I imagine myself on a wild bronco. I slow for a moment and watch as he goes in and out of me, but with me on top and the head of his cock buried inside me, it is easy for me to feel like his penis is mine and I am fucking his hole. I feel powerful with my new imagined penis. In and out I go. I wonder if this is how men feel? Are they powerful just because they have a penis and can put it into holes of all sorts? I wonder if Paula felt that power with the strap-on, fucking me from behind. She seemed very confident with it. I wonder how many times she has used that and with whom? I want to know the answer or maybe I don't. I am not sure I have the nerve to ask anyway. She did seem very adept at its usage – and she did make me cum while using it. I struggle to change my focus to Drew. He enjoys being fucked by my/his big cock. I thrust my hips and tighten my glutes as if I'm giving it to him as hard as I can. It's nearly violent. He licks his lips, raises his shoulders off the bed, and grabs my ass to finish off deep inside of me. As soon as I am sure he's finished, I roll over onto my back and bring my knees to my chest. I read in a magazine that will help the sperm stay inside and reach their destination. We had been trying to get pregnant for a year and I am willing to use any old wives' tale or witch's trick to make this pregnancy happen. I stay curled up in a ball for fifteen minutes. His sperm slowly leaks out of me onto my side of the sheets.

"Is your head better?"

"Which one? The little one really took a beating. I thought for a minute that I was in a John Wayne movie."

"And you were the horse? Haha. I was just trying to get the job done efficiently. It felt good, right?"

"Mostly, I am a little sore."

"Sorry, honey." I kiss his cheek.

While we spent the next three weeks waiting to see what happened, there was an explosion at another mine in West Virginia. This time it was the Upper Big Branch mine in Raleigh County. Twenty-nine miners were missing. The mine has rescue chambers with special ventilation units and food supplies if something happens while the miners are deep underground. When an explosion occurs, people in the mining community pray that the men made it to the safety in one of those chambers. Then we all hold our collective breath and wait for rescue workers to be able to reach the chambers and save the miners. Sadly, after two days of searching, eleven bodies were recovered. The next day, the search was suspended because of the high level of methane and indications that a fire was still burning in the mine. The rescue chambers had enough sustenance for a dozen miners for four days, so we remained hopeful that the others had reached safety after the explosion. Two days later, the other bodies were found. No one survived.

This was another instance of our investigators having cited the mine owners for hundreds of serious safety violations prior to the explosion. A state-funded independent investigation would put the majority of the culpability on the mine's owner but also blamed our office for not notifying the mine's employees that the mine was not operating safely. I worried what the ramifications of that would be. We didn't like to have any negative press, trying to do our jobs and staying under the radar but this would obviously result in someone being called to explain to the Secretary of Labor. Poor Edwin. It's likely he would be the one under fire. It's sad to think that people never think of rules and laws that are put into place not just for general safety of its citizens but also safety of specific types of workers. No one talks about the work we do in Mine Health and Safety until there's a tragedy.

For the first time in almost nine years, my period is late. I am cautiously optimistic that our latest attempt was successful. We wait an additional week before I take my first pregnancy test. I don't want to get Drew's hopes up, so I do it quietly early one morning before work. I had the tests under my bathroom sink for a while in anticipation of this day. I urinate on the First Response early pregnancy detection stick and wait for two minutes to see whether two pink lines appear. Two minutes can seem incredibly long. I brushed my teeth and returned to the stick to see the tell-tale two pink lines! It worked – I am pregnant!!!

I climb into bed next to my sleeping husband. It is remarkable how child-like he looks when he is sleeping. I rub his stomach to wake him and whisper "Daddy, I think our days making John Wayne westerns are over!"

"What? What! You're pregnant?!"

"Yes!" I squeal with joy.

"I'm so happy, Catherine. We still get to practice baby-making occasionally though, right?"

"Yeah, honey. We can still practice." I kiss his cheek and let him return to sleep.

I get dressed and go to work. The only person I would tell this early in my pregnancy is Bonnie. She is equally excited. "What about your favorite judge? Are you going to tell her?"

"No, not yet. Maybe during the conference in June. I don't want things to change between us yet. I know that sounds selfish, but I just can't."

"You have to do what you have to do. You know I'll support you know matter what."

"That's why I adore you so. You are the best friend ever." I try to tell her that frequently so she knows I mean it.

The next few weeks go by with little discomfort. I only seem to feel sick after taking the prenatal vitamins. I start taking them before bedtime so I will sleep through any nausea. I didn't have much morning sickness with the twins, so I wasn't anticipating having much this time. But then I worried – if my pregnancies were essentially the same, did that mean I was having another boy? Of course, we would be happy with a healthy baby, but both Drew and I really wanted a daughter.

"Drew, what happens if it's another boy?"

"Then it's another boy. What can we do?"

"If it's a girl, I want to name her. Ok?"

"Sure, babe. You can name her as long as I have veto authority if it's too wacky."

"Ok, I think you are talking about the names I had chosen for the boys if they were girls – Summer and Sunshine?"

"Right and Calypso, Lilac, and Meathead."

"I never said Meathead! But that is an interesting choice. Thanks for the idea!"

"I get veto authority over boy names too then."

"Of course. We have to say these names forever so I think we should both approve of them."

"We are in agreement then. My next prenatal appointment is tomorrow. We'll get to pick a date for the ultrasound for next month. Then we can find out if it's a girl or boy. Can you come?"

"I can't come tomorrow because of the meeting with the consultants from Baltimore. But I'll definitely clear my calendar for next month's ultrasound appointment."

"Ok, that sounds good. After tomorrow's appointment, let's tell the twins about their little status as almost-big brothers."

"Great idea. Let's take them out for ice cream and we'll make an announcement."

"Perfect."

The following day, I went to see my OB/GYN, Dr. M. She had a long Persian name so she just preferred to be called Dr. M. She delivered the boys after my long-time doctor, who recommended her, retired. It was the first female ob-gyn I ever had and I liked her a lot. She always listened to me, took extra time with her patients against the wishes of the insurance companies. She was young, beautiful, gave free samples of medicines and seemed to be on top of emerging treatments and diseases.

Dr. M's nurse weighed me, took a urine sample and my vital signs. Then I disrobed and went to wait for Dr. M in the examination room. She had already given me a due date around the new year. I wasn't looking forward to being nine months pregnant at Christmas or during wintertime. I have an irrational fear of falling on ice. Not being able to see my feet compounds that phobia. Maybe it will be a usual winter involving minimal snow.

While I was planning for the winter that would be coming in six months, Dr. M. came into the exam room. She asked how I was feeling and noted that my weight gain was on target. She listened to my heart and lungs. Then she checked the fetal heart rate. She moved the stethoscope around my nearly still-flat stomach. I definitely felt more bloated than I was at 10 weeks last time. I have heard that women look pregnant earlier the second time around so I was expecting it. She looked a little concerned.

"Is everything ok?" I asked.

"I'm not sure. Let's go into the other exam room. I'd like to do a quick ultrasound. Have you had any cramping or bleeding?"

"No, nothing."

I wrapped the gown around myself and went to exam room three down the hall. Dr. M's office was painted mauve and had pillows with inspirational sayings scattered around the chairs and couches in the waiting room. It looked like a Victorian parlor. There were fresh flower arrangements, soft music and fragrant odors almost like a spa. It was a departure from a usual sterile environment that most doctors' offices had. She had a flair for decorating and making patients comfortable. That was another reason I loved her.

I got on the exam table and put my feet in the stirrups. She returned wearing latex gloves. She warmed the ultrasound gel so it wouldn't startle her patients and their delicate tummies. She opened my gown and squeezed the gel onto my bare belly. Then she pressed the wand on my stomach. She saw a tiny dark spot.

"It is usually too early to do a standard ultrasound before ten weeks gestation and you are around ten weeks based on your last menstrual period and our calculations. I'm going to have to do a transvaginal ultrasound, ok?" Dr. M asked.

I wish Drew were with me now.

"You have to put the wand inside me?"

"Yes, Catherine. It won't hurt. I think you had one during your last pregnancy."

"Yes, I did. It's ok."

She put a condom on the wand and added some gel to it. I guess that was a lubricant. She inserted the wand in my vagina. Then she moved it around and around.

"There is the embryo. Do you see it?"

"Yes."

"It seems to be measuring smaller than ten weeks and the heartbeat is very faint."

"What does that mean?" I asked, tears welling in my eyes.

"Catherine, I'm not sure if the embryo is viable. I'm sorry."

"What do you mean? What can we do about it? Are there other tests?"

"No. We will have to monitor it. Return in three days for another ultrasound. Stay on bed rest until I see you again."

"Is that it? What else should I do?"

"There's really nothing else. It's a wait and see game. I don't want to make any predictions. Let's just see what happens in three days, ok? Hopefully, the embryo will grow, the heartbeat will strengthen and everything will be fine. Don't stress out. There is nothing you can do to help it, but you can hurt it if you are stressed."

"Ok. Thank you, Dr. M. I'll see you in three days."

I put my clothes on and left the office without checking out. I went home, climbed into bed, called Drew and asked him to come home. I explained what happened, even though I wasn't exactly sure what happened.

He was so sweet with me, waiting on me hand and foot, bringing my favorite foods, and magazines I liked to read but never had time. The boys were extra nice, too. They were cuddly and on their best behavior. I spent three days trying not to blame myself for whatever was happening, but how could it be anyone else's fault? The baby, or embryo, was inside of me. I was the only one responsible for it. I didn't drink or do anything harmful like eat soft cheeses or shellfish or whatever else was on the prohibited list this week. I took my vitamins regularly. I'm sure Dr. M. would say that sometimes these things just happened. I think my own mother had a miscarriage before or after I was born. I can never remember. Of course, I doubt these things are genetic, but maybe they are? I haven't even had a miscarriage yet, but I am fighting the urge to be pessimistic. For three long days, I stayed in bed and thought of everything I did since conception day. I know what day it was. The day the window cleaners came. The day I rode Drew like a bareback cowboy. Was this karma that I was horny because of Paula and then I had sex with my husband to create a baby that wouldn't live? Did I bring this on? I'm not much of a believer in a higher power, but I wondered if I should – dare I think it – pray for a positive outcome? Or, worse yet, bargain for it? No, I believe everything happens for a reason. It will be sorted out the way it's supposed to. I have got to chill out and stop trying to place blame. It's not helping the baby or me to worry about things over which I really have no control.

Drew came with me to the next appointment. Dr. M. whisked us into room three immediately.

"Has anything changed?" she asked.

"No bleeding or pain if that is what you mean."

"Did you stay in bed since I saw you last?"

"Yes, I barely got up to use the bathroom,"

"Change into the gown and I'll be back in five minutes."

I waited on the examination table for her to return. Poor Drew sat helplessly by. I wasn't sure if he ever witnessed a transvaginal ultrasound. I guess I should have warned him.

Dr. M. returned, took the wand and put it into a new condom, then lubed it up.

Drew started turning green.

"It's ok, honey. They have to do it inside because of how early it is in the pregnancy."

I doubt that comforted him.

She inserted the wand again and moved it around to find the hidden embryo.

"See that?" She pointed at the screen.

"That's your embryo. I want to measure it. There is still a weak heartbeat, but it's a heartbeat!"

I guess this was the new measure of success.

"At this point in your pregnancy, the embryo should be doubling in size every three days. Yours is 10% bigger than three days ago. It is still viable, just not growing at the usual pace."

"So...?"

"I don't want you to stay in bed anymore. Just go back to work, continue your routine. Come back in 3 days and we'll measure her again."

"Her?"

"Sorry, Catherine. I don't know what it will be, but I assumed you wanted a girl after your two boys."

"Yes, we do want a girl."

"Seeing a heartbeat and growth however minimal it is, is a positive sign.

We'll go with that for now."

"Thank you, Dr. M."

We waited another three days. I worked as usual, picked up the boys from school, drove the carpool to soccer practice, made dinner, did laundry, just like everything was perfect. I felt like a fraud knowing that nothing was perfect. Maybe nothing would be perfect again. I was exhausted trying to keep up the façade.

The appointment three days later was identical to the previous one. The embryo had a weak heartbeat and grew a tiny bit. Dr. M. wanted me to return in another three days. That night I started talking to the embryo. I told her that she needed to get stronger. I was eating healthy for her and giving her vitamins. Bonnie called my stomach "Thor" because "he" was such a strong embryo fighting to survive. I told her that we expected it to be a girl. That is how her nickname became "Thora." I talked to Thora all day, willing her to be a resilient girl who could overcome everything. I rubbed my stomach and sang to her. As it turned out, none of it helped.

At the appointment three days later, the embryo measured smaller for the first time. Dr. M. no longer saw or heard the heartbeat. It seemed that Thora failed to thrive. I stifled my sobs in room three.

"What does that mean?" Drew asked innocently.

"It appears that the embryo is no longer viable. I'm very sorry."

"What do I do?" I really didn't know how to deal this new situation.

"There are two ways to handle this. You can wait until the body expels it. Or you can have a D&C to remove it."

"What are the benefits and risks of each option? How long do I have to make a decision?" I need some answers, but I'm not prepared to make decisions right now.

"If you wait for the body to reject it, your body will handle it naturally. That means that you will start bleeding, maybe cramping and it will come out probably like a heavy period. It will happen when your body is ready. You have no control over the timing. You should probably relax for a couple of days afterward. If you choose to have a D&C, that is a surgical procedure. You will have to make an appointment and go to the outpatient surgical center. You will be put under using general anesthesia, I will perform the procedure to remove the embryo and some of the surrounding tissue. You will be a little sore and have the same heavy bleeding. You will probably need a few extra days of bed rest, but you can really return to your routine when you feel up to it. Why don't you think about it overnight and call me tomorrow? Is there anything else you need to know before making your decision?"

"How risky is the D&C? Is there a chance anything can go wrong? We still want to try again so I want to ensure my chances to conceive again are not compromised."

"Catherine, there really is a minimal risk with either option. Clearly undergoing surgery is riskier but this procedure is very common."

"Ok. Thank you for being so patient with me."

"Catherine, again, I'm very sorry. But the good news is you are young. I don't think there's a genetic problem. You have delivered healthy babies in the past, so I think you are in a good place to try again. Of course, you need to wait at least three months before trying again. In fact, you shouldn't have intercourse for at least 6 weeks. You have my cell phone number if you have any questions. Please don't hesitate to call me. I'm always available to you."

"Thank you, doctor," Drew said.

Dr. M. left the room. I put my clothes back on, a totally different person than when I removed them. I now was a person who lost a baby or suffered a miscarriage. I guess the term "lost a baby" isn't really accurate since I didn't *have* a baby. I didn't even have a fetus. I created an embryo that failed to thrive. That sounded so distant. It didn't really capture the grief I felt.

For the first time since they were born, I wished I could send the twins to someone else's house for the night. I wanted to be alone with Drew and plan our next move. I didn't want to make this decision on my own. I felt like I might choose the emotional response instead of the rational one. Or maybe I'd be rational and not proactive or thoughtful. I just didn't feel capable of considering all of the pros and cons of the situation. I knew Drew would know what to do, but we needed time alone to talk.

He took care of dinner. I sat numbly nearby. I wasn't hungry. I wasn't engaged in conversation. I didn't feel like faking being happy for the boys. I felt like a terrible mother. I just wanted to cry, go to bed, and have this whole awful day behind me. Yet I knew that there would be many more awful days to come.

Drew was very good at cutting though complex information and determining the optimal course of action. I was so glad to have him on my side when it was necessary to make an important decision. Tonight, we didn't have to decide which dishwasher was the best to purchase or how to deal with difficult people in a PTA meeting, but the future of my body and our no-longer-living embryo that was still inside of me.

I sat pensively propped up on my bed while waiting for Drew to join me and wrote the words I was feeling.

Still
My belly churnings are absent
The desire my heart once felt gone
Swimming emotions in my mind have drowned
My insides are still
My embryo is no longer
Now I walk the path to unpregnancy alone
And longingly wait for tragedy
Only to return to my private hell of stillness
Still nothing is alive within me
Yet still it is within me
Still.

The conversation didn't last as long as I thought it would. Drew thought the best idea was to let the embryo come out naturally. I admit that deciding was easier than I thought it would be. Why go through the expense and uncertainty of surgery if it wasn't necessary? I called Dr. M. the next morning to let her know our decision. Now we just had to wait and go about our life until the inevitable occurred.

The next few days passed slowly and emotionally. Waiting was awful. I didn't know how it would happen or when it would happen. I tried to go about my days how I always did, but it seemed artificial, like I was in no man's land.

Four days later, I felt crampy. I asked Bonnie to tell Edwin that I went home because I didn't feel well. She offered to come with me, but I told her that Drew would come home. Bonnie would be very comforting to me and I'd love her company but it's likely Drew would prefer to be alone with me when we officially lose our "baby."

I went home, tried to watch a movie on the couch to relax and wait. Dr. M. didn't give me a sense of how long this could take. Each body does its own thing. I felt ill-prepared and unhappy about the lack of control. Maybe the D&C would have been a better option? At least I could have selected a day to have my embryo ripped from my body.

The movie I watched ended and Drew still wasn't home. I called his cell phone. He didn't answer. I didn't want to waste energy worrying about him. If he was nearby, he wouldn't answer anyway. I felt a very sharp cramp and went to the bathroom. I sat on the toilet, not sure if that was the right thing to do. I had a pain in my lower back, a feeling I often referred to as watermelons. I felt like watermelons were going to emerge from my back when I had PMS. It was the same sensation but a little stronger, like big watermelons were growing out of my back. I rubbed my back to ensure there were no large fruit emerging. Then I felt an odd movement followed by a splash on my privates. I stood up and saw the toilet filled with blood. It looked like some large clots. Maybe one of those was my embryo? I felt nauseous and melancholy. I sat for a while longer wondering where the hell Drew was. When I felt strong enough to stand, I cleaned myself off and put the toilet paper in the trash can so the bloody mess would be undisturbed in the unflushed toilet. I fumbled for a maxi-pad, somewhat pleased with myself for remembering where I kept them since I never used them. I put on some comfy sweatpants and got into bed.

The front door opened and I heard Drew come up the stairs two at a time.

"Drew? I think I just lost the baby."

"What do you mean 'you think'?"

He entered the room with flowers and my favorite candy. I wasn't sure whether to be surprised or pissed off that he was shopping while I was miscarrying.

"I've never done this before, so I'm not sure if that is what happens or not. Go look in the toilet."

Drew entered the bathroom, then gagged. Geez, I forgot how he is bad at handling bodily fluids. He returns looking worse than I do. If I have to comfort him after I have a miscarriage, I'm going to scream.

"How are you feeling?" he asked.

"A little gross. First, I felt the watermelons, then there was blood everywhere. I felt nauseous. Now I just feel an extreme sense of loss. Are we supposed to call Dr. M?"

"I'm sorry, hon. What can I do?"

"I guess I'd like some Advil or something. Did Dr. M. say I can take something for discomfort?"

"I'll call her to tell her what happened and see what to do next. I know this is awful, but I'm going to take a photo of the blood in the toilet and send it to her to see if that is what we should be expecting."

"Thank you. I know the blood isn't something you want to deal with, but I appreciate your help."

"Don't worry about me. Just rest and I'll be back with information. Can I get you anything? Water? Wine?"

"I'll just wait to see what the doctor says."

Drew disappeared down the stairs. I wonder if he even has Dr. M.'s phone number. I guess he'll find it. He's resourceful like that. I fell asleep while waiting for him to return. I was exhausted waiting for this to happen. After it did, there was a slight relief to not worry about it anymore. But now I'm drained and depressed.

When I woke up, I went back to the bathroom and more blood came out. I think gravity helped it flow with vigor. This time it was less clotty but just as disgusting. Even though blood doesn't bother me, I was feeling slightly lightheaded. I cleaned up again and returned to bed. Where the hell was Drew?

"Drew?! Where are you?"

He rushed back to the bedroom.

"After I talked to Dr. M., I returned and you were asleep. I didn't want to wake you. She looked at the photo and thinks that is the bulk of it. You will continue to bleed for up to two weeks but it should be like your regular cycle after today. If the bleeding is heavier than usual, you might be hemorrhaging and will have to see her ASAP. She said you can take whatever pain killer you prefer. She also advised to drink wine and relax. And, sadly, no sex for a couple of weeks."

"Thank you for calling her. I just had some more bleeding. It's in the toilet. I feel very tired. Will you get me some Advil and water? I'm going to try to nap again. Oh – it's almost time to get the boys from school too!"

"Ok, one thing at a time. I'll get you some meds and water, then I will get the boys. I don't need to look at anymore bloody toilet water. Do you mind if I flush it?"

"Go ahead. I guess we don't need to be reminded any more of what could have been."

"Catherine, just because the blood is gone doesn't mean we won't mourn. We lost our baby-to-be. It's ok to grieve."

"Ever since I found out I was pregnant, I started making plans. I thought about what she would look like, what we would call her, where she would go to preschool, when she would enter kindergarten. I didn't tell you before, but I even bought a little pink dress. I really felt like it was going to be the daughter we wanted. I feel like I jinxed it. Like it's my fault she's gone. I feel like we are flushing our dreams literally. I didn't know it would hurt so badly to lose someone that I didn't even know."

I started to cry, then sob, then wail. I just let it all out. It wasn't pretty, but it was necessary. I let every emotion that I ever had in my body out just then. It wasn't really cathartic. It was more like a carousel of crazy. Drew held me and comforted me, cradling me in his strong arms. He was a pillar of stoicism when I needed that. I knew he was upset too, but it was happening to me directly and him indirectly. If I was going to be an irrational mess, then he needed to be the strength to hold our shrinking family together. He stroked the top of my head and kissed my forehead. It was a little pejorative, but I didn't have the energy to be offended. I know that wasn't his intention. He was trying to be a calming influence. When I was out of tears, I stopped crying. My nose was both stuffed and runny. I put my head on Drew's pillow and closed my eyes.

When I woke up, it was dark outside. I heard a faint noise and followed it. Drew was on the phone downstairs. I tiptoed toward him. I missed dinner and felt hungry. I was also queasy and unbalanced. I made another trip to the bathroom and changed my leaky pad – why do maxi-pads suck so much? I guess I can't use tampons during this. Maybe I need to ask Dr. M. I'm not sure I can live through two weeks of bleeding into pads.

"Who are you talking to? Can you make me dinner?"

"Bonnie. Yes."

"I forgot I was supposed to call Bonnie. Is she ok?"

"Yes, she's fine, just worried about you. Do you want a grilled cheese?"

"That sounds good. Will you add some ham and spicy brown mustard to it please?"

"Sure. I put the boys to sleep a while ago. They were worried about you. I told them that you were really tired and had a stomach ache so you went to bed early. They skipped their baths tonight because I didn't want to deal with it."

"Ok. I'm not really worried about baths."

"Sit on the couch and I'll bring you some food." I sat in my own living room feeling like a stranger. Everything seemed different. The photos of Drew, the boys and me looked foreign. For ten weeks, I had imagined that there would be another person in photos by the same time next year. I thought the twins would make great big brothers to a little sister. I envisioned them teaching her to walk and talk. They would tell her jokes, pick out funky outfits for her and someday check out her boyfriends to ensure they passed muster. It wasn't only Drew and I who lost a child, the boys lost a sibling. I was grieving for them too and they didn't even know it. My brain was swirling with the ideas of all I had lost. I would never have believed suffering a miscarriage could be so paralyzing. How is it that I became so attached to something I didn't even know about three months ago? I only had the promise of a future with my baby and it was taken away. I began to cry again. I felt so pathetic.

"Cath, be there in a minute. Do you want water with that?"

"Yes, please. Do you still have movies saved on the dvr? I feel like I need something to focus on so I will do something other than cry."

"Yes, we'll find something. Here you go." He handed me a plate with my sandwich cut into butterflies, like my grandmother used to make for me. He is the most thoughtful person. My nose was still significantly plugged up so I couldn't taste much of the sandwich, but I was glad to have something in my stomach. After finishing, we went to our room to watch tv in bed.

Drew scrolled through the movies on the dvr and suggested a few different options. Some were things he had seen before that he really liked and wanted me to see. One he recorded so he could see it because he had read an interesting review of it. I didn't really care what we watched except I wasn't up for a foreign film. I'm not sure I could read the subtitles because my eyes were shot. He chose an action film that he loved. I nodded off a third of the way through.

I woke the next morning, hoping the day before was a nightmare. Then I felt the bulky pad in my panties. Did I mention that I hate maxi-pads? I could feel blood dripping out of me. It was an extremely unpleasant feeling like a rush of thick, warm water exiting my body. I walked slowly to the bathroom to see what accumulated during the night. I sat on the toilet and heard more blood drip, drip, drip into the toilet water below. It had slowed down a bit thankfully. I changed the pad and went back to bed.

The next two days were more of the same. Blood, tears, unrealized dreams. I decided that I had to get myself together. I needed to return to work. I hadn't told anyone about my pregnancy, besides Bonnie, so my absence was probably seeming suspicious. I was grateful that the government had free assistance if I needed to talk to anyone if I couldn't shake off my grief in a reasonable amount of time. I decided to go for a half day and see how it went.

My first half day went well. I had enough to do to catch up on what I missed. I was so busy that I didn't have time to worry or grieve. I realized that keeping distracted was the way to deal with this. I returned full-time after the first half day. Spending half the day wallowing in sorrow was not productive. I needed to be busy even if it meant pushing my grief aside to function properly. I am certain that I will mourn in my own way when it was necessary. I didn't have to dwell on it every day.

Drew and I had sex for the first time about two weeks after the miscarriage. I stopped bleeding several days before. I wasn't sure how long we should wait exactly but it seemed like if I felt up to it, we should do it. One night I felt really aroused for no particular reason. I told Drew that I was ready to try it. He was very delicate during foreplay; we took our time and enjoyed each other's bodies in a way that we hadn't since before having the twins. It was gentle yet playful and felt like genuine lovemaking. We weren't rushed to make a baby or get it in before sleeping or worried about being interrupted. He entered me gingerly when I was ready. I felt very connected to him and complete in the love we shared that night. I was secure in knowing that he would protect me from everything the cruel world offered. He was and would always be my knight in shining armor.

For the first time in five years, I wasn't counting the days until the judges' conference. I hadn't told Paula about the pregnancy or miscarriage. I wasn't sure how she would take it, although I wasn't planning on keeping it from her. I wanted to tell her in person. I was a little worried about acting enthusiastic when I talked to her before she came. That is when she usually gave me instructions about what she wanted me to do or wear or when to come to her room. I was looking forward to seeing her, I just wasn't sure how the conversation would go. I knew I would have to act very interested, which I was, but I was guarded too. I didn't want to betray the seriousness of our impending talk until I was ready to have it with her. On the Thursday before the conference, she emailed me.

Catherine:

I hope to see you at the conference next week. I'm looking for some information on restaurants in the area of the hotel. Are you able to talk today?

Judge Marlon

I was sure that this was a coded email to have an official reason to talk. She could research restaurants just as easily as I could. It's one of the benefits of being in an illicit affair, I get to also be a detective.

Judge Marlon:

It is so wonderful to hear from you. I'd be glad to talk to you about restaurants. How about 2:00 p.m. today?

Catherine

As usual, I could set my watch by Paula's timeliness. At 2:00 p.m. on the dot, my phone rang.

"Good afternoon," I answered.

"Catherine, it's nice to hear your voice. I miss you."

"I miss you, too." It was the truth. I just didn't feel the excruciating longing for her that I had felt for most of the last decade.

"I have some bad news. Garrett is coming with me to D.C. He has some meetings to go to, but I'm not sure how much alone time we'll have."

"Oh no! That is terrible." I tried to sound more upset than I was.

"I know, sexy. I think we'll find some time; I just can't tell you when at this point. His schedule isn't set yet. I just wanted you to be prepared for it. Maybe we can meet in the lobby on Tuesday morning and have coffee or breakfast?"

Monday was the travel day for the conference participants this year. The conference was brief like last time, only Tuesday through Thursday, then the attendees traveled home on Friday.

"Tuesday for breakfast sounds good. Let me check on timing. I have the agenda here somewhere on my desk. Crap! There are files and papers everywhere. Ok, here it is. The opening remarks are at 9:00 a.m. Do you want to meet at 7:30 a.m. or 8:00 a.m.?"

"8:00 a.m. sounds good. I don't want to act suspicious. Are you ok? You sound distant." I guess I can't hide much from her. We've known each other for too long.

"I'm fine. I have a lot on my mind. I'm so sorry for being distracted." She understood my apology as being sincere yet playful. I know she appreciated when I used one of our secret phrases. It was almost as good as plain old phone sex.

"Catherine, you are very naughty for being distracted while talking to me. I think I will have to punish you for not giving me your full attention."

"Yes, ma'am. I understand completely." My clit tingled even though I wasn't really interested in pursuing that path today. Too often it happens that my brain and Pam have different plans.

She lowered her voice to almost a whisper, "what type of punishment do you think you deserve?"

"Um. I'm not sure. It sounds like it's going to be a long week of withholding sex."

"Catherine, remember you can suggest a punishment, but it doesn't mean I'm going to take your suggestion. That was too easy of a response. Tell me what kind of punishment you want."

Even though I didn't want to have this conversation, my mind was up for the challenge of conjuring a response that would please my mistress. Spankings? Erotic, but boring. Nipple clamps? That's been done. I remembered something I saw on a BDSM website after reading the article about the Montgomery County S&M house.

"I want you to restrain me on a spanking bench and then spank me with a paddle."

"Wow! Where did you see that? You are a very naughty little submissive girl. Tell me what it looks like."

"I looked on a website. I sort of found it accidentally. There are different types – some are wooden and some have leather pads. The person – me in this instance – would be on her stomach on one of the planks, like a pommel horse. There are places for the arms and legs to be restrained with leather straps to limit mobility. My ass and Pam would be on display and accessible to you for anything. It looks like a piece of furniture you would really enjoy, ma'am."

"Catherine, I am very pleased that you took the initiative to discover something that we could both enjoy immensely. I would love for you to be restrained on a spanking bench and I would love to beat your ass until it turns pink. You make me so horny. Damn, girl."

I felt a little proud of myself for suggesting something that may have surprised her. My panties were dripping wet at the idea of a spanking bench and about making her horny, but I still feel conflicted about the loss I've suffered and my desire to share that information with her in person. I feel like I'm betraying the memory of my dead embryo by playing this game. What was it about this woman that prevented me from having a normal conversation? She makes me swoon with desire, even when I am opposed to it. I lose all sense of right and wrong, common sense, good judgement. What has she done to me?

"Thank you, Judge. It is my goal to make you horny and achieve the best orgasms of your life."

"If you only knew how true that was. I love every second we are together, exploring each other's bodies and the limits of what is possible. I have so much more I want to do to you, Catherine. My ideas for scenarios are endless."

"I hope we have the opportunity to try more of them next week."

"So do I. One of the other judges just popped his head in here. I'd better see what he wants. I'll see you next Tuesday at 8:00 a.m. Catherine, will you wear something pink for me? I love how you look in pink."

"Yes, ma'am. I'll wear pink. See you then. Have a safe flight."

"Goodbye, perfect little sub."

Tuesday arrived in the blink of an eye. Weekends always flew by with the twins. Soccer game, birthday parties, play dates, and sleepovers kept us busy. We barely had time to do anything around the house. Laundry was piling up, there were dishes in the sink, the yard appearing unruly, and there were weeds in our flower beds. I am considering hiring a cleaning person. I just don't know whether it is a good use of our extra money. I think about the sad shape my house is in as I drive to the conference hotel. It is in Arlington this year, not very far from my house. Even though it is unlikely we will be intimate today, I made sure I shaved my armpits, legs and bikini area and trimmed my nails with my Pittsburgh nail clipper keychain. I decided to wear a short pale pink skirt with matching pumps and a black somewhat sheer blouse with a hot pink bra beneath it. I had a suit jacket to match my skirt but I think it will be too hot to wear it. I want to look sexy enough that she will desire me even if we can't fuck. I realize how ridiculous that sounds given the fact that I have to have a very serious conversation with her. I also know that I am under her spell, so clear thinking is not a possibility.

Parking is easier than I expected, so I arrive in the lobby and find the café by 7:45 a.m. That is another thing I've learned. It is not a good idea to keep Paula waiting. I am glad to have a few minutes to decide how I'm going to tell her about my miscarriage. I hate having to inject reality – particularly this reality – into our carefully constructed fantasy life. But I think I owe it to her. I hope this isn't a miscalculation on my part. How much honesty did we promise each other? I understand how much fidelity means to her, meaning only that I can fuck her and my husband and no one else. And sometimes I can only fuck my husband when I have her permission – which sometimes I agree to, sometimes I pretend to agree to and sometimes I blatantly disregard. Most of the time, I am honest about my transgressions. While I have been worrying about how to tell her this, I realize a little too late that one thing I have not considered at all is what her response will be. I cannot anticipate her response. She will likely be a little angry that I hadn't confided in her before or maybe I'll get lucky and she will be comforting in my time of loss. Or maybe she will say that she's only in it for sex and she's not really concerned about what happens to me when we are not together. "I love you when we are together. You are nothing to me when we are apart."

I nearly started to cry at the thought of that possibility. It was my intention to not become emotionally involved with her. I think I am mostly successful at that. I don't sit around daydreaming about being with her, although I do occasionally imagine her voice when I'm trying desperately to cum with Drew. Sometimes she urges me on "Catherine, you may cum now." Or "Catherine, you are so inept that you don't deserve to cum." "Catherine, you have thirty seconds to cum or you will forfeit your opportunity today." In my imagination, she always starts with saying my name. It is sexy in its simplicity while sounding regal and demanding. A cornucopia of feelings inundates me when I hear her voice say my name.

"Catherine?" Her voice interrupts my thinking about her saying my name. How coincidental.

I turn on my heels to see her. My breath catches in my throat. She cut her hair to a long bob. It's wavy and full and bounces when she walks. She is a rare woman who gets more attractive with each passing year. How can it be? She looks stunning, radiant. I second guess whether we should have this conversation or just reserve another hotel room and get naked. Why didn't I think about getting another room? I am disappointed with my lack of ingenuity today.

"Judge Marlon, you look beautiful." I stop short. Is this something one woman would say to another? My cheeks flush with embarrassment. She wore a fitted peach chiffon dress that looked like perhaps she was going to a garden party rather than a conference. She had the air of aristocracy and confidence. I was drawn to her like a moth to a streetlamp on a warm summer night.

"So do you. I like your pink."

"I do like following directions, ma'am."

"You will earn some good girl points. Do you want to eat at the café or go to the restaurant down the hall?"

"If we have time, I'd prefer the restaurant."

"The restaurant it is." I follow her to the right. We pass the elevators that undoubtedly go to her room with her sleeping husband inside. The restaurant is tucked in the corner beyond the jewelry shop. Why is it that the nicer hotels have all of these amenities now? Salons, spas, boutiques. There's no reason to ever leave there.

"Table for two," Paula informs the hostess.

We follow her to the back of the restaurant. She leaves menus on the table and disappears. There are only a few people dining at this hour, which pleases me. I don't want any of our colleagues watching our interaction. My lack of a poker face causes problems frequently. I don't want people to make assumptions about us, even if they are true. I sit with my back toward the center of the room. She prefers seeing the whole room anyway. It's an Army thing – always being prepared. I guess if an attack were to occur in the hotel restaurant, she would be my knightess in shining armor to save me from whatever evil lurked, as I would sit blissfully unaware looking at a wall.

I glance over the menu realizing that perhaps I don't have much of an appetite after all. Our waitress appears.

"Hi, I'm Lindsay. I'll be taking care of you today. Can I get you some coffee?"

"Yes, two coffees," Paula answers. I half love when she takes control. I guess her authority is part of the game. Maybe I'll let her order my breakfast for me, too.

"I would like some water, too," I tell Lindsay.

"Be back in a flash." Lindsay disappears.

"What are you going to order?" I ask Paula.

"I am pretty hungry because I missed dinner last night. I think I will get the daily special with eggs, pancakes and bacon. What about you?"

"You choose for me."

"Ok. I will." I knew that she would approve of my relinquishing control over my breakfast options.

Lindsay returned with two coffees, cream, and two water glasses. I thanked her as she placed the beverages on the table.

"Are you ready to order, ladies?"

"Yes. I would like the daily special, eggs over medium so that the yolks are runny but the whites are not, with whole wheat toast and crispy bacon. My colleague would like avocado eggs benedict with no meat."

"Sounds good. Thanks for your order." Lindsay was off again. I wanted to question her choice of food for me, but I really needed to start the conversation while we had a break from interruptions. I decided that eating in the restaurant with constant interruptions was probably was not an ideal location for this topic.

I picked up the creamer to add to my coffee, but Paula said "no."

"No what?" I asked.

"No, you may not have creamer. You may have your coffee black today."

I see. Our game was starting early and I wasn't sure if I could even continue it to any reasonable fruition. I was foreseeing a long frustrating day.

"Yes, ma'am," I croaked. She looked pleased with herself. Tingle. Dammit. No tingle, I begged my clit to listen.

"Paula, I have something to tell you."

"Continue," she said half interested.

"Uh, I, uh, recently had a miscarriage."

"You what?" Paula asked incredulously.

"I was pregnant and I miscarried. I'm sorry I'm really devastated. I'm grieving. I want to be with you, but I'm not sure I can deal with any of this right now."

"I'm sorry that you are going through this. But you aren't the only person who has ever grieved."

"You aren't even a parent. I don't think you can speak about this."

"You've never asked me why I am not a parent. Did you think I was just selfish and I wanted to travel the world and play tennis all the time? Nothing is further from the truth. Before you get all high and mighty on your parental horse, maybe you should hear a little more about me. You want to know why I am not a parent? It's because I can't have kids."

Her tone changed to disgust and impatience. She continued, "You want to know why I can't have kids? One night when I was at the refugee camp in Thailand, I had to use the bathroom after dark. I was scared to go alone, so I woke my dad to escort me. When we left the covered area of the compound to use the makeshift toilets, a group of men grabbed us. My father was held at gunpoint and forced to watch three men rape me repeatedly. I was young. I hadn't even hit puberty yet. My dad was screaming in Vietnamese, but they didn't understand him. I felt like I wasn't in my body any more. I had to separate myself from the pain of being ripped apart from the inside out. My mind left my body. I thought I was dying. I could see a bloodied child beneath me fighting while being held down. One rapist after another took turns brutally fucking me until I passed out. When they were done, they left. My father ran to me and cradled me in his arms, his tears wet my cheeks. There was no medical help. I was bruised, bloodied, and broken. My vagina was destroyed. There was no way I could carry a baby because of the damage. Eventually my uterus was removed after we moved to the U.S." She looked indignant. I had no idea. I wasn't even sure what to say.

"Paula. I didn't know. Why did that happen? Did the men ever get caught?"

"There were rumors that I was targeted since my father was well-known in Vietnam. The Thai people did not want any more refugees coming from Vietnam. We were draining their very limited resources. They expected word to get back to Vietnam to keep boat people away. They didn't know that it wasn't our plan to land in Thailand. Storms brought us there. No, the men were never brought to justice."

Lindsay returned with our breakfast. I lost my appetite completely by then. I mumbled something in her direction. Tears filled my eyes. I'm not sure if I'm crying for myself or Paula or all of the words that should have been said before now.

When Lindsay left, Paula continued, "After we moved to the U.S., my dad did everything he could do to protect me. He didn't want me to leave home. He wanted me to dress in baggy clothes to hide myself and not be noticed. He insisted that I wear a bra before I even had breasts. He would touch my back each morning before school to ensure I was wearing a bra. I felt trapped in his protection. It was humiliating for me to wear something I didn't need, that is needlessly uncomfortable. But I did as he wished. I became a great student, I studied and learned as much as I could. When I got the chance to leave home to go to college, I went as far away as I could to escape the confinement my dad created to protect me."

I started to eat my food to do something productive with my hands and energy. I didn't know how to react. I was looking for sympathy from her and I didn't get it. She turned the tables on me so quickly that I wasn't even sure what happened. Now I had to be sympathetic to her. I don't know why I never asked her about having kids. Some people just don't want kids. We talked about so many private and personal things; it is odd this topic never came up. But it certainly did not and now I appeared to be uncaring or indifferent. How am I going to fix this? She didn't seem to be sad or even angry, but resigned to the truth about her horrific past. I wanted to know more yet I was unsure what to ask.

"Paula, I'm so sorry. I didn't know. I guess I made an assumption that you just didn't want kids. I don't know what else to say."

"You don't have to say anything. I just thought you should know."

"I want to hold you and comfort you for something that happened decades ago. It seems your pain is fresh still."

"I have only told three people about the rape. It is not something I want to discuss or remember. I'm sorry how it came out. I wasn't trying to diminish your feelings. I just wasn't sure I could give you the empathy you needed. It was more than I could pretend. My memories washed over me and came spilling out of my mouth in an unpleasant way. I am ashamed of my reaction."

"Please don't be. We know each other too well for that. I am honored that you shared that traumatic event with me."

"I hate that we are here in this restaurant. This discussion deserves a more intimate setting."

"I hate that we are here when I can't even touch you the way I want to. And it's almost time for the conference to start." I reached across the table and caressed her hand for a moment in a way that would not seem strange to a casual onlooker.

Paula glanced at her watch and started eating her food. She didn't seem to have lost her appetite after telling me about her rape. I guess she has spent years of her life coping with the aftermath and perhaps it was no longer that hurtful to her? Even though the talk didn't go in any of the ways I had imagined it going, the outcome may have been better. I know I didn't get the sympathy I craved from her, but I did get a deeper insight into her whole being. The conversation made us closer than ever before.

That first morning of the conference passed by quickly. There was a new employee to manage the Continuing Legal Education paperwork so I had nothing to tether me to any specific place. I spent hours thinking and re-thinking about what happened to Paula in Thailand. I couldn't fathom how frightened she must have been or how helpless her dad must have felt being unable to protect her. I imagined different outcomes: someone interrupting the rape, Paula wetting the bed instead, tracking down the rapists and bringing them to justice. I wonder if that is why Paula went to law school. Did she have a vendetta? Was there any way to prosecute them? Had she explored any of the options? It seemed impossible since it happened decades earlier in an unfamiliar environment and the only eyewitnesses were a child and her father who didn't even speak the language of the attackers. I wondered if there was any precedent to bring them to justice? How would that even occur in an international case? I was unsure whether to discuss any of this with her. I'm certain she would have already gone through the exercise of investigating options, determining the best course of action and implementing it. Unless she concluded that the most appropriate response was to do nothing. Could it be? Had she sought counseling? I really wanted to spend a lot more time discussing this, but I'm not sure if the window of transparency with her had elapsed.

"Earth to Catherine!" Paula was in front of me.

"Sorry, I was thinking." I didn't even realize that people had left the conference room.

"You looked like you were a million miles away. Are you ok?"

"Actually, I was thinking about our conversation from this morning. I would like to talk about it more if you are willing to," I confessed.

"Maybe someday. It was draining to discuss it once. I don't want to revisit it any time in the near future."

"What are you doing for lunch?" I asked sheepishly hoping for another private meal with her.

"I'm afraid Garrett is joining me for lunch. Do you want to come along?"

"No, I don't think I would be comfortable with that even though I would like to be with you."

"Ok. I think he'll be going out after lunch to do some research or meet clients. Maybe we can have a few minutes alone during the afternoon break?"

"I would like that a lot."

"Let's plan on it then. I can't give you a key to my room, but maybe we can go there if he goes out."

"Sounds good. Enjoy your lunch." I didn't mean it. In fact, I was pretty jealous. I thought of the conferences as being the time we had together. I didn't like Garrett's infringement on my time with Paula.

"You are beautiful when you're pouty." My lack of a poker face gave me up again.

"Thanks. I think." I smiled, mostly because she knew me well enough to know that I wasn't happy with the current situation.

She walked away slightly swinging her garden party dress in an alluring way that made me miss our lunchtime dalliances even more. I had an hour and a half to myself until the conference's afternoon session began. I went back to the same restaurant where we had breakfast, then decided I would take a walk around the block instead. I had my newspaper in my purse in case I wanted to enjoy the sunny day and read outside. Fortunately, my shoes were comfortable enough for a brisk walk. I left the hotel with purpose in my stride.

As I walked out of the lobby, I noticed an alley that led to a courtyard that I hadn't noticed before. There was a fountain, several restaurants with both indoor and outdoor seating and nicely landscaped flower beds with tulips, daffodils, and lilies. It was a small oasis very near the busy streets in Arlington, yet totally unseen by passing traffic. What a gem I found. I decided on an Ethiopian restaurant and asked for a table for one. I wasn't hungry enough for a regular lunch, but I knew I'd be starving if I skipped lunch all together. Their fitfit salad would be perfect for this occasion. The server brought me the mixture of lettuce, onions, injera and berbere sauce that was more plentiful than I expected, but delicious nevertheless. I enjoyed the salad as I read the Washington Post. I couldn't eat it all, but it wouldn't last long as a leftover. As I was paying my bill, I looked up and saw Paula and Garrett walking by on the other side of the fountain. I don't think they saw me. They seemed very involved in their conversation. I watched their body language. I felt like an interloper analyzing their interaction. They seemed comfortable with each other, although there was no obvious affection. They could be colleagues or siblings. There was nothing about the couple that screamed married partners in love with each other. Or maybe I was reading too much into it? Maybe I wanted to see no obvious romantic love between them because I wanted her romantic love to be saved for me? Did Drew and I hold hands when we were walking somewhere alone together? Would casual onlookers assume we were a couple in love? Or maybe Paula didn't really have the capacity for love after all she had been through? I know when we are alone together that she loves me. I can see it in her eyes and feel it in her occasional selfless actions. Maybe it is all for the reward of sex? My head hurt thinking of all of the possibilities. Sometimes there is nothing good in overanalyzing things. Let our relationship play out how it will and enjoy it while I can. That is my new mantra. We agreed years ago that our relationship would be something separate from other relationships, kept in a little box that didn't interfere with our marriages, our work, our friendships or anything else. We also agreed that we would be in it for sex games only and no emotion, but we sort of failed on that plan. It felt safe to love her when I was with her. It didn't seem unfair or unrealistic. I think I have done a very good job of keeping my feelings for her only evident when I was with her. Kudos to me.

I paid my lunch check, folded my newspaper and walked back to the hotel. Everyone was waiting outside the conference room mingling. I looked for someone to talk to so it wouldn't appear I was alone. I saw Colby, the young attorney, and Duncan standing near the coffee service and walked their way. After engaging in small talk for a few minutes, Duncan started encouraging people to enter the conference room for the afternoon session which focused on recent updates of investigations of mining accidents. I definitely wanted to hear about this, so I entered the room and sat in a chair in the back. Paula rushed in and took her seat next to Judge Hernandez just before the door closed indicating that the session was beginning. I don't think she noticed I was in the room initially, but she began playing with her pen in a seductive way that I knew was meant for me. She held it in her left hand and formed a circle with her right thumb and forefinger, like a tight okay sign. She pushed the pen in and out of the small hole she created. The participants were very interested in the speakers that I was certain only I knew what she was doing. She was teasing me in a crowded room. I squirmed in my seat wishing that it was her finger entering me. I felt dampness build in my panties and then my clit tingled. I tried desperately to listen to the panel of speakers from federal and state government agencies who discussed investigations of each mining-related fatality including determining the root cause and contributing factors, but the flirtatious spectacle performed by Paula required my attention. She was great at foreplay even when we weren't near each other. I hated her and loved her for it at the same time. My heart was beating wildly and my mouth felt like a sandbox. I actually thought about leaving the room, grabbing a glass of water and heading to the bathroom to finger myself in semi-private. Only 20 minutes left until the afternoon break. Could I make it? What if Garrett was in their room? She couldn't be enticing me like this if she had no intention of letting it play out. Or could she? Another dominant-submissive head game like getting me so freakin' aroused and then withholding sex just to prove the power she had over me. She really had a way to turn me on like no one else. She made it seem simple. I am not really that easy. Or so I tell myself. She dropped her pen and turned toward me to pick it up. She winked at me as she grabbed it. She knew exactly what she was doing – and I fell for it hook, line, and sinker.

Finally, it was time for the break. The speakers stopped talking, the audience gave an appropriate round of applause and I left the room, waiting very impatiently for Paula to exit. She walked out with Graciela Hernandez and politely excused herself to approach me.

"Do you have a minute to talk?" she asked.

"Yes, ma'am." I was louder than I meant to be.

"Follow me." We walked toward the lobby and got on an elevator ascending the hotel. She pushed the button for floor fourteen. We turned left out of the elevator and I followed her to room 1412. She opened the door with her key card, I entered and she slammed the door unintentionally behind herself. Before I could say a thing, she pushed me up against the wall and kissed me. My tongue felt like a beached whale devoid of moisture, but I didn't care. I was beyond horny and wanted to be with her any way possible. I was a little afraid to be too aggressive but it seemed like the situation and lack of time called for it. I fondled her breasts and tried to remove her dress at the same time. She reached between my legs searching for my dripping hole and entered me with two fingers at once. I pulled her toward the bed but tripped on something on the floor. I fell, Paula entangled with me. Ouch. That hurt, but I would assess my injury later. I hiked my skirt up around my waist and pushed my panties toward my ankles. I wanted my shoes off but couldn't afford to use my time for that. We kissed for a moment and she moved toward Pam. Her fingers re-entered me and she kissed my clit. First it was a gentle kiss just to have a soft sensation in my most sensitive area. I was moaning and lost the ability to think clearly. I wanted to have an orgasm so badly.

"What's wrong, baby?" she stopped to ask me.

"Nothing. Don't stop." I urged her.

"I don't understand. Did you ask me to please continue what I was doing?"

I did not want to play a game. I was desperate to cum. But I knew, particularly in this situation, and perhaps in all situations, she had the power and I did not.

"Yes, ma'am. I am so sorry. You make me feel so horny. I really want to have an orgasm. Will you please allow me to?"

"Yes, of course, I will. After you make me cum."

I was so close. I need to make her cum instead. If I do it quickly, there will be time for my orgasm as well.

"Yes, mistress. Tell me how I can please you."

She rolls over. She is on the floor next to me. I push my panties off to have more freedom of movement and I remove her thong as well. She is wearing a sexy peach push-up bra and her heels and nothing else. I am a wrinkled and disheveled mess.

"I want you to suck your thumb and then put it in my ass. Your nails are short, right? Then put your tongue inside Sawyer. Reach your index finger around to my clit and massage it until I explode. Can you do that, little sub?"

"Yes, ma'am."

Making my thumb wet was more difficult than I expected because of the dryness in my mouth. I coerced my saliva glands to produce anything resembling liquid to moisten my thumb. It might be easier to put my thumb in my own pussy to lubricate it, but I was afraid to make such a bold move as it might be misinterpreted that I was trying to satisfy myself. I pushed my barely-damp thumb into her asshole. She moaned in the sexiest way. I would give up my own orgasm to hear that sound again. I prided myself on my altruism in this moment and experienced profound pleasure in attempting to provide her with the best orgasm ever. My beached-whale tongue went in and out of Sawyer, accessing more juice each time. I discovered that I could make my tongue really hard, almost penis-like or soft and mushy like a pile of mashed potatoes. Clearly this called for a hard tongue. I fucked her with my tongue and her hips rode the wave while her clit craved my attention. I reached my fingers to her clit. It was hard yet elusive, but I had a mission to complete. My thumb and finger rocked in unison fucking her gorgeous ass while rubbing her clit and my tongue did its job in between the two. She moaned, arched her back and shuddered. My job was done.

As her breath slowly returned to normal, she said, "Catherine, you are beyond spectacular. There is no one like you."

I smiled. "You made me this way. There is no one like us."

My clit was still throbbing through the excitement of pleasing my mistress and being praised for my skills. I wondered selfishly if there was time for my orgasm.

Click! There was a key in the door. It was pushed open and the maid was standing there with the cart of clean linens. We are partially clothed on the floor. We forgot to put the other lock on the door. She immediately noticed her mistake and left without saying a word.

"Holy shit!" Paula exclaimed. I barely had time to react. The whole thing happened so fast. I was on the floor between her legs. There was no doubt what was happening.

"She must see things all of the time." I said, trying to mitigate the fear, even though I was just as freaked out. We both knew that it could have just as easily been Garrett. The maid's intrusion was a quick way to obliterate my horniness.

I started to get up, straighten my skirt and find my panties.

"Just lock the door. I still want you to cum."

"Are you sure? That sort of dried me up."

"I think I can change that in a minute." She was right. She could change that in a second. I locked the door as instructed and returned to Paula.

She stood up in her heels and bra and motioned toward the bed. I joined her there.

"Lie on your back and lift up your skirt," she advised.

I did as she suggested. She went to the bathroom, turned on the water and then returned to the bed.

"Catherine, you trust me, right?"

"Of course, ma'am." What was she thinking?

"I just washed my pen. I want to put it inside of you. It's so small you will barely feel it. I just want it to smell like you. Whenever I use it, I will know where it has been. Whenever you see it, you will know that I fucked you with it. Is that ok?"

I knew that in reality she didn't have to ask permission. Since it was clean, I had no objection. I liked that she would have something to remind her of me.

"Yes, please fuck me with your pen."

"Catherine, you are so hot."

"Yes, ma'am."

She was right that I barely felt it. She pushed it in and out a few times, then put it aside so that my unique scent would dry all over it. She then put her two fingers inside of me and fucked me roughly with them.

"Do you like that better, Catherine? Can you feel my two fingers?"

"Yes, mistress. Fuck me harder."

"Catherine, we don't have a lot of time. Can you cum in one minute?"

"Yes."

"Can you cum in thirty seconds?"

"Probably."

"I'm giving you thirty seconds."

She put her lips on my clit and sucked it into her mouth. I knew I could cum if she would put one finger or thumb into my asshole. I was craving a good ass-fucking. I knew that would increase both the intensity and the speed of my orgasm, but she wasn't doing it and I couldn't ask. I needed to focus on my clit and the fact that I was submissive and couldn't always get what I wanted. The desire of wanting something – anything – in my ass and not getting it was enough to make me cum. I had become the perfect submissive because I really thrived psychologically and sexually on not getting what I wanted when I wanted it. Her tongue flicked my clit, my asshole remained empty and I resisted the urge to push her face deeper into my crotch as I writhed in orgasm. It happened so quickly that I didn't have to experience my usual climb up the cliff and free fall into the sea of orgasm below.

Paula moved to put her lips on mine so I could taste myself. It was a sweet satisfying mixture of her scent and mine that I loved having in my mouth. I wish I never had to wash my face or brush my teeth, so I could relish this flavor for eternity.

"I love you when we're together," I said it first.

"Same here. I love how you make me feel. I love the closeness we have, the trust we've built, and you're pretty good in the sack, too."

That was a great compliment coming from Paula. She made me feel pretty special, too. I hesitated to look at the clock knowing that our twenty-minute break was up.

"Thank you for the fun break. What time is it?"

"Ugh, it's 2:40."

"I think the break ended at 2:30. I'll get cleaned up and out of here."

She had more clothes to put back on than I did. I went to the bathroom and attempted to tidy my appearance. I had to be careful not to leave any evidence of my visit, particularly since Garrett would be returning at some point. I didn't remove any jewelry or clothes except my panties and I certainly wouldn't leave the room without them.

I returned to the bedroom to see Paula looking perfect. How does she do that? Every hair in place, no makeup smudged, even her dress was wrinkle-free. She smoothed out the bedspread to not betray knowledge of the activities that occurred there.

"Come here, Catherine." I loved how she said my name. It was demanding, intimate, sexy.

"Yes, ma'am," I said it playfully this time. I enveloped her in my arms, cradling her from all of the pain she had in her life, being her protector for an instant. I felt powerful in my ability to provide her safety within these walls. I knew it would be over in mere minutes. Our lives would return to the chaos that they were. Our double identities would resume. But for a brief time that afternoon, I was hers and she was mine and nothing else mattered.

She pulled away first. "Back to reality." She read my mind. What an amazing half hour we shared. It contained all of the intimacy, intensity, passion and love I had ever known in my life. I wonder if I would ever be the same.

I picked up my purse, she put her newly-scented pen in her purse and we left room 1412. We walked silently to the elevator. I wondered if we should not enter it together or if I should take the stairs to another floor to prevent suspicion, but neither of us spoke of it. Something felt very different but I couldn't put my finger on it. I felt calm, almost at ease. Then I remembered that we had been caught by the maid. I didn't think anything would come of that. It was quite jarring honestly. She couldn't report it. What would she say? She had no way of knowing if we belonged in that room together anyway. I suppose she could talk about it with friends or colleagues when those conversations came up. What was the strangest thing you saw or found while cleaning rooms? Drugs? Weapons? Sex toys? People fucking? It was part of her job. I didn't have the energy to worry about that. I pushed it out of my mind almost as quickly as it entered. I was getting good at pretending things didn't happen when they didn't benefit me psychologically.

When we left the elevator, I walked toward the lobby. We didn't need to return to the conference together. I went to the café and looked around. I think there were coffee and snacks outside the conference room, so it didn't make sense to spend money here. I took my time perusing their food, then went to the bathroom to spend a few more minutes, then sauntered back to the conference area. There were granola bars, fresh fruit, brownies and cookies, coffee, water and soda. I acquired a small plate and placed a brownie and some strawberries on it. I put a granola bar in my purse for later. I stood in the corner alone and munched on my snacks. It is interesting how hungry I get from a little mid-afternoon roll in the hay. After feeling quite full after lunch, I felt famished two hours later after a cathartic orgasm. I thought about having some coffee to stave off the inevitable exhaustion I will feel once I sit down and my body realizes it is no longer in fight or flight mode. I'm not sure I can manage going into the current session if I don't have the energy to stay awake. I check the agenda and see the topic is legislative and regulatory updates – no chance that will be exciting enough to keep me entertained.

I decide to look around for Duncan and see if he needs any help. I walked down the hallway away from the lobby. I didn't see Duncan. I visited the CLE table and see how that is going this year. There are a few employees there, arranging and rearranging forms and folders. They hadn't seen Duncan. I returned to the snack area and sat down. I pulled the newspaper out of my purse. There was an advice columnist I liked to read. She gave witty responses to all of the conundrums her readers faced. Today's question was about having an affair. I wasn't convinced that I could objectively look at it. The person who wrote in said that she wasn't hurting anyone by having an affair because her husband didn't know about it. She wondered if she should confess when the affair was over. The response was neither polite nor clever. The columnist indicated that the writer was a selfish horrible person and should take a look at herself to determine why she embarked on an affair if her marriage was fine as she claimed it was. It was harsh and probably true. I didn't want to look inward enough to have this be related to me at all. I started to feel withdrawn and depressed. Why did I read the paper? I had been feeling the post-orgasm contentment, not only physically but psychologically and emotionally. Now I feel like a piece of shit. There are many opportunities for me to feel bad about myself, I don't need the advice columnist adding to that. I thought about my life, my marriage, my family, my woman on the side. Was I really hurting my marriage if I wasn't spending time away from my family to have this other relationship? I wasn't actively loving Paula or withdrawing from my emotional bank for her? I was merely showering her with temporary love and affection. Was having a sexual relationship with someone else detrimental to my relationship with Drew? I don't think so. In fact, sometimes being aroused by her led to greater intimacy between him and me. He didn't need to know that he wasn't the catalyst for everything we did between the sheets, particularly if the outcome was the same. I'm certain lots of people – of both genders – become excited by a plethora of stimuli often unrelated to their significant other. I'm not going to let any of this bother me anymore. I can justify doing whatever I want. What Drew doesn't know won't hurt him. I feel certain about that. He will never know about Paula because I will never tell him and I will never get caught.

"I heard you were looking for me. Are you ok?" Duncan appeared out of nowhere and was likely confused by my expression.

"Oh, yeah. I was just thinking about something I read. Not a big deal. I was wondering if you needed any help. I wasn't sure I wanted to hear about regulations this afternoon and I wanted to justify my existence at the conference."

"We're pretty good now. You can leave if you want. Why don't you go home and hang out with the twins? I'll see you here in the morning." Duncan wasn't my boss, but I guess I could leave especially if he suggested it. I really wanted to say goodbye to Paula. I shouldn't leave in the middle of the session, even if I wasn't in there. However, being at home sounded good. I think I should go home. I was feeling worn out because of the afternoon activities – both sexual and mental.

"Sounds great. Thanks. I'll see you tomorrow." I picked up my bag, threw out the newspaper and left the hotel. I drove home in 15 minutes, picked up the boys from school and put a roast in the oven. I turned on the tv and sat on the couch. Moments later Drew called out "Hello! Anyone home?"

"Yes, I'm in the living room," I said.

"What's the smell?" he asked.

"There's a roast in the oven. It's only been in there for – what time is it?"

"Almost six o'clock."

"What?! Oh my god, I fell asleep. Where are the boys?"

"I think they are in their room. Exhausting day at the conference?"

"I guess more than I thought. Let me finish up dinner." I don't know the last time I took a nap alone, years maybe? It's something I frequently fantasize about, but it just doesn't happen. I'm glad the boys played nicely – there could have been disastrous results if they were left unattended.

After dinner and dishes, I told Drew that I was still feeling tired and I went to bed. He didn't question me. It hadn't been that long since our miscarriage so he was still a little watchful over me. I would use that to my advantage tonight.

The next day I slept in a little and got to the conference after the morning session had started. Only Paula would be looking for me. I saw her at the mid-morning break.

"Well, there you are," she said.

"Yes, I slept in a little."

"Did you leave early yesterday?"

"Yes, Duncan told me to go home. I was feeling really tired in the afternoon, so I decided to do it."

"Were you alone?"

"What do you mean? When I left here, I was alone. Then I picked up my sons from school and took them home."

"I noticed Colby wasn't around after the conference."

"Are you serious? Do you think I'm interested in him? Haven't we been through this before? I don't like him. I like you. Only you. Why don't you believe me? Is this because of G.I. Joan?"

"Shhh! We aren't talking about her."

"The only time you get paranoid and jealous is when you think about what she did to you. I am not her!" I was unintentionally getting louder. There were too many people around for me to behave this way.

We walked down the hall toward the restaurant to continue our conversation. I didn't like how my morning was starting. It was tiring having to convince my mistress that I was faithful to her. It was insanity. How could she be so powerful yet insecure? Are they opposite sides of the same coin?

"What is this about?"

"Nothing," she said. She suddenly looked small and vulnerable yet alluring. I felt like a ball of contradictions myself. I want to comfort her and shake sense into her. She was infuriating.

She continued, "you know being with you is a huge risk for me. I have the best job that I've ever had. I can't be caught with you."

"Yes, I know. It is risky for me too. I have a family. We aren't going to get caught. We are very careful. Are you worried about the cleaning lady yesterday?"

"No, I hadn't even thought about her again honestly. That was scary though," she giggled.

"What then?"

"I really feel irrational sometimes. When you aren't where I expect you to be. My imagination goes sort of crazy. I think you are with someone else. Maybe someone who can give you something I can't. Like a young guy."

"I don't want a young guy. I have a guy already. I don't need another one. Haven't I told you that before? I don't have time or energy for anyone but you. I'm happy with you and the limited time we have together. Please believe me. I'm not Joan. I'm not going to hurt you. I don't want to stop seeing you. I have way too much fun being naughty with you – the way only we can be."

"Catherine. I believe you. I do."

"Then act like it." I have never been stern with her before. I didn't feel that good about saying it, but it was tedious having to reassure her so often.

"I'm going to spank your ass for talking to me with that tone," she responded.

"I'm happy my old mistress is back. Do what you will with my ass, you know I will enjoy it anyway."

"You can bet on it if Garrett leaves the room today. I think he's doing some work in there. His plan was to be there all day."

"Oh no. Really? No fun time for us?" I was genuinely disappointed. Nothing would remind her how much I am committed to her than a bit of sex to prove it. I am happy to be putty in her hands to be molded to be her perfect submissive.

"Not today, sexy Catherine. You will have to wait until tomorrow."

"Delayed gratification, my favorite," I said without much irony.

"What choice do we have? Maybe I can send him out to do something?"

"Why don't we rent another room?"

"Interesting idea, naughty girl. Did you bring cash? We can't use a credit card."

"So I really didn't think that plan through. I guess I'll wait until tomorrow. Don't play with your pen in front of me or I won't be able to wait."

"Did you like my suggestive motions yesterday during the conference?"

"Like them? Not really. You are lucky I didn't jump your bones during the talk about mine fatality investigations. That would have been scandalous!"

"You are a funny lady. I'm glad I can still make you horny without even saying a word."

"Your gestures say thousands of words. You should be more discreet though. You talk about risky behavior while you are pantomiming fucking with your pen."

"No one was watching me but you. I knew where everyone's eyes were. Did you notice the one inspector with the ridiculously low-cut blouse? That is what they were looking at, not me."

"Oh no. Is today the session on Sexual Harassment? You know what happened last time, right? During one of the briefings on Sexual Harassment, participants were asked to write questions on pieces of paper so they could be confidentially asked to the presenter. She was supposed to answer the questions. One of the judges or law clerks wrote 'please tell the judges to stop looking at my boobs when talking to me.' The speaker gave it to me at the end of the session. Looks like we'll have an EEO complaint on our hands if everyone was staring at the speaker's breasts rather than your lewd actions!"

"I don't think you told me that. How awful. Some of the male judges are a little old-school and expect women to be subservient to some degree. They, of course, don't get away with that with me or Graciela. Maybe we have to do a better job of protecting the young attorneys?"

"Or maybe the old judges need to behave appropriately?" I suggested.

"I think we won't have a lot of control over this crop, but many are preparing to retire. I think the next generation will be different."

"Unless we've allowed a culture to exist that doesn't have ramifications for poor behavior? Have we done that?"

"I don't know. I'll talk with the women judges separately to hear their opinions and get back to you."

"Ok. I'm not sure what I can do about it, but it would be good to be aware. Another secret mission for us!"

"I'd like to be undercover more often with you," Paula had a way with words.

"Same here. But back to the conference for us now." I hated bringing us back to reality, but I also didn't want a repeat of yesterday when we returned very late together. Once again, I went to the restroom while Paula returned to the conference meeting room alone. That was definitely the safest approach to take.

Paula ate with the other judges for lunch. I wandered around the same courtyard as the day before. This time I found a small Peruvian restaurant. It was a rotisserie chicken and yucca, cash-only type of place. The food was fabulous. I spent the hour wishing I was in Paula's room instead of enjoying the delicious chicken. I didn't read the newspaper during my lunch hour after too much time spent mentally debating the rationale of my illicit affair the day before because of the advice columnist. I didn't need that kind of negativity or overthinking occurring again, especially not when Paula was in town. I beat myself up enough when she's gone. I don't actually think that I'd stop seeing her, but I wonder why I need her in my life. I honestly don't think I'm missing anything with Drew. It's just the excitement of having her. And, I guess she is a little more creative sexually. I wasn't unhappy before, but I am more fulfilled now. If we ever stopped seeing each other, I would never forget her. We've been through too much. She's taught me too much. I like how she smells. I like her crooked mischievous smile. I even like when she tests me or challenges me to experience things I never would have known about. I daydreamed about some of my favorite scenarios – both in person and on the phone. I wish her husband hadn't come with her. We could be making new memories instead of me reliving old ones alone in a Peruvian chicken place.

I finished my food, threw out the chicken bones and paper plate, placed the tray near the trash can and meandered back into the pretty courtyard. I walked around the block before returning to the hotel. One of the little shops I saw was a lingerie shop. I wondered if it had sex toys and porn videos inside. I have never been interested in porn videos, it just seemed like those things were sold in tandem. I should have walked inside to see what was there, but it could wait for another day. There was one more day of the conference. Maybe Paula could go with me tomorrow? That would be fun. We have talked about what we would buy if we ever went to a sex toy shop or party together but I never thought we'd actually do it. I have a new goal and I can't wait to tell her. When I saw her again, she was talking to other people and I knew it would be difficult to get her attention so I decided I would wait until the afternoon break. I would not take risks or engage in suspicious behavior. We cannot get caught. That is one reason I don't complain when she has to have lunch with other colleagues. I don't want to spend much time in public with her. It is likely that onlookers would know my every thought. I would unintentionally undress her with my eyes. I'd rather be alone with her and purposely undress her with my hands.

When the afternoon break began, she found me through the crowd and inquired how my lunch was and who I spent the hour with.

I told her that I was alone and ate at the Peruvian chicken place.

"Is that it? You look like a cat that ate a canary."

My expression gave me away yet again. "Well, I did see a little boutique that had lingerie."

"And? Did you go in there to buy some?"

"No, I think it might also have vibrators and other toys!"

"What do you mean 'you think'?"

"Well, I didn't go inside. I thought maybe we could go together tomorrow."

"What a naughty idea. I'll award you some good girl points for that."

"Is Garrett still in your room?"

"I'm afraid so. He texted me during the session and said that he has a lot of work to do."

"What about tomorrow?"

"I don't know yet. You are very anxious, Catherine. I think I like that."

"You make me crazy! I really want to be with you."

"Be patient, sexy. Didn't you have enough of me yesterday?"

"I will never have enough of you, ma'am."

"It makes me very happy to hear you say that. I'll see if I can get him out of the room tomorrow. The reality is that I don't have a lot of control over him or his work."

"You just have control over me."

"That's the way I like it."

"I hate being this close to you and not being able to touch you or kiss you."

"I agree – it's difficult. Try to control yourself. We'll fuck soon. I promise."

"Promises, promises. I'll see what I can do in terms of controlling myself."

"Good girl."

Those are two of my favorite words that come out of her mouth. Even though it sounded condescending, it's very sexy as well.

I spent the afternoon controlling myself. It wasn't something that I enjoyed. I considered having sex with Drew that night, but it might be odd on a Wednesday night. I controlled myself a little longer. I was certain Paula would figure out a way for us to be alone on Thursday, the last day of the conference. I wore a dress for easy removal, a thong for easy access and a slightly tight bra for all day arousal. Not that I needed that. I had been thinking about her and being alone with her for more time than I had been with her on this trip. I went to the hotel's café early in the morning just in case she would stop by. We usually didn't leave anything to chance. We planned meticulously. But Garrett's presence threw a wrench into our whole week together. I'm not one for praying, but I heartily wished that he would have someplace to go and their room would be empty. Then we could go there and remember to employ the security lock to prevent intrusions! Lascivious behavior would ensue. As I planned our fun lunch time hanky-panky, Paula snuck up behind me. I jumped with surprise.

"What are you so focused on?" she asked.

"I was daydreaming about having a private lunch with you."

"That explains the look on your face."

"Another poker face, huh?" I really had to work on that.

"I'm glad that you can't hide anything from me."

I wanted to say that she should trust me more, but it didn't sound like a good idea to start our day with a statement like that. Instead I looked her over like a hungry dog looking at its next meal.

"You look stunning. Although, you'd look better without that nice suit on. I can't wait to rip your clothes off."

"Down girl, it's not looking good for us today either."

I felt like I was going to cry. I have been waiting to be with her. She promised she would make it work. I wanted to be with her and feel her skin next to mine. I wanted to kiss her cinnamon lips. I even wanted her to find a reason to spank my ass. I could think of a million tiny infractions that could result in punishment. I felt a heady desperation that was examining all of the possibilities. Could I find a bank, withdraw cash that wouldn't be noticeable to Drew so I could get us a room and spend our lunch hour together? Was that too risky? I feel like Paula would discourage it.

"Ma'am..."

"Catherine, please don't cry. I want to be with you too. I just don't think it's going to work today."

"What if I get another room using cash? You are leaving tomorrow."

"Do not withdraw cash and get another room. That is not a good choice.

We can have phone sex as soon as I get home. This isn't the end of us, it's just an unfortunate bump in the road."

"I don't know when we'll be together again. The next conference isn't for two years! I don't have another reason to go to Pittsburgh. Are you coming back here for the dentist or anything? I feel like a baby, but I don't want you to go without us being together again."

"It's ok. Remember there is no one like us. No one naughty like us."

That wasn't really consoling me. "Can you get some breakfast with me now?"

"Let's get something from the café."

I felt like an infant, crushed because I couldn't have what I wanted. I wanted to pout, have a tantrum, make Garrett go somewhere – anywhere – to get out of their room. Why was this bothering me so much? Clearly, he infringed on our time together. But my reaction didn't seem rational. I was desperate for her. I had to temper my feelings and gain some control. I didn't like her power over me when she seemed so calm. I guess it didn't make sense for us both to be irrational. Then we would get caught. I closed my eyes and took a deep breath. I imagined meditating like I did in a training class we hosted a few years ago. I breathed in deeply and thought of the teal of the Caribbean. Then I breathed out completely and let the stress leave my body. I repeated these deep breaths until I felt revitalized.

Paula brought me a latte and a blueberry scone. She really is in tune with what I need. Or maybe I give her too much credit. Either way I felt calmer, the food was good and I could still sit with my favorite woman for a little while. We made small talk. I heard about Kenickie's latest adventure, the progress on the ALJ union, her travel plans for the summer. We conversed like two friends might. It was nice to hear her voice, share her excitement and just talk about regular things. Too often our conversations were just sex talk, which was fun, but I did like to hear more about her life, her thoughts and opinions. Sometimes I wasn't sure she wanted to hear mine.

The day ended with no sex between Paula and me. She hugged me goodbye at the end of the conference and promised to call soon to chat. There were people around so I think those were code words for something else. It was safe, not risky. That night I went home and tried to act normal again. I engaged with the twins, made dinner for the family and even suggested a game of Yahtzee afterward. I loved playing the game when I was growing up and wanted to instill the love of board games and card games in the boys. I felt successful so far. It did seem that they needed constant interaction. No downtime or boredom for kids nowadays.

The remainder of the summer sailed by until August. In late summer, when things usually quiet down in my life and around the globe, another mining disaster occurred. On August 5, there was a collapse in a mine in Chile. This did not impact my office directly, but we offered guidance and blueprints of safety schematics. Many other U.S. government agencies, most notably NASA, were engaged in the rescue efforts. When two parts of the San Jose copper and gold mine shaft collapsed in Copiapó in northern Chile, there were two sets of miners ascending the mine. One group was able to escape, but thirty-three miners were trapped three miles from the entrance to the mine. There was a rescue chamber located 2300 feet under the surface of the earth. Rescue efforts were slow and produced no results for days. Rescuers attempted to drill large boreholes, but the drills did not reach the miners. Finally, on August 22, a hole was made in the ramp near the shelter where the men were huddled. The trapped miners attached a note to the drill indicating that all thirty-three of them were alive and living in the shelter. The rescuers were shocked when they learned that all of the missing men had made it to shelter. The people of Chile and the world rejoiced, but their jubilation was short-lived as their ability to bore a hole through the ground to reach the miners was hampered by the depth. Literally the whole world watched as this drama unfolded. Chilean officials worked to create a drill bit that was strong enough to pass through the rock to reach the miners. They were able to send notes, videos and food, but getting the miners out was a nearly insurmountable challenge. Summer turned to autumn and citizens of the world watched with rapt attention. After sixty-nine days, they were freed, raised one at a time from the depths of the mine. All were in remarkably good shape except losing weight and gaining beards.

Everyone in the mining community was thrilled at the positive outcome. While I'm certain their investigation would take years to determine the cause, there was a collective sigh of relief that there were no deaths or serious injuries. During all of this drama, Drew and I started to talk about trying to get pregnant again. It had been six months since the miscarriage. I was ready to try again. I made an appointment with Dr. M. to ensure I was healthy enough. It didn't appear there were any lingering complications from the miscarriage. I felt fine physically and emotionally. I had finished grieving. Sex with Drew was enjoyable, and not painful, nor were there any other issues. We decided we would start after the new year. That way we could enjoy the holidays without having pregnancy stress. I was a little worried about the space between the kids. The boys are eight and in third grade. Of course, we'd be starting all over with diapers, sleepless nights, and baby-proofing the house. But a woman's ability to have children is limited time-wise so we thought we'd give it another try. If it didn't work, we could always adopt. Both of us were willing to adopt. That at least would allow us to choose the gender of our baby. But for now, we'd spend 2011, and potentially 2012, trying to make our own.

2011

The year started with a plan to start having sex on day ten of my cycle again. We decided that we would only try that for three or four months before moving to day eleven. I didn't want to waste six months on day ten. By the time March arrived, nothing had changed. My period came every month on the 28-30 day of my cycle. We discussed changing to day eleven. That was when I got pregnant the year before. I felt that day eleven was going to be lucky for us. I remembered that the day we got pregnant was the day I was horny because of a failed phone sex attempt with Paula, then Drew came home with a headache. I did not want to repeat that. I hoped day eleven did not correspond with a phone sex day. Occasionally Paula and I would start having a very naughty conversation at work, I could close my door and masturbate with her guiding me. Once in a while, she would tell me to go to the private bathroom on our office floor. It was there mostly for important guests. But I used it to follow her directions. She might tell me to go in there and finger myself or take my panties off for the remainder of the day and sit in the wetness she created. We still had phone sex on my days off when I could use a vibrator and have an orgasm into her ear. She loved instructing me how to make myself cum. It was an erotic experience for us both.

In April, Edwin and Duncan came to my office with information that two of our judges decided they were going to retire at the end of the month. One had already been scheduled for a June retirement. This was unprecedented! We had to hire three new judges very quickly. The hiring process in the government was not fast. We already had a job announcement ready and we had approval to hire. Those were two big hurdles. It would take 4-6 weeks to advertise the positions, get a list of eligible candidates and interview. It would take several more weeks to get them cleared through security. Some of these steps could go quicker if we hired a judge with a clearance or one in an agency with which we had security clearance reciprocity.

I don't know why Duncan and Edwin thought of me as the go-to person for rectifying all calamities. Of course, I could handle most anything they threw my way. I guess competence has its benefits. After we discussed how to fill the soon-to-be vacant positions, we turned to the issue of training the new judges. Usually we just assigned them to their new courts and it was handled in-house at their new courts. Since there could be three judges starting at once, it made sense to train them together at headquarters. That meant we would have to ask a few experienced judges to come to D.C. to lead the training efforts. The wicked wheels in my mind were already turning to see how this situation was going to benefit me. I offered to help Duncan set up the training modules and coordinate with the judges which topics should be covered based on their familiarity or expertise with those subjects. With three more seasoned judges retiring, Paula was one of two with the most seniority of our remaining judges. She would have to conduct part of the training. Her areas of competence focused on the impact of mining on the environment. This includes ensuring water and air quality and prevention of the introduction of toxic substances like chemicals and hazardous materials into the areas surrounding mines. She has prepared testimony for Edwin when he has testified before Congress on environmental issues as they pertain to the mining industry. If we hire experienced judges, we will not have to train them on the Administrative Procedures Act or judicial conduct and ethics. We can instead target material related just to federal mining laws. I strenuously recommended that we choose qualified candidates who are already administrative law judges. Learning the new area of the law is much easier than learning to be a judge in addition to learning the new area of the law. Edwin agrees with my approach particularly because our time to get these new people in place is limited if we want to mitigate the impact on our proceedings.

Even though it is too early to go into detail, I decide to email Paula with the news that it's likely we will have our annual rendezvous.

Good afternoon, Judge Marlon:
I hope you are well. I have some interesting news if you have time to talk.
Catherine

Catherine:

It is so nice to hear from you. I'm sorry but I have a decision deadline tomorrow and I must complete this case. It is high profile and precedent-setting. I will contact you as soon as it is finished.

I hope you have good news to share.

Judge Marlon

I'm disappointed that I can't tell her about her impending visit yet. Maybe more details will be fleshed out before I talk to her. That would be advantageous. After all of these years of our pseudo-togetherness, I still get turned on by seeing her signature line on her emails. "Judge Marlon." Oh, what Judge Marlon does to me. I hope these new people get hired before I get pregnant. That would really put a damper on my summer activities with Paula. I feel really conflicted when I think about my future plans for my family and my intense desire to be with my Mistress. I know I can manage them both for a while longer. Sure, I might have to take a break when I'm pregnant. I am certain it would be very bad karma to be with her while pregnant with Drew's baby. I won't risk that. It might be strange to see her soon after the potential baby was born, particularly if I was still breastfeeding. I think she would enjoy sucking milk out of my tits though and I would enjoy the intimacy of that, but breast milk is liquid gold. I would feel guilty if I skimmed milk from my baby's cache to share with someone else. Maybe I do have a touch of morality? So perhaps allowing Paula to steal milk from my baby was off-limits. That could mean nearly two years without her. I can't be with her when I'm pregnant or breastfeeding. What was I thinking having another baby? I'll have to give up an important part of my life to do that. Didn't I think this through before? I'm disappointed with myself. Everything happens for a reason. If I get pregnant, I have to take a break. I must have a really honest conversation with her when she comes in two months. Thinking we can hire three judges in two months is optimistic, but today I'm attempting optimism.

I spent two days working on an agenda of topics for the training. We had some modules that had been developed in the past that needed modernizing. They were quite useful. No one likes to reinvent the wheel. In the meantime, we advertised our positions using a vacancy announcement. The announcement would be open for ten days and was for status candidates only, meaning the applicants had to be current government employees. That should limit the number of eligible candidates, allowing us to evaluate the resumes quicker, select a group to interview, and offer positions. Then we only had to wait for the background investigations to be completed.

Finally, Paula wrote back.

Catherine,
I am sorry I was unable to contact you sooner. The intricacies of my case required a lot more research than my law clerk or I anticipated. We actually finished it a day after our deadline to meet our case completion goal. Are you available to talk this afternoon? I am anxious to hear your news.
Judge Marlon

Judge Marlon:
How wonderful to hear from you. I am available to talk whenever you can. I think you have my office phone number.
Yours truly,
Catherine

I waited anxiously and, moments later, she called. I hadn't spoken to her for about two weeks, yet it seemed like forever. I felt like a kid waiting for Christmas morning when I knew she would call. I should be too old for feeling this level of anticipation. I had a surge of teenage hormones when I heard her voice.

"Catherine? How are you?"

"I'm great. Guess what?"

"Do we have to play a guessing game?"

"I'm so sorry, ma'am. I don't want you to guess anything. I have some news that I think you will enjoy. But, as with most of our conversations, it has to be confidential at this time."

"Certainly. Our own permanent Vegas Rule. You know you don't have to tell me that every time there are secrets from headquarters."

"I know I don't. Somehow it comforts me to request secrecy. I know I can trust you with anything. I already trust you more than anyone else in my life." I realized as I said it that it was true. I trusted her more than I trusted Drew or even Bonnie, my long-time best friend. Because of the nature of the intimacy we shared, I had to trust her more. I felt a little sad about the truth, but it is what it is. Don't get hung up on the details, I told myself. Compartmentalize! It's the only way to survive an affair.

"Go on, you're killing me with the suspense."

"You know that Judge Kowalski is planning to retire at the end of June? Judge Gelman and Judge Jackson announced they are retiring too. We have to hire three new judges!"

"I heard whispers that they were considering leaving. I can't believe they put in their paperwork without notifying the rest of the judge corp."

"I think they wanted to ensure it would be authorized before making an announcement. We have put out the advertisement to hire new judges. Edwin and Duncan asked me to help them arrange new ALJ training here in D.C. for all three new hires. We are going to have experienced judges come in to train! That means you will have a paid trip to D.C. this summer!"

"That is great news! Except... I do have a trip planned with Garrett this summer. He's having a big birthday."

"Way to put a damper on my excitement. We can plan the training around your trip. Do you have the itinerary already?"

"Yes, I can share it with you later. It's on my home computer. Please don't misunderstand, I'm very happy that I will be able to come there for a bonafide purpose. In fact, I will tell you about a new scenario I have dreamed up for us to act out. Well, of course, I won't disclose all of the details, but there are a few items I'll need for you to acquire."

"This is starting to sound more like the Mistress I adore. I can't wait to hear."

"Sounds good. I'll have to work out all of the specifics and then I'll get you a list of things to get. Let's have phone sex soon. Are you off this Friday?"

"No, next Friday."

"Let's plan on having a conversation that day. Will you have some time?"

"Yes, ma'am. I will make time for you. Speaking of time, did you hear what happened to Graciela Hernandez?"

"No. Is she ok?"

I knew she and Graciela were friends in addition to being colleagues. There was a time they were the only two female judges in our office.

"An attorney in one of her cases propositioned her."

"That is not an unusual occurrence."

"She gets propositioned a lot? Has she told you of other times it has happened?"

"No, not specifically. I mean it happens to me a lot."

"It does?" I asked incredulously.

"Sure. Sometimes the government attorneys flirt with me and sometimes the private ones do. Sometimes it's really overt and unprofessional and other times, it's a subtle suggestion. Either way I would never even get a drink with someone who appears in front of me. It smacks of impropriety and is borderline unethical."

"I had no idea that ever happened. Am I being naïve or do all of these people fall under your sexy spell?"

"I think they are trying to garner favors. They don't understand that I would not risk my career for any of them. If I was seen with an attorney who appeared in my courtroom, other people would find out. I would lose the appearance of impartiality. My whole professional life depends on my ability to be fair and credible."

"I agree. I just can't believe attorneys do that – and in court! How unprofessional. I feel a little jealous that men are hitting on you all day."

"It's not just the men," she admitted.

"What?! Why would women make that assumption? Are they just desperate for attention?" I was nearly seething at the idea that women were making passes at *my* woman.

"I don't pretend to understand human psychology. Why do people do what they do? I could spend all week trying to analyze the actions of these people. Frankly, I don't have time for it."

"Can these attorneys be reported?"

"I don't think that would help anything. They have to appear in front of me. Sometimes I see the same ones over and over. We aren't a huge subset of the law, you know. We get to know each other, make small talk and sometimes it goes too far."

"Are you saying you are complicit in this behavior?" Maybe my anger was misplaced?

"No, as I said before, I have to maintain my judicial demeanor. Seriously."

I am surprised that we never had this conversation before. I felt a bit dejected and unhappy about the turn in the conversation. I started it with happy news and now I was feeling distant, like I didn't even know who I was talking to. I was experiencing some kind of lack of understanding of object permanence. Maybe I thought when I wasn't with her, she just sat in a room and waited for me to reappear. But instead she was looking gorgeous sitting on the bench in her robe while men and women alike were trying to seduce her. Why would I assume that all people would display some type of professional behavior in a professional setting? It was a courtroom for chrissakes.

"If you say so."

"You sound like you don't believe me. Are you doubting me?"

"No, ma'am. What choice do I have anyway? I am here and you are there with the snakes in the courtroom."

"People are people. If they would flirt with me in a grocery store or on a running trail, they don't see the line that they are crossing in a work environment."

"Thanks for clarifying that. Do you see these attorneys in the grocery store or on a running trail?"

"Pittsburgh is smaller than you'd expect. So, occasionally I do see people from work in other places." I guess she thought that answer would pacify me. It did not.

Edwin knocked on my door and pushed his face between the crack of my door and the jamb. Even though he was almost old enough to be my father, he was still boyishly handsome. His wife was a lucky woman and she knew it.

"Edwin is here. I have to go. I'm not sure if I hope that we'll resume this conversation. Talk to you next week?"

"Yes, Catherine. Be a good girl and don't worry about me. I can take care of myself." Now I definitely was concerned.

"I'm sorry to interrupt your call. Duncan and I were talking about where to host the new judge training. Do you think we should do it on-site or just get a conference room at a hotel? The judges who travel here to execute the training will need to stay in one of the nearby places, so I bet they'd give us a discount on a small conference room. We don't need much space."

"I can make a few calls for you and see what kind of options there are. Clearly, free is the best choice and that would be hosting the training in our office. We would have to justify doing it elsewhere for the budget folks."

"Right. I'm glad I run everything by you. You always think outside the box at all of the options that I hadn't thought of."

"No worries, Edwin. That's what you pay me the big bucks for!" This is a common joke among feds. We don't get paid as much as our private sector counterparts. None of us gets paid the big bucks, yet we all continue to work for the government because we think our work for the American people is important. The reality is that I prefer the training is at our office in a conference room. That way there won't be lots of my colleagues hanging around the hotel at weird hours when I want to have private time with Paula. I can help sway Edwin's decision. I just have to find the perfect conference room. I will reserve a few different ones, even though it is probably two months early. It's better to be prepared ahead of time than attempt to find space at the last minute.

The next month flew by. My homelife was very stable. Drew and I had our usual sex on day eleven of my cycle, Paula and I engaged in one episode of phone sex which was not on day eleven and resulted in a fabulous orgasm. Bodie fell off the swing set and cut his leg in a way that required stitches. We all rushed to the hospital's emergency room. Our wait time was minimal and the doctor seemed quite competent. However, Drew and I had to hold Bodie down to allow the doctor to suture his leg. He was more scared than injured. It was an awful experience for all of us. Logan was worried about his brother. The bigger problem was Bodie couldn't play soccer or even take PE class. Keeping that kid still was a challenge.

In the meantime, we received sixty-four applications for our three vacancies. Edwin decided to interview eighteen candidates. I sat in on a few of the interviews since we preferred using interview panels to decrease the potential for unconscious bias in the selections. We had some really great options. Edwin cut the pool in half and decided to engage in a second round of interviews. He would then rank the remaining interviewees. Of the nine, six were women and three were men. All were willing to move if necessary. These vacancies gave us an opportunity to see where we should place the new judges. They could be at headquarters, Denver or Pittsburgh. The retiring judges were from different places, but it is possible that our needs have changed and we would need two in one location based on our current caseload or emerging trends. That is another analysis that I'll assign to someone to look into before we make decisions.

Day 28 of my cycle came, but my period did not. I wondered if I was pregnant. The timing would not be ideal. I'd like one more tryst with Paula before having a baby. But I may not have the choice. I debated what to tell her or if I could have sex with her if I was just barely pregnant. It started to seem like it wasn't a terrible idea. Her visit would be in the next month or so.

I've been waiting a year to see her again. I hated thinking that it might not happen. I thought of her cinnamon breath and her beautiful, yet mischievous smile. I imagined her giving me instructions on how to behave or what to wear and I felt my clit tingle. I had been anticipating her sharing vague details about what she was going to do to me. This magical thinking was getting me nowhere, except aroused with no outlet. I had to actively will my period to come. I needed a few more months of not being pregnant to enjoy her at least one more time. And if a pregnancy didn't happen for another year, she would be back again for next year's conference. Maybe I'm being greedy? I wouldn't sacrifice my family for her, but the thought of being with her and enjoying every touch, scent and magnificent orgasm with her made me second guess any plans I had to enlarge my family. My attention is being diverted from one of my priorities – my family. I must remember to keep Paula in her little box in my mind, heart and clit. Occasionally she escapes and affects every part of my life. She impacts how I do my job, what I do on my day off, and often she coaches me through climaxes with my husband. None of that was my plan. But sometimes the best laid plans do not pan out.

My period finally came at day 35. That was confusing my cycle a bit. I was grateful that I wasn't pregnant just yet. I hated being dishonest with Drew, acting like I was disappointed that I wasn't pregnant, but I really wanted to wait just a couple more months. I could probably "forget" the day eleven next month and that would buy me another month. He wouldn't remember if I didn't. I had to remind him each month when it was time to try. Then I would be home free until Paula's visit.

It was settled that the training would occur in the middle of July. Paula's trip for Garrett's birthday was in August thankfully. A week before the training, she emailed me.

Catherine:
Good afternoon. I have a list of things that I will need for the upcoming trip. Please let me know when you are available to discuss these items.
Judge Marlon

Judge Marlon:
I am looking forward to helping you acquire the materials you need. I am available after 2:00 p.m. today if that works for you.
Catherine

I knew that she did not mean training supplies, but rather things I should get for our private time together. She had alluded to a scenario she was plotting for us. I was both excited and worried for her call. I was excited that she has things planned for us, but worried about my ability to get what she wanted, keep it hidden and then get it to her room undiscovered.

At 2:15 p.m., my phone rang.

"Hello?" I answered. I should have identified myself, but I was pretty sure it would be her.

"Catherine?"

"Yes, ma'am, it's me."

"I will be arriving on Sunday night. Have you seen my travel arrangements?"

"No, but I selected the hotel and made sure that the training would be held in a different location. Since it is not a huge conference center like the conferences we hold every other year, I thought it would be best to not have headquarters' employees hanging around the hotel. I want people away from the hotel so we can have privacy. Sorry, I got side-tracked. When you do arrive?"

"You are a smart woman. You earn good girl points for ensuring our safety. My flight gets in at 7:00 p.m. at National Airport."

"When do I get to cash in my points? Maybe there's something I'd like to get with them."

"Maybe if you obtain everything I ask for, we will play a game of your choosing next week. Would you like that?"

"Yes, ma'am."

"We will have a tentative plan for 'Catherine Day' at the end of next week."

"You make me happy." Even though I knew the good girl points were meaningless, the idea of Catherine Day sounded fun. I could pick what we do for a change. Secretly, I knew my plans would never be as good as hers. I didn't have time to sit around and dream up things to do. Also, I liked the element of surprise that existed since I didn't know what she would do next. That was one of the best things about being with her. She always had great ideas that left us both feeling beyond satisfied. I was already feeling stressed about having to come up with ideas. I definitely had a sub mentality. I am not cut out for a role with power or authority. It is the one time in my life that I am not in control and I relish the loss of control. So maybe Catherine Day would be a disaster. I guess I'll have to purposely not earn that privilege.

"You make me happier." She was competitive. Maybe it was the military background or always trying to be the best to overcome her past, doing well in school, becoming a lawyer then a judge. There are some things I don't want to compete in and this is one of them. I'll let her statement go unanswered.

"What is your shopping list? Do I need paper?"

"I think you can remember. First, I'd like you to go to the store you mentioned near the last conference hotel and get a double dildo. It can be made out of silicon or jelly, bent or straight. I'd prefer one that vibrates but that could be harder to find. It should be at least twelve inches long. Do you know what I'm talking about? It is one that can penetrate us both at the same time, so it's for two people not two holes on one person. I can't wait to use that with you. It will be one intense session, hopefully resulting in simultaneous orgasms. Bring one of your husband's belts – do you think you can take one without his noticing? Canned whipped cream – the refrigerated kind. There are a few other things I want, but I think I can bring them. They are multi-purpose items so they won't cause suspicion."

I had a very vague idea of one thing she was planning and it sounded intriguing. I felt my breathing deepen just listening to her list. Then I felt the dampness in my panties. Thankfully, they had a cotton panel to absorb some of this moisture. If I were wearing a thong, it would have become a soupy mess. Just the anticipation of her visit was going to make me crazy. I was already losing focus regarding the other things I had to accomplish. How many more days until she gets here?

"I will call you early on Monday morning from the hotel lobby to get your room number. The training starts at nine. Are you going to go for the opening session? I know you aren't scheduled to train until later that day."

"Yes, I think on the first day I should be there all day. Maybe on subsequent days, I can go later. I think it's good for all of the judges who are trainers to demonstrate a united front to the new judges. That reminds me, can you send me the resumes or some biographical information on each of the new judges? I'd like to read up on their backgrounds beforehand." It was just like Paula, leaving nothing to chance. She wants to know who she's dealing with and what they already know so she can tailor her training to their specific needs. I wish all of our trainers were prepared similarly.

"Yes, of course, I'll send that to you after we hang up. What time should I come then - 7:00 a.m.?"

"Coming at 7:00 will give us about an hour and a half for scenario number one. I think that will work. I can't tell you how much I am looking forward to seeing you."

"Me too. Last time seems like a long time ago. Of course, it was rushed and brief since we didn't have much alone time. Hopefully we can make up for it this time." Then I remembered the maid interrupting us. I do not want a repeat of that. That was horrifying.

"We definitely can. We have five days with no spouses in the way!"

"Are there any other requests you'd like to make? I'm not sure if we'll talk again before Monday morning?"

"Do you have a cami or something like that? Maybe a lacy tank top?"

"Yes. I have a few."

"Hmmm. Can you wear one of those with no bra? I want to see your nipples through your blouse. I want to bite them and then know they are rubbing against your cami with no protection. That sounds so hot and maybe a little ouchy. Do that for me."

"Yes, ma'am." I realized by the end of her request it was no longer a question, but instead an order. It was an easy one to comply with.

"Anything else?" I didn't want our call to end and just hearing her make erotic plans for us was titillating.

"I like how we can use everyday items and turn them into something to enhance our sex play. Let's just see what is in the hotel room and we will improvise. I still have my special pen. I smell it every day just to see if I can get a whiff of you. I keep it away from the others in my desk. You remember my pen, right? I shoved it inside Pam so it would be covered with your juices."

"How could I forget? You taunted me with it during the conference, sort of like mentioning it now is making me very horny."

"Poor little sub, did I make your clit tingle?"

"Tingle? It's at a full-on throb! You make me ridiculously horny, just the slightest thing you say."

"You may thank me for that."

"Thank you, ma'am."

"You are welcome. I don't have to tell you not to fuck your husband because I made you horny, do I?"

"No, ma'am. I won't have sex with him. But maybe I'll rush home and use my old vibrator before he gets home. May I do that?"

"No, you may not. Thanks for asking. You will wait for me next Monday. I want your next orgasm to be with me."

While there was something erotic in withholding, making me wait seemed like cruel and unusual punishment. I know I had the choice to obey or not and then be truthful about my obedience or lack thereof. I wasn't really that good at being dishonest. I am more likely to tell the truth and let the cards fall as they will.

"Yes, ma'am. I understand completely."

"I will know if you cum without me and lie about it. So I hope you don't consider that to be an option."

"No, ma'am. I have never lied to you and I don't plan to." Even as I said it, I wondered if it was 100% true. I think it was. But we have been together for many years. It is possible that I fibbed about something.

"Good girl, Catherine. Continue to be good and you will be rewarded."

"Yes, Judge."

"Do you remember everything I asked you to acquire?"

"Yes, ma'am."

"Ok, then, I will see you on Monday morning."

"Yes, ma'am, you will. I can't wait."

"Me neither, Catherine, me neither. Goodbye."

"Goodbye." She hung up before I got both syllables out. I think she liked the dramatic ending to our phone calls. She demonstrated that she even had power over when we would stop talking. That is ok. It makes me want even more of her, like I can never get enough.

The next day was Friday, but it was the Friday that I had to work. I decided to take a long lunch break to go over to the lingerie shop to see if they also sold sex toys. I asked Bonnie if she wanted to join me. I might need moral support for this purchase. She was not interested. She often joined me on strange adventures, like the time I wanted to try to make a favorite Indian dish and we went all over Arlington County to find an Indian market to buy obscure ingredients. But today did not include a hunt for ingredients, it was a search for a specific sex toy. I raced across town, found a rare parking spot without a meter and entered the store. I felt slightly awkward, but knowing I was on a mission to please my lover made it palatable. I passed the lingerie and, as suspected, there was a large hidden area behind a beaded curtain that contained every sex toy imaginable. There was a girl who was about twenty-two years old who had twenty-two visible tattoos and piercings working there. Her name badge said "Hannah." She, of course, asked if I needed help. I told her that I was going to look around for a while and I would notify her if I required assistance.

I passed the bondage area with a variety of restraints, gags, blindfolds, collars, cuffs, and chastity devices including cock cages. Next was the S&M section containing whips, paddles, riding crops, floggers, and a variety of electric shockers. I had no idea such things existed. Admittedly, this store visit was making me incredibly horny. Was I really going to manage to withhold for yet another day? I think this was part of her plan and she was challenging me. Do I have this much control over my libido? At this point, I feel like masturbating in the office's parking garage since my car is currently in the street at the store and not in a very private location. I don't know if I could be that discreet if I needed to. I am almost afraid to walk another step through this pleasure palace. I could spend my whole paycheck here and still not try everything that looks remotely interesting. The next part was focused on anal play. Surprisingly, I had seen many of these things at the sex toy party. Although there were butt plugs that were the size of a bottle of water here. I'm not sure that would fit into anyone's ass. It seemed a bit naughty and definitely erotic. I imagined how it would feel, even with a ton of lube. Painsure or maybe just pain. I suppose some people enjoyed testing the limits of everything, even their assholes.

Finally, I was in the regular old vanilla dildo and vibrator section. There were hundreds, if not thousands of options. Every color, size, texture, and material imaginable. I perused the selection, knowing that I was not looking for a typical vibrator. I remembered the erotic humiliation of purchasing zucchinis from the farmer's market in Pittsburgh, followed by condoms at the drug store while Paula watched. She wanted me to carefully touch and select each vegetable. Both of us knowing that those zucchinis would be used to fuck me. It was part of the foreplay. This activity was designed for the same purpose. I see that clearly now. She wants me to be embarrassed buying a double dildo in public. There is probably only one use for it and the cashier and I will know exactly what that is. I can barely contain my dual and opposing feelings of arousal and shame. There were about 12 double dildos to choose from. Only two were vibrating. One had veins and appeared to be made of silicone, it looked more or less realistic particularly due to the flesh color. The other was clear with some red coloring inside. I'm not sure what it represents. The more natural one was larger maybe even a bit larger than she requested. It looked like a nice size for filling up Pam and Sawyer. The switch to turn it on was located in the center and both tips twisted off to insert batteries. I worried a little that they could open up and the batteries would pop out. I decided that would be the question I could ask Hannah. It would undoubtedly make her feel useful. After making my selection, I glanced around to see if there was anything else I wanted to get either for Drew and me or to surprise Paula with – or potentially both. It seemed that I had taken too much time there, so I would make my one purchase and leave. Now that I knew where this place was and all of the fun merchandise they had, I could certainly come back another time.

I went to the register hoping to maintain my solitude in the store. Hannah was waiting there. I handed her the big double vibrator and asked how to ensure the batteries wouldn't come spilling out. She assured me that there was a safety latch that would prevent that. She asked if I needed batteries. Of course, they are not provided and I certainly did need some. The entire purchase was $75.00 and I had only $80.00 in cash. This was not the type of purchase I would like showing up on my credit card bill. This was also my lunch budget for the week so it looked like I was going to have PBJs or grilled cheese for the foreseeable future. She packaged my purchase in a black bag with no identifying information on it. Where the hell was I going to hide this for the weekend? I had a few more hours to contemplate that. For now, I had to get back to the office. I sat in my car my panties dripping wet. My clit was no longer throbbing thanks to the conversation about batteries, but that didn't dry up my wetness. It was going to be a long afternoon. I hope buying whipped cream won't cause a similar reaction. That should be an innocuous trip to the grocery store.

When I returned to the office, Bonnie asked how my shopping trip went. I told her about all of the varieties of sex toys in that store. She promised she'd return with me sometime. I think she would like it. She is the only person, besides Paula and maybe Drew, that I could envision entering a store like that with. I guess I have to own my sexuality and be willing to ask for and buy what I want to achieve my goals whatever they may be. I decided to keep the vibrator in a locked drawer in my office. I would have to temporarily move some confidential files out to make room. It's not ideal, but necessary. It also means that I have to stop in the office before 7:00 a.m. on Monday morning to retrieve it before going to Paula's hotel. Even though that was inconvenient, I think it is the least risky option. What a dramatic shift of thought to be making decisions based on the least risky option. I can pick up the whipped cream over the weekend and keep it in my home refrigerator and I can easily borrow one of Drew's belts that morning without notice. I spent a few minutes wondering what the belt was for. Would she use it for bondage purposes or was she going to slap my ass with it? Would she use it to connect two things together? There were so many choices and my guess is she has thought of something that I never would have picked.

I really lack sexual creativity. I'm so grateful to have her do the thinking for us both. What about the whipped cream? I hope she loads Sawyer up with it and allows me – no, demands me – to lick her clean. That would be insane – in a good way. What else is she bringing with her? I know she can't pack the clarinet case of goodies. That really is too bad. I love the objects she manages to smuggle in that thing. How clever of her to have a traveling orgasm carrier. Maybe she has other personal belongings that she wants to slide into my wet pussy so she can keep them as trophies. Perhaps I will think of something of mine that she can masturbate with so I have a little innocent token to remember her. That will give me a goal for the weekend and something to think about so I don't just obsess incessantly about what we will be doing for the next week, how she will challenge me, bringing me to the edge of climax cliff over and over and occasionally allowing me to soar over the precipice to experience an explosive orgasm. I would never have guessed that I could be so enamored with this incredible woman, yet so conflicted about the situation. Nothing has changed with my family. Drew and the boys are my priority, except for the one week nearly every year that I see Paula. Then I go to extraordinary measures to become one with her.

I spent the weekend in a self-induced daze trying to get to Monday unscathed. I looked around my house at seemingly ordinary tchotchkes to see if one could be used as a trophy for me. It was a meaningless task designed to distract me. I knew we would go to a soccer game and hopefully celebrate the win with a dinner out and maybe ice cream or the new local craze, frozen yogurt. I did laundry and went grocery shopping, cleaned the house, made lunches for the boys, and worked on other household chores. I picked out an outfit to wear to see Paula on Monday, deciding on a pencil skirt, lacy cami, thong, sweater and open-toed slides with kitten heels. I'm thinking it's demure yet slightly sexy. Maybe librarian chic. It says work, but not serious work. I usually don't put so much thought or effort into selecting outfits, but I feel the need to do it for her.

I went to bed shortly after the boys did. It's better to get all of the rest I can in case I need extra strength for tomorrow's escapades. It took me a while to fall asleep because I kept thinking about Paula. But finally sleep came. Unfortunately, it wasn't for long. Around 3:00 a.m., I heard a thud, then crying. Drew and I ran to the boys' room. It appeared Logan had fallen out of bed. Upon turning on the light, we saw his bed covered in vomit. Poor thing must have vomited in his sleep. As Drew took him to the bathroom to clean him up, I removed the soiled sheets from the bed and put them in the washer. I put fresh sheets on his bed. I found clean pajamas in his dresser and brought them to the bathroom. The look on Drew's face gave away his concern.

"He has a fever," Drew said.

"How high?" I asked as I touched his forehead.

"102," was the response.

I think the doctor told us to not be concerned until the temperature reaches 103 or 104 unless there are other symptoms. I believe vomiting is one of those symptoms. He felt hot and appeared listless. Of course, it was the middle of the night.

"Do you think we should take him to the ER?" I asked Drew.

"I would prefer to wait until the morning and see what happens."

"I agree."

We put Logan in his clean pajamas and gave him a drink of water. He said his stomach was not upset any more. Drew carried him to his bed. We both kissed him goodnight and returned to our room. I wondered whether I should sleep in his room to be nearby, but decided to set my alarm for an hour later to check on him. After a restless hour of sleep, I returned to Logan's room. He was sleeping peacefully, but was still very hot. I once again planned to wake up an hour later to check on him. Nothing had changed.

When I checked on Logan at the time I would usually get up for work, he is still quite warm. It looks like a rash is developing on his face. I call the pediatrician's all-night nurse to schedule an appointment as soon as possible. I'm certain Drew has important meetings at work so he can't stay home. I would prefer to be with my sick baby anyway.

"Honey?" I guess it's time to wake my sleeping husband.

"Yeah, oh, how is he?" Drew asked as he was waking up.

"Still feverish and it looks like there's a rash on his face now. I made an appointment with Dr. Swanson at 10:00 a.m. I'll stay home with him. Can you get Bodie to camp?"

"Yes, sure. I better get showered." He gets out of bed slowly. It is 6:45. When I hear him in the shower, I look up the phone number to the Hampton Inn by the office. I need to let Paula know that I will not be seeing her that day because Logan is sick. I feel awful disappointing her, but I am disappointed as well. However, I know that my family will always be my priority. This is the first time I really had to demonstrate that.

I dial the number. A strange tone indicates the number is no longer in service. I check the number and dial again. I get the same response. That is weird. I doubt I misdialed twice. I try a third and fourth time, same result. I have her cell phone number but we agreed to never call each other's cell phone unless it was a real emergency. I don't think this qualifies. I call Edwin's number and leave a message that I will not be in. I am not certain if he will check his voicemail before the training, particularly since he will be doing the introductory remarks welcoming our new judges. I text Bonnie to tell her the same. She asks me if she should tell Paula that I'm home with a sick kid.

"NO WAY!" I text back to her. Paula would be furious if she knew that I discussed our relationship with anyone. She doesn't know that Bonnie is my best friend and that I tell her almost everything. I spare Bonnie some of the details, but she pretty much is fully aware.

"Ok, down girl," was her texted response.

"Sorry, she would flip out if she thought you knew anything about us. In fact, delete these messages right away. No proof should exist. Then empty your trash can. Please let Edwin and Duncan know that I won't be there today. I left Edwin a voicemail, but I don't know if he'll get it before the training starts."

"You got it."

"Thanks! You're the best."

"Don't you forget that. I always have your back."

"I won't ever forget. Hope to see you tomorrow."

I try the Hampton Inn phone number one more time. Still not in service. What the hell? That is so frustrating. The shower stops. I'll have to figure out what is going on later.

"Mooooooom!" Bodie shouts from another room.

"What do you need? Please don't shout! Come here and talk."

"Logan's barfing again!" he yells again.

I rush over to their bedroom and Logan has vomited again. This time some of it went into the trash can we placed by his bed.

"Are you ready for camp, Bodie? Dad is going to take you soon. Get some breakfast and brush your teeth. Then get your backpack together and make sure you have a snack and a bathing suit in there. I think it's pool day."

"Yes, mama."

"What's going on?" I ask Logan.

"I guess I'm still sick," he responds.

"How is your stomach? Did it feel upset before you threw up or did it just happen with no warning?" I'm not sure what difference it makes except if he knew it was coming, I hoped he would react quicker next time.

"I didn't really have any warning."

"Ok, go into the bathroom and take off your pajamas. Put on some shorts and a t-shirt. I'm going to take you to the doctor in a little while. I'd like to see if you can keep some food down. Are you feeling hungry?"

"Yes, I'm starving and thirsty."

I try to remember if this situation is the one that we feed the kids BRAT – banana, rice, applesauce and toast. Drew usually remembers these things better than I do. What else could BRAT be for if it wasn't vomiting? I wish I had remembered to ask the nurse at the doctor's office when I called earlier.

"Drew? Is this when we do the BRAT diet?"

"I think it's for diarrhea, but vomiting is sort of the same – problems with the gastrointestinal tract. That is what we probably should try."

"So now I have to see which of those items we have and he will eat! Thanks, hon."

"Logan, are you in some clean clothes? I want to get you some food. Do you prefer bananas or applesauce?" I already knew I'd make plain toast – not even butter on it.

"Applesauce please." I heard his small voice coming from the bathroom.

I went to the kitchen, retrieved a cup of applesauce from the pantry and opened the fridge to get the bread out to toast. The first thing I see is the whipped cream in the spray can. Even though I put it off to the side, it had a bright red label. Clever marketing ploy. My eyes were drawn to it and my thoughts shifted to what would have been happening right now if I were in a hotel room several miles from here instead of preparing a bland breakfast for my vomiting child. Paula and I could wait until tomorrow. It wasn't ideal, but it would be fine. I forced my focus to return to my current situation instead of the fantasy world in the Hampton Inn. Almost robotically, I toast the bread, get a plastic cup of water and put both of them next to the applesauce and spoon on the kitchen table.

In a flurry of activity, Drew enters the kitchen with Bodie following behind him trying to gather all of his things and find his sneakers. I hand Drew the coffee that I made for myself. I can make myself more later. Drew slurps down the coffee. The noise annoys me. It's a relatively new habit that he has acquired. He used to be so proper, as his own mother taught him manners. Occasionally he belches loudly and has taken to slurping hot beverages and soups. When did this become the norm? Now is not the time to bring up the irritating tendency, but I'll do it soon. I don't want the boys to think this is appropriate behavior.

"Thanks, babe. Bodie, are your shoes on?"

"Almost!"

I get up to find Logan coming down the hall. He looks sickly and pale in spite of the rash.

"Come and get some food and water, little man." I kiss Drew and Bodie goodbye as they head out the door.

"Feel better, buddy! I'll see you later," Drew says to Logan.

"Ok, Daddy." He almost sounds cheerful.

I fix another cup of coffee as Logan sits down at the table, pitifully eying his plain toast and applesauce.

"Can we put some butter on this? Or peanut butter?"

"We can't put butter on it, but I can add a little peanut butter." I scrape a miniscule amount of peanut butter across the top of his toast.

He gobbles down both the applesauce and toast.

"Make sure you drink your water, too. You can get dehydrated after vomiting."

"Ok, Mama." The boys only call me 'mama' if they are sick, tired or want something. I really like when they do, even though it's usually to request ice cream, a toy or a sleepover. If we ever have another baby, I want her to call me 'mama' all of the time.

"Why don't you sit on the couch and watch tv while I take a shower? Do you feel well enough to do that?"

"Yes, Mama. Can I take my water cup to the living room with me?"

"Sure, just be careful with it."

I go back to my bedroom and try the hotel one more time before getting into the shower. I still get the no longer in service message. I wonder if I have the wrong number. Instead of checking the hotel website, I check the nationwide Hampton Inn website and then select the one in Arlington near the office. It has the same number listed. Ugh. There must be a problem with the phone lines. How frustrating.

I shower and dress, not wearing the outfit I planned for work. Since it's quite warm, I put on a pair of shorts, a shirt and sandals. There's no need to wear a skirt to the doctor's office. I try the hotel again. No longer in service.

Logan is still in front of the tv, mesmerized by whatever he's watching. I make another cup of coffee and eat some yogurt. It's almost time to leave for the doctor appointment.

At 9:30 a.m., Logan and I get in the car to drive to the pediatrician's office. It takes about fifteen minutes to get there. They have changed their waiting room so now there is a sick kid area and a place for children who have well visits scheduled. I can tell Logan isn't feeling well because he is listless and clingy. I don't mind him wanting to be cuddled because I know those days will be coming to an end soon enough. But maybe we will all have a new baby to cuddle? It's likely the boys will become more dependent then because they will see us giving the new baby attention that they want. Who knows? There's a ton of psychology behind growth and development, but I'm certain not every child follows an identical path.

"Logan?" the nurse calls him.

"Come on back. What's going on today?" she asks as we walk down the hallway painted with bright cartoon animals.

"He vomited during the night and again this morning. He has a bit of a fever and a rash developing on his face." I explained in response.

We entered room six which was the dinosaur room. The boys used to love the dinosaur room when they were smaller. The fact that dinosaurs have gone out of favor in my boys' lives indicates that they are no longer little guys anymore. It's funny how little things like this make a difference in our lives. They used to love Go, Diego, Go and his baby jaguar, but now that show is "for babies." They are more interested in iCarly, a show with actors not cartoons.

"I'm Frannie and I'm the nurse. I would like to take your temperature and see how tall you are and weigh you."

Logan looked at me to approve the next steps.

"Sounds good," I replied.

He stood up next to the hash marks on the wall to indicate his height and stepped on the scale to determine his weight. Frannie entered the information on an iPad. Logan climbed onto the examination bed where Frannie took his temperature and noted the result. When she finished, she said Dr. Swanson would be in soon before leaving.

"The stefiscope was cold on my chest."

"Stethoscope. There's a "t-h" in the middle, not an "f." They always seem to be cold. I'm not sure why. We should ask Dr. Swanson."

"Can I play with your phone while we wait?" Logan asked.

"No, baby, let's just talk. Tell me how you feel right now. Does your stomach feel better after eating? Have you felt like you might vomit again?"

"I'm still hungry, but my stomach doesn't hurt. I only felt a little sick on the way here, but maybe I was car sick."

"Is that supposed to be a joke about my driving?"

A sly smile crossed his mouth. It's an ongoing family joke about who the best driver is. I know I am because Drew is really hard on his brakes. He is impatient in traffic, always changing lanes to get ahead. It's exhausting to ride with him. I prefer to drive when we are all in the car going somewhere. I guess it's another thing that I expect to control within my family.

Dr. Swanson knocked on the door and then entered. We hadn't seen her since the boys' annual check-up.

"How are you guys? Probably not very well since you are here for a sick visit!"

"This guy has been vomiting and seems to have a fever and a rash." I explain. I'm sure it is all written on the chart. I never know if she expects him to describe his symptoms or wants me to do the talking. Sometimes my twins are shy and don't want to talk to adults, so I figure it's better for me to start the conversation.

She looked into his ears, nose, and mouth and listened to his heart, lungs, and stomach. After evaluating his symptoms, she suggested that he rest for the remainder of the day and return to camp tomorrow if he feels up to it. She suggested children's Tylenol for the fever and thinks the rash is environmental. We haven't tried a new detergent or soap, but maybe he was next to something at the camp. It isn't an allergic reaction to a plant or food. I'm happy about that. It doesn't seem to be contagious either.

We drive back home and plan to spend the day together on the couch watching movies and maybe napping. Sounds like a pretty good day to me, not exactly the day I had planned however. Once Logan is settled on the sofa, I decide to try the hotel again. Same aggravating tone. I had another idea. I will call the national 800 number and see if they can connect me. The national reservation agent answered. I explained that I was trying to reach a guest at the Hampton Inn in Arlington, Virginia and have been unable to get through. She tries and gets the same answer I did. The number is no longer in service. She reports the problem with the number and tries another number. Someone answers and she connects me. I tell the local agent about my difficulty getting through to her hotel. She admits there are problems with the phone service today and they think it is being worked on. She says she can try to connect me to Paula's room to leave a voicemail but isn't sure it will work as their internal system is not operating consistently either. She asks if I want her to put a note under her door, but I decline. I don't think that is safe. I'll go with the voicemail. I leave a voicemail indicating that my son is sick and I will call her later. I'm looking forward to seeing her tomorrow and I'm excited to bring her the items she requested. After hanging up, I feel relieved that I was able to leave the voicemail. At least she will hear my voice, understand how sorry I was, but that I needed to care for my family. Neither of us wanted to wait an additional day, but I will make it up to her tomorrow. There's no doubt about that.

While I was thinking about it, I looked through Drew's belt collection and selected one that looked too small for him. I'm not sure why he keeps stuff that doesn't fit him anymore. I wrapped it around itself in a tight coil and placed it at the bottom of my bag for work. I just have to remember the whipped cream in the morning, then get to the office early to get the new double vibrator from my locked drawer and get to the Hampton Inn before 7:00 a.m. If Logan is still sick tomorrow, I'm hoping Drew can stay home. I have to presume that will happen. I'm so looking forward to seeing Paula.

I returned to the living room to start our movie marathon and my little angel was asleep in the sunlight that was flooding in through the window. He looked so sweet and perfect. I guess that will give me the opportunity to get other things accomplished. First, I'll text Bonnie to see how things are going around the office. I would guess she is in her office and not at the training. She does have to present to the new judges later in the week.

"Hey chica! What's up?" I texted.

There was no response for a very long time.

"Sorry. I went to lunch and forgot my phone. How is Logan?"

"He's going to be fine. He's taking some children's Tylenol and napping. He's not contagious and it's not serious. I'll be back at the office tomorrow."

"I'm so glad to hear that."

"Thanks. How is the training going?" I asked.

"It's seems like everything is fine. I stopped in to meet the new judges. They seem nice. Judge Levy is so young. Did you interview her?"

"Yes, she is very qualified. Did you see Paula?"

"Very briefly. She was in good spirits. I, of course, didn't mention you."

"Thank you. I couldn't reach her at the hotel. The phones aren't working. I finally left her a voicemail. I hope she gets it. I'll call her later."

"Be careful."

"Of course, I will. I'm not risking my family."

"If you say so. I have to run. I'll see you tomorrow. Love you, girly."

"Love you back!" She was the greatest friend. I don't know what I would do without her.

I remembered that I didn't clean up the vomit from the second episode this morning. That was a huge mistake. Not only was it caked on the rug and bedspread, it smelled like it had fermented. Some days I felt like I should be paid for this motherhood job! This was one of them. I had to spray and spray the cleaner to get the odor and stains out. Even after using a lot of elbow grease, it still wasn't clean. I gave up.

I check on Logan. He's still sleeping peacefully. He feels warm, but I think it's more because of the sunlight than his fever. I feel very hungry, just realizing that the yogurt I had for breakfast wasn't enough to nourish me. I prepare an omelet with some vegetables, ham and cheese and devour it.

It's been another hour, so I try the hotel phone number again. Not surprisingly, I hear the same angry signal that the phones are no longer in service. I hope there is no real emergency that anyone would have to reach someone at the hotel. I suppose everyone has cell phones now so it probably isn't a problem. It's only a problem for people who are trying to be secretive and not use their cell phones.

I sit on the recliner near my sleeping Logan and think about Paula and the vibrator I purchased. Not knowing exactly what she has planned is enticing, but I also know that Sawyer and Pam will be sharing different ends of the same double dildo. That will be taking our pleasure to a new level. I'm certain of it. I remembered the one time we sixty-nined and climaxed at the same time. It was transcendental. Capturing those moments defies time and space, I enjoy my memories of them and reminiscing with Paula about them. She remembers everything.

"Remember the first time I told you to assume the position?"

Or "Remember when you gripped the sheets in anticipation of pain?"

Or "Remember when I told you to answer me with 'Yes, ma'am' or 'No, ma'am'?"

Or "Remember when I made you request permission to cum?"

Or "Remember when we went to the farmer's market and you chose the zucchinis knowing that I was going to stuff them inside of you?"

Or "Remember when I told you not to fuck your husband and that you must wait for me?"

Or "Remember what happened when you disobeyed me and I smacked your ass?"

Yes, I remember. I remember every single time we were together. I remember everything you said to me. I remember every time I orgasmed with you on the phone or in person. I remember what you smell like and feel like. I hear your voice in my head more often than I will ever admit. I remember feeling a connection to you like I have never felt before with anyone else and that I will never feel again because I remember how naughty we are together and that no one else will ever be naughty like us. I remember you telling me that you wanted to be the best lover that I ever had or ever will have. And you are. You know me better than I know myself. You understand my needs and you fulfill my desires without my having to ask. What more could anyone ask for? I guess there's love. But I love you when we are together and you love me when we are together. That is perfect for us. If we were together every day, our relationship would not be as special. I sometimes fantasize about what it would be like if we lived together. If we could maintain a dominant-submissive lifestyle every day. Is that sustainable? As a concept, it sounds exciting. But it likely is not a workable situation.

I wore myself out with all of the what-ifs and memories and fell asleep. I woke up to Logan poking my stomach.

"Hi Baby. How are you feeling?"

"I'm still tired, but hungry too."

"How about a grilled cheese?"

"Yum!!" That was enthusiastic.

I went to the kitchen to prepare food once again. He finished the first one in only a few bites and asked for another. His increased appetite makes me think he is on the mend. I gave him some chocolate milk to drink. He finished two full sandwiches and a big glass of milk. I called Drew to let him know that Logan was improving. He was relieved.

Once again, I tried the hotel. Since it was late afternoon, I hoped the situation there would have changed. Even though Paula should still be in training, I could leave another voicemail if she didn't answer. The phones still didn't work. I was frustrated.

It was time to pick up Bodie. I figured Logan could stay home alone for a few minutes while I went to the day camp. I hoped he would be ready to go when I got there and not procrastinating with friends. Fortunately, he missed his brother so the pick-up went smoother than usual. He wanted to know how Logan was, if he could play with him, if they could go outside, a thousand questions. I advised him to let Logan choose the activity and it would likely be inside play for today.

I left the boys alone in the living room and went to my room to try the hotel again. The training should have ended by now and maybe Paula was back in her room. I dialed. It rang! Yippee!! A hotel operator answered. I asked for Paula's room. She attempted to transfer me and the phone went dead. Christ! I dialed again, got the same woman, and explained what happened. She said that they have been having problems with the phones today. I wanted to say "no shit," but decided that would be impolite. She transferred me again and the phone rang.

"Hello?" Paula answered.

"Oh my God! I finally got through to you! I have been calling all day!"

"Really?"

"Yes, the phones weren't working in the hotel all day. Did you get my voicemail?"

"No," her answer was curt.

"My son was sick, so I couldn't come today. I called the hotel to tell you, but the phones weren't working. I tried a dozen times and couldn't get through. I finally decided to call the nationwide number and they put me through to the local hotel. She transferred me to your voicemail but wasn't sure it would work. I left a message telling you that my son was sick and the phones weren't working. It was so stressful."

"I didn't get your voicemail."

"I'm so sorry. I left one."

"Catherine, I'm not interested in hearing your excuses. I thought you would be here and you weren't. This isn't worth the risk for me. I don't want to see you tomorrow. Do not come to my room."

"What? Are you kidding me? Ask the woman at the hotel desk. The phones haven't been working all day!"

"No. I'm serious. I can't trust you. I don't believe you. How do I know you weren't out with someone else?"

"Why would I be out with anyone else? I only want to be with you."

"I can't do this anymore. Goodbye, Catherine." Click.

"Hello? Hello! Hello! Paula?!" She was gone. Just like that. She hung up on me. And she broke up with me. I had the double dildo that she requested in my locked drawer at work. I felt sick. I put years of my life into this relationship and diverted energy from my family for this? How could she could just walk away from me so easily? What happened to "There is no one like us"? I slid down the wall and cried in a crumpled heap on the floor. I wanted to vomit. I felt devastated, angry, and betrayed.

Maybe she would reconsider when I saw her tomorrow at the training? Maybe she can't resist me after all of these years? I grabbed a pillow and screamed into it just to get the frustration out of my body. I was drained. All the years of emotions that I had been putting into my little Paula box came rushing out, spilling on the floor like marbles rolling away from me. Should I collect them all or let them go? I don't have much time to experience all of the emotions that I'm feeling. I have to get myself together before Drew gets home. I call his cell phone quickly to see where he is and ensure that the hotel number is not the last one on my phone. He'll be home in fifteen minutes.

Fifteen minutes is not enough to sort through the isolation and abandonment I feel. I have to proverbially dust myself off. I will see what happens tomorrow. I can't believe that our relationship is over just like that. Because phones didn't work at the hotel, really? I can't even make sense of what just happened. Maybe she was looking for an excuse to break up? But why make me go to all of the trouble to buy the items for her scenarios? Did she think it wouldn't matter? That I could just move on like it never happened? I spent years, YEARS! with this woman. Was she better at compartmentalizing than I was? I'm being swept under the rug like a pile of dirt for no one to see. Didn't I mean more to her than that? I knew her darkest secrets. I shared in her deepest desires. I played her naughty games. I assumed our annual shenanigans would occur forever. I was wrong.

The next day Logan was well enough for camp, so I went to work and the training sessions that I helped plan. Paula ignored me. I wore the outfit I had planned for the day before, so she could see my braless cami and make out the shadows of my nipples. That tactic did not entice her. I showed my bravest face all day long while my insides had crumbled like ancient Roman buildings. I wondered how my backbone kept me erect when I felt like a spineless jellyfish floating in a current with no direction of my own. I didn't know whether I should look upset so she could see the impact of her callous dismissal of our relationship or if I should attempt to be stoic when there wasn't a stoic muscle in my body. I didn't know the right thing to do. Should I try talking to her, telling her that I am only faithful to her, to us? Would that make me appear even weaker? I am partially defined by my relationship to her. I was her sub. I don't want that part of me to die or be removed like a useless appendage. My mind swirled in a tornado of conflict. Admit my vulnerability that she would see as frailty and hope for her forgiveness? Give up on her as if none of this was important? Move on? But to what? There would never be another Paula. She was right. We were two of a kind. It is not possible to cultivate another relationship like ours. Nor would I want to. It was too special and too perfect.

The next two days I only visited the training for a few minutes each day to see if Paula's reaction to my presence had changed. It hadn't. I couldn't fathom being near her and not touching her and talking to her. On the last day, she approached me for the first time that week.

"Thank you for all of the effort you put into the training." She paused then said, "It was nice."

"You're welcome. It was." Tears welled in my eyes. I am not sure what she meant by her last statement, but I know exactly what I meant.

Epilogue

Weeks and months went by. I tried to resume my life as it was pre-Paula. It was a challenge to grieve for the loss of our relationship while acting as if nothing in my life had changed. I obviously had Drew, the twins and the new life growing inside me to focus on. However, her absence had created an unmistakable yet seemingly invisible void since she never really occupied any actual space in my life. She definitely occupied space in my head and likely occupied more space in my heart than I had admitted even to myself. I had to force my life to go on uninterrupted. Except it had been interrupted by a force unlike anything I had ever experienced, nor do I believe I will ever experience again. I tried to remember the snippets of the happiest times, the explorations of things that were possible, the cravings for things I didn't know I had that were fulfilled without my making a known request.

Sometimes I think Paula was all in my imagination. Except I can hear her voice in my head, coaxing me to cum, demanding that I say "Yes, ma'am" or "I am so sorry, Mistress," telling me that there is no one like us in our shared naughtiness. I enjoyed our salacious secrets. I loved being her sub. I relished the time I spent not having to be in control of my life. She made all of the decisions for how we spent our time together. It was so freeing. But, alas, it's over. I have only cried once or twice. I didn't want to feel that deeply about her and I believe I was fairly successful at compartmentalizing, but occasionally I allow myself to think of the might-have-beens. I knew our relationship was a fantasy with no real future. Even so, I didn't expect it to end when and how it did. I am certain Paula had many more scenarios dreamed up for our times together.

As fall turned to winter, Drew and I discovered our new baby-to-be was the daughter we were hoping for. We prepared a pink nursery which even made the boys excited about their new sister. One day I was pulling some baby quilts out of my closet that we had packed away after the boys outgrew them and I knocked over the briefcase that I used for conferences. An envelope fell out. It was curious there could be something in there since when? The conference the previous summer? A letter from whom?

I felt a little lightheaded and panicked as I ran my fingers over my name written on the envelope. Catherine. It wasn't polished handwriting, nor was it rushed. It was deliberate, elegant somehow. I unsealed the back, not taking the time to determine what I hoped the contents would reveal.

Catherine –

I struggled all weekend before the conference trying to determine the best course of action. I knew I would have to end our relationship. I loved all of the time we spent together. You are perfect for me in almost every way. I have never said this outright, but I think you knew that my marriage was far from satisfying with Garrett traveling, making our sex life almost non-existent. Even when we were intimate, it was more like doing the deed to check a box. It wasn't designed to make us closer; it was accomplishing something on a to-do list. I knew that was what I was getting into when we were married. Garrett was a safe choice. I hadn't known thorough intimacy until you. You make me feel complete. But I understand that your loyalty was always with your family. I trusted that you loved me when we were together, but I will love you always. I could have easily left Garrett to be with you. But I knew you could not make that sacrifice and I would never ask you to. I knew I had to let you go. I had thought about it several times before. I even told you that I couldn't see you for parts of almost every conference when I knew that I could. I tried to push my feelings aside so I wouldn't get in too deep. But I failed – repeatedly. The only way to stop this affair was to end it once and for all. I had to find the strength to do what I knew you couldn't do. I had to let you go. You have to be with your family – they need you more than I do. Telling you on the phone that I didn't want to see you anymore was the most difficult thing I have ever done. I could feel the disbelief and devastation in your voice. It was one hundred times worse for me. I couldn't stand to be near you the next few days at the conference knowing the pain I caused you. I avoided you, trying to appear aloof, but dying inside. I felt like a selfish piece of shit, but I was doing this for you. You needed me out of your life. And I needed you more than ever. On the last day of the training, I thanked you for everything you had done. I hope you understood what I meant. You made life worth living. You pushed me to find the depth of passion that I will likely never experience again. You inspired me to feel again, not to float through life uncaring and indifferent. I remember every minute we spent together. I have my whole lifetime to relive and cherish our years of passion.

I love you even though we will never be together again.

Paula

About the Author

When Patsy Snowdale is not writing erotic fiction, she is busy living in suburban Washington D.C. working for the government and keeping up with her active family which includes her husband and three children.

Read more about her and her fiction at patsysnowdale.wordpress.com.